I0691831

Please don't tell my parents
I SAVED THE WORLD AGAIN

by Richard Roberts

OTHERSIDE PRESS

Dr. Biotic raised a finger, sounding amused again. "Ditto. Welcome to being a villain one minute and a hero the next, Deathette. Unlike my squeaky-clean colleague here, I can relate. Maybe we'll get together for soft drinks sometime."

I wasn't sure how I felt about "Deathette," but I'd celebrate it replacing the last villainous title someone stuck me with—"Redneckromancer." Ugh.

Tonika's super power might be calmness rather than baldness. She turned those dark, eyes to me now, and said, "So you saved me, using necromancy, which is not as bad as its reputation." She sounded like Sherlock Holmes analyzing a case.

I snickered, happy to have the tension be over. "Nope. It's as bad as they say, or worse. Black magic. Blood sacrifices, violatin' the spirits of the dead what deserve peace, gross zombies, and a craving for powah y'all would not believe. Ah do the best ah can. Ah'm Avery Special, by the way."

"And I'm Dr. Biotic, mutagen junkie," the cat filled in for the girl who didn't know. "I won't be the same species tomorrow, let alone in the same frame of mind. I have a stabilizing serum waiting for me at home right now. Fortunately for you, my friend here is a pure and true superhero, as smart and noble as it gets. No sarcasm. He's a very good guy. He'll take care of you."

CHAPTER ONE

Other teenage girls have normal after school hobbies, like sports or the chess team or training turkeys for combat. Me, I was kneeling inside a circle drawn on the floor of a pitch-black room deep underground, about to pour a bucket of ice water on my head.

First, I chanted a magic spell. Chanting was important. Spells were more music than words.

"O Pluto, quamvis per vallem mortis ambulo, nihil mali timebo, quia canis in valle sum vilissimus."

I dumped the wooden bucket of ice water over my head. Oh, yeah, what a great hobby.

UGH.

So.

Cold.

Miserable and shivering, I chanted again.

"O Pluto, q-quamvis p-p-p-per v-vallem—"

My teeth were chattering too hard. Even if I managed the bad Latin most spells were written in, I couldn't get the rhythm or tone.

Breathe deep, Avery Special. Don't be tortured by the chilly air on your wet skin. Welcome it. Focus on your super power, on its cold energy. You are the cold and nothing else.

My teeth stopped chattering. My body stopped shaking. That's it. I was cold outside, and cold inside. I was pure magic, as dark as this sub-sub-basement chamber.

Close enough that my body was merely uncomfortable, anyway. The rhythm, the notes, they flowed like liquid instinct as I repeated the spell.

"O Pluto, quamvis per vallem mortis ambulo, nihil mali timebo, quia canis in valle sum vilissimus."

My magic swirled inside me, not chained, not wild. Disciplined and mine to control.

My teacher stepped into the doorway. Green light from the single glow stick in her hand did little more than highlight her short, paper-pale body and black hair. The only feature that stood out was the large, single eye above her button nose. In the darkness, it looked pure black.

The glow stick, feeble as its light was, was for me. My teacher didn't need it. Her name was Schleimy, she wasn't even close to human, and she preferred darkness, which is why she lived so far underground.

Maybe I'd gotten used to LA, because all that only seemed a little weird these days.

I stood, filled with cold, and walked calm, even steps to meet her at the doorway. Ice water dripped off of my body, off of my matted and still stubbornly puffy red hair, off of the ridiculous purification costume. It was a tabard, just a sheet of fabric that draped over me front and back, with a hole cut for my head and a rope belt tying it down around my waist. Black symbols in elegant calligraphy lined either side, a spell I didn't know in a language I didn't know. Chinese, maybe. This ritual was cobbled together from a dozen magical traditions.

I looked down at the soaked white cloth and me in it, and smirked. "If Sue saw me wearing this, there wouldn't be enough ice water in the world." If Chris saw me wearing this, a bucket of ice water would at least slow him down enough he'd ask politely.

To my satisfaction, my words held only a hint of Southern accent. My magic was under control.

Schleimy growled in her hoarse voice, "If you can think about such things, the purification did not work and the spell is canceled."

I shivered, not just from the cold still tingling my skin. Bowing my head, I said with soft, even calm, "It was only a joke, Master. I swear. I can do this. I have been planning this spell all month. Please, Master, let me continue."

She hesitated, then stepped away, leading me through the black underground complex.

Whatever this place had been before Schleimy moved in, it sprawled with enough rooms for a mansion. Schleimy lived in the rooms at the center, and we passed through two of those. The glow stick's green light hinted at a crown on a mannequin, a basket of fishing poles, a refrigerator, a knee-high stack of comic books, head-high stereo speakers, a massive cassette tape player, boxes of music cassettes, boxes of vinyl discs, boxes of CDs and DVDs. No television. If she owned a computer I'd never seen it. She didn't like the light from the screens.

I had no idea how Schleimy read the comic books. Or where she went fishing, for that matter.

We reached another room reserved for teaching magic, bare except for a magic circle painted on the concrete floor. Much more elaborate than the purification circle, five unlit candles decorated the outer ring of the central diagram.

I sat down at the very center, legs crossed.

Honest truth, I didn't need any of this. I could cast this spell in my bedroom. I could cast it on a crowded bus. Regular folks needed these preparations to cast a spell, if they could at all. Me, I'd inherited necromancy as my super power. The incantations, the circle, they didn't make my spells work. They made my spells safe. Magic draws trouble like a magnet. Maybe I wasn't a powerful necromancer like my great-great-grandmother Alicia Blackheart, but a big spell like this would be the start of something terrible without these protections.

Speaking of my great-great-grandmother Alicia Blackheart, the barely visible blue outline of a slender woman in a dress drawled in a florid Carolina accent, "Ah really don't see why you'd bothah with this spell, honeysuckle. Poltergeists aren't hard to make. Call up a few tragic ghosts, make them angry, and hahvest the corporeal bits. Then you stitch them togethuh."

The purification ritual must be working if I could hear my dead necromancer relatives. I didn't answer her. My evil great-great-grandmother would never understand that even more than safety, I treasured that Schleimy taught me to treat ghosts as people, not as raw materials.

Swallowing hard, I said to myself instead, "Reckon here goes."

Schleimy and the glow stick were gone, and I was glad for the darkness. Even by my distorted necromancer's standards, this spell was creepy as all get out. I had to remind myself that it wouldn't actually hurt me.

Raising my right hand, I flowed my cold power into the shape of a knife. One sharp claw. Alicia had taught me this spell, and I poured magic into the blade, honed the edge like a razor.

Then I cut off my left hand with it.

Or rather, my ghost's left hand. It appeared in a blue outline, drifting away from where I knew my arm to be.

I tried to move my left hand. The ghost hand moved instead, fingers wiggling, then clenching into a fist. It floated from side to side as easily as waving my arm.

My right hand took hold of my flesh and blood left hand. My right felt it. The left didn't. I pushed magic into the blank appendage, filling it with cold, until I could feel the shape of palm and thumb and fingers in that magic at least.

After some struggle, I felt my flesh and blood fingers twitch. Thank goodness. I'd known it would work this way, but thank goodness.

As I practiced moving my living left hand, I reached my ghost hand through the doorway to knock on the outside wall. Schleimy entered, dropping the glow stick in the doorway to kneel in front of me, reaching for my living left hand. With the feeble light behind her, I couldn't see what she was doing.

Ow. I could sure feel the sting. Did she poke me with a pin?

My teacher rasped, "Good. Excellent. You were right, Apprentice. I was not sanguine about this spell, but you'll have full use of your hand in two days, I'd guess. It may be clumsy for a while, until you get used to which hand is which."

YES! Squealing with glee, I lunged forward and hugged the cold little cyclops paper golem, or whatever she was. Finally! I'd been wanting this magic so bad. I could move things without touching them! Just for fun, I picked up all the candles from the magic circle and laid them next to the door, without unwrapping my arms from Schleimy's shoulders.

Completely, one hundred percent worth the super creepy spell and all the ice water.

From the basement entrance, a man asked loudly, "Avery, are you here? Hurry up, it's time to go."

"Not ready! Hurrying up! Don't look!" I shouted, running out of the casting chamber to the entrance hall, which was actually just the hall where the elevator and emergency stairs descended from the empty building above us.

Distant glow stick light hinted the vague shape of the superhero Mech standing by the elevator. Hopefully facing away. I would die of embarrassment if the second-most-handsome guy in LA saw me in this getup.

The handsomest was my boyfriend Chris, and wasn't I smug about that. Uh-huh.

Grabbing my clothes, I ran into another room. From the feel of carpet under my toes, this had to be Schleimy's bedroom, and I would apologize for dripping on it later. Right now I threw my absurd purification costume out into the hall, where it went splat. Then, wet or not, I struggled into my regular non-wizard clothing. Shirt, overalls, socks, shoes, and finally my backpack, because I might be a necromancer, but I was also a high school student with an essay about the Byzantine Empire to write.

My ghost ancestors would love to help with that. One of them could tell me first-hand stories about Byzantine zombie armies. My teacher at Pepperidge Preparatory School for Girls had no sense of humor whatsoever and would give that a solid F.

I ran back out to the entrance hall, clothes sticky and shoes squelching. My giant hair, of course, was already almost dry and bouncing around.

I found Schleimy standing in front of Mech, her hands on

her hips and single eye glaring up at the full-sized human. Her already-scratchy voice rasped especially hard with anger. "Turn that light off, human."

Mech fiddled with something on his face. His normally warm voice dipped in apology. "Sorry. I thought it would be a good compromise. I should have known you can see it. How is this? No emissions, just amplified signal on my end."

Schleimy poked him in the stomach. "Bring another light into my house, Mech, and you'll be standing upstairs waiting for Avery from now on."

Mech bowed, stiff with shame. "Again, I apologize. I was trying to respect your wishes. I'll do better next time."

That was Mech. He was such a nice guy. Rigorously nice. Superhero nice.

The elevator dinged, and the door opened, spilling actual bright light into the hall. Not hurt by it, just annoyed, Schleimy turned and stalked off into her home.

Mech and I crowded into that elevator and rode it up three floors to ground level. Even there, it let out into an interior hall lit by fluorescent ceiling lights. No windows. No direct sunlight, even here.

My eyes had adjusted by this point, and I could see Mech, dressed casually but stylishly in pressed slacks and a buttoned silk shirt, both in blue, with the sleeves up to show off his muscular arms. Stereotype brown leather and brass rim goggles hung around his neck. South Asian dark, Mech was absurdly pretty for an adult twice my age. I couldn't understand how he maintained a secret identity. He not only looked like the paragon of justice regular people would imagine under his power armor. You could tell at a glance how nice he was. He radiated strength, charm, and sincerity. Even his voice did. You'd have to be blind and deaf not to know he was a superhero.

He started moving as soon as the elevator opened, apologizing to me as we stepped briskly through the door from one hallway to another, "I'm sorry we're in such a hurry. I'll explain in the car."

We entered the front room, where finally windows opened up onto a bright downtown Los Angeles street. This looked like the front desk of a momentarily abandoned business office. In a sense it was, since while she avoided this room, Schleimy sometimes sold magical relics in the windowless interior rooms on weekdays. Figuring my fingers were dry enough, I fished my phone out of my backpack and glanced at the screen.

"Y'all ain't kiddin' about the hurry. It ain't even five o'clock!" Ah. My accent, thick as mud and wandering all over the South and some of the West, was back. At least hardly anyone laughed at it here in LA.

We made it out into the sunlight and fresh air, warm even in January, and Mech held open the door to his car just long enough for me to climb in. I didn't know car brands, but it was nice, well kept, but not a fancy sports car or anything. This was definitely a mad scientist's car, though. I'd seen the second, hidden dashboard with all the cool buttons.

We pulled out into traffic. Mech drove fast, but politely.

"So why all the hullabaloo?" I asked, and wondered where my accent got the word "hullabaloo." It spit up some weird ones sometimes, without my knowing what I was saying until it was already out.

With a friendly and considerate smile and his eyes responsibly on the road, Mech said, "I hope the timing wasn't too awful. I'm expecting an expert to help me with an important experiment today, and she'll be arriving ahead of schedule."

Delight bubbled up inside me again. "Nope. I had just exactly enough time."

"For what? You know your parents want me to keep tabs on your progress," he pressed with just the right amount of curiosity to not feel like a snoop.

Not that I would have cared. Grinning stupid big with pride, I used my ghost hand—invisible to regular people—to pull his goggles up from around his neck. Twirling them on my spectral finger, I then returned the goggles where they belonged.

Experienced superhero Mech wasn't shocked and his driving didn't waver an inch. He did smile a lot, echoing my pride. "Well, I don't know how happy your parents will be about a daughter with telekinesis, but I'm impressed. You're flourishing, Avery Special."

I sprawled back in my seat as best a seatbelt would let me. "Spec ah am. It's a most exhilarating feeling aftuh fourteen yeahs of barely controlling my powuhs."

It was a sign of how safe Mech made people feel that I was willing to talk so much in front of him without worrying about my chaotic accent.

Lightly, he changed the subject. "I hope you won't mind spectating a little mad science before I take you home. My expert gave me barely any warning."

My grin remained strong. "Sounds like a hoot. Is this expert Barbara?" I adored that eldritch horror haunted goth girl.

Mech shook his head. Not so much as to take his eyes off the road, of course. "No, a woman named Dr. Biotic. Actual doctor-ate, by the way. PhD in biochemistry. You'll like her."

Which meant she was a weirdo.

We pulled around the back of a hospital halfway along the curving trip between the West end of downtown and my home at the west end of Glendale. The hospital was a huge, tangled nest of individual buildings and catwalks, and Mech took a parking spot labeled "Reserved For Super Powered Specialists.' Sure enough, as we got out he attached an ID card to his shirt. I didn't have the right angle to read the card, but it did not say "Mech."

But then, in his superhero work his highly identifiable face was always hidden by a metal visor.

The inside of the hospital looked like a hospital. All hospitals look the same. Wide halls in random colors. Wooden counters. Everything was clean and bland. Except for the occasional sign only pointing out something very important like "Emergency" with an arrow pointing at a corner that leads to another corner and then another corner, you had to either know where you're going or get lost until security dragged you off.

Security did not drag off Mech, so thankfully he knew where he was going. It only took four corners, two elevators, and two security doors to get there, not in that order.

Our final obstacle was a grid of red energy beams right behind the security door to an otherwise ordinary-seeming medical ward. L-shaped nurse station, various doors into patient rooms, that kind of thing. And this laser grid.

Mech walked right through it. A nurse walked through it the other way, not giving us a glance. Assuming it was fine, I walked through the beams myself.

It was not fine. A horrible computerized screech rang out of the nurses station.

A stocky, freckled, red-haired nurse—a good description of me, except the nurse part—whose ID card read "Sofia"—rushed up to the counter, looking between the computer and us with a worried frown.

I gave her a resigned, apologetic smile. "Guess this is 'cause ah don't have a badge, huh?"

She just looked more worried, and her voice was cold. Not hostile, but cautious. "No. To get measurements like this... You're not an extradimensional being of horror and darkness, are you?"

"Necromancer," I corrected.

The nurse crossed herself and hurried into a back room. I'd gotten worse reactions.

Another nurse approached us. Well, maybe not a nurse. She wasn't wearing those paper pajamas nurses wear, but a subdued floral print dress, shoes with heels, and an ID card reading "Judy." She combined heavily lined age and athletic poise in a combination I wasn't used to. Also strictly controlled enthusiasm as she greeted, "You're early!"

"My colleague is going to be early," he explained.

"Your colleague is early for being early," another woman's voice announced, dry and whimsical, from one of the patient rooms.

We followed that voice into a normal looking hospital patient's room. The room itself was normal, that is. Funny plastic hospital trash cans. Shiny plastic-surfaced couch. Pale brown walls. Television mounted up in a corner. And of course the hospital bed, with maybe a thicker, nicer looking mattress than I was used to.

The inhabitants were slightly less normal. Standing by the bed, wearing a ragged denim vest and shorts, stood a woman with cat features and scraggly blue fur. A metal plate decorated the left side of her abdomen and where her left ear should be. Her right ear poked up in a triangle out of the top of her head. Her right eye was the same navy blue as her fur, but the left a solid ruby red. The blue eye's slit pupil wandered over me curiously. Her tail lashed, and whatever kind of tail it was, it wasn't a cat's. Cat legs weren't thick, pointed, and lined with alternating red and purple feather stripes.

The patient sleeping on the bed was mostly covered in sheets and a hospital gown, but that only called attention to her baldness. Not just regular baldness. Regularly but not closely set holes, like audio jacks in computers, ran in lines down her smooth scalp. Not only was her scalp bald, she had no eyebrows, or even hints at eyebrows. Leaning a little lower, I squinted, and... nope, no nose hair. Boy howdy, somebody hated hair. Probably not this girl herself. She lay eerily still, except for a subtle blue blurriness around her skin. That kind of sleep suggested she hadn't done any of this to herself.

Mech stopped by the bed, looked down at the girl, said, "Then I guess there's no reason not to get started," and didn't get started. He just looked uncharacteristically nervous.

"Do you need nurses to assist you?" asked Judy, professionally cheerful, helpful, and distant.

Mech shook his head slowly. "I hope not, but have... just have everything standing by, except security. You don't need to worry about violence, at least."

Despite her feline face, the blue cat woman's raised eyebrow and smirk were easy to read. "I don't have the same upgrades that I had when I went toe to toe with Rage and Ruin, colleague." Her gaze turned to me. "Hey, girl. Nice to meet you. I'm Dr. Biotic."

I extended my hand. She shook it, not thrown for a second by a left-handed handshake.

As she did, she flicked her head up and looked past my shoulder. Dryly, she added, "So, I have to ask. What is that thing floating behind you?"

Well, hush my mouth. I was keeping my poltergeist hanging behind me so I didn't get distracted by it. I floated it up front, and asked, "You can see it?" I barely could. I wasn't sure where

I'd gotten Ghost Sight. I didn't have it two months ago. It was still a feeble version. "How many fingers am I holding up?"

Folding her arms under her chest, Dr. Biotic grinned mismatched teeth, some fangs, some human. "Two." She grinned especially hard because her eye had tracked my ghost hand the whole way, and she must see it making bunny ears behind Mech's head.

She didn't say the bunny ears part, which told me everything I needed to know about this woman's personality. Mech was right, I liked her immediately. Just to be sure, I slid my ghost hand around Dr. Biotic's head to give her the same bunny ears. Yep, her eye tracked until it passed behind her, and her grin never wavered. This woman could laugh at herself, too.

So, fair's fair, I moved the poltergeist back behind me and left it doing the bunny ears over my fire-engine-red mop of fleece. I had plenty of hair for me and the girl on the bed both, alas, plus some extra for Dr. Biotic and Mech if they weren't content with their short hair cuts.

Mech might not know what we were laughing about, but he watched us be amused at each other until his patience ran out and he declared with only a hint of irritation, "I'd like to get started."

Dr. Biotic's gaze back snapped to him, and she frowned in surprise and concern. "You're nervous."

Mech grimaced, staring hard at the girl in the bed. "Of course I'm nervous. The whole superhuman community failed this girl, heroes and villains both. My procedure should work. I'm almost positive it will work. If it doesn't, I'm out of ideas."

From silliness to concern, and now Dr. Biotic flipped to a firm, encouraging smile. "You're the expert on override codes, my friend. You've got this."

At last, I had an excuse to ask, "What happened to her?" Blue blur and extreme baldness were a strange combination, after all.

Dr. Biotic immediately held up a hand, palm out to Mech. That kept him silent as the cat woman explained, "She's an innocent high school girl with no super powers. The kind of villain who other villains hate put cyborg implants in her brain to control her. Shutting off the control was easy, but now she won't wake up."

Mech gritted his teeth and clenched his fists at his side. "She's been like this for four months. Four *months*." His voice husked, like he just might cry.

Hand still up to him, Dr. Biotic murmured, "It's okay, my friend. You'll save her. If you don't, someone will. She doesn't seem to be aging. The wait isn't making anything worse."

Taken aback by just how upset Mech was, I asked, "Y'all're tryin' ta get the implants out?"

Controlled again, but still dour, Mech answered, "I know of only two cyberneticists who could do that and leave her alive. One did this to her. The other is dead, I hope. I'm going to upload a new operating system in her implants that will ignore the signal receivers designed to control her. Right now, she can't function without them."

Increasingly curious, I pried, "How d'ya do that?"

"Like this," he said, emphatic. Out of his pocket he pulled a little bitty computer tablet, not much bigger than a phone. A phone, and a bundle of wires. He plugged one end of three wires into the holes in the girl's head, and the other end into his little computer. A thumb swipe lit up the screen, and Mech raised it to his eye until it unlocked. When it did, the screen showed a big green button. Mech held his thumb over it, but hesitated.

"Waiting only makes it worse," Dr. Biotic warned, with a sad, sympathetic smile.

Mech pushed the button. A spinning activity symbol replaced it, and a progress bar. It took about three seconds for that bar to fill.

When it did, the superhero very gently unplugged the sleeping girl, leaned over her, and asked with the quiet voice you use to wake sleepers, "Tonika? Can you hear me?"

No response. Not even a flutter. Dr. Biotic put two fingers against the sleeping girl Tonika's throat. After a few more seconds the cat shook her blue head. "She's still out. Not asleep, suspended animation."

Mech's fists clenched again, and his pretty face pulled tight as he barked, "Do something!"

Dr. Biotic gave him a wry, disarming smile. "What do you want me to do? Have you tried unplugging her and plugging her back in?"

"That's not funny," Mech hissed.

Attempt to disarm failed, Dr. Biotic looked him straight in the eyes and said solemnly, "I don't know why I'm even here, friend. You know more about cyborging than I do. I'm a geneticist. I could mutate her until the implants fell out, but the person who woke up wouldn't be the person you're trying to wake up now. You wouldn't like that solution."

Mech jabbed a finger in Dr. Biotic's direction, and growled, "You're filled with implants."

I took a breath. I didn't know I'd been holding it. Seeing Mech, so kind and gentle, lose his cool was... scary. I wasn't scared of him. I was scared of a situation so bad it would upset him like this.

Dr. Biotic was starting to sound exasperated too, shaking her head and spreading her hands. "I didn't make them. I have them installed when a mutation goes bad. It's one of the downsides of being my own guinea pig. I know how to live with having implants. When she wakes up, I'll be able to give her good advice. I wish I could help wake her. You know that. But I can't."

My voice squeaky, but feeling like I had to do something, I said, "Ya know, it might be worth tryin'?"

Mech was way too nice to yell at me. He merely gave me a puzzled frown. "What?"

Dr. Biotic held out a warning hand to him. "Shhh!" He nodded, watching me, listening attentively.

I waved at the sleeping girl's head and the blue fuzzy effect that I'd realized Mech couldn't see. "Her ghost ain't lined up right. It's in her body but not part of it. Never seen nothin' like it, never nohow."

Yeesh. My accent got so ridiculous when I was nervous.

Mech stepped back, clearing a path between me and Tonika. Gently, with a tense but encouraging smile, he said, "Try, Avery. If it goes wrong, it's my fault, not yours."

I shuffled up to Tonika's head and peered closer. Normally I couldn't see people's ghosts, even in the dark, because they were just… part of the person. Now I not only saw the outline, I saw something else, a shape I couldn't make out, inside her head. An intruder, not part of this girl.

Normally I'd have to think about how to deal with that, but today I had just the tool. I reached my ghost hand into the sleeping girl's head, grabbed tight what felt like a metal spider even if it had no physical existence, and yanked the squirming ghostly thing out. As it came free, it squawked harsh, electronic noises, then faded into nothing.

Figuring that thing had been blocking the girl's ghost like a wedge in a door, I did what Dr. Biotic suggested. I took hold of her ghost in my flesh-and-blood hands, pulled it out a couple of inches, then pushed it back flat into her body.

The blue outline matched her skin surface, and disappeared, merging into her like it was supposed to.

The bald girl's eyes snapped open, dark brown eyes looking up at us, flicking between me, Dr. Biotic, and Mech.

The superhero gasped. "Tonika!" He raised both hands, and his voice went low and soothing. "You're going to be okay."

She didn't look like she was going to panic. Her body didn't move, but her head tilted slightly to the side and she said in a thoughtful murmur, "Tonika? This isn't the kind of setting where you would lie to me, so that must be my name."

Dr. Biotic smiled again. She sat down on the edge of the bed, looking down at Tonika, so obviously taking over that Mech and I took two steps away. Friendly, calm in an easy-going rather than hushed way, the blue cat woman told Tonika, "You're a brave girl. Hold onto that. Amnesia is scary the first time, and no, that's not a joke. What's important is that you are you. No matter what you forgot, you're you, this person listening to me. Everything else is just labels and details. You know who you are, and you have a future waiting to be discovered like everyone else."

No longer at bedside, the heroically nice Mech still raised his hand to add, "And I'll take care of you while we discover your past. You're safe now, Tonika. Thanks to Avery."

With that Mech suddenly spun around and grabbed hold of me in a tight hug. Furiously tight, desperately tight, and he might not be bulky but he was strong. So was I, for a fifteen-year-old, or it might have hurt. While I wheezed, Mech whispered, "You did it. Thank you. You're a hero."

"Ain't whatcha said after that undead lizard thing last month," I gurgled.

Reluctantly, Mech let go and stood up straight again. He still couldn't stop smiling. "I wasn't happy, but when it comes to accidentally unleashing monsters, I'm in no position to throw stones."

Dr. Biotic raised a finger, sounding amused again. "Ditto. Welcome to being a villain one minute and a hero the next, Deathette. Unlike my squeaky-clean colleague here, I can relate. Maybe we'll get together for soft drinks sometime."

I wasn't sure how I felt about "Deathette," but I'd celebrate it replacing the last villainous title someone stuck me with—"Redneckromancer." Ugh.

Tonika's super power might be calmness rather than baldness. She turned those dark, eyes to me now, and said, "So you saved me, using necromancy, which is not as bad as its reputation." She sounded like Sherlock Holmes analyzing a case.

I snickered, happy to have the tension be over. "Nope. It's as bad as they say, or worse. Black magic. Blood sacrifices, violatin' the spirits of the dead what deserve peace, gross zombies, and a craving for powah y'all would not believe. Ah do the best ah can. Ah'm Avery Special, by the way."

"And I'm Dr. Biotic, mutagen junkie," the cat filled in for the girl who didn't know. "I won't be the same species tomorrow, let alone in the same frame of mind. I have a stabilizing serum waiting for me at home right now. Fortunately for you, my friend here is a pure and true superhero, as smart and noble as it gets. No sarcasm. He's a very good guy. He'll take care of you."

With the day saved, Mech was going back into "nice guy" mode fast and hard. Standing tall, with a comfortable but politely apologetic smile for everyone, he put an arm around my shoulder and said, "After I get Avery home. That shouldn't take more than an hour. You'll sit with her, Dr. Biotic? I'm sure the nurses will want to check her vitals."

For the first time, Tonika moved something other than her head. Her arm rose, sliding free of the crisp white hospital sheet. She had one of those little tubes in her arm for attaching IVs, even though nothing was plugged in at the moment. Her fingers flexed, slowly extending and then making a fist. "Yes. I've never felt so weak. I mean—" For the first time, her analytical calm cracked, eyes fluttering wide with panic.

Dr. Biotic pounced on that panic, metaphorically and almost literally. She laid her hand on Tonika's forehead, telling her with frank, sympathetic friendliness, "It's fine. People without amnesia get half memories like this all the time, they just aren't worried about what it means. These are a good sign."

Mech's own expression, momentarily tense, returned to a smile. He squeezed my shoulders, then guided me out of the room. "Come on, Avery. You did good today."

I let out a huge sigh. "Ain't that a relief. The way mah powers work, ah was afraid ah might'a set off a world-threatening disaster there."

Chapter Two

"I'm looking forward to telling your parents how well you're doing," said Mech as he pulled his car, and us in it, out of the hospital parking lot.

I opened my mouth to be proud of myself, only to be interrupted by a telephone ring coming from the dashboard. And sure enough, Mech reached out to touch a button on the dashboard, then frowned, head tilted slightly to the side in a reflexive copy of listening to a real phone.

Just the slightest bit exasperated, he told no obvious microphone, "Is someone else available? I'm delivering Avery home by land."

Mech paused, listening to a voice I couldn't hear. His thoughtful almost-frown turned into a harshly disapproving definitely-frown. With the strain of parental style worry, he argued with the caller, "She's fifteen. She's not a pro. We can't—" Pause. "Alright, but we shouldn't."

Another pause, and Mech stopped at a light and turned to look at me directly, his expression solemn and every other hint of bias locked down tight. His voice came out just as even. "Avery, the University is testing children's powers this week.

We do it occasionally to learn more about how super powers work. One of the children released an undead monster. No one on site has the right powers to control it."

My fire-red bramble thicket eyebrows shot up, and I asked breathlessly, "Undead? Ah'm the only livin' necromancer in the world." Please, please don't let this mean another dead necromancer had gotten out of their grave.

Mech shook his head, eyes back on the road as the light turned green. "One of the teens being tested has unpredictable powers." His voice remained flat. The guy was trying so hard to be nice and not push me in any direction.

Which was sweet, but I didn't see this as a choice. Taking a deep breath to prepare myself first, I said, "Ah'll do it. Necromancer duty, and all that."

Mech didn't look at me or answer immediately. He scowled, the guilty kind of scowl, and turned left at the next street. We were heading West now, practically under the hills, towards one of the gajillion downtowns LA seemed to have.

After a few blocks, Mech reached under the dashboard and pulled a switch. A compartment in the door next to me opened, small and sleek and lined with black cloth. I hadn't even seen the seam.

Subdued, Mech said, "Thank you. You've already saved the day once. We're asking too much of you. If you're going to do this, wear that."

I pulled the contents of the compartment out, dangling from my fingers a black strap with a white oval at the end., until my brain made sense of what I was holding. "A… collar?" Of the kind called a "choker," if I remembered correctly the clothing-obsessed ramblings of two of my closest friends.

Well, Mech wasn't keeping it in a hidden compartment or asking me to wear it for fashion reasons, so I slid it around my neck and fiddled with the buckle under the "cameo," the white oval. As I worked on that, Mech explained, "It fit the original owner's look. It's a disguise."

Was it? It was. I couldn't actually see what it did from the inside, but when the buckle clicked in place I felt dampness hover around me like mist, and caught hints of shadows moving at the edge of my vision. Then inspiration hit, and I raised my hand up enough that I could see it in the rear-view mirror.

I whistled, long and low. Black smoke hid my hand completely, and dripped off my fingers like slime, only to dissipate a few inches away. Yes, this would keep anyone's secret identity, and I appreciated it. Maybe I was the world's only necromancer, but hardly anyone knew that.

Mech turned again, and I realized my muscles were all bunched up and tense. We were close.

Another turn, onto a street of buildings averaging around five stories, in various flavors of shiny. Mech sighed, "A parking space. That's a miracle." As he pulled into it, he told me calmly and firmly, "The monster is on floor—"

White light flashed out of the front door of the white tower one building down. A gust of cold followed, a wash of necromantic power I could feel from here.

"Never mind," amended Mech.

A girl wreathed in white flame backed out of the tower's door. In each outstretched hand a shining white ball sparked and grew to the size of a softball. She threw it inside, and another ball began to form, over and over. All while she backpedaled in a long but plain white dress.

I climbed out of Mech's car in time to see the monster follow Light Girl out of the building. It had to duck low to get through the door, flinching but otherwise unharmed by the balls of light the girl threw at it.

The monster could not possibly look more undead. Shaped like a headless man in plate armor, it loomed a good third taller than any regular man, with beefy broad shoulders and chest. No muscles supported that size. The transparent, dark-blue armor contained transparent lighter blue filling around a transparent, pale-blue skeleton. In its right hand it held a long, skinny metal pole with a transparent, flickering blue scythe blade at the end and a fancy spike on the other side.

All of those could be undead cosplay. I knew this thing was real necromancy because of the mass of writhing blue flame half the size of its body that floated where a head should be. Dark, shadowy impressions of faces appeared and disappeared in that blue, all directed at Light Girl.

That blue flame was what you got when you infected fire with necromancy magic. They fed on each other, creating this erratic, almost-alive power. A lot of erratic, almost-alive power.

It didn't say anything. It trudged after Light Girl, who back-pedaled a good twenty feet down the sidewalk from it, and raised both hands, palm out.

Heat, unpleasant, dry, and penetrating, like the worst summer sun, pushed away the chill of necromancy emanating from the monster. A heartbeat later, the girl lit up in a white corona so bright it hurt to look at. A heartbeat after that, she unleashed a white ray as thick as her waist into the spectral knight.

I winced at the sound, like a distant chorus distorted into shrieks. Was anyone else hearing this, or was it one of those mage-only things? There were plenty of bystanders. I could officially declare Los Angeles residents insane as they stopped and gawked rather than running away. Gawked from across the street or way down the sidewalk, sure, but that was all the caution they displayed.

The spectral knight thing hissed like water added to boiling bacon fat as the beam hit it, and paused, hunched up in pain.

But that was it. It wasn't getting any smaller, or dimming, or cracking, or anything else. The light attacks caused it pain, but no damage. Meanwhile, I felt the flickering of the heat aura given off by the girl's powers. No matter what my grimoires written by centuries of drug-addled occultists said, hard experience had taught me that magic comes from the inside, and Light Girl was running out of strength.

I approached the monster slowly, ready to take over when Light Girl's strength gave out. Mech got there first, literally, by running down a line of cars and scooping Light Girl up in his arms. Her flames went out. I and everyone on the street could hear Mech tell her, "You did well. You saved lives. Let Deathette finish this."

Yep. Totally time for me to do that.

I stepped in the monster's way. It flooded the space around it with the cold of necromancy. This thing's raw power dwarfed mine. What I had was the exact abilities it was vulnerable to.

Also one more advantage I was deeply grateful for. I'd watched its relentless focus on the girl attacking it. This specter was nearly mindless. I wouldn't have to worry about it coming up with plans. It did the simplest, most obvious thing, swinging its scythe down to chop me in half.

I really, really hoped I was ready. I'd been pouring my own power into my flesh-and-blood left hand. Now I raised my arm and caught the blade, not with the hand, but with the magic inside the hand.

Ow. Yeah, that hurt. The edge sawed at my magic, trying to get through it to my flesh. I couldn't keep this up for long, but I had a little time.

So, I used that to reach into its writhing head and yank out a wad of power. The power came free in a struggling mass of blue flame. It felt like slippery ice, twisting around and trying to get free. It felt angry and hateful. Those shouldn't be physical sensations, but they were.

At the top of my lungs, I shouted, "So many've us have ghosts. This's yer chance, folks. Who d'ya wish you could speak to again? Speak their name!"

A woman behind me yelled, "Robert Pedreira!" in the squeak of someone taking a chance they couldn't believe would work.

I declared, "Robert Pedreira, yoah loved ones miss you. Yoah loved ones call you. Rise! Take this sacrifice'a powuh and rise! Take these few precious moments to speak t' them agayn!"

My words and my super power backing them called something. I felt a touch, the literally ghostly touch of a sliver of the dead's memory. Gritting my teeth, I sucked the blue flame into my arm. It didn't want to. I hauled it in anyway, and pushed the power back out into that trembling spirit, which surged into a fully fledged ghost and floated away to the woman who had called it.

In the process, I wrung the wild malice of flame out of the magic. That was the most important part.

"Again!" I shouted. Someone in the crowd shouted a name, and I did it again. And again. And again.

Until finally, I held the scythe blade easily, and grabbed the last grapefruit-sized ball of flame, pulling it away from the spectral knight's body. Unpowered, that body evaporated, weapon and all.

Oof. Tired as I was, I needed the power in this mass of angry flame. I squeezed the energy out of it and into me, until the blue disappeared like regular fire did when you blew it out.

That helped, as did letting go of all the power I'd held tense in my left hand. Making and relaxing that fist produced an unpleasant pins-and-needles prickling, but after the whole chopping the ghost off to make a poltergeist thing, I had no idea if this was a good or bad sign.

Was that poltergeist hand still around? What if I'd disintegrated it—no, I floated it around in front of me. A barely visible blue outline, its fingers wiggled for me more easily than the ones on my arm. So, no damage to me from that struggle. Behind me people were laughing and crying and yelling at and being yelled at by their ghosts, but they could do that without me until the power animating those ghosts gave out and they dissolved.

Stretching my arms and back, I stomped up to Mech. Walking more carefully with Light Girl in his arms, he met me in the middle.

"Where'd this start?" I asked them.

"Sixth floor," the girl said in a heavy accent I didn't recognize. She looked as tired as I felt, but she had already started wriggling in Mech's arms, making him put her down on the sidewalk.

They could figure that out themselves. I left them behind and entered the building, following the dark, oversized, slimy boot prints in the carpet until they disappeared on tiled floor. I couldn't tell what this building was for. It had hallways and a lot of rooms and the occasional little lounge area. Mech had said "university"? Yeah, schools didn't need to explain their buildings.

Too tired for the stairs, I found the elevator and went up to the sixth floor. As I stood in that elevator, looking at the fake wood paneling, I realized that if the monster came from the sixth floor, Light Girl either lured it down five flights of stairs, or held it off in the tight space of an elevator long enough to go that same distance. Dang, girl. Either way, I was impressed.

The elevator opened on the sixth floor. I emerged into a level pretty much like the first floor, with white and blue paneled walls and floor, lots of doors distinguished only by numbered metal plates, and a niche set aside nearby with a withered potted plant and two not-very-comfortable-looking, plastic-covered yellow couches. The big difference here were the, oh, dozen middle and high schoolers spaced around looking curious and maybe a touch anxious.

An undersized door I'd dismissed as a closet without even noticing clicked and swung open. Out of it walked a high school boy with lurid scarlet skin, little sharp horns on his forehead, gleaming black hair and eyes, and a skinny tail that ended in a heart-shaped spearhead.

My boyfriend, Chris, as sleek and graceful and infernally pretty as ever.

His sister Annie peeked out of the door behind him, the female version of his devilish beauty. As always they were dressed fancy and to match today, in a ruffled yellow gown with red edging on her, and a similarly red-edged ruffled yellow blouse and pants on him. Behind Annie I made out not a closet, but a large stone room. I had given them access to magic they could use to find me in an emergency. I couldn't argue with them thinking this counted. I adored Annie and Chris enough that I wouldn't argue if they used that magic to go buy donuts.

"Avery?" he asked, voice raised, which made me realize I was still wearing the drippy black illusion or hologram or whatever.

"Chris?" answered an even more unexpected voice. The sharp-edged, vivacious voice of my girlfriend Sue.

Sue rounded the corner of one of the hallways, greeting Chris with wide-eyed surprise. Chris was gorgeous. Sue was flawless. Not beautiful. In one sense, she was beautiful. In another sense, she was the most generic-looking high school girl imaginable. She had no exceptional traits, but nothing wrong. No hint of acne or scars, she had fluffy and shiny but generically brown hair, she wasn't too fat or too skinny or too muscular or too anything. I had grown very fond of that perfect evenness, myself, and when you got close enough to look into them she had lovely hazel eyes.

That was all her physical looks. Sue flaunted a wolf pack's worth of sharp, intelligent stares, long strides, and poised stances that bristled with attitude. She was also still wearing the uniform of the high school she and I went to, a blue sweater vest over a cream blouse and a knee-length pleated blue skirt.

Sue and Chris locked eyes, smiled, and walked up to clasp hands, then lean in for a quick kiss on the mouth. They made the picture of a happy teenage couple in a serious relationship.

That is, until I unbuckled the choker around my neck, the disguise turned off, and they turned to look at me.

My knees went weak. They prowled towards me together, like hunting jaguars. Their eyes stayed locked on me with that same ferocious hunger.

Chris took a place on my left side, and Sue on my right. They both kissed me on the cheek at the same time and took gentle hold of one of my hands.

My head swam. My heart raced. Would I ever get used to them doing this? Hopefully, no.

And "hunger' undervalued the way they looked at me. Their expressions included something lost, like they couldn't believe they were lucky enough to be dating me. I was the one who should be asking that. Two extraordinary people crazy in love with me? I was okay looking if you liked girls with muscles and big hair. I had asked, and would have to keep asking, because the answers never made sense. I had been forced to accept "beauty is more than skin deep."

Chris broke the silence, flashing me a grin of brilliant white teeth on red skin. "People were streaming the fight online. I knew it had to be you."

Okay, I had my self-control back, enough to raise an eyebrow and ask in amusement, "Mah accent?"

Chris grinned even wider, like I had fallen into a trap, and shook his head. "Couldn't make it out on the video. I recognized your fearlessness." And mercy me, he was serious. His smile looked so *proud.*

"What were y'all doin' thatcha saw the video so fast?" I asked, curious.

"Annie and I were shopping for clothes online," he answered, simply enough.

Honestly, it made sense. You couldn't be as fashionable as the Domingo twins without putting a lot of work into it. Their clothing sense wasn't a super power. They just really, really liked dressing up for its own sake.

Sue squeezed my hand tighter in both of hers and tossed her hair. With a touch of sneer, she said, "I totally can't believe they sucked you into fixing this. Don't the heroes of this city have any pride?"

Oh, wait. Pride! Yes! Aw, Annie had gone. I had to speak to that girl and explain to her that I liked her company and it didn't always have to be Date Night when her brother and I were together. It left me an excuse to brag to Peggy and Annie together later.

Right now, I had Chris and Sue, and I gushed, "Wait, if you're here, look! Look what I can do! I just got this power today!"

Folding my flesh-and-blood arms, I reached out my ghost hand down to the closet door and turned a plant pot upright that had been knocked over in the fuss. While their eyes tracked to watch that, I drew my ghost hand back, grabbed Chris's tail near the end, and tugged. Then I followed up by ruffling Sue's hair.

Chris let out an extended, bug-eyed squeal at the pull on his tail. That got a cackling laugh out of Sue, and she kept laughing so long I wasn't sure she noticed the hair ruffle.

Entirely secure enough to laugh at himself, Chris did just that, with an amused snicker. He followed that up with a sincerely delighted smile and a nudge with his elbow. "A poltergeist! I know you've wanted one for months. Congratulations! Did Schleimy help you get it?"

I preened under my boy- and girlfriend's happiness. This had been a tiring but highly rewarding day.

Chapter Three

As I prepared to explain everything but the purification costume, an elevator ding interrupted me. Mech and the girl I'd been calling Light Girl stepped out. The latter came out of the elevator, peering around suspiciously, echoed by an equally sharp comment in Spanish.

Sue jerked upright like she'd been stung by a bee. Twisting out of my grip, she said something in Spanish back to Light Girl. Something angry.

Light Girl retorted. Sue shook her head, glaring furiously. I spoke maybe three words of Spanish and had no idea what they were saying, but it sounded vicious and probably profane. Light Girl was out of her depth, though. Sue had sharpened her wit on the meanest mean girls in the city. After a few exchanges she said something with a lifted chin and a cruel sneer that left Light Girl sputtering.

Sputtering with fury. Light Girl's head lit up, almost like a halo, but more like a bright light was always right behind her. I felt a touch of hot wind. She was drawing in her power to fight.

I drew in mine. I was going to have to step in.

Mech did instead, literally stepping between the two girls.

He said something to them in Spanish, which made them both look away, scowling but quiet. Light Girl's aura didn't drop, but it stopped building.

Spanish. If I was going to live in LA, I badly needed to learn Spanish. The problem was, I needed to learn Latin first. It seemed like every book about magic in the world was written in Latin. Really terrible Latin. Sixteenth-century occultists didn't have grammar guides on hand.

Hot wind kept tickling my skin. Light Girl may have stopped fighting, but she stood facing the other way with fists clenched, and yes, the light around her was getting brighter again.

I dealt with that by pulling my friends into the hallway Sue had come out of, around the corner and out of sight. With any luck also out of earshot.

Spinning around, I faced Sue directly. "Okey-dokey. First—" Lifting my hands, I cupped Sue's cheeks and kissed her warmly on the lips for a couple of seconds before releasing her again. "—thanks for standing up for me."

Only one thing would have gotten Sue that mad, that fast. Light Girl had said something insulting about me.

Raising my eyebrows, tilting my head forward in both pleading and reproof, I went on, "But second, please allow me try and make friends fuhst. That might'a just a bad moment. She was just in a fight and her power was ridin' her mighty hard. I've been theyah."

My cursed, wandering accent changed with every sentence there, hadn't it? Well, I had no time to feel stupid about it.

Sue waved a hand, lifted her chin, and sneered in disdain. "No way. She's just like my parents, obsessed with being a hero rather than, like, heroism. The mad scientists pretending to be regular nerds in this place had me and her comparing powers, light to shadow. She was totally snotty about it the whole time."

I looked Sue in the eyes, raised my voice slightly, and told her firmly, "*Third*—" Dropping to a gentle murmur, I took her hand in mine and gave it a squeeze to go with my soft smile. "Thanks for standing up for me."

Sue's righteous anger deflated into a weak, awkward grin. Rather than say anything, she bumped her shoulder against mine. Chris took Sue's other hand and added his own affection-ate squeeze. This relationship existed because they were both in love with me, but Chris and Sue were good to each other. Chris was good, period.

Ahem. Business. I tried to run my hand through the tan-gle of my hair, and asked Sue, "If you were heah already, do ya know wheah that undead monstah came from? Ah kinda thought ah was the only necromancer around."

Perking back up, Sue flapped a hand down the hall. "Oh, for sure. Down there. It came out of room eighteen. I was in fifteen and the thing tried to eat my shadow and I was so totally terrified."

It turned out I hadn't needed to ask. By the time we reached room sixteen I felt the itchiness on my skin. The sensation led me straight to the melted door of room eighteen. Inside, in the middle of a big square room white room that a school could rearrange for any purpose, sat a middle school boy on a tall stool, kicking his feet idly while he scratched his torso with both hands.

I put him at… probably thirteen. He hadn't hit a big growth spurt yet. On the other hand, he'd outgrown the old jeans he was wearing enough that they showed half his calves. That mismatched with an adult's t-shirt that hung off him like a tent, bedecked with the unintelligibly faded emblem of what I thought might be a band. I definitely made out skulls and light-ning bolts. Two little metal bead earrings decorated each ear. His arms showed some muscle despite his size, his short yellow hair skewed wildly in all directions, and he scratched all over with an obsessive ferocity.

An obsessive ferocity that I couldn't blame him for. His power filled the room, a sensation like a cloud of bugs whirling around me. Bugs that couldn't get into my eyes and nose and mouth, at least, but I for sure felt the itch.

Raising my hand, I asked the boy cautiously, "Black magic kids club?"

He jumped in surprise, arms and legs flailing, rocked back-wards and nearly fell off his stool before grabbing it tightly and recoiling back up straight. A wide, ecstatic grin split his face, and he held up his left hand, palm out. "Black magic kids club!" he squealed with glee.

I high fived him, then we both yanked our hands back and massaged the palms. Ugh. The wriggly sensation touching him left on my skin was intense despite that hand still being a little numb.

"Oof, cold!" he hissed, reacting to my power. Glancing up past me at Chris and Sue, he must have seen expressions of confusion because he pointed back and forth between me and him, chattering an explanation. "Oh, okay, so, there are four teenagers with black magic powers in LA. Me, her, Barbara, and the Godchild of Despair."

I flashed him a grin and lowered my voice to confidential level. "Ah think we've found a fifth. Ah saw th' light girl strugglin' with her power. You can tell she wants moah, wants to let it devour her. Ah bet her power doesn't heal, only destroys. Black magic is still black magic if you paint it white."

The kid pulled his feet, in sneakers with untied laces, up to the edge of the wooden stool and rocked forward and back on it as he chattered enthusiastically, "I saw you fighting the underworld harvester on a science camera because they wouldn't let me melt a window and you were super cool! In that costume I thought you were Barbara."

Sue grinned her favorite wicked grin, and I tried not to blush at being compared to Barbara the ultra-curvy goth eldritch sorceress. I'd been wearing a dripping black smoke disguise! Chris at least had never met Barbara and had no idea why Sue would tease me over it.

I changed the subject, fast and hard. "So that theah thing was an undahworld harvester?"

The boy had gone back to scratching, reaching his arms all around himself to get at the itches. I was tempted to join him. Whatever he had done absolutely drenched this room in that gnawing power of his. While he scratched, he half-answered, "I don't know. That's what I'm calling it. I summoned it, I didn't make it." Straightening up suddenly, he held out his left hand. "Oh, my name's Hodir."

I shook. We both put up with the sensation of each other's

magic. I gave him a grin. "Mah parents named me Avery, so ah reckon ah've got no room to judge. Chris 'n' Sue got the normal names."

When our handshake let go, Hodir bounced on his chair, causing the wooden legs to clack on the tile floor as he asked eagerly, "Oh, hey, ooh, do you want to see my power? I got to see you use your power, but you only got to see the thing that came out of my power. Watch this!"

The little blond-haired boy thrust both his arms straight forward, palms out and fingers splayed. Black lines drew themselves in the air in front of him, forming into circles, triangles, lines connecting them, an elaborate design like the circles Schleimy used to keep my magic contained. Chris and Annie took a step back, eyes wide and impressed. I understood the extra layer of what was going on. Like me, Hodir didn't have to research and calculate and design these magic circles, didn't have to draw them himself or worry about what they were made of. He did it the same way I did necromancy, like flexing a muscle. The circles weren't the spell, they were the visual side effect, like a car's wheels turning if you pushed it rather than a car moving because its wheels turned.

Cause or effect, the diagram completed, only to twist. Lines wriggled and bent. A dull, ugly rainbow of colors ran through the lines, replacing the original black. The cloud of bugs sensation disappeared as all of Hodir's free-floating power was sucked into the spell.

The design split in three places, like the seam on a doll tearing, revealing a strobing kaleidoscope through the gaps. Some other space.

Something clicked, and the whole design disappeared. The swarming-bug feeling came back so hard I barely kept my hands at my side.

The man in the corner said gently, "I think you've shown off enough for this afternoon, Hodir. Wait until I've got my experiment set up for the next one, okay?"

Well, didn't I feel like a goof. I'd been so totally fixated on meeting whoever else was doing black magic, I hadn't noticed anything in the rest of the room, including that we weren't alone. The room might be unspecific and white, but that didn't mean it wasn't empty. Weird electronic devices lined the walls, with antennas and lenses and masses of wiring, often bare metal wrapped around something hundreds of times.

The room also contained a middle-aged man in a white lab coat, with a short brown beard and a friendly smile. Huge glasses perched on his nose, but he also wore brown-leather goggles with brass trim around his neck like an amulet. In one hand he held a cream-colored plastic device that reminded me more of a hand vacuum than anything else, while his other hand fiddled with its many buttons.

Hodir may have forgotten him, but the boy knew him. Tucking his feet under the stool, Hodir went back to rocking. Quiet and guilty, he mumbled, "Okay, yeah, you're probably right."

The bearded guy pointed his device at me, and said cheerfully, "I'd like to hear more about Miss Special's powers. Are you aware you have an autonomous energy construct following you around?"

Sheer reflexive cussedness made me move my ghost hand out from behind me and around the room. Sure enough, the goggle guy followed its progress with his little device. Bemused and amused, I declared, "Well, bless my soul, I didn't think any'a that ghost hunter tech stuff worked. Yes, sir, that's my poltergeist."

His vacuum-looking toy must have had a monitor, and the results of pointing it at my poltergeist must have been fascinating. He stared and stared as he said with increasing enthusiasm, "Getting the data we need to make it work is one of the reasons we're here. Could I convince you to join our tests tomorrow?"

I hadn't heard him approach, but behind me Mech said, "Brian, Avery here has had a full day of high school, two hours of magical tutoring, woke Tonika from a coma—"

The lab-coat-and-goggles guy, Brian, knew who Tonika was. He gasped at the news.

Mech just kept talking. "—and defeated a rampaging ghost when we weren't smart enough to have the right tech on hand. She doesn't need any more pressure. I'm going to take her home to her parents now."

Suddenly solemn, Brian laid his little vacuum thing on a tiny table and folded his hands. Inclining his head, he said with quiet respect, "Thank you for helping Tonika, Miss Special. You are as big a hero for that as anyone who puts on a costume and vanquishes evil. Maybe bigger. I hope your parents are as proud of you as you deserve."

Okay. Well. Um. I scratched the back of my head, not used to this much seriousness from adults. Apparently, Mech wasn't the only one as hardcore about the "good" part of "good guys." Not sure what to say, I fluttered my fingers and offered weakly, "If y'all're being all science-y, ah guess ah oughta say, that harvester thingamajig wasn't a ghost. That word, 'construct,' that's a better description. It was a thing made'a necromancy power itself, not a dead person necromancy got back up."

Still grave, Brian nodded. "Thank you, Miss Special. That kind of information is useful."

Mech laid his hand on my shoulder and gave it a gentle tug. "Let's go, Avery. You must be exhausted."

Okay, get your balance back, Avery. I flashed the chaos magic boy a friendly grin. "Nice to meetcha, Hodir."

Bouncing in place, he corrected, "Hodir Deathshriek Thorvalsen! My parents were super really crazy big into death metal when I was born. They always say they wouldn't name me that now, but they know I'm going to grow up to be so cool, everyone will wish they had a name like mine."

Okay, maybe I was the lucky one on the name scale after all, but Hodir and I sounded about equal in the "good parents" department.

I turned to look up at Mech, only to have Sue put her hand on Mech's wrist and ask him, "Hey, can I take Avery home? Like, I can call Winnifred to pick us—" She waggled a finger at herself, me, and Chris. "—up and take us all home at once."

Mech, all affectionate smiles and slow, careful movement for the tired hero girl Avery, shook his head. "No, Miss Perrier. I promised Avery's parents that I would deliver her home personally, and keep them updated on her training. I've already had to call them and tell them we'll be late."

I put on my own big, loving smile, and addressed my

girl- and boyfriend. "It was great ta see ya both, and y'all've been a peach of patience lettin' everyone else talk, Chris, but let the man do his job."

Chris took hold of Sue's waist and carefully, firmly pulled her backwards until her hand came free of Mech's arm, and Sue was out of arm's reach of me in general. Black eyes on mine, Chris promised, "We'll see you soon, Awesome Special."

I turned away. I wouldn't say it out loud, but I was intensely relieved by Mech's intervention, because Mech was right. Normally, Chris's and Sue's affection was very welcome, but I'd had too much of everything today. I was looking forward to going home and relaxing and letting it all be over.

Chapter Four

It wasn't far to my home in Glendale. At least, not far by LA standards. I was from Lexington, Kentucky, and the size of this city kept shocking me. Official city names might keep changing, but one unbroken metropolis stretched over so much land it could cover a third of Kentucky.

I lived on the West end of Glendale, near the hills, on a dusty little street of nearly identical small, pale houses. I saw my friend Peggy as we drove by, and gave her a wave.

Mech pulled up in front of the small, pale house that belonged to my folks. They came right out, and Mech got out of the car declaring, "I apologize again for bringing Avery home late, Mr. and Mrs. Special. Us big name superheroes had to ask a teenage girl to bail us out twice. I hope you'll be half as proud of Avery as I am."

Me, I'd heard this story, and ignored it to go meet Peggy. Peggy Pendleton only lived a few houses down, so we didn't need much of a walk to meet in the middle. Peggy had plain brown hair, plain brown skin that might just be a tan, and while she wasn't wearing plain brown clothing today, the hoodie sweater and floppy, oversized jeans were a muddy green that wouldn't stand out anywhere. She walked with a small cloud of little green bugs flitting around her feet and clinging to her pants legs. Hoppers, I figured. Plant, grass, tree, or just cicadas, the world was full of little bitty hopping bugs and Peggy's super power drew them to her like she was the insect goddess.

Peggy had her hands stuck in the pocket of the thick hoodie. After all, it was January. It might get down to sixty degrees tonight. I had no clue how Peggy could handle wearing this much in the Southern California sun.

Okay, all my friends wore at least as much. My necromancy came with a cold side-effect. Annie was fireproof. Chris must have had a little of that, being her twin. Probably part of the "devil boy" look, anyway. Sue had been trained by her parents and her life to endure terrible suffering.

Sometimes I thought Sue's parents were great and super-humanly supportive. More often I wanted to show them what black magic could do to someone.

But Peggy was the friend in front of me, and I ditched any brooding to give her a lopsided grin. "Hey there, Pegs! What's with the new crowd? Figured y'all'd emptied the whole dang neighborhood by now."

She knew what I meant, of course. Lifting one flip-flop clad foot, she peered down at the green specks sticking to it with a mellow smile. "It's the rainy season. There's always something new sprouting, so there's always new bugs moving in. I'm going to try and shoo them out of the neighborhood. Want to come? We could get a frap-a-lap on the way back."

I shook my head, sending my hair flailing like a rug. "Not today. Jes' got home an' ah am exhausted. Magic trainin', then savin' a coma victim, then whuppin' an undead monster. Craziest afternoon ah've had in at least a month." I paused for a second, reached into my woolly hair to scratch the back of my head, and sighed, "Wish ah could, though. Saw Annie today, and realized ah've seen hardly hide nor hair 'a you two lately. I spend all mah time on Chris 'n' Sue."

Unfazed and smile unbudged, Peggy leaned a little to one side and asked, "Why don't we all go out for a movie? I want to see the one about dancing cats, and Dave and Moonshine don't like theaters."

That made me jump, or anyway jerk half an inch straighter up. "Now, why did ah not think of thayat?" Literally. It hadn't even popped into my head.

"Because your hobby is magic," Peggy answered matter-of-factly.

I didn't jump this time, I just stared. Peggy had me again. She threw out the big truths so casually. I'd finally gotten control of my powers last October, and was so thrilled I'd thrown myself into it more and more. Had I even read a book that wasn't a grimoire or watched a web show since Thanksgiving break? My life had been school, magic, and romance lately, and nothing else.

"Ah may need an intervention," I declared, still boggled.

Peggy nodded amicably. "I'll tell Sue."

Who if she had a choice would spend every second of every day with me, but cared more about making sure I was okay.

Behind me, I heard Mech's pure, friendly, and noble, "By, Avery! Thanks again!"

I looked around and saw my parents standing near the front door of our house, looking at me back. Very intently.

I flinched theatrically and flashed a grin again at Peggy. "Oops. Time t' go. Movie good. We'll all see a movie."

I trotted over to my folks, and we all bustled inside as I chattered, "Hi, Ma! Hi, Pa! Ah got a cool power to show you, but maybe after a nap. Reckon Mech told you, ah've had me A Day."

We got into the front hall of our house, with its walls as pale and dust colored on the inside as the outside. The door closed behind me with a sharp *clunk*.

"We need to talk," said Dad.

Oh, no.

Seeing my expression, Mom gave me a gentle smile. "You're not in trouble, honey child."

I couldn't remember any time I'd been put through this before, but I knew what that meant. It meant they weren't mad about the trouble I was in, and the punishment I was about to face wouldn't be called a punishment.

Dad put his giant hand on my shoulder, and gave me a warm smile, slightly hidden by his beard. Dad was as big as he was sweet. Heaping tons of both. "We're proud of you for the good deeds you did today."

Mom was only small compared to Dad. She had the kind of lean intensity I'd seen on heroes and villains. She took my hand and squeezed it as she added, "But also relieved."

"Special girl…," Dad started, his smile turning pained and awkward.

Mom interrupted him by laying a light hand on his beefy bicep. Her eyes were turned solely me. Her tone and expression were inscrutably sober. "Avery, you've spoken to your great-great-grandmother."

There was only one great-great-grandmother Mom could mean. Alicia Blackheart. "More'n ah care to."

Mom squeezed the hand she was holding again, and told me slowly, "I used to be sad when I was your age that I didn't inherit our family's necromancy legacy, or any super power for that matter. Then I stopped thinking about it. While your powers were only flickers and episodes, it was cute and I still didn't think about it. Now I've had to learn as much as I can. We have a lot of necromancer ancestors, Avery."

I knew the best way to reduce the horror of where this was going was to be cooperative. I looked up at the concerned parents walling me in on either side and admitted, "Ah've spoken to a few of them."

Mom's mouth tightened. She gave me the hard look parents use when they want their child to take information seriously. "They're all evil. All of them. I can't find a single reference to one of our ancestors who had the power and didn't at least kill people under dubious circumstances. Alicia was a legend for being friendly and fun, but she had blood on her hands. The best you could say is that most of it was debatably justified."

Dad covered his face in his hands. I couldn't tell if he was really that upset or not. I just wanted to know how much trouble I was in. He groaned, "I can't believe we're having a 'don't give in to the dark side' conversation with our daughter."

That brought a little of my spirit back. I propped my fist on my hip and told my folks impatiently, "Ah'm not gonna turn evil." How could they even think that?

Mom still had that "take me seriously" look, and it drained the brief spark of rebellion out of me as she said, "You're going to face times when you have to make choices that are debatably justified. Everyone has to make difficult moral choices at some point, but necromancers make more of them. I don't know why."

I did. This afternoon was a perfect example. I hadn't listened when Schleimy said casting the spell wasn't safe, and trouble had fallen on me like an avalanche, worse and worse as I had to use magic to get out of it. This squirmingly unpleasant conversation was just one pebble in that rock fall.

"I—" I started to say, and stopped.

I'd already broken a few laws because I loved my powers so much. I'd stolen, broken into and just plain broken people's homes, encouraged my boyfriend to mind-control difficult adults. Yes, it all felt completely justifiable at the time, but that was what Mom was saying, right? And fights. I kept getting into fights.

Dad hugged me, which involved leaning down, wrapping his big arms around me, and hoisting me up into the air. Mom joined in. With a warmth that made me hope the worst was over, she murmured, "You're not in trouble, Avery."

Dad agreed, "We're warning you, while we try to figure out what can be done. Right now, we just think you need to cut back a bit. Take your dating situation—"

My blood turned to ice. The worst was not over. The real horror was just getting started. My parents were about to take the best thing in my life away from me.

My folks couldn't miss how I froze up. Mom gave me a sharp look and corrected me emphatically, "We *like* Chris and Sue. They're obviously good for you, and they're the last thing we want to take away. But you also jumped into the deep end of the dating pool feet first."

Dad laughed, and I jumped in surprise, or at least tried. He was still holding me off the ground. As if this was some minor, amusing topic, he said, "We are the luckiest parents alive. So many of the physical dangers parents have to worry about with their daughters, we don't, thanks to your necromancy powers."

I could kill people with a touch. Heck, I'd had to work hard to learn how to only hurt people with a touch. No mean or pushy boy or girl was going to be a threat to me, Dad was right there.

Mom hugged me tight again, then took a half step back, returning to the serious adult explanation stare. "But emotionally, you're in for a whirlwind no one is ready for the first time. Usually, we're not ready for it the tenth time."

Dad added, "And we would much rather that be what you're confused about than how hard to hit back when some self-proclaimed witch hunter shows up to destroy the dancing skeleton project you were putting together as an innocent birthday gift for your girlfriend."

"Shoot, Sue wouldn't be interested nohow in dancin' birthday skeletons, but I getcher point." The girl with the light powers who had taken instant offense at the powers of darkness leaped to mind.

Firm but less severe, Mom said, "At the very least we're going to cut down on your magic lessons. Maybe try to get you into more regular social situations, even if those are social situations with your super powered peers. We don't want to punish you, just make sure you don't drown."

"Unless it's in flapjacks," declared Dad suddenly. Tucking me under one arm like a bag of flour, he carried me swiftly towards the kitchen. "Negativity over. Avery has gotten the point. Now I am going to make everything better with flapjacks. Delicious, delicious flapjacks."

My anxiety eased. My pulse slowed down from a race car whine. The only punishment I was facing looked like something I figured I should do anyway.

I sighed. "Then after ah'll go work on mah Byzantine Empire essay, which ah assume is normal an' non-evil 'nuff for everybody."

Chapter Five

Say what you will about Pepperidge Preparatory School for Girls being a blood-soaked arena of sharks pretending to be human teenagers, the teachers were astonishingly good at teaching. By the time the class finished a page of complex math problems, my teacher was walking down the rows, passing back our history essays.

Not complicated math. Complex math. It's the name of a type of math, like algebra or geometry.

Looking down at my essay, I saw a ninety-three circled in red at the top. Well, wasn't that a marvel. I felt a lot better about my chances of getting a hang of equations with "i" in them. Maybe this was what my parents meant by Sue and Chris being good for me. My grades were certainly going up.

One of the good things about this teacher were notes telling me exactly what I did right and wrong. Let's see. A note saying that picking Kievan Rus and its relationship with the Byzantine Empire was a good choice. Another saying... she took off five points for unnecessary information? I should avoid what doesn't support my conclusion?

I'd never heard of a teacher complaining that an essay was too long. Was that even a thing? I'd have to ask Sue about it.

Fortunately, it was almost lunch time already. Soon the bell rang. Girls filed out into the hallways, sniping nasty little comments at each other and pulling subtle, sadistic practical jokes. Sue and I drifted through it, untouched and taking no part, the only two people dangerous enough to carve out a neutral role.

As always, bumping shoulders with each other affectionately, Sue and I processed through the line of the school's deli, bought meals with our food cards, and walked down the cafeteria like invulnerable champions to the far wall. On either side of us girls butchered each other with gossip and snubbing. As always, Sue opened a hole in the wall with her shadow powers, and we stepped out into the courtyard and left them to it.

Except today, one of the girls stood next to a tree, waiting for us.

Sue snarled like a wolf, teeth bared and body tensed to attack. The girl threw up her hands and squeaked, "Wait, please, I'm not your enemy! I've never tried to hurt you, have I?"

Sue didn't answer instantly, so the girl must have been telling the truth. I didn't recognize her at all. I had trouble telling any of the students here apart. Did they bleach their hair blonde, or leave it brown? That question covered the differences between ninety percent of the student body. The school uniform of blue knit sweater vest, blue pleated skirt, white knee socks, and white button up blouse sucked the individuality out of nearly everyone. Not bright blue or white, either. Washed out colors as dull as the costume was uncomfortable.

With no specific vengeance to dish out, Sue merely glared at the girl and snapped out, "You are intruding where you're not welcome."

I slipped my hand into Sue's and gave it a tender squeeze. Sue's glare dimmed from imminent violence to merely suspicious and resentful.

The merciful partner, I warned the girl, "Better 'splain yourself fast, missy. Don't think you'd make us angry like this without a mighty good reason." I personally wasn't angry, but it had to be "us" because Sue and I were a team here. And everywhere.

Hands up, palms out in a sign of peace, the girl squeaked desperately, "I need your help."

At that I squeezed Sue's hand again. Sue needed me to be the kind one. She didn't know how. I was vividly aware of her more slender hand in mine, even without needing it to communicate. As obsessed as Sue was with kissing me, holding hands remained intensely intimate.

The girl couldn't see any of this, of course, and just kept on with her plea. "I just don't know who else to ask. That's all I want, a direction. Someone else to talk to. I have trouble controlling my super power. I don't have any friends with powers. Just tell me where to start and I'll never bother you again, *please!*" That last word came out with a squeak of agonized fear.

"What sorta power ya got?" I asked as gently as I could in a situation so tense.

She looked down at the grassy courtyard lawn, gritting her teeth. The answer came out like an embarrassed confession. "Precognition. Sort of. Mostly I see how dangerous things are."

That made me smirk. "Which is whah you avoided us." I almost dropped my smirk for a wince as my accent played up, turning that "us" into a Carolina "uh-us" as thick as grits.

The girl grimaced, teeth flashing and head tucked down between her shoulders. "It tells me to avoid everyone here. And how. Kind of. The truth is, most of the time I don't understand it. It told me to be here, and I only figured out why when we started talking."

"Hmmmm," I mumbled, considering. I sure knew people who could help her. What I didn't know was how to contact any who would be willing to help her.

To my delighted surprise, I heard Sue's backpack unzip. Sue's shadow pulled out a notepad and pencil. After a quick scribble, Sue ripped off a page and her shadow drifted it over to the girl. Stiff and irritable, Sue told her, "Here. The college nerds running the place will totally love to see you. There will be other super powered kids there. You can try to make friends. Just not with us."

The girl bowed. "Thank you," she whispered.

Then she ran for it, around the corner of the building out of sight.

I raised a curious caterpillar-thick eyebrow at Sue. "Us?"

Letting go of my hand, Sue grabbed my elbow instead, pulling me down for us to sit side by side on the little garden wall, where we always ate. I understood her hurry and desperation. We'd lost precious alone time to helping a stranger.

"I'm taking you home today," she explained. Sue did that so often I'd stopped making any attempt to keep track, and let her do the remembering and the negotiating with my folks. Uncertainty she would never let anyone else see crept in as she added, "I agreed to, like, go to that power testing thing again, and I figured it would be more fun bringing you along. We'll totally skip it if you want."

I shook my head. "Naah, 'spec that works. Mah folks want me t' socialize moah anyway. Peggy suggested we see a movie togethuh. Maybe we can do that aftuh." There wasn't time to explain all my complicated feelings about that. Such as, was this really the smartest thing to do, going straight to a super power specific event the day after my parents told me that my powers take up too much of my life? Even if I was doing it to branch out and be social?

If my anxieties were audible, Sue pretended not to notice. She flashed a grin, whipped out her phone, and started typing. "I totally love that idea. I'll make arrangements."

Chapter Six

Which is why, two hours later, I was closing down the expensive tablet I'd been given when I was mysteriously scholarshipped into this definitely-not-a-reform-school for rich girls. My parents weren't on the way, so I was in no hurry.

It was never a bad idea to wait until last to leave in this place, anyway. Someone might have lost their memory of what happened to the last person to mess with Sue and me.

Stuffing the darkened tablet into my backpack, I hoisted the strap onto my shoulders and looked down at the still-seated Sue. "Yoah in even less of a hurry than me. Ah take it ah'm providin' transportation today?"

With all the other girls gone and the teacher doing teacher things, Sue gave me a warm smile and slid to her feet, pulling up her own backpack. "Winifred will be picking us up from the Ivory Tower, but you're getting us there."

We dawdled on our way out of the room. We dawdled as we walked down the hall. I pointed out to Sue, "Winifred must know by now."

Winifred was Sue's family's live-in butler, a wiry, grey-haired old woman as stiff and hard as steel, and the most competent person I'd ever met. Or imagined.

Sue grinned easily back at me. "But she'll totally never admit she knows, or tell my parents. Discretion is her life. The same with my parents. Like, I'm sure they suspect something? But we have super powers, and friends with super powers. That we have a way to get around by ourselves won't be weird to them. They just don't know how good that way is."

My parents would not be that jaded, especially with magically influenced, questionable moral decisions on their mind. If there had ever been a safe time to admit that I could go anywhere I wanted whenever I wanted, without my parents ever knowing… this sure wasn't it.

The last visible student turned a corner out of sight. I ducked aside to the nearest door, whispered, "Alice, let me in!" and knocked on it with my knuckle.

The door clicked and opened a fraction. Sue and I slipped inside quickly, and the door shut behind us. By the time I gave it a glance, it had gone, leaving bare stone.

We weren't in school anymore. Sue and I stood in the cool air of a weathered stone mausoleum, all pale beige and dusty. Burial niches lined the walls. Four pillars held up the vault, and between them a low staircase rose to a single sarcophagus covered in clockwork, like a lock with a shining white jewel at the center.

Set into the floor by the only entrance lay a bronze plaque engraved, "Here Lies Alice." That was her name, the name of the ghost who haunted this crypt, who was this crypt, and could move it anywhere that had a door to hook up to.

I'd picked up Alice within days of arriving in LA. Picking up magical tools seemed to be built in to necromancy. In an empty burial niche lay my magic staff and magic hat. All the other niches were blessedly empty, except one.

In one shadowy oblong hole in the wall lay Revivienne, a skeleton in an elaborate purple dress and a huge hat. I left the hat covering Revivienne's skull and crossed arms to comfort my friends, who I knew found the skeleton creepy. They couldn't see what I see. Traceries of necromantic magic wove across and between every bone, a masterpiece of magical crafting that could raise Revivienne as a seemingly living person of ethereal beauty, infinite style, worshipful loyalty, a brilliant mind, and a genius for clothing-related magic.

Alas, I had the power to awaken that wonderful creation for a few minutes at a time, tops, by straining all of my limited abilities. I'd done that a couple of times when my friends weren't around to be freaked out. It had been completely worth it.

Look, these school uniforms were horribly sweaty, even in LA's winter. A few little spells I could cast but never understand made my wardrobe a lot more comfortable and me less likely to pass out. Oh, and the fabric tore less and resisted stains.

Enjoying the room's chill, I stretched my arms and asked Sue, "Who all d' we pick up next?"

Sue reported, "Peggy, Chris, and Annie are going home the regular way, then getting ready to meet us. They'll call Alice when they're ready. Like, if you'll convince this thing to listen to anyone but you and Annie." She ended with a resentful scowl at the walls.

"Aw, I reckon she jes' needs a bit'a feeding," I assured Sue with a grin. Alice had plenty of power, enough that I could feel the cold of necromancy drifting around and through me. It got her attention, though. Stroking a hand affectionately down a rough-surfaced wall, I trickled cold out of myself into the stones and murmured, "Alice, honey child, ah do need you to remembuh to take mah friends places too, and listen foah them when they call."

Alice didn't respond. I still wasn't sure how much mind she had. But I knew she heard me, so I shot Sue an encouraging smile. "Alrighty. Give it a try."

Folding her arms and shooting suspicious glances up and around at the ceiling, Sue called out, "Alice, take us to the Ivory Tower. That place we were at yesterday."

The door that hadn't been there a second ago swung open.

We crept out of it into a blue-tiled institutional bathroom. Alice had taken over a miniature door at the back of the bathroom. What was that door normally for? I had no idea. But... "Good choice," I whispered, patting the door before pulling it closed so Alice could disconnect.

The bathroom was empty of people, and so was the hall when we shuffled out into it, looking scrupulously casual. Out of a window at one end of the hall I saw the tops of buildings and nearby hills. We were on the same floor I'd visited yesterday.

Heading to an inner hallway, Sue jerked a thumb down it. Doors stood open with lights shining out, and a college-age guy in a lab coat stood in one. Sue said, "I'm in the room at the end of the hall. Maybe, like, if we get started early, I can get done early and we can go out and have fun."

We walked down the hall together. Most of the rooms we passed held high tech, medical-ish equipment and an adult connecting wires. A couple had kids already being tested. In one of those, a boy in an iridescent suit played a violin with furious passion, sending balls of colored light rushing around the room. I kind of wished I had time to check that out.

I didn't. Sue clung to my left arm hard with both hands. She needed me, and I didn't have a clue why. Would it be better to probe, or leave it be?

I decided to err on the side of knowing my girlfriend's feelings. "The way ya folks—"

That was how far I got before a middle-aged man in a lab coat with mad-scientist goggles hanging around his neck burst out of the room we were passing, grabbing me by the shoulders. "You're here! You got Manipulator's message?"

"What who, now?" I asked, trying to catch up. Oh, right, this was that guy, Brian, who'd been examining Hodir yesterday.

Sue let go of my arm, folding hers tight under her chest and scowling.

Brian let go of my shoulders, maybe figuring out he was being a tad too enthusiastic for comfort. Science geeks did love their specialty, even the adults. Settling into a more fatherly calm but still smiling big time, he asked me, "First, what do you want to be called?"

Sue gave him a hard look with her soft hazel eyes, and snapped, "She's not part of the Community and she doesn't have a secret identity." Woo, some passion there.

I backed her up, but with a friendly grin. "She's right. Yesterday was jes' me helpin' out in an emergency. Ah'm plain old Avery Special, nothin' else."

Brian's head tilted an inch, and his smile changed. I couldn't read it, but it reminded me of parental pride. "I'm glad to hear it. I don't think anyone should be encouraged to get into this life before they're eighteen. Dealing with the extreme personalities on both sides warps you."

I had to agree with him. Sue's parents were a perfect example, and Sue was a perfect example of the damage that did. So I put my arms around Sue's shoulders and gave her a quick, firm hug. My girl needed love.

Although a touch of my own anxiety tickled me. I'd shown up and immediately been treated as an official necromancer and supervillainess, not just a girl who happened to have necromancy powers.

Well, then, maybe coming here had been the right idea after all. I could squash rumors like that in the bud. So stop worrying, Avery, be here for the girl who loves you, show everybody that you're just a teenager like any other, and have fun.

The brown-bearded scientist guy drifted back to conversational, with maybe a little lecturing tossed in. "When we found out Mech knows you, the whole research team was excited. Necromancy is a mystery. No one has gotten a chance in modern history to take measurements. If you'd be willing, one of my colleagues would like to take some readings while you use your powers."

The name from the beginning of this conversation popped into my memory, and I asked hesitantly, "This... Manipulator fella? That there's quite a name."

Brian held up a hand, palm out. "You're safe. Playing twisted games with regular people isn't fun for him anymore. Only heroes and other villains are exciting. That happens to most villains, thank goodness."

Sue's pout softened, and her eyebrows rose in hopeful curiosity. "Hey, he was the guy examining me. Does that mean I'm, like, off the hook today?"

"We thought you'd prefer to accompany Avery," said Brian, with a "trying not to make a big deal of it" smile, which meant the canny old guy knew more about us than that we were dating. Now that he wasn't spazzing out over Science, he had a relaxed, detached air, standing very upright but with his hands in his lab coat pockets.

Someone else took over the spaz duties. A woman with ink-black skin, ragged denim clothes, and a mass of floppy spines instead of hair running down the back of her head leaned out of Brian's testing room. "Did someone say Avery?" Spotting me, she squealed, "YES!"

The woman was quite a character, with pebbly teeth that weren't quite sharp enough to be fangs, and a metal plate around an obviously artificial red left eye. Her right eye was a dark, regular human blue.

I would definitely remember someone this strange looking, but despite that she seemed naggingly familiar, so I asked, "Do ah know you?"

Grabbing my right hand, the woman shook it enthusiastically as she explained, "Doctor Biotic. I told you yesterday I was going to do some stabilizer. Look, I got all my internal organs back!"

Letting go of my hand, she grabbed her denim jacket and pulled the hem up not quite far enough to be indecent, showing off a stomach as pitch-black as her face, her hands, and apparently all of her skin. Other than the color, her stomach was smooth, human, and visibly muscular, but only enough to look fit.

Staring at her stomach felt weird and uncomfortable, so I turned my stare up to her face and tried to think of something to say. I failed.

It didn't matter. She pointed at her robotic eye and chattered on as if I'd asked a question. "Oh, yeah, that. It's stubborn. I'll grow a new one, one of these days. But you're not here to hear about my powers. I have a favor to ask of you. Technically, Mech has a favor to ask of you and I'm passing it along because he's out defeating the forces of evil. Something weird happened at a home where supervillains with mental health issues were being treated. Explosively weird."

I tried to grasp at meaning as the words flew by me, and it didn't help when Doctor Biotic grabbed both of my hands and dragged me into the room.

The room hadn't changed much. It was still big enough to be a classroom. A small classroom, but still. If the equipment lining the walls had changed, I couldn't tell. This time Tonika sat on the wooden stool in the middle of the room, with wires sticking out of the sockets in her head and running back to the computers and machines and who-knew-what-all being fiddled with by Brian.

Her face tight with anxious embarrassment, Tonika gave me a wave, just a shy little flutter of her fingers.

Doctor Biotic scooted backwards far enough to point back and forth between the wires in Tonika's skull and Brian typing at his computers, all the while explaining, "We're trying to find out who Tonika's family is and where she lived, so we can reunite them. She had a boyfriend, but we can't find his contact information to ask him. Mech was hoping Brainy Akk here could get something out of the computer in Tonika's head. Any luck, Beardy?"

Beardy—ah, Brainy—ah, Brian Akk straightened up from peering at his little computer on its wheeled stand, and gave us all a sad grimace. "No. Nothing. If the information was ever there, it's in the parts of the implant that burned out. Those damaged segments were mostly memory. I'm sorry, Tonika."

Clasping her hands in her lap, Tonika answered, "I was prepared for it. I remember Organism One's—"

I jumped. Organism One!? I'd thought I had troubles with undead conquistadors! Organism One was the kind of villain who tried to take over the world, and a powerful enough mad scientist to maybe pull it off.

While I reeled, Tonika kept talking. "—intentions in erasing my memories. Personal information about my life wasn't useful to my role as a cyborg slave agent. It had no reason to back up that information, and complete erasure removes the possibility I would try to find a way around whatever security restrictions it put on that information in my head."

Wandering over to her, Brian patted her bald head, then got busy delicately removing plugs from Tonika's sockets. Sounding fatherly again, he said, "I'm relieved you're taking this well."

"I'm terrified, but panic makes things worse and the

implants make it easier to control my emotions," she answered, sitting still as he removed the last few plugs. The final one was a USB port right at the top of her neck. With them all gone, he took a purple wig out of his lab coat's copious pockets and fastened it onto her scalp. It had little buttons that fit into the sockets to hold it in place, and the hair hung down like thin plastic strands rather than real hair. Thanks to the way it plugged in, it did look just like it was growing out of her head when attached.

Me, I walked over and took Tonika's hand in mine, giving it a reassuring squeeze. She looked up at me with a weak smile. She was tiny and thin, to match that smile. She had to be thirteen. Someone had dressed her in a black jumpsuit that was more like a catsuit, although the rubbery fabric was thick enough it was completely modest. Modest or not, I wanted to beat with a stick whoever thought it was a good idea to dress a girl already nervous about being a cyborg in an outfit that made her look like one.

Doctor Biotic jerked back into perky attention and launched into another speech. "Right, right, and that's where you come in, Avery. Mech's a good guy, but he's not a teenage girl. He wants me to ask you to be Tonika's friend. I know you can't just walk up and stick friendship to somebody, but you're a social butterfly, and in about fifteen minutes this building will be packed with kids with super powers who for pretty good reasons feel like nobody understands them. Show Tonika around and help her make introductions, okay?"

I gawked up at one blue eye and one red eye. "Me. A social butterfly."

Doctor Biotic pointed a shiny black finger at me, then herself. "You. Social Butterfly. Me. Og. Good at flint chipping."

Tonika giggled, lifting her fists to her mouth.

Draping her forearm over my shoulder, Sue drawled, "Like, she has a point."

I gawked at her now, mouth hanging open. "Ah'm the definition of a wallflowah!"

Sue smiled, proud and a little teasing, like a cat. "Only in a hostile crowd. Don't argue with me, Avery. I totally know you better than you know yourself."

Probably true.

Sue's smile widened, and now she purred like a cat, sly and smug. Raising a hand with a finger pointed, she told me and the room, "For example, you have a big freckle right—"

I froze up in mortified horror. What did Sue know!?

She jabbed me in one shoulder blade. "Here!"

I shot Sue a scolding glare. She dissolved into squeaky giggles.

Ignoring those giggles was the only way to hold onto any shreds of dignity I had left, so I turned my attention and my smile back to Tonika. I even managed to mostly ignore how Tonika's mouth was clamped tightly shut in barely restrained laughter. I just said, "Reckon if ah can help, ah'd be happy to. Y'all'll be less nervous wandering 'round with kids your age than adults what sees ya as a science experiment."

Doctor Biotic propped her fists on her hips and stuck out her lower lip. A skinny tail I hadn't noticed before lashed sharply behind her. "Not fair. I see me as a science experiment!"

Brian the professor guy gave her a very solemn, thoughtful stare, and asked, "What did you dose yourself with, Biotic? You're hypomanic."

She grinned all her odd little bumpy teeth at him. "It's the other way. This is what I was like originally, when I was completely human."

Brian took a deep breath and rolled his eyes. "Why am I not surprised?"

Me, I glanced between Sue and Tonika and jerked my thumb at the door. We tiptoed out while the adults argued.

Nibbling my lower lip, I looked up and down the hall, and went, "Hmmm. Figger the social stuff'll have to wait 'til the kids with slower rides get here. Where's the room you were bein' tested in, Sue? Ah figger Tonika'll feel a might better seein' other folks get stuck with electrodes, right?" I gave Tonika a friendly grin, and she smiled back.

Sue pointed. We followed that finger, down to a room near the end. Inside, a man with spiky black hair, mad-science goggles over his eyes, and an armored jumpsuit in purple and black, hooked much less goofy machines that were mostly white plastic together with bundles of cords.

Not expecting this, all I could do was ask, "Ahem?"

He jerked upright—but fluidly, with the poise of someone used to conflict and surprises. Turning to face us, he twined black-gloved fingers together and gave me an evilly gleeful grin that matched his drawling voice. "Deathette, I presume?"

Sue pushed her way in front of me, waving her arms in violent negation. "Nope. No way. Like, forget it, bozo."

My girl's scowl was rapidly becoming seriously angry. I intercepted one of Sue's hands, squeezing it reassuringly as I stepped in front of her instead, addressing the outrageous supervillain. "Ya got me confused with some'n else, Mister. That Deathette girl was most likely doin' a favor and nobody'll see hide nor hair of her again. Me, mah name's Avery Special, and ah spec it'll stay Avery Special."

He straightened out his index fingers to lay them against each other, looking down at me with only traces of dry, evil amusement in a mostly serious voice. "That's a shame. Battling a necromancer superheroine would be something for the bucket list."

Letting go of Sue's hand, I put my fists on my hips and shook my head slowly. "Yall'll have ta hope for the next life, 'cause it ain't likely gonna happen in this'n. The good news is, ah happen to have the same kinda powers and that Brian fella talked me inta substitutin'."

Manipulator whipped his right hand up in a clenched fist and crowed, "Yes! That's why we're here! For *Science!*" And, very suddenly, the supervillain theater ended. With ordinary, easy-going, even casual cheer, he tapped a box on a stand and explained, "I'm still setting up. I won't be ready for you for a few minutes, but you can sign in now." He waved a hand in vague dismissal, his tone reassuring. "It's all optional. Whatever name you want to give, and whatever information you feel comfortable sharing. It will all be kept confidential and we only use it for research purposes."

He gave the box a gentle push, and its stand rolled a couple of feet towards me on the five tiny wheels at the bottom. The box had a monitor. It was just a little mobile computer, really, like something you might see in a hospital. The questionnaire on the screen also looked like something out of a hospital, with questions about health conditions, age, exercise, and whatnot. The top two questions were "Name" and "Super power(s)," and then in big red letters NOT REQUIRED before moving on to address and the rest.

I typed in Avery Special as my name, and Necromancy as my super power. I figured I might as well fill the rest out honestly, too. I had nothing to hide.

I had just finished typing in my address when my eyes scanned up and I noticed my name read "y pil" and my super power was "Nomny."

Scratching my head, I asked, "What in Sam Hill!?"

Sue leaned over to read the screen over my shoulder. Her teasing leer grew and grew on her face, and she asked, "That new ghost hand you've got?"

"Yeah?" I asked, confused.

"You were typing with it instead of your left hand," she finished.

...what, really? Putting my hands back on the screen, I typed in—

Well, boy howdy. Sure enough, typing was such an automatic process I'd moved my ghost hand in to type instead of my flesh-and-blood hand, and a touch screen wouldn't register the ghost fingers.

Sue leaned around me to smile with vicious sweetness up at my boggled face. "You picked up your backpack with it when we left school. It was adorable."

"And you didn't tell me?" I demanded.

Sue shrugged. "Why? I pick up my backpack with my shadow all the time. Now we both have the same power." Her smile radiated satisfaction at having that in common now.

I scratched my head again, and had to spend a flicker of concentration to do it with my flesh-and-blood hand and not my poltergeist. I must have been focused enough in school that I used my real left hand for typing and writing. It was eerie how less than a day later, having a poltergeist felt automatic, like something I'd always had rather than a new toy.

Manipulator flipped on a screen on one of his rounded white machines, and stared at that monitor while he plugged and unplugged a cord in different sockets. A touch of teasing couldn't quite leave his voice, but otherwise he sounded like a sincere, professional scientist as he said, "Hard as this may be to believe, Miss Perrier, but I'm sorry about yesterday. I was hoping the interactions with a power set we do understand would help us understand Miss Cruz's powers. I of all people should have noticed the personality conflict."

Sue didn't answer. She didn't even look at him.

Tonika, standing by the door, lifted a hand hesitantly, and asked, "Um?"

I gave her a big, encouraging grin and a nod. "Go on, Tonika. Cain't be more ignorant'n me, nohow."

A little more firmly, Tonika asked Manipulator, "Did you say that you understand shadow powers?"

The supervillain turned to face us again, lifting his goggles to give the three of us calm, curious looks. He looked and sounded like a teacher now. "Not how the human body produces and controls them, but the shadow itself uses the energy differential between a more lit and a less lit surface to generate an imaginary Dirac network. That's imaginary as in imaginary numbers."

I nodded. "We just got ta those in clayass."

You know, this Manipulator guy deserved more credit than I'd given him. He was completely unfazed by how ridiculous my accent could get. I hadn't seen him even wrestle down a reaction.

Sue was at least willing to look at the villain now, propping a fist on her lip to give him a skeptical glower. "So do those words mean anything besides 'shadow powers'?"

Manipulator barked a wry, cynical laugh, and grinned at us. "They mean a lot of math. Welcome to physics. The math does work. Brainy predicted a number of things that enhanced shadow powers like yours can do, Miss Perrier. They contain their own space, which they superimpose over existing space to make it look like they're opening holes in solid objects. They can apply physical pressure. Once the network is created, it can lift off of the surface the shadow was cast on, and transfer sight and sound from a distance. It can act as a conduit for other types of energy. There's no reason you're limited to your own shadow, either. Your powers may not be able to access all these abilities, but we know the imaginary Dirac network can produce them."

As snippy as if she were being told she wasn't good enough, Sue answered, "Yeah, I've got the first two, and, like, that's it."

Which was a lie. I'd seen Sue lift her shadow off the ground today, and she had never said it directly, but I was pretty sure I'd seen her using it to listen in on another room.

Tonika, her bravery increasing and her voice getting more firm with each question, asked Manipulator, "So I suppose it's difficult to directly measure these things, but you got some readings that reminded you of shadow powers? It seemed reasonable that a power that looked like light but didn't act like it might be another imaginary Dirac network produced by the opposite energy differential type? And if you superimposed the two, rather than canceling out, you were expecting a change in perceptible readings that would let you graph the complex number equations involved? Not only would that give you information on a new power, it would be hard confirmation that the math you're using for shadow powers is correct?"

Flabbergasted, I gawked at Tonika and said, "Is that cyborg brain genius y'all're showin' off, or were y'all that smart already? And in case it ain't clear, either way ah think y'all're the bee's knees."

Tonika lowered her eyes, but also grinned. Pushing her hanging purple plastic hair up around an ear, she mumbled, "Organism One wanted me because I think in unusual directions."

Manipulator golf clapped with gentle admiration, and a brighter, fiercer pride in his smile and stare. "Correct directions. Correct about our thinking, at least. Our thinking was dead wrong. The results of Miss Cruz's and Miss Perrier's powers overlapping were nothing like interacting imaginary Dirac networks. It looked to me like—"

"Magic?" I inserted confidently.

And now Manipulator grinned. Some of the villainous

drawl returned, and he waved the fingers of one hand like a magician preparing for a trick. "Physicists prefer the term 'strange energy.' More accurately, a very small core of physicists flip their wig if you use the word 'magic,' and the energy is certainly very strange. That's why I wanted to meet you so badly, Miss Special. No one in modern history has gotten to take readings off of a necromancer. The last person to even try was Professor Fitzwidget in 1922, and the technology available to him might as well have been chalk drawings." His lips curled up, somewhere between a smirk and a grimace. "Apparently he got into distracting trouble after only a few days of tests anyway."

I smirked back at him. "Mah great-great-grandmama Alicia was powerful distractin' and loved her some trouble, yes sir." Looking over at Sue, I asked, "Sweetheart?"

All the paranoia and anger melted from Sue's face when I called her that, and for a second she looked as shy and vulnerable as Tonika as she asked back, "Yes?"

I waved at the door. "This fella's serious. Go get me mah hat 'n staff, wouldja?"

She didn't discuss it further, just rushed out the door.

Turning my attention to Tonika next, I said, "I reckon you'll feel downright normal once ya see how this fella hooks me up with wires and doohickies. Lookit all this junk."

Manipulator pulled his goggles back down over his eyes and raised a gloved finger. "Junk I still haven't set up. You're pretty distracting yourself, Miss Special. I suppose Deathette would be so distracting I wouldn't be able to say this: Shoo yourself. Stand outside for five minutes. I'm never going to get ready if you two keep me talking."

I snickered, and Tonika and I did just that, stepping out into the hall to stand and wait. We even closed the door behind us. There were teenagers arriving now, half a dozen of them shuffling into their various rooms to be tested. Sue was nowhere to be seen.

Smiling lopsidedly down at Tonika, I asked, "Well, he's a hoot and a half, ain't he? Mighty likable for a supervillain."

She nodded, frowning and furrowing her brow in serious

thought. "With the name 'Manipulator,' perhaps that's deliber-ate. In fact, I'm sure it's deliberate, but speculating what his goal is for us liking him would be futile. There are too many possi-bilities, many of them innocent."

My smile turned into a huge, approving grin.

Tonika watched it for a few seconds with a weak smile, then mumbled, "And, uh… thanks."

My grin pulled an inch wider. "Gonna have ta be specific. Been a mighty busy twenty-four hours."

An awkward but not actually shy grin sparked on Tonika's face. "For all of it, but I mean making me feel more comfortable."

I looked up and down the hall and nodded at the teens and preteens peering at door numbers, exchanging greetings with the scientists on the other side of those doors, and occasionally chatting with each other. "Well, look around. Every one'a these kids has powers, and most of us feel lahk freaks. We got permis-sion to poke 'round and you're bound ta click with somebody."

Chapter Seven

Somebody drifted out of the crowd, headed for us. A girl in the same bland school uniform I was wearing, in fact. After a couple of seconds, I recognized her as the girl from lunch. Honest truth, my classmates did all look alike to me.

She looked almost as desperate as the last time I'd met her. Clutching the straps of her blue backpack, she scurried up to me and sighed. "Thank goodness, it's you. Do you know who I talk to? I don't even know what to say. I feel like I'm here on false pretenses."

Shy little Tonika quivered, grabbed my sleeve, and squeezed my arm for strength. It worked. Voice quivering, she addressed the newcomer. "Did you—are you—did you come without an invitation? Or just bad instructions?"

The new girl gave Tonika a searching stare that drifted into blankness, like she was looking through Tonika at something beyond her.

Still squeezing my arm ferociously, Tonika asked, "Your super power is doing something, isn't it?"

The new girl's eyes snapped back into focus. She shifted her weight, shoulders tensed and wriggling an inch to either side.

Low and abashed, she said, "It's telling me you're safe."

Tonika's death grip on my arm relaxed. Solemn and calm, she responded, "No, I'm not, but maybe I'm the specific kind of safe you care about. I didn't get the kind of invitation the other kids got, either."

Me, my grin never budged. Both girls needed encouraging. "Spec that's easy to fix. That Brian gentleman gave quite thuh impression of being in chahge."

Tonika's smile returned too, hesitant and hopeful. "Even if he's not, he's very friendly, and Doctor Biotic would love to help. I think she finds scientists funny, which is funny itself, since she is one. The real kind, not just the mad kind."

"And in the process, moah folks foah both of you to meet," I encouraged. "Ah must stay out heah in the hallway so Sue can see me when she gets back."

The new girl's back jerked straight and stiff, her eyes widening in shock. She squeaked, "Too late!" Taking three steps to the side, she placed Tonika between me and her, folded her arms in convincing casualness, and focused her eyes entirely on the smaller girl with the long, purple wig. "So, what's your super power? I'm Delphine, by the way."

Tonika answered, "Tonika. And I don't have one, unless you count cyborg brain implants. Right now, all they do is improve my memory. Going forward, anyway." The bitterness in that last sentence was unmistakable.

Delphine didn't mistake it. She smiled with a puppy-dog mix of hope and encouragement. "If that means you have amnesia, I can help keep people from making fun of you for it."

And lo and behold, Delphine's prediction proved itself true. Sue rounded the corner of the hallway, eyes locking immediately on me and calling out, "Avery! Look who I found!"

She'd found Chris, and dragged my delightfully handsome devil-boyfriend along by one hand, while he dragged his sister Annie by her hand, and Peggy followed them all with her own hands in her pockets but looking around at everything with a faint, curious smile.

The (retired) fashion-model twins normally favored loose clothing with lots of ruffles and lace and such. Perhaps because of where we were, today they were dressed in more villainous fashion, in sleek, figure-hugging black jumpsuits marked by lines of yellow and orange flame pattern on the sides. Nearly knee-high laced boots and half a dozen loose belts each broke up the simplicity, with spiked leather bands at their wrists and dog collars at their throats. Two little bitty bands decorated their tails, out near the spade tips.

Not their usual style, but as always, they wore it with elegant confidence. They stood out starkly next to Sue still in our bland school uniform, and Peggy in her dirt-colored t-shirt and corduroy pants. As if they'd planned it, Tonika's bodysuit looked completely natural and plain, with Chris and Annie in a more elaborate version nearby.

Annie had my magic hat on her head, and my staff in her free hand. The latter looked like a shoulder-high wooden pole with a brass cap on one end and faint abstract engravings giving the wood texture. The hat was a wide-brimmed sun hat, currently black, with a ring of pinky-high skulls around the crown.

I held out my left hand. Annie swept off my hat and tossed it like a discus. It floated more than it spun, and I hardly had to lean to the side for it to settle right onto my bushy mane. While teenagers crossed between me and Annie I thumped the woven brim, turning the hat from black to the blue of my school uniform. Then the way cleared for a few seconds, and Annie spun my staff like a cheerleader's baton and tossed it as truly as the hat. I grabbed it easily out of the air and thumped the base against the floor.

Caution hit me, and I thumped the hat with a finger again, this time on the skulls. "And ah do not want to heah from the peanut gallery."

The ghosts haunting my hat successfully chastened, I clapped Tonika on the back and introduced, "Tonika, meet mah boyfriend Chris, his sistah Annie, and Peggy, who is the greatest."

"She is," echoed Chris immediately.

Annie nodded furiously, her liquid black hair bouncing.

Sue scowled, and a second later nodded. "Yeah."

Peggy said nothing, just smiled a little wider as she watched us all.

Chris, always friendly, took Tonika's hand and gave it a warm shake. His smile was warmer still. Which was good, since Chris was tall and Tonika was short, and he had to look almost straight down at her and she almost straight up.

I explained to the group, "Raht now weah taking Tonika's new friend heah—"

"Delphine," Tonika supplied, while the actual Delphine did her best to lurk in the background.

"—to get signed up foah testing," I finished.

Sue gave our fellow Pep Prep student a suspicious glower, but her eyes quickly slid away and she merely stepped up shoulder to shoulder with me.

It didn't exactly take long to walk everyone down to Brian Akk's testing room. It was, what, twenty feet away? But just like last time, as we reached the door Doctor Biotic lunged out with a crazed grin on her face. She grabbed Chris's and Annie's wrists, hauling them into the room. Annie let out a squeal but didn't resist. Chris just looked amused and confused, and as soon as they were inside the room and Biotic let go, he slipped a calming arm around his sister's shoulders.

A couple of hurried steps and I reached the door and could see what was going on. Doctor Biotic stood, gesturing furiously back and forth between the twins and Brian Akk, who stood by his machines and watched her with a bemused expression.

The pitch-black, mutated ex-superheroine babbled gleefully, "Brian! Brian, photograph their feet!"

Mister (Professor?) Akk's confused smile solidified into a warning frown. "Biotic, I'm serious. You need to give yourself something when you get home. You may be genetically stable, but not mentally."

She flapped a hand in easy surrender, while the fingers of her other hand pushed back the limp spikes, or tendrils, or whatever she had instead of hair. "Okay, okay, fine. I've been thinking about what would be fun to be next anyway. I'll go for something chill. Maybe mix a slug of capybara with scorpion and sphynx cat. But but but! Their feet, Brian!"

I couldn't help it. I broke out in giggles. Chris picked it up with compulsive, bubbly chuckles. Annie giggled too, with her head tucked down bashfully. Then the girl sitting on the stool in the middle of the room being tested laughed. Soon everyone but Peggy, Doctor Biotic, and Brian were chuckling in some fashion, and Peggy at least wore a big smile.

Patient and resigned to his colleague's mutagen-induced madness, Brian asked, "Fine. What about their feet?"

Jerking her hands in sharp back and forth motions towards Annie's high-heeled boots and Chris's regular-heeled boots, Doctor Biotic gushed, "Isn't it obvious? They have partial hoof morphology. I've been trying to find an example you can document since mine reverted. Why do you think teenagers are wearing heels like that? It's the shape of their bones!"

I was gobsmacked. No lie, I gawked at Biotic with my mouth open and my eyes wide like saucers. I'd seen Chris and Annie barefoot and learned the secret, yes. Their feet looked perfectly human, but they walked on tiptoes all the time if they could. It had something to do with their powers making them look like devils. The real secret was, Chris would wear heels as high as Annie's if fashion allowed a boy to do it.

As goofy as Doctor Biotic sounded, she'd spotted it in less than a second while they were wearing shoes. Thick, concealing shoes. Her mania sure hadn't made her stupid.

The explanation got Professor Akk's interest. Eyebrows raised, he asked the twins, "Only if you two consent?"

I scratched the back of my neck as Chris and Annie exchanged glances. After a second of that, Chris answered, "Sure. Should we take off our shoes?"

Brian shook his head, hoisting the hand vac looking thing he'd used on yesterday off a table, or a device that looked just like it to my eyes. "No need. My camera takes several kinds of pictures at once, some of which are effectively x-rays."

As Brian took photos, Tonika wandered silently into the room. Scratching behind my ear, I watched her pad closer to the girl on the stool.

Oops. Doctor Biotic had been so distracting, I'd ignored the actual test subject we were interrupting. A little middle schooler no bigger than Tonika, her purple t-shirt with a green unicorn pony (okay, a cyborg pony, but still sparkly) and dark-blue jeans stood out against the room's white tile and the greying wood of her stool. She wore her long black hair pulled back in a ponytail, and had a pair of glasses up on her forehead and leather and brass goggles around her neck.

The leather and brass goggles were a mad-scientist thing, right? Which explained why around the girl, floating in the air, stretched a complicated geometric figure made out of strings of translucent, shimmering, rainbow-colored light. Tiny metal joints marked the corners.

Slowly, gently, and cautiously, Tonika reached her fingers towards one of the light strings. The girl on the stool watched her, but gave no warning, so Tonika kept reaching until her fingers passed through a strand, with no visible effect.

Softly, Tonika told the girl, "This is beautiful. It must be important. Why aren't you proud of it?"

The girl answered with an edge of sulky frustration, "I am, but I don't know what it does, and it's the only invention I've ever made. I don't know if I even have a power anymore."

That got Brian Akk's attention, or maybe he was just finished taking photos of my friends' feet. He took a couple of steps to the edge of the web, and gave the girl a fatherly, encouraging smile. "It's not rare for a thirteen-year-old mad scientist's power to have only activated once, Miss Benitez. It will grow. As for not knowing what it does, you're in good company, because neither do I. This is what we call Tier Three mad science. It uses physics humanity hasn't guessed at yet. Half my machines are telling me it doesn't exist at all."

Man, my head itched. I dug both hands into my mass of hair and scratched furiously.

Tonika tightened her lips in thought, and after a few seconds told the girl on the stool, "I bet mad scientists have written about what they do to inspire their powers and make them activate. You might be able to find a common element, or advice that works for you. I could help you look it up. It sounds fun."

The girl's face lit up like her web. Metaphorically, at least. "You would? Please!"

I grinned at Tonika while trying not to scratch my leg. "Y'all didn't need me ta help you make friends, Tonika. Look at you."

Tonika turned to smile back at me over her shoulder. "You make me feel brave."

"She does that," confirmed Annie in a shy but emphatic squeak.

Sue nodded, sounding begrudged. "Yeah, she totally does."

The girl in the chair blinked suddenly in surprise and looked past me. "Wait—Sue!?"

Sue leaned forward a few inches, staring at her hard, until light dawned. "You're, like... Olga, right? From Northeast West Hollywood Middle?"

I fidgeted. Good gollies, I itched, all over! It was driving me crazy! Did one of the kids on this floor make itching powder or something?

No.

I knew this sensation. I should have recognized it sooner.

"Everyone out! Get down! Whatever!" I yelled.

I rushed forward, grabbing the two most defenseless people, Tonika and Olga, and dove to the floor in the back corner of the room with one of them in each arm. Half-turning to shield them with my body, I held my staff out towards the invisible source of violently itchy magic in the center of the room. My friends had left the room entirely, but I felt the cold pressure as Sue's shadow flowed over me.

Good. I poured even colder necromancy into that shadow. It was a crude shield, but the erupting magic would have to burn through it to get to the girls I was hiding.

The air cracked, splitting into a series of interconnected circles right where the chair Olga used to be sitting in had been. Strobing, multicolor light showed through the gaps. The center circle ripped wider and wider, with a squeaky tearing sound.

Hodir, death metal t-shirt and all, stepped out of the rip. He looked around until he saw me, and raised his fists in triumph. "Yes! YES! I did it! This is exactly where I wanted to be! Avery, look, I created a rift that was completely controlled by using you as an anchor on the other end! It worked perfectly with no problems!"

The rift behind him let out a cracking noise, like breaking wood. The gap Hodir had stepped out of lurched wider. Some of the side circles broke completely open. Itchy magic flooded over my magic barrier, but shadow and staff kept it from penetrating and doing who knew what to Tonika and Olga.

"Okay, that's a problem," Hodir admitted, turning around to give his portal an anxious frown.

At which point the hovering light web, which hasn't moved an inch until now, collapsed. It went through Hodir. It went through the knocked-over stool. But the portal caught on the strands, and in less than a second was crushed into a glowing rainbow ball tied up in glowing rainbow threads. The little metal corners were gone from the web. Maybe they'd been illusions to begin with.

The pressure of Hodir's chaos magic faded rapidly. Thank goodness. When it was low enough I was confident it wouldn't mutate someone or drive them insane or whatever, I let go of the younger girls and climbed slowly to my feet.

Olga, sitting up and staring at her floating, compressed web and the portal it caged, said, "It's never done that before."

"Did it ever have the chance?" asked Tonika, sitting up next to her. Olga giggled in response.

Walking up to him with a growing smirk, I told the little black-magic wielder, "Well. Howdy, Hodir. You sure can make an entrance."

"I know, right?" he replied, giving me an open-mouthed smile so wide and proud of himself that he ought to light up the room.

I didn't quite know what to say to that misplaced enthusiasm. After a couple of seconds Brian Akk stepped out from behind some of his equipment and asked, "Is everyone okay?"

From inside and outside the room we all chorused, "Yes."

Brian nodded. The man was sure calm. He also had a couple of devices in his hands I couldn't possibly identify, and finished wiring them together, then locked them into one device at a pair of twisting joints. "I'm relieved. Normally these testing events are a lot quieter, I promise."

I grimaced and hung my head. "Yep, that's mah powah's fault."

Hodir cleared his throat loudly and stuck his chin out in bulldog pride. "Uh, excuse me? Chaos mage, here? *My* power, *my* fault."

"It was crazy before you showed up," I argued, pointing at him with one finger of my hand holding my staff.

Undeterred, he nodded sharply. "Right. Chaos magic."

I gawked at him. I was doing a lot of that this afternoon. It was just so bizarre to meet someone in exactly my position. Switching my staff to my right hand, I held out my left. "Black magic kids club?"

Hodir grabbed my hand and pumped it enthusiastically. "Black magic kids club!"

My friends were filtering back into the room. Sue stepped to the side and watched me fixedly, her mouth a thoughtful scowl. Chris stepped up next to me and held out his own left hand to Hodir.

Aw, shucks. He'd noticed Hodir was left-handed. Chris could be sweet like that.

With his most winning smile, Chris introduced, "I'm Avery's boyfriend, Chris Domingo. I didn't have a chance to say 'hello' yesterday. Avery has mentioned the black magic kids club a few times. I've always wanted to meet another member."

Hodir shook his hand back, turning his enthusiastic smile up to Chris. "That's me. You saw what I did? I totally ripped a hole from one place to another with my bare hands." Hodir's eyes kept widening as he looked up at Chris, and now he looked down at where Chris's hand held his. The blond boy's voice turned into a squeaky stammer, fast. "That hand. I, uh—you saw it. It worked. Mostly. But someone was here to stop me from destroying... uh, I'm Howdy. I mean Horns. I mean Hodir. And you're—"

Throwing his arms over his head, Hodir wailed, "AAAAAH!" and ran for the door. He bumped into Annie, rebounded off of her, and lifted his arms away from his face long enough to see hers. Leaping away, he fled down the hall squeaking, "Don't look at me! Nobody look at me!"

I sighed. "Guess it don't stop." I'd really hoped my power was done flinging trouble at me.

Chris nudged me with his shoulder, leaning his head over to touch my hair. "This one isn't your fault, either. That... happens sometimes. I hope he'll be okay. If I go looking for him, he'll just be more embarrassed. Or he might take it wrong."

Tonika held up her hand, and announced with only a hint of sheepishness, "I'll do it."

"If you're going, I'm going," declared Delphine from the doorway.

"I need to give him back his... this," said Olga, grabbing her web and the scrunched-up portal it held trapped. They moved as easily as if she were holding a hamster ball.

"We'll figure it out together," Tonika told Olga, taking hold of her other hand.

Tonika and Olga rushed out, with Delphine close behind.

Brian Akk and Doctor Biotic were focusing on putting science doohickies back upright and in place, so my friends and I drifted out into the hall.

Chris spoke first, with a lopsided smile. "That reminded me of how we all became friends."

Sue eyed him with a skeptical, sidelong scowl. "Fighting for our lives in an illegal reality show?"

Undaunted, he replied, "Scared and out of place until two of us took the lead and showed that we could face anything as a team."

Sue's scowl turned into a pout, and she looked directly away from Chris. Poor girl didn't know how to handle a compliment. Maybe especially from a boy watching her with such a warm smile. It had never occurred to me before, but... maybe Chris had more feelings about Sue than just partners in loving me?

I approved, but I also had no idea what to say about that, and somebody needed to say something. I tried, "So. Guess we all're free for a few minutes."

Chris turned his black eyes back to me, and chuckled, "Want to wander around and gawk at the normal-compared-to-us having their innocent, not evil powers tested?"

I let out a faint groan. "Ah'm already drownin' in super

powers today, thank you kindly. Ah need some regular life stuff."

"This is regular life stuff for us," he shot back, with a joking rather than pushy grin.

I scratched above my ear, this time out of pure awkwardness. "It ain't that. It's..."

Sue picked up where I couldn't find the words. "Avery's parents are being difficult."

And suddenly everyone's smile was gone. My friends clustered around me, everyone with a concerned expression and a comforting hand on me somewhere.

"It's not that bad," I lied. Worse, I could hear the strain of lying in my voice. Maybe it really wasn't that bad, but it felt like it. Then it all came out in a rush. "They think ah've been focusin' on mah powahs too much, and they're afraid ah'll go evil lahk mah ancestors. Theah right about the powahs part. Plus, Annie and Peggy've seen hardly hide nor hair of me."

Chris's smile came back, gentler this time, but with enthusiasm. "Well, Annie might have a cure for that."

The feminine devil twin nodded. "I know you've been missing tree climbing here in LA."

I managed a small, wry smile. "Sue's parents got this crazy machine that gotta've been made by a mad scientist for me to exercise on, but it ain't at all the same."

With a hopeful smile, Annie explained, "I've found the gym with the tallest rock-climbing spire in LA. I thought we might all do it together."

"Ah ain't leavin' Peggy out," I said flatly.

Peggy shrugged. "I'll try it."

Well... I had to take her word for it. I smiled a little wider. "Thanks, y'all. Thanks, Annie. You're a peach, do you know that?"

Now it was Annie's turn for a tight, embarrassed smile and to look away rather than see anyone's expression.

But I didn't let it go. Putting a hand on her shoulder, I said, "Ah kin go out for coffee with Peggy. Is theah somethin' you'd like to do together?"

Too flustered to speak, she pointed at my woven red

backpack, which I'd never actually taken off.

I nodded, leaning forward. Annie unzipped the pack and pulled out a notepad and pencil. After a few seconds of sketching, she held it up for me to see.

Two stick figures lay on their backs with their legs stretched up a wall, reading, and two arrows pointed at them with the label "same book."

I grinned big. "Now, don't that sound like a mighty good time, and just what ah need to get back into."

There was only one other teenager in the hallway, down at the other end. Everyone else was either done, or in rooms being tested. Having noticed that, I sighed. "Think we ought to check if that Manipulator fella is ready for me?"

Cheerfully practical, Sue gave my shoulder a squeeze—nobody but Annie had actually let go of me yet—and pointed out, "We need to get it done before the movie anyway. Then we can go out and be totally regular non-powered friends."

Chapter Eight

So, trailing my friends, I trudged back to the classroom or laboratory room or whatever academic room it was originally meant to be, now converted into an examination chamber. Tonika leaned against the wall near the door, arms behind her back, silently waiting.

I addressed Manipulator, who was grinning toothily and wringing his hands in anticipation. "You ready yet?"

He nodded slowly, eyes alight with fiendish anticipation. "Very much. Stand here, please? And take off your sweater."

That turned out to be so he could fix white plastic rings around my arms and stomach, with little clasps that buckled them in place like belts. Not simple white plastic, either. Shiny white, with what looked like strips of copper on the inner curve, except copper wouldn't be so flexible.

While he did that, and fixed electrodes to my throat and hands, and put a thing like a tiara around my head, I said to Tonika, "Weren't expectin' to see you here. Y'all get some new friends?"

She nodded, her smile hardly shy at all. "Yes, and Hodir feels much better. They're getting tested, and I wanted to see how your testing goes. You're an inspiring person."

"That she is," Chris agreed. Sue smiled.

Now it was my turn to feel hot and awkward and not know how to deal with a compliment.

Which left me standing in the center of a white-tiled room brightly lit from fluorescent ceiling bulbs, with two walls crowded with machinery and a dozen wires snaking from those machines to the sensors on my body. The air conditioning in this building worked well, and a cool draft played over me, accompanied by peculiar chemical smells from the machines.

Brian Akk's machines had mostly been straight up and down racks of computers. Manipulator's tended to sleek, medical-looking machines covered in rounded white plastic. He turned a lot of them on, and built-in monitors lit up with lots of readings I didn't recognize. I did see a lot of zeroes and flat lines. Some were crazy bouncing lines, or more mysterious numbers. I spotted my pulse rate, blood pressure, and wasn't sure what O2 measured exactly, but I knew doctors liked to test it.

Peering at a screen I couldn't see from this angle, Manipulator asked, "Is your power active—" He hesitated for half a second and continued with a self-deprecating chuckle that turned to sly humor. "Sorry. Deathette is such a good name, I have trouble remembering I'm not testing her."

And yes, I was amused this time, smirking as I answered, "It never completely shuts down."

"Are the hat and staff magic?" he asked next, moving to a different machine.

I nodded, but just a little, because I didn't want to dislodge his equipment. "The hat does all kindsa things, but mostly it's a ghost cage. Mah staff's like a battery. It's full up. Thought that might help the testing."

All the supervillainous goofiness gone again, in sober and focused scientist mode, Manipulator held out his hand. "Can I and may I hold it?"

"Yep, it's safe," I assured him. Crossing over to me, he took the staff and laid it in something that looked like a cradle-sized MRI, with a big white ring around a thin, padded bed. It had its own monitor, which Manipulator watched as the machine hummed.

Naturally, I was curious, and asked, "What's the readings say?"

With just a touch of solemn resignation in his voice, he reported, "That it's an ordinary piece of wood, which is what I expected them to say. I'm getting no readings of active super powers from you, either. We still can't directly measure magic, so we have to analyze its effects. I have some remains you can animate, but I'd be most interested if you can summon a ghost."

"Ah do believe ah have jes' the thing." Grinning at his sober despair, I reached up and thumped one of the skulls on my hat. "Who's awake?"

A young man's voice yawned, and the Horse Skull Kid said, "Figgered you were never going to let us talk again, little missy."

Smooth and coy as always, Alicia Blackheart said, "Yoah mah closest heir, Avery dahling. Ah will watch ovah you until you join me watching ovah ouah descendants. Right now it's just mahself, the Horse Skull Kid, and... well..."

A gravely, booming man's voice I'd never heard before cut in when Alicia faltered. "Ah am shamed before the gods that a daughter of my line stayands before others with an unshaven head and such heavy clothing! A skirt was enough for me and my ancestors as the heavens and the waters decreed, and—BAH HA HA HA HA!" I swear I could hear the man clutching his belly with glee as he laughed. "Ah cannot keep this up. I am Namluh of Many Titles, Avery. The world has changed so much since the time of Ur, but the joke of talking like my parents talked to me never goes out of fashion."

And of course, my ancestor from who knew how many thousand years ago had a Southern accent. "I'll get to know you later. Great-great-grandma, if you would care to step out?"

I felt a subtle tug, and let Alicia take the power she needed. I held out my hand, and in her form-fitting gown and spectral copy of my hat, she appeared in a blue outline in front of me, her hand at first in mine but then stepping away to stand alone.

"I take it you're using your powers now?" Manipulator asked, looking between me and his screens with a serious but also casual frown.

"Still nothing?" I asked back.

He turned his head towards monitors, whose mysterious numbers must have backed up his answer. "Cellular respiration rate up. Some nervous system action. Generic signs a super power is active, but nothing else."

Alicia Blackheart gave me a winsome, transparent smile over her shoulder. "Sweetie pie, ah do believe the gentleman would lahk to meet me in person, if you'll supply enough powah?"

Giving the shade of one of history's greatest and most famous necromancers more power was not the smartest thing in the world to do, but I could take the power back if necessary. Anyway, in her twisted way, Alicia loved me. I closed my eyes, filling myself with cold, holding it focused and tight within me, then let it flow only out of my right hand directly into the ghost's left.

Everyone gasped.

I opened my eyes to see Manipulator walk in slow steps with wide, awed eyes up to my now only slightly see-through spectral great-great-grandmother. Voice barely above a whisper, he said, "It's true. Alicia Blackheart."

She smiled at him, more sinisterly playful and teasing than his theatrics had ever managed. "Ah'm sure yoah wishing ah was in the flesh. Ah do so love a man with a spahk of deviltry in his eyes."

Alicia walked with serpentine, hip-swaying steps up to meet him, raised her hand, and took hold of his jaw. Manipulator went suddenly stock still at the unpleasant touch of necromantic magic. The sweetness in Alicia's still-playful voice turned acid. "Except when it's directed at mah sweet, naive, and well-meaning great-great-granddaughtah." She raised the index finger of her free hand, and twirled it in a small, complex spiral, leaving a knot of blue magic. Leaning closer, her eyes staring into Manipulator's, she murmured, "Whatevah mischief you were thinking of dropping onto huh gloriously maned head you had best forget, suh. Othahwise—" Her hand on his jaw tilted his mouth open, and she pushed the newly-formed spell into his mouth and then back into his throat with her finger, as if it were a candy. "—you will live just bayahly long enough to regret any malicious action. Do you unduhstand?"

He didn't respond. I could see the spell lodged in his neck, glowing through his skin, just sitting there. Like a bomb.

Releasing him, Alicia Blackheart turned to give me a loving smile, tugged on the brim of her hat, and said, "Ah'll see mahself out."

And she disappeared, even to my ghost sight. Back to haunting me like my other necromancer ancestors.

Wondering why I'd ever expected anything else, I cleared my throat and said, "Right. Uh. I imagine you'd rather we're done?"

Manipulator rubbed his throat and returned to full animation. Smiling hugely, he swept his eyes over his machines and their many monitors, and threw his arms out with dramatic joy. "Yes, but only because this session was such a wild success. I'll be tabulating this data all night. Maybe for weeks. I hope you'll come back again soon, Avery."

Sue rolled her eyes and growled, "Supervillains." Grabbing my wrist, she dragged me out. I struggled in a hurry to unfasten the sensors, and the ones without clasps were ripped off me to fall loudly to the floor as their wires ran out of give.

Just before I got yanked through the doorway I saw Manipulator rubbing his throat again, where the knotted blue ball of Alicia's curse still floated inside.

Chapter Nine

The pale-blue painted hallway was slightly more occupied than when we'd gone in for testing. Now three teenagers stood in it, two of them talking to each other and one poking at his phone.

Tonika closed the door to Manipulator's room behind us. With him out of sight, I put my face in my hands and groaned. "Let's all agree to not tell my folks about this."

Sue slid her arm around my back and nestled close to me. With her soft smile came soft, confident words. "It's fine. Tell your parents I dragged you to an event where school kids were getting their powers tested, and you volunteered to further science. They couldn't read your powers. You sound like a good girl, it's technically true, and they won't find out anything to contradict you."

I blinked, and raised my face from my hands. "That's right. What am I complaining about? Your parents are a hundred times worse."

Our friends started to converge around Sue, but she waved them off. With a hard, determined smirk, she lifted my chin and told me, "I'm used to managing mine. For you this is new and sudden."

Shivering, I pushed myself up completely straight, then took a deep breath. "That's what scares me. Everything was fine, and then they come out of nowhere with this. I've been dating you two and using my powers for months, and all of a sudden it's a problem now? If they didn't like it, why did they wait?"

Sue smirked wider. "Like, because they're scared of you. Duh."

I gasped, recoiling, and squealed, "I would never hurt my folks!"

Chris put his arm around my other side, giving me his own reassuring squeeze and speaking in his own calm, reasonable, reassuring tone. "No, I get what she means. What can your parents do to you?"

I turned my head to give them both a sarcastic and probably haunted glare. "The same things parents can do to other kids? Ground me, take away my stuff, lecture me and make me feel like a jerk?"

Chris accepted this with a barely visible nod, and prompted, "And if you don't care? If you decide to not obey?"

"Uh..." I had no answer. It was too weird to think clearly about.

Chris continued for me, quiet and gentle. "They know that if they push you too hard and you rebel, they can't do anything about it. You're powerful."

I shook my head. Nuh-uh. "I just barely squeak over the line as a fully fledged necromancer, you all. I'm as weak as it gets."

Chris smiled, his affection breaking through. "The weakest necromancer is scary and dangerous and awesome."

On my other side, Sue rolled her eyes in exasperation at Chris's enthusiasm for my powers. Still, she flapped a hand and admitted, "He's, like, not wrong."

Chris's black eyes looked straight into mine, and with his smile wrestled low he said, "If they do the worst and kick you out—" I shivered in horror at that thought. "—what happens? Either you move in with your rich girlfriend—" On the other side of me, I felt Sue stiffen, her grip on me tightening. I knew that idea filled her with excitement and hope. But Chris kept on soft and reasonable. "—or you become a supervillain. They'll have pushed you into exactly what they want least."

Sue snapped impatiently, "And don't tell us you couldn't do it. You have invisible weapons most heroes don't have defenses against."

I snorted, feeling good enough again to push free. "I know, this is just getting to me because it came as a surprise. Nobody can really think I'd be a supervillain. Like I'm going to move into a mausoleum and send hordes of zombie rats to steal food from gas stations while I kidnap passersby one by one to build—"

A little girl's voice sing-songed, "Lullabye!"

The sensation of invisible bubbles rolled over me, but I pushed it out of my body automatically with the cold of my necromancy. My friends and two kids behind them couldn't do that. Their eyes fluttered closed, and they collapsed to the floor on top of each other, asleep.

All except Tonika, who wobbled, blinked several times, and as the magic spell ended, stabilized again.

Because that's what it had been. A magic spell powered by a kinder, less destructive magic than mine. A magic spell cast by a girl even shorter than Tonika and younger than Hodir, standing feet apart and one hand extended towards me. On her head sat a black top hat slightly too big for her, and in her left hand she clutched a fat, brightly colored book titled *Pudgy Bunny Defends Himself.*

A fake book. The spells in it might be real, but the art was all wrong. I had an official Pudgy Bunny grimoire, and that was not Pudgy Bunny.

"Woah, there!" I shouted at the girl, holding up my hands, including the one holding my staff.

She cursed adorably, "Oh, beans," and sang, "Blast!"

I hit her with my necromancy claws.

It happened so fast. I couldn't let her finish the word, finish the spell. The claws were the quickest weapon I had available, and the one that wouldn't kill her or render her a mindless vegetable. It was the same spell as the claw I'd used to make my poltergeist, but without the power and precision necessary to sever a ghost. These were just three flimsy blades of magic gouging her life force.

The little girl dropped to the floor, curled up in a ball shivering and gasping for breath.

On the other side of the hall a door flew open and an equally little boy with crystal gauntlets shouted, "Evildoer!" and leaped at me.

I grabbed his face with my ghost hand, shoved him hard back into his room, yanked the door shut, and held it.

Someone ran up behind me. I hit them with my claws before turning around to look. An adult, one of the professor types, lay on the floor next to my friends, shaking and wheezing.

This was so out of hand. I needed to find a way to calm this down.

Which made this exactly the wrong time for the girl with the light powers to run around the corner, see me, point an accusing finger, and snarl, "You!"

But that's what happened.

What did the little girl with the top hat say? Right. "Oh, beans!"

The girl with the light powers raised her hands, and a glowing ball appeared over each. Hot wind flooded out of her, ruffling no one's clothes, not even her own. This was the sensation of her magic building.

I was not going to let her finish those light orbs, and my claws wouldn't cut through a power rush like that. I sucked all the power out of my staff, lunged forward, and grabbed her hands with mine. She grabbed back, and we wrestled, not with our muscles, but to force our magic into each other.

This was the first good look I'd gotten at the girl. She was cute. Not in the attractive sense. Well, yes, that too, but she had a round, smooth face and long black hair nearly as shiny as Annie's. Dark brown eyes glared with earnest ferocity. Her anger looked innocent and passionate and noble and foolish, like mine usually was. The adorable look was greatly heightened by her clothing, a tube-shaped, off-white dress that covered from throat to wrists to ankles, chosen by someone who was aiming at modesty without realizing the girl under the dress wasn't tube-shaped. A tiny gilt cross on a thin gilt chain hung around her neck over the dress. It didn't flare dramatically with light. It just lay there.

It took about three seconds for it to become clear to both of us that the light powers girl was winning this contest. That was how long it took to burn through the extra magic I'd absorbed from my staff. I struggled harder and harder to keep her magic out, while her eyes literally shone with ferocity.

Losing the fight wasn't the problem. I did not want to find out what that baking hot power would do to my body, tuned to the cold of necromancy.

But… I'd given my great-great-grandmother's ghost a lot of power, and never taken it back. "Alicia!" I wailed.

The transparent blue ghost of Alicia Blackheart flickered into existence behind my opponent. Alicia sighed, her voice thick with pity and disgust. "Honey child, we have got to teach you combat magic. This slap fight is embarrassing me."

Reaching out, the ghost touched the back of the light witch's neck. The girl's eyes unfocused, then closed. The rush of power trying to invade me slowed to a trickle and stopped faster than that.

She dropped to the floor, with my still holding onto her hands. Crouching over her, I felt her throat for a pulse. Alicia never cared if her enemies lived.

There. I found it. Thank goodness.

In the silence of the ended fight, I heard clicks. Looking over my shoulder, I saw Brian Akk standing in the doorway of his testing room, fastening the last clasp on what looked like a skeletonized white plastic glove. In that glove's grip he held an old, worn, ordinary fire extinguisher, which somehow seemed far more sinister and dangerous.

He looked sad, but completely calm. Poised.

Other kids and a couple more adults lay motionless on the hallway floor. I hadn't hit them. The burst of light girl's magic must have knocked them out. Anxious faces of children and adults peeked out of most of the examination rooms through barely ajar doors.

Jerking upright, I waved my hands desperately and wailed, "It's not my fault!"

Tonika, leaning against a wall but upright, wheezed, "It's not. I saw it all. Angel Cruz assumed Avery started it, but she didn't."

"It's not her fault, Brainy," echoed the voice of Doctor Biotic, much more calm than Tonika or myself.

Brian Akk looked through the doorway into his testing room, face and voice blank as he asked, "How do you know?"

Doctor Biotic stepped out. She leaned a forearm against the door frame, and gave him a wild grin with those round little teeth in a mouth whose tongue and palate were just as jet-black as her skin. "What does it mean when someone shouts 'evildoer'?"

Brian Akk sighed. His shoulders slumped. He let the hand with the glove and fire extinguisher hang by his side. The readiness drained out of him. Grimacing at Doctor Biotic, he answered her, "That they're so eager for a fight they don't care if one is actually deserved."

Doctor Biotic nodded, and winked at me. A metal shutter closing over her red robot eye was visible even down the hall.

Rubbing his face sourly, Brian Akk pointed out, "I still have to tell Mech about this."

I hated that they talked about Mech as if he was my parole officer.

I hated that they were right. Nobody trusted a necromancer. My parents weren't the only ones watching in case I turned evil.

"So will I," Doctor Biotic told Brian, her voice holding a promise that Mech would hear a much more redeeming story. Which would mean Mech would tell my parents a much more redeeming story. Hopefully.

Coming here at all had been iffy. That it ended up in a magical brawl where I'd knocked out three other teenagers and an adult… this was exactly the kind of debatably justified violence my parents were worried about.

I got reassurance about one thing. My friends were moving. The original sleep spell hadn't lasted long. Scooping my staff up, I pulled them to their feet one at a time. Angel Cruz, the girl with the light powers, was still out like a light, thank goodness.

However much my friends had or hadn't witnessed, Sue gave my hand an extra squeeze, and pressed her shoulder to mine even as she gave the hallway and all its inhabitants a haughty scowl. "Come on, Avery. We don't have to be welcome here. We have a movie to catch. I'll call Winifred."

Nothing could be more soothing than the feeling of Sue at my side. She made it possible to hide my worry. Flicking my hat to make sure my ancestors stayed quiet, I groused, "At least ah had mah hat 'n staff. Ah'da been toast without them."

Chris took his place at my other shoulder, smiling down at me. He had bounced back fast, and it was hard panic about anything while sandwiched between the two people who loved me most. Plus, he knew exactly what to say. "No dwelling on super powers. I want to see this dancing cats movie Peggy is so enthusiastic about, and then persuade my rich girlfriend to take my not-rich girlfriend and our not-rich-or-romantic friends out to dinner."

Annie's tail curled around my calf, gave one squeeze, and then withdrew. Her smile held nothing but admiration. "Thank you for protecting us."

Peggy nodded approval. "Ethiopian sounds good. And the movie looks emotional, but lots of fun at the same time. I like the hippopotamus in the trailers."

The movie was good. We walked out of it laughing, and sang its songs while we ate spicy-but-not-hot beef dishes I didn't recognize. I forgot all about what my parents would say about the fight.

That is, until well after midnight, when my phone beeped. All my fears came rushing back as I rolled over and looked at my phone where it had fallen on the floor.

A text message showed on the lock screen.

I think I've found a way to make your parents see you're using your powers for good. A non-violent way.

Snatching up the phone, my heart pounding, I texted back.

Who is this? How did you get my phone number???

Chapter Ten

Sue also liked to take me to school in the morning. It's a thing you can do when you're willing to get up early and have a butler who never needs sleep or personal time.

It meant I had to start the day with a confession. Squirming in my seatbelt, I looked across the backseat at Sue, and tried to give her an apologetic smile. It came out as a grimace. "Ah got me a text from Tonika last night."

Sue reacted the same way I had, but adding a raised eyebrow. "How'd she get your number?"

Which at least meant I had the answer. "From Mech's phone."

Eyebrow still up, she asked, "Cyborg hacking powers?"

"Didn't ask." Clearing my throat, I moved awkwardly to the real topic. "She had this suggestion. Or request. Or. Uh." Grimacing again, I asked in a rush, "Wouldja mind if tonight I went 'n purged a haunted house?"

Sue groaned, and I recoiled in guilty shock. This wasn't even the part I was expecting to be the problem!

Laying her head back against the seat's headrest, Sue complained to the ceiling, "I can't come tonight! I'm seeing Marcia!"

The mysterious Marcia, the best friend too dangerous for Sue to introduce me to. Not that I cared. Marcia made Sue almost as happy as I did. I cared about that.

I did frown, pressing my overgrown eyebrows together. "On a Friday night? Don't y'all usually see each other on Saturdays?"

Still staring hopelessly upwards, Sue said, "I told my parents I'm spending the night with you."

Which was more disturbing, that Sue used that as an excuse, or that I knew her folks would accept it instantly?

Forget that. It took all my effort to force out the next few words. "Actually, ah oughta do this one alone."

Sue lurched upright, hazel eyes wide as saucers. Palms raised, she leaned towards me and shouted, "No! I'll cancel Marcia. I will always be there when you need me, Avery. Always."

I closed my trembling hands over hers, making myself look into her eyes that were already shiny with tears, and explained slowly, and a touch hoarse, "It's a haunted house. It's ghosts. Murderous ghosts. That's whah ah'm goin', 'cause ah'm the only person what can fix it an' be safe. Ah want mah folks to hear 'bout me doin' stuff to help folks without fightin'."

Sue was starting to shake. Her voice fluttered with panic as she squeaked, "I won't abandon you."

My heart stung like a fist squeezed around broken glass at the desperation in her expression. For her sake, I had to keep control, and keep my voice tender and slow and only a little fluttery. "Sue, the place's been sealed fer nigh on twenty years. It ain't no supervillain nest."

That at least startled Sue out of her panic. Confusion crowding out her misery, she asked, "Twenty years? Like... an empty building in LA for twenty years?"

I have her hands a tight squeeze. Her face had gone almost as pale as mine, and tears rolled slowly down her cheeks, leaving tracks in her subtle makeup. I murmured, "An empty house. That's how haunted it is. Ah don't want ta take you inta thayat. Ah'm the only person what's safe. Ah want you ta be havin' fun with Marcia. Y'all'll have fun, right?"

She sniffed, calming down, but still shivering and clutching my hands like a lifeline. "I... we... yes. I've told you how totally obsessed Marcia is with her powers. I'm going to make her take a break. We're going to go shopping for swimsuits, swim in her pool, like, do all the cliché sleepover stuff. Paint our toenails. Watch the dumbest horror movies we can find on the internet. Order pizza delivered from a restaurant chain. Sleep in sleeping bags." She shivered, jerking forward and declaring, "It doesn't matter. I can cancel."

I raised my chin imperiously, managing a glare backed by honest outrage. "Don't y'all dare. Ah want this for you."

Sue sniffed again. The stiffness in her downturned face relaxed to a slack, unhappy frown. She raised begging puppy dog eyes to me and husked, "You're not angry?"

Maybe angry with myself. I didn't know what I was feeling, only that my heart churned with it. "No! Ya can't watch mah back against ghosts, Sue. Ah'm doin' this 'cause it's the thing only I kin do. Tomorrow ah want ta call you an' ah spec to hear about all the totally normal fun y'all had with Marcia, okay?"

I leaned far forward, wrapping my arms around Sue, and squeezed her in a ferocious hug. She clung to me, and I held her—

—until an awkward thought broke through, and I looked at the slim, black-clad Winifred in the driver's seat. "Should we, uh..."

Prim and cheerful, Winifred said, "I did overhear Mistress Avery and Mistress Sue talking about ways Mistress Avery could use her powers to help people, but traffic was difficult and I didn't hear any details."

The car pulled up in front of Pepperidge Preparatory, and Winifred stepped out to open Sue's door. Sue took a moment to smudge her makeup back into something not obviously tear-stained, and we both slid out that side.

That began a strange and ominous day. All morning I was intensely aware of how the fingers of my left hand hesitated when they typed on the tablet that came with this fancy school. When I had to write with a pencil or pen, I let my ghost hand do it rather than deal with my nearly illegible printing.

We didn't dare talk during class, but I could see the tension in Sue's figure sitting in the next chair.

At lunch, the moment we were out in the courtyard and the shadow hole closed behind us, Sue grabbed my arm and cuddled up against it. She didn't let go as we sat down on the planter wall like always, or open up her food box.

"Sue…" I said softly, hunting for words.

I didn't find any, and Sue didn't respond, but she let go with one arm to pick up her fork and poke at her food. She took a few bites. I ate my whole meal, but my body crawled with awkwardness inside and out the whole time.

The end of lunch bell rang. We stood up, and Sue reached out her arm towards the school wall to open our way back inside. She paused just long enough to whisper, "I'm sorry," as if she was about to cry.

When the hole opened, Sue's face betrayed no sign of weakness or upset to our classmates. She maintained that mask the whole rest of the day.

I spent the whole time feeling guilt clawing at me from the inside. I'd expected to feel guilty for telling Sue that I wanted to do this alone, and making Sue feel left behind. Instead, I felt guilty for making Sue feel guilty.

School finally ended. As I pulled my backpack onto my shoulder, I realized I'd picked it up with my ghost hand again.

As Sue and I walked down the hall towards the front door side by side, I reached out and took hold of her hand, squeezing it tight. I felt her tremble, but was sure no one but me knew.

When we got out into the warm sun and cool breeze, standing on soft grass, I turned and cupped my hands over her cheeks. Leaning so close our noses touched, my green eyes looking into her brown, I whispered, "You got nothin' to feel guilty 'bout."

Then I kissed her. I kissed her so fiercely that despite their terror of us, a couple of the other schoolgirls whistled and clapped.

It was an embarrassing time to see my father pull up to the curb and beep for me, but I didn't let that hurry up the kiss by a single second.

Finally, I let go. Slowly, so Sue would know it was reluctant.

Her face still only inches from mine, Sue asked softly, "You mean it?"

"Ah mean it," I whispered back.

Sue threw her arms around my back, pulled me close, and kissed me just as hard as I'd kissed her.

I'm embarrassed to admit that I lost track of anything else going on until the kiss ended. I was even more embarrassed, after Sue let me go, to get into the car with my father. I picked the back seat so I didn't have to see his expression.

After we'd been on the road for a couple of minutes, he let me off the hook with a cheerful declaration. "Your mom found a restaurant that serves cliché British food. What do you think of the three of us going out, seeing Alicia's star on the Hollywood Walk of Fame, taking a walk by the ocean, and then eating eggs covered in sausage before coming home?"

Relief practically flattened me, and I grinned as wide as my face would bear. "Ah believe ah kin put off mah homework long enough for that."

Chapter Eleven

I returned home contemplating that I hadn't known there were superhero and villain stars on the Hollywood Walk of Fame, much less that Alicia Blackheart was one of them. My parents still hadn't mentioned the fight at the research building.

A rush of gratitude struck me. Thank you, Tonika. By the time my folks found out about the fight, I'd have proof I could do more productive things with my powers.

Being out all afternoon and into the evening helped me keep from being too tense, and I went to bed at the normal time. Then I just lay there until my phone beeped with a text.

It read:

I'm ready. Mech will be out all night.

Followed by an address and a building diagram drawn in pencil.

Well, I *had* told Tonika I needed to know where I was going, not just have a name. Simple as the sketch was, the secret passage inside a bank downtown was perfectly clear.

Leaping to my feet and dressed in regular overalls rather than my goofy school uniform, thank goodness, I knocked on my door, whispered, "Alice?" and slipped inside when it opened.

In the cool, comfortable quiet of the crypt I held up my phone, flipping between the address, a street map, and the diagram. "Take me here?"

The door opened, and lo and behold, in front of it stood Tonika in a plain black dress and a fancy mirrored visor over her eyes. Very fancy. The glass blended into coppery side struts to hold it onto her head. Padded coppery side struts, no less. Faint colored dots moved on the dark glass, suggesting the view from behind them included more than the view in front.

Tonika was standing in a dark, circular living room. It looked fancy, with doors into other rooms and a counter blocking off a miniature kitchen. That was all I got to see before she put her finger to her lips, whispered, "Shhh," and scurried into the crypt with me.

I shut the door behind her.

With all chances of being observed gone, Tonika straightened up and gave me a bright smile. The high-tech goggles looked natural on her, especially with her long, purple hair. After a couple of quick glances around, she broke into an eager chatter. "So, this is your secret method of travel? However it actually works, it's effectively teleportation. No wonder you don't want anyone to know. Is it okay to ask how it works? It's necromancy themed and you have necromantic powers, but I've learned from Mech's computers that while most mad scientists like a high-tech or crudely experimental theme, disguised technology with a different aesthetic is common."

"Uh...," I said as I tried to catch up. "Her name is Alice. Ah don't know how she wuhks, but ah know theyah's a ghost involved, and a great deal of necromantic powah whose source ah haven't figured out, since ghosts don't make theyah own. And you ah freaky smart. Can ah ask mah questions now? Ah have a lotta questions."

Tonika nodded, up and down, very serious, and clasped her hands behind her back. "Of course. I'm certainly smart, but mainly I have an unusually roundabout direction of thought. I found out about our target the same way I got your phone number. So I don't get bored, Mech has been letting me use his computers to help direct him in his crime fighting. I enjoy it, but he doesn't need much help and I have a lot of time to learn from his files. The help I do give him makes an obvious difference, so I'm taking one of his scanners in case I can help you during this exorcism. Once I turn them on they will probably keep a record Mech will eventually see, but we're going to do a good deed which makes that a plus, not a negative. What else did you need to know?"

It might have been less intimidating if it all came out as a rush, but instead Tonika explained it all in perfect calm. Completely off balance, I stammered. "That, ah… reckon that covers it. Gonna repeat you're freaky smart, though."

Tonika giggled, head tucking down meekly between her raised shoulders.

"Guess there's ain't nothin' to do but get a move on, then. Alice, take us to…." I raised my phone again and fiddled with my maps. Clumsily. Drat my new left hand. "That's in Pasadena, ah reckon?"

Alice clicked. Her door swung open onto a dimly lit night-time street.

I had to chuckle. Well, I'd known it wasn't the address Alice responded to.

In an impressive new trick, Alice had taken over the passenger door of someone's minivan. When we stepped outside that put us a short driveway on the quietest street I'd seen in LA so far.

Also the greenest. This was crazy. Pasadena was on the northeast end of LA. We should be in a desert. Instead, there were trees and rolling hills all around us. The cool January night smelled damp and green. It was like a miniature version of being back in Kentucky, except that at this time of year Kentucky was a bunch of grey dead stick trees and brown dead grass, with grey overcast skies or maybe a little snow.

Something else grabbed my attention. I pointed at a house across the street. "That one."

Tonika looked at the charming little two-story house opposite us, then up at me. "Necromancy vision? What does it look like?"

"Ah don't have words." I didn't. I wasn't sure even myself

why it leaped out at me, as if that building was the only thing clearly in focus on the street.

Pulling my thoughts away from that strange sensation, I prompted, "So, uh... haunted house?"

Tonika went still. Almost... computerized, as she recited, "It was before Mech's time, so his files didn't have much information. The house was owned by a serial killer who meddled with mad science, whatever that phrasing means. After the killer died, the house contained violent ghosts. One person died, and two superheroes were attacked. With no necromancy experts available, the heroes at the time decided to magically seal the building." The stiffness faded, and she cocked her head, probably looking up at me sidelong behind the fancy glasses. "Maybe they were waiting for you."

Okay. Well.

I ducked back through the van's door into Alice, grabbed my staff and hat, and only then returned to the street and shut the door, dismissing Alice. I wasn't expecting a fight. I was expecting the ghosts to have decayed into incoherent spooky whispers. But fight or not, I'd be doing magic, so I might as well have my tools.

Staff in my left hand, skull-decorated sun hat wedged onto my hair fluff, I glanced up and down the street but saw no traffic. We were way, way out of the heart of LA. The only cars I heard whispered down a distant freeway. This street was dead, just the way I like it.

We jaywalked across the street to stand in front of a densely overgrown yard. Not a huge yard, but a yard, another sign of how far from the center of LA we were. My house back in Glendale had a back yard, but only because there wasn't much else anyone could do with a gully leading down to a freeway.

This house was fancier than mine. White, with peaked roofs and a second story, multiple windows decorated both stories, and an only slightly overgrown stepping stone path led to the front door. Unlike the yard, it looked fresh and well taken care of.

When we reached the front door itself, I could see faint rainbow symbols laid over the wood. A similarly subtle opalescence covered the windows. Someone really had decided to wrap this building up like a birthday present and leave it for me twenty years later.

I took a couple of deep breaths, remembering what I'd learned, first from Pudgy Bunny, then from Schleimy. Focus. Raise the cold inside me, but keep it inside me, until my whole body was a still statue of ice. Feel the cold magic stored in my staff, mingling it with mine, so that there was no place where I ended and it began.

Control.

Okay. I was ready. Tapping my hat, proud of the lack of accent in my voice that I was sure meant my power was fully disciplined, I asked, "Any reason I can't just rip the spell off?"

A touch exasperated, my great-great-grandmother's voice answered, "Othah than style, no."

"Go for it, missy," the Horse Skull Kid encouraged.

"Are you all mad!?" bellowed Namluh. "The walls are threaded with serpent manifestation BA HA HA HA HA no, it's harmless." After a faint sigh of satisfied humor, he continued, "Silly little mages of air and water always do this when they meet the power of death: Cover it in mud and go run and hide."

I grabbed the door handle, turned, and pushed the door open. The spell ripped exactly like wrapping paper as I did. The magic felt prickly, fizzy, on my hand before it dissolved. Above and around me, transparent rainbow strips peeled away from the building and disappeared.

A cold draft of necromantic magic rolled out of the entrance hall. After twenty years? Well, they did seal the place.

I glanced back over my shoulder at Tonika. "You might want to stay out. There might be still dangerous ghosts in here after all. There's got to be spores and stuff."

"HA!" Namluh burst out a laugh. "Don't worry, your little client is safe. Take it from a man who has built, sanctified, and robbed many a tomb. The blessing of death purifies the air. Haunted tombs are the only ones safe for regular men and women to enter."

I was relying on my natural necromantic energy to kill anything that might try to infect me, so that made sense. Besides, the place didn't look like a rotting tomb. It looked like the residents moved out last night.

Honest, the inside was as nice as the outside, from what I could see. A main hall led back to a living room, judging by the huge television and plush leather couch. To the left a funny little side hall ran parallel, just big enough to hold some doors. Opposite it, a large oval mirror hung on the wall, next to one of those special closet doors that look like wooden window blinds. On the right side, by the entrance, a carpeted staircase climbed up to the second floor.

Right here by the door a small table and two dressers had been spilled on the floor, smashing a flower vase and scattering small knickknacks like an ash tray, a framed photo, and a block-shaped clock. The only definite signs of violence were a couple of long, five-clawed gouges, one on each wall of the hallway, and a black drippy stain half-overlapping one of those gouges. Years-dried blood.

But no corpses, or anything, and what I could see of the living room looked perfectly intact.

I stepped over the threshold, gripping my staff tight, ready for anything.

Nothing happened. The place sure was full of cold death magic, though. It felt like the best kind of cool bath, just cold enough to be refreshing. Except not. The cold pressed, scraped, instead of soothing.

Out loud, I said, "One thing is for sure. Something terrible happened in this house. It's filled with pain and rage. I guess you're safe from spores, but don't come in until I clear out the ghosts. This place really did need a necromancer."

Me. This was exactly what Tonika said she'd found for me: A non-fighting, non-morally-challenging way that only a necromancy could help. The kind of story I wanted my parents to hear. Plus, something it would make me feel good to do, as a person. I had no intention of becoming like my ancestors, using my powers to hurt other people so much that I learned special spells to do it better.

Another thought struck, and I told my own ghosts, "And you three might want to wait outside, too."

Three blue figures appeared in the hall in front of me, more highlights than silhouettes.

The tall, skinny one in the Stetson folded his arms, and the Horse Skull Kid said, "Not happenin', little lady."

A man with a bulging belly, bald head, and fuzzy skirt grabbed his stomach, which wobbled when he laughed. "You think the Great Namlah is afraid of the angry dead? BA HA HA! That was me laughing at danger!"

Alicia lifted her hand to touch her ghostly mimic of the same hat I was wearing. "If theyah is something in heah dangerous enough to hurt us, ah am certainly not abandoning mah great-great-granddaughtuh to fight it alone. Ah personally expect this to be more like necromantic maid service." A prospect she sounded disgusted by.

Numlah made a throaty rumble before speaking. "Yes, that goes all the way back to Ur. 'Clean out the spirits of the last king I murdered and his warriors from the palace!' It did pay well."

Horse Skull Kid *tsked* philosophically, "And stealin' ever-thin' you need gets ta be more trouble than it's worth pretty ding dang quick."

"Heh." Numlah's latest laugh came out in one bubbly chuckle. "And then it would be the old king's wife who kills my client anyway."

I could definitely hear the sharp edge of Alicia's smirk in her voice. "Ah see dying because you forgot women have opinions is a six-thousand-yeah-old tradition."

I felt encouraged that they were taking this so lightly, but... "Okay, I have to get to work."

Tonika stood right outside the doorway, fingers playing with the ear rests of her fancy goggles as she rotated her head up, down, and side to side. Crisp and businesslike, she reported, "There are energy sources that read like mad science upstairs and in the basement, and something quite strange in the living room."

It took all of seconds to walk down the hall to the living room, even taking care not to step on the debris on the floor. That gave me a look at the "something quite strange."

Which was, I had to admit it, something quite strange. A wall of intertwined ghosts. No, one central ghost wrapped in a web of other ghosts. The capturing ghosts were what I would normally expect, vaguely defined human shapes, mostly just from the waist or even shoulders up, in smudged blue with their arms wrapped around their captive.

The captive, while definitely a ghost, was an odd one. She was brown. Sepia-tone, even. She looked like a very old photo of a girl younger than me, but transparent. I couldn't see much of her dress with all the other ghosts covering it, but she had a funny hat, a tiny little thing like a top hat but with a forward brim like a baseball cap, and covered in flowers. If there were such a thing as antique sneakers, she was wearing them.

Her eyes tracked me, and she wriggled in the arms gripping her. Both hands of one of the ghosts holding onto her covered her mouth, keeping her from talking, but I was sure she wanted to.

Beyond her, an absolutely tiny hallway was just big enough to contain a door on either side, the left door open onto stairs leading down. The hallway ended in a spacious kitchen.

Well, the easiest thing to do was—

My body seized up like I was choking, but reflexes saved me. I stopped pulling in the magic around me as soon as I started. Breathing hard, relaxing my muscles and focusing my own power again, I wheezed, "This isn't necromancy. I've felt this before."

Alicia, noticeably more visible now, a short and lithe woman in an elegant gown, agreed, "It is rather like that powah in those funny catacombs last year, isn't it? But not quite."

Behind me, Horse Skull Kid observed, "Good for ghosts. Reckon any livin' fella tries to mess with you in here, we'll teach him a lesson he won't forget in a hurry."

Numlah, who looked like exactly the same grinning, big-bellied, completely bald man in a sheepskin skirt the outline had hinted, flopped down on the couch, licked his finger, and raised it into the air. "Odd, yes. Well, your power is true. This feeble imitation won't slow you down."

Out of the corner of my eye, I saw movement. A blue humanoid figure congealed out of the air, picking up a clock on a low bookshelf.

Pushing power into my voice, I snapped, "Don't you dare!" at it, and it vanished like steam blown by a fan.

"We'll keep a watch fer riffraff. You help the little missy, there," offered Horse Skull Kid.

I was being way too cautious. The weird power in the air had thrown me. These were ghosts! I needed to act like a necromancer, which meant abandoning silly spellcasting, stomping up to the ghost web—oh, they were welcome to try to grab me, if they were that stupid—grabbing the spectral blue hands over the brown ghost's mouth, and prying them off like tape.

They came away exactly like tape, with the same tearing noise. The vintage photograph ghost underneath grimaced, eyes squeezed shut for a couple of seconds as she squeaked, "Ow! Ooh, ow ow ow!"

But also like pulling off tape, the instant the initial sting was over, her eyes snapped open and she was all serious, attentive, and smiling with gratitude. "My heroine! Can you help my cat?"

I looked down. There was an extra lump on the side of the mass of ghosts holding her, and sure enough, when I looked closely those dozen pairs of hands encased a ghostly cat the same brown as the girl.

I pulled free the hand covering its head. As the tape sound snarled, the cat said, "HISS!" and then settled into a bland, "Meow."

Straightening up, I asked the girl, "You aren't like the rest of these ghosts. You aren't like any ghost I've ever met before. What are you doing here?"

She gave me a proud, even slightly smug smile. "Looking for clues, of course. There was a hole in the spell in the chimney, but I wasn't expecting this. I'm so glad a necromancer showed up. I thought I'd be stuck like this for decades!"

Behind me, Horse Skull Kid exclaimed, "I reckon I know that voice!"

The girl looked over my shoulder, and her proud smile became a huge, delighted, open-mouthed grin. "Horse Skull Kid!"

Thumbs in his belt, Horse Skull Kid strolled up next to me,

and leaned down to give the girl a quizzical smile. "Well, if it ain't little Gumshoe! I never reckoned I'd see you again. How ya been? How'd things go after I left?"

They might as well have run into each other at a fast-food place, she picked up the conversation with such casual cheer. "It turns out it was Old Man MacGuffin all along! He wanted to stop Laura and Miguel from marrying. You won't believe it, but when I wrapped up the case everyone was happy, even him!"

Kid nodded approval. "I'd love ta hear all 'bout it sometime. Nice ta see you made it to the West Coast."

"I'd love to tell you, but I'm a bit tied up right now," she replied with deadpan graciousness.

"Meow," muttered the cat in disgust.

Gumshoe's attention returned to me, all polite wide eyes and hopeful smile. "Can you help me out? I came here to find out if my client's brother was one of the victims twenty years ago. If you wake up the ghosts, they'll let me go and I can ask them."

"It's perfectly safe, honey child," Alicia assured me.

Numlah, now so well defined I could see his toothy grin, got up from the couch and cracked his beefy knuckles. "They'll be angry, but we'll protect you."

"Hooey, they'll be angry!" agreed the Horse Skull Kid, but followed up with a smirk. "But you're the necromancer. Don't matter none what's keeping 'em mashed up and active like this. Ain't no fancy sorcery or crazy doodad can stop you from takin' control iff'n you put your mind to it."

I held out my right hand and ran it over the crude shapes holding Gumshoe. Crude and blobby as they were, they were so strongly manifest that it didn't take much magic in my fingers to actually touch them. They twitched at contact, the pain and fury in their bodies cold, tingly and unpleasant to touch, like a bed of needles. So much pain. So much rage.

This was going to take a lot of power. Taking two steps out, I held both my arms out straight at my sides. Pulling stored magic from the staff, I unleashed it like a fire hose in every word as I chanted, "Spirits of this place, hear me! Hear the words of the Queen of the Dead and obey her! By right of blood I rule you!

With the power of my ancestors I rule you! Your killer has no authority over you. Your murders control you no longer. Mine is the power that enfolds you."

It was a lot of power, blasted into a house already full of death. Winds gusted, then spun around me. Spectral faces hovered in the air, appearing, moaning, and fading out. My body felt light, then floated up a foot in the air. All the time, I kept chanting. "I order you now to let go. Let go of this child. Let go of your anger. Let go of your pain. Move on, spirits in this house. With my power I break the chains your murderer placed upon you, the chains of science and magic and revenge. Leave this place, and be at peace!"

Wind roared, throwing open doors, knocking items off shelves and tables, until it stampeded out of the house and into the gentle, balmy January night. Upstairs, glass broke as ghosts that didn't want to take the long way broke out of the windows on their rush to freedom. I dropped out of the air and felt rather proud of landing neatly on my feet. The spirits holding Gumshoe and her cat peeled away in a torrent, leading the stampede out of the death house. Unaffected by my spell, those two floated gracefully to the floor.

My ghostly ancestors were already dimming and fading as the unnatural power in the building drained, but I got to see Alicia touch her fingers to her forehead in exasperation. "Honestly, Avahry."

Horse Skull Kid's grin glinted as it faded out of sight. "Girl's got a soft touch. Ain't nothin' wrong with that."

Numlah didn't have a comment. He just looked jolly. He looked so jolly that even after he completely disappeared, he left an impression of jolliness hanging in the air.

That left me, Gumshoe, and her pudgy cat. Without an obscuring mass of other ghosts, the girl's dress proved to be at least a little more elaborate than I thought, with a crisp mantle around her shoulders, a tight belt at her waist, and buttons down the front. The dress didn't go far past her knees, and puffy pants went the rest of the way to her leathery, rounded, thick-soled shoes. It might have once been in pretty colors. Now it was all lighter or darker shades of sepia.

The cat was pudgy, but otherwise a normal cat. Not even particularly fluffy. It did have a severe, wide-eyed stare. Not so much accusing as giving the impression it could See All.

The girl fiddled with her hat, tucking it just so in place over her short, curly hair. She smiled like a calmer version of Namluh. Like it was her natural state. "Jinkies. I wasn't expecting that. Good for you doing the right thing, and shame on me for wanting to keep them in pain just so I could ask them questions."

I was on edge enough to jump at movement in my peripheral vision, but it was just Tonika, peeking around the hall's corner into the living room. "Is that... you're the Gumshoe Ghost Girl, aren't you?"

"That's right!" the ghost answered gleefully, and gestured with both hands at the feline next to her. "And this is Ghost Cat Solvin' Mysteries."

"Meow," said Ghost Cat Solvin' Mysteries.

Gumshoe Ghost Girl put her hands on her hips, then raised one in a fist. Ghost Cat Solvin' Mysteries jumped up onto her shoulder as she declared, "And together we're the Bubblegumshoe Detective Agency!"

"Meow!"

They posed like that for three seconds before Tonika said, "I know. Your receptionist said you left to investigate this house two weeks ago, and didn't come back."

I jumped again. "Wait, you knew she was here!?"

With the visor on, I couldn't fully make out Tonika's expression, but she sounded earnest and just a touch apologetic when her face turned to me. "That's how I found out about this place. I had some ideas about how to find out who I am, so I looked through Mech's files for private detectives with unusual talents. I found out the Gumshoe Ghost Girl had gone missing, and it seemed like I could help several people all at the same time."

Ghost Cat Solvin' Mysteries raised its head proudly, uninterested in our human quibbles. A spectral blue outline of a cardboard box faded into existence in front of it. Ghost Cat Solvin' Mysteries climbed inside, sitting regally upright as the box levitated an inch off the floor and floated away and down the stairs.

Gumshoe Ghost Girl looked around the room she had been

tied up in the last two weeks, and grinned sheepishly. "I don't think I can turn you down."

That launched Tonika into a guilty squeak and frenzied hand waving. "No, no, I didn't want to obligate you! I was just trying to help everyone!"

Unfazed, the Gumshoe Ghost Girl walked past me to Tonika, and past her into the hall, telling her, "Well, now that the morass of vengeful spirits is cleared out, we can split up and search the house for clues. Why don't you come with me and tell me what you need?"

"Please," accepted Tonika, scurrying to catch up.

I started to follow, took two steps, and then stopped. That sounded like a private conversation and none of my business.

So instead, I peeked into the kitchen. A bowl of fruit sat on the little dining room table. A half-prepared peanut butter sandwich lay on the island counter. They looked incredibly, brick-hard stale, but not rotten or moldy. The same with the flowers in the vase on the table.

I crossed the room and opened up a couple of windows to help air out the last dregs of that weird pseudo-death magic.

They might not be visible, but I knew my ancestors were still here, and asked, "Kid, you know that ghost. Who made her? How can a ghost that strong hold on more than a hundred years?"

"Two hundred and change, I reckon," his voice answered brightly. "Don't think she *was* made. Sometimes ghosts like that happen."

"Avery, darling, you've bayahly begun to learn about your powahs," Alicia chided.

"HA!" barked Numlah. "Don't let her make you feel small. The bloodline of necromancy runs as far back before me as it does from me to you, and in all that time we've barely scratched the surface of death's mysteries."

Hope built inside me, lightening my heart and bringing out my own smile. Walking back into the living room, I asked them, "But I did it, didn't I? I exorcised a house full of murderous ghosts and put them to rest. No dangerous battles. The only moral choice I had to make, I made the decent way. I guess I can go wait by the door for Tonika. My work here is done."

Man, did it feel good to say that.

"YOWL!" shrieked Ghost Cat Solvin' Mysteries from downstairs. The spectral cardboard box came zooming up the basement steps, past me, and out towards the front door, with Ghost Cat Solvin' Mysteries clinging desperately to its sides.

Slow thumps, scrapes, and clanks announced something else climbing the stairs.

My shoulders bunched up, and I slumped my head forward. "Well, crud. Had to open my big mouth."

Chapter Twelve

The thing in the basement reached the top of the stairs. It was tall. It was shiny. It was humanoid. In a house where nothing else had rotted, it smelled gross.

I backpedaled to the entrance hall as I resolved the details. The thing paused now in the basement doorway was a robot, maybe six feet tall, with long white hair. An elaborate robot, in the rough shape of a human woman, slim but not very detailed. At least, not detailed in the human-woman sense. It was made of way more shiny, segmented metal plates than it needed to be. White hair, puffy atop its head but straight as it hung down its back, cascaded all the way to its waist.

The smell probably came from the black, gooey gunk leaking between many of the plates. I couldn't see the robot's back, but the hair wasn't thick enough to hide a sharp blue-white glow that something back there cast on the nearby walls and ceiling.

But weirder than all that, I saw the outline of a human ghost inside, vibrating like a struck tuning fork.

The robot's face had eyes and a mouth, but the former were featureless and shiny like the rest of its surfacing. The latter didn't seem able to move. That left it with a dead, emotionless stare as it turned those eyes to me.

It took a step towards me. And then a second. And then a third. Each faster than the step before.

I did the first thing I could think of, plunging my ghost hand inside it to yank out the ghost. Except the ghost hand bounced off the metal surface, unable to reach the ghost I could see inside.

What a great time to learn my ghost hand couldn't pass through metal. Or something. No time to figure out the meaning now.

At least the robot felt the pressure and had to react to the obstruction. It shoved the ghost hand out of its way, which took some wiggling as I kept the distracting hand in place. If I'd been smart, I could have pushed the robot down the stairs and kept it down there. Too late now.

Like this, my ghost hand was only a distraction, but as the robot twisted to get a double-handed grip and push the poltergeist away, I got a glimpse of the source of the light. A glass tank full of blue liquid and white lightning had been clamped into a depression in the robot's back. It didn't just glow like a fluorescent light, either. It radiated that irritating, artificial necromancy chill.

Was there a glass cover over the cavity? Glass wasn't metal. Whatever, I went for it, swinging my ghost hand around behind the robot, grabbing the cylinder, and yanking as hard as I could.

Pain exploded in my left hand, dropping me to my knees, grabbing my wrist with my other hand. Light flashed bright enough to leave spots in my vision. Cold roared over me.

But all three faded, disappearing in mere heartbeats.

"I just GOT that hand!" I wailed at an unjust universe, because my flesh and blood hand was fine. It was my poltergeist that had just burned away. The pain had faded because there wasn't any ghost hand left to feel.

The ghost inside the shiny exoskeleton didn't vibrate anymore. It flopped, bits of it straying out, moving like a badly handled marionette. That was how the robot moved as it began lurching towards me again, arms outstretched.

I'd used up a whole lot of power cleansing the house, but not all of it. Getting a grip on what remained, I commanded, "As Queen of the Dead, I order you to stop!"

The robot stopped. The badly connected ghost directing it had to obey me, but the whole thing twitched like some evil madman's broken, mistreated toy.

I would only get one chance at this. I hoped the merciful option was still the right one. Darting up to it, I filled my hands with icy power and got a grip on the malformed human outline of the ghost where it poked out of the metal. I pulled, drawing it halfway out, all of its torso and head, until only the forearms and legs were still connected. Then I slowly, gently, pushed the ghost back into its shell, smoothing it out like dough so it fit properly.

Unlike with Tonika, the ghost didn't fade completely when I reattached it, but it became a barely visible blue edge to the robot's physical outline, following it perfectly as the metal moved.

The robot's upper body lurched forward. I threw myself back against the wall, watching it suspiciously as its metal arms closed over its metal chest. It whined in a boyish voice, "No! You sick old—" The agonized, delirious tone disappeared, replaced by wonder. "It doesn't hurt anymore."

I let out a heavy, relieved sigh. "It worked."

Alicia commented sulkily, "Ah suppose you can't argue with success."

Namluh let out a curious harumph noise. "A ghost powered statue. I've seen it before, but there is something twisted to this one."

The robot, still hunched forward, let go of itself and instead raised its hands to clench and unclench its fists, staring at its fingers with that still empty, expressionless face.

I took a careful step forward, raising my hands palms out, and tried to sound reassuring. "Take it slow. It'll be okay. Someone did something awful to you, but—"

"I know he did it, I was there!" the robot snarled, head twisting to look at me.

I only kept its angry attention for a moment. Standing up tall and straight, it strolled past me into the hall to look in the mirror still hanging on the wall. Metal fingertips touched metal chest, metal shoulders, metal face. The movements and hushed words were finally peaceful as she said, "I'm beautiful."

Definitely a girl's voice. I'd been mistaken about "boyish," but sometimes that's an easy mistake to make, especially when people are freaking out.

Relaxing myself, I hazarded, "Well... yes, I suppose so. I guess giving you your mind back is what you wanted?"

As if I hadn't spoken, the robot balled up a fist and punched it into the wall right up to the elbow joint. "And I'm strong," she murmured in vicious, dreamy satisfaction.

I didn't know what to say about that, which gave her time to withdraw her fist, straighten up, and smack that fist into the opposite palm with a painfully loud clang. Her head rolled back, and the expressionless face laughed in a giddy stutter. "Ha! Ha ha ha! Ha! I know what I'm going to do with this strength."

And with those ominous words said, she ran out the front door of the house and out of sight.

I followed her to the front door, where I stopped because there was no point. Tonika and Gumshoe Ghost Girl lurked on the stairs nearby, staring owl-eyed at what had just happened. In her arms, Tonika carried an awkward, poky bundle wrapped in a bedsheet.

The confidence she'd started this mission with gone, Tonika asked in a shy, soft voice, "What do we do now?"

I took off my magic hat and wiped my forehead with my wrist. Ugh. I hated what I had to say next. "Reckon there's only one thing we can do. Confess."

Chapter Thirteen

Which left Tonika and me standing on the not-completely-overgrown walkway at most fifteen minutes later, when a red and copper suit of shiny, angular armor swooped down out of the sky to land in front of us.

Mech crossed the last few feet with quick footsteps, throwing his surprisingly warm metal arms around our shoulders and pulling us against his chest plate for a tight, worried hug. Then he jerked back, helmet tilting up and down as he looked us over, no doubt with the assistance of high-tech medical scanners. As urgently as if we were his children, he asked, "Are you girls okay?" The power armor subtly distorted his voice, but not beyond recognition. Besides, could anyone else sound so sincere?

Tonika nodded, her borrowed visor clutched in both hands, revealing her expression of awkward anxiety. The running lights of Mech's armor cast little moving dots as they reflected off her purple plastic hair.

I made myself look Mech in the eye indents on his mask. No, I wasn't okay, but I wasn't freaking out. I'd been steeling myself to be open and honest instead. "Weah not even scratched. Ah ain't in much danger from ghosts, even ghost robots. Us bein' in danger ain't the problem."

Mech put a hand on one of my shoulders, and another on Tonika's opposite shoulder. He lifted his face to look past us at the open door of the house. "And you really cleared the place." Surprise turned to impressed approval, and a squeeze from those gauntleted hands. "Good job."

Why did his being nice make this even harder? I wanted to bathe in his approval, but I couldn't ignore the important part—my failure. Mixed feelings struggling in my heart, I said, "Ah was all proud'a myself too, except the part where I set free—"

A car zoomed up the road and pulled to a scratching but not quite screeching halt at the curb next to us, which completely wrecked my train of thought.

The driver's-side door opened, and out climbed a woman who moved with eel-like slinkiness right up until her tail got caught in the hole cut for it in the driver's seat, and she had to yank it free. To be fair, the curving, savagely sharp stinger on the tip of that black, segmented tail would tangle with anything. My skin crawled as the tail curled up to head height behind her. I would not be comfortable with that pointing at the back of my own head, ugh. It lowered as she approached us, extended back, a little low, and with the tip twitching from side to side out of sync with her sinuous steps.

The rest of the woman… well, she had peach-pink skin, but it was too eerily even a color for any human skin tone. Her body was smooth, unnaturally smooth, except where black shell plates decorated her shoulders, the sides of her hips, her forearms, around her jaw, and completely covered her fingers, making them look like clawed gauntlets. A wild mane of three stripes of pale purple, hot pink, and deep blue puffed around the top and back of her head. Small black domes that looked suspiciously like eyes decorated her temples. Her real eye was also completely, featurelessly black. Just one eye, the right eye. Her left eye was red and obviously artificial, set in a grey metal socket.

Doctor Biotic—because it had to be Doctor Biotic—raised her arms and clasped her hands behind her head, purring, "Hey, check it out, Mech. Only two arms, and my heart pumps just fine. Admit it. I'm hot." I was sure she was curvier than the last time I'd seen her, and she had reduced her clothing to shiny red shorts and a red bandeau to show it off. Well, more likely to show off the black bug plates decorating her skin.

Mech's mask hid his expression, and the armor most of his body language. He just stood there, and when he didn't respond Doctor Biotic lowered her arms and continued with casual, almost languid confidence. "I've got some options set aside in case my digestion fails, and the hair's a wig. I also lost all my tattoos again." Reaching us, she laid a hand on my head and another on Tonika's, so she could push us gently aside and peer past us into the house. Her voice dropped to a near whisper. "Holy moly, they did it. The Murder House is open."

Looking past us apparently wasn't enough. Pushing Tonika and me out of the way, she walked the rest of the way to the front door and stood on the threshold, staring inside.

Just in case, I asked, "Doctor Biotic, ah assume?"

"That's me," she answered distractedly, not looking back.

Mech patted our shoulders, getting my and Tonika's attention back so he could tell us, "I can't comfortably carry you both home, and you said I might have a villain to chase."

"Er..." I wasn't sure what I wanted to say, now.

With the warmth that made me think of his so-friendly smile, Mech continued, "So I called someone I knew would be awake to take you home. I wasn't expecting her to arrive so fast."

Doctor Biotic's scorpion tail lashed once, from left to right. She leaned back and tilted her head enough that together she was able to give him an exasperated stare without moving her feet. "I live around here, Mech."

I had to say something, and threw words together in an anxious jumble. "Mech, ah ain't sure about the villain part. Ah think she was one'a the victims put into a robot body. Ah don't even know how that would work."

Unruffled, Mech gave my shoulder a reassuring squeeze. "It's okay, Avery. We'll catch it. Rampaging robots are nothing new in LA, even intelligent ones."

"But she's more'n that," I insisted, my foot twitching as I

fought the urge to stomp it. "There's a ghost controlling that there 'bot. Ah got the feelin' she's vengeful, but that don't mean I was right. Or then again, she might be huntin' folk down to kill 'em right now. Ah coulda exorcised her, but ah woke her up instead. Ah didn't have time to think—"

Mech let go of Tonika's shoulder to take hold of both of mine. He leaned forward to bring his face closer to my level. He was naturally tall, and the armor made him taller still. "It's *okay*, Avery," he repeated, in the warmest, gentlest voice a man could have. "It's not your problem anymore. Or yours either, Tonika."

I boggled, mouth hanging open, and flapped my arms erratically. "How can it not be mah problem? Ah'm the necromancer!"

Mech's voice firmed up, but only with solid approval. "You've done enough, and I mean that in the good way. You can let go."

Behind me, Doctor Biotic said pensively, "I remember the aura of... evil in in this place. You knew it wanted to kill you just standing on the doorstep. That's all gone. You did good, kids."

Apparently thinking I'd be fine now, Mech asked in a more practical and curious tone, "You said the ghost detective was here?"

I pointed a thumb over my shoulder at the house. "She 'n Ghost Cat Solvin' Mysteries are still inside lookin' for clues."

Still mournful, Doctor Biotic said, "I hope they find some. One of the worst parts of that mess was that we were never completely sure what happened to the killer. We thought he died in there, but couldn't get in to find out."

Mech gave my and Tonika's shoulders a pat, then straightened up, now all noble and heroic business. "I have to set up surveillance to catch the robot as fast as possible, Biotic. Take care of the children, would you? And Avery, you did a hero's job. I mean it. Let the adults handle the rest."

And with that he leaped off the ground as if he hadn't paid his gravity bill, and flew away into the night sky.

"Ah wasn't tryin' to do a hero's job," I told the spot he'd been standing in.

Doctor Biotic walked past us again, this time to open the

doors of her shiny but slightly battered grey sedan. "Come on, kids. In the car. You can put your loot in the trunk, Tonika."

Tonika jerked in surprise at being caught, but didn't argue. She scurried over to the corner of the building and came back with her bundle wrapped in a sheet, which she dumped into the trunk when Doctor Biotic opened it by clicking her key.

I slid into the back seat on the right, and Tonika on the left. I wouldn't have minded sitting by Doctor Biotic, I just felt like as partners in this misadventure, Tonika and I should stick together.

Doctor Biotic's driver seat had a hole in the back to accommodate tails, and she slid hers through it, then hooked the stinger into the island between her driver and passenger seat to keep it from stabbing Tonika. The car pulled out into the street as smoothly as it had pulled in savagely.

And during that whole process, Doctor Biotic explained, "I'm not going to tell you the full story of that house. It wasn't a supervillain, just a death-obsessed psycho messing with other people's mad science. Catching a supervillain is a lot easier than catching a random crazy."

Tonika and I sat there, silent. Not sure what to say. I didn't even know what time it was, and I was too afraid to pull out my phone and find out at what crazy hour I'd be getting home.

Raising her voice, Doctor Biotic told us firmly, "You did a good job."

I grumbled, "Mah parents won't think so. This was supposed ta be dull. Jus' doin' a good deed, no big deal."

"No, they probably won't," the scorpion-tailed woman agreed sadly, "But I appreciate it."

"Why…" Again, I wasn't sure what I was asking.

Positive but not quite cheerful, Doctor Biotic filled in, "Did we seal up the house like that? It was that or burn it down, and we seriously considered burning it down, but we weren't sure what that would set off. Sacred Constellation knew a little necromancy, but not enough to deal with ghosts like that. She could put a barrier around the house to keep all magic inside, so we did that and hoped that, well… you would come along some day. Thanks for coming along some day."

Tonika sat up a little straighter in her seatbelt, and half-stated, half-asked, "So the idea was right, at least."

Anger bubbled up like stomach acid, and I burst out, "How could ah have known there'd be an undead robot in the basement? Nobody told me those were a thing!"

Tonika shrank back into her seat. A few seconds of silence passed. As we merged onto the freeway, Doctor Biotic said in a flat, even tone, "There's something you'll need to learn if you want to be a superhero."

"Ah don't want to be a superhero," I shot back, crossing my arms like a sulky child. Why not? I had plenty to sulk about.

"Might be a little late, Deathette," Doctor Biotic said with dry amusement.

Still scowling, I grumped, "Ah know. Mah powah draws me intah messes."

Doctor Biotic laughed, and I jumped in my seat from the surprise. Her voice bubbly, she corrected, "What? No, kid, Deathette, Avery, whatever, it's nothing to do with your power. This always happens to everyone."

Tonika tilted her head, frown suddenly sharp and inquisitive. "Always?"

In the front seat, Doctor Biotic shrugged her bug-plated shoulders. "Most of the time, at least. No matter how smart you are, nothing ever works out like you planned, especially when you throw super powers into the mix."

Still angry, still acid, I spat out, "What, so there's no use planning?"

My anger rolled off of the older superheroine. "You'd better have some kind of plan, but it had also better have room for surprises, because there's going to be some. Guaranteed. That robot you released might turn out to be a hero. Or she might stalk you, isolate you, and beg you to release her from her suffering."

"Mech sounded pretty sure it was dangerous," Tonika pointed out.

"It's Mech's job to protect people," Doctor Biotic non-answered.

Silence settled in again. My anger drained back down to sullenness, then started drifting into anxiety again.

This time, when Doctor Biotic spoke up, she did it in a warm, if matter-of-fact tone. "I agree with Mech. You did good, even if it wasn't quite the good you expected. The robot is not your responsibility. You should let it go, leave the rest to the adults, and just be proud of yourselves."

"I suppose," I mumbled, looking out the window. Two, then a third drop of rain landed on the glass. It was night time in January, after all. I hadn't seen actual rain since I'd arrived in California.

Up front, Doctor Biotic sighed, heavy and sad and philosophical. "But you're not going to let it go."

Scrupulously blank, Tonika asked, "How do you know that?"

Hints of pain scratched in Doctor Biotic's lowered, voice. The sound of confession. "I've made more mistakes than Mech has. Worse mistakes. Done things I regret. No matter how much I tell you that this isn't your responsibility, it feels like your responsibility, and you think you have to fix it. You're going to think things like only you understand the problem or have the powers to fix it. Or that you just have to. And maybe that you still have to fix whatever got you into this mess originally."

My stomach churned, feeling guilty for feeling angry that the older woman had predicted thoughts that had been starting to form in my head.

I halfway surrendered, or at least retreated. "Can ah jes' have a few minutes to concentrate on the problem in front'a me?"

Tonika looked across the seat at me curiously. "Which problem?"

I shuddered, guilt and anxiety making my stomach squirm. "What ah'm gonna tell my parents!"

Chapter Fourteen

Which led inevitably, the next day, to a five-way phone call with my friends.

I complained to the tiny video windows on my phone. "So they're callin' Schleimy, or callin' Mech ta tell Schleimy, or I don't know what-all, but they're cuttin' mah magic lessons down ta once a week on Saturdays."

I adjusted my legs a little. I tended to slip out of position slowly when I sat cross-legged like this on my mattress. Which led to adjusting my huge, floppy, plaid flannel shirt I kept for lying around and sulking indoors. All while holding the phone out at arm's length with my other hand. Technically it was the only light in my room, but no amount of drawn curtains blocked out the Southern California sun. Someone in LA must have solar-powered super powers, and that would be terrifying.

"I should have been there," declared Sue, looking off to the side from her camera, tiny face scowling and voice hard and merciless in its guilt.

I waved my free hand sharply. "Absolutely no way, no how, nuh-uh. Y'all didn't feel that place. If any livin' human'd walked in, they'da been attacked."

Sue's eyes returned to the camera, glaring. "You're a living human."

"Not for this," Chris pointed out, his tone and expression mild.

Sue's face twisted in anger, eyebrows plunging, and her mouth opened in the beginning of a snarl. The gentle tone had worked, though. She relaxed into a mere sullen pout, which probably matched mine. "Yeah, okay."

I didn't give a sigh of relief only because I didn't want to upset my friends. I did lean back on my right hand, to hide a fit of trembling, and just had to hope it wouldn't be visible on my left hand holding the phone. My parents had taken this... okay. Okay enough that I could be annoyed rather than horrified. I'd had all the best intentions and heroes were telling her I'd done a good deed. For crackdowns on living too magical a life, this wasn't awful.

Now my friends had taken all the news with nothing but concern for me. The worst was over.

Annie's face pushed Chris's aside in their window, her frown compassionate and sad and a lot more noble than mine or Sue's. The same with her soft voice. "I'm sorry you lost your ghost hand. I wanted to see you using it."

Chris peeked over Annie's shoulder while she had the phone. They shared one telephone. Around them, I could see the lush, green potted plants that divided their bedroom in half. One phone, and one bedroom. Even as big as it was, sharing a bedroom with a sibling would drive me batty. It didn't seem to bother them. At times like this, they passed the phone back and forth like teammates handing off a basketball, with perfect cooperation.

Since I hadn't said anything, what with trying not to think about my disappointment at losing my poltergeist, Peggy said, "You'll just have to do the climbing thing this week."

Switching my phone to my right, I sat up and flexed my left hand speculatively. My dexterity was coming back, and some heavy exercise would be just the thing. Of course, I could do the ritual on my other hand, but I wasn't going to mess up both my real hands at the same time. I wasn't sure about the safety of casting the spell more than once, anyhow. A girl's ghost can only heal so much.

I perked up a bit, managing a wry smile. "Maybe ah'll even see y'all more'n once. It ain't so bad. Ah've learned a lotta what ah need from Schleimy already anyhow."

While I talked, I stilled my body, all the way to the core. I focused on the cold inside me, on my awareness of my magic and how it moved in currents up and down me. Stirring them, I raised more cold, and more, a current of freezing slush that perfectly traced my body under my skin, but not escaping. Then I let that power relax again, fading rather than releasing it. No spill-over to cause weird side effects.

With any luck, my friends hadn't even noticed the tiny pause before I continued, "The punishment is mah folks're even more upset about mah necromancy, not that ah'm spendin' Saturday mornin's in Chinatown."

"What!?" screeched Sue, jumping in the air and nearly falling off the treadmill in her parents' exercise room.

I rolled my eyes, feeling like I should back up Sue's freak-out with at least mild exasperation. "Yeah, Schleimy works there on Saturdays."

Sue's background rolled as she slid off the treadmill, shaking her head and waving her free hand. Cold and ferocious, she snapped, "No. Absolutely not. Totally no. Not happening."

Annie's face filling her and Chris's phone looked concerned. So did mine, I'm sure. So did Chris's when he took the phone back from Annie. Peggy's face at least showed a faint frown.

Chris merely sounded puzzled. "Yeah, Chinatown is closed on weekends."

That couldn't have been Sue's point, but it sure got my attention. "How can ya close a whole neighborhood every week?"

Peggy shrugged. "They do."

Annie nodded, and murmured, "Five p.m. Friday to nine a.m. Monday. Barricades on the streets."

Their window flickered to Chris, who said, "Every week."

Aghast, words thick with horrified sarcasm, Sue lectured us, "Yeah, because it's full of supervillains on weekends. Like, why do you think your creepy little sales goblin mentor is there on Saturdays? Who do you think she's selling to?"

Despite myself, I grinned. "Aw, Schleimy's a pip. You just gotta get ta know her."

Sue's face set as hard as old oatmeal and as smooth as a marble statue. "I'll get the chance. I'm coming with you."

My style didn't exactly die, but I did look back her hard. "Ah 'preciate the thought, darlin', but that's yoah Marcia tahm."

Chris frowned, too, suddenly very serious indeed as he told Sue, "Your parents aren't going to be happy if they find out you're spending several hours in a supervillain convention. I don't want them to take you away from us."

That hit. That hit hard. Sue clenched her jaw, then nibbled on her lower lip. Then her jaw set defiantly. "Just next week, then. You're totally not ready for these people, Avery. They're crazy. They pretend to be nice, but it's just a trap. Everyone and everything is a target to them. I'm not sending you into that alone. I can at least, like, back you up the first time. Mech will think it's a good idea, because they won't let him in to protect you."

Able to be just as stubborn as Sue and with a much less delicate jaw to jut out, I warned, "Just don't you risk gettin' your parents as upset as mine are."

In her role as The Calm One, Peggy suggested, "Scaling back could be good for you."

I leaned back, propping a hand on the mattress again and sighing at the phone as the tension lowered. "Ah know. Ah want to."

Everyone gave me a look through their phones, like they could see right through me. Chris and Annie pulled their phone back far enough that they could press their faces together and both look skeptical.

"But...?" prodded Peggy.

I half-grimaced. The left half. "Ah'm worried 'bout the ghost robot."

"Mech can take care of it," Sue answered immediately.

My half-grimace turned into a full grimace. "By melting it down?"

"You said ghosts run out of power by themselves," murmured Annie.

I half-shrugged. "Ah dunno with this one. Ah don't know anything."

Taking the phone from Annie, Chris murmured equally gently, "I think this is what your parents meant. You have to learn to let go, or being the only living necromancer is going to rule your life. It will never end."

Peggy nodded from her window.

Lurching back upright, I complained, "There ain't no one else knows how ta handle this! What if it needs help? What if it's delusional an' starts murderin' folk? Ah could stop it in a second. Ah don't know if heroes can do that afore folk get hurt."

I knew Chris's mind control powers didn't work over a phone. His smile really was that sincerely loving and calm as he answered, "This is what I mean. What your parents mean. There's always going to be trouble begging for your attention, and that trouble is always going to come with risky decisions that you'll regret forever if you get wrong. Leave that to the adults who want the job." Peggy nodded, but let Chris continue. "I'd rather you spent all your time on us instead."

Now everyone nodded, Sue emphatically.

My eyes suddenly stung with tears. I rubbed at my wet nose as I started to sniffle. I was an ugly crier, but it hurt to feel cared about this much. "Thanks, everybody. So, uh... Monday?"

Chapter Fifteen

Monday. Monday afternoon, specifically, when the final school bell rang. I sat at my classroom desk flexing my left hand again. My writing was now completely legible. It would be nice if losing my ghost hand had returned all that natural precision to my real hand. No such luck. It did force me to practice, so I was recovering fast.

Sue tugged on the shoulder strap of my sweater vest. "Don't dawdle. Winifred will be waiting for us already."

I scooped up my backpack and slung it over my shoulder, asking, "Uh...?"

As soon as I was on my feet Sue grabbed my hand, pulling me out into the hall. She laughed. "Rock climbing, remember?"

I nodded. "Ah remember that part."

As she dragged me along, Sue deigned to answer my real question, if with a teasing grin. "Regular friends fun. We're not taking Alice. Peggy, Chris, and Annie will meet as at the gym, and Winifred will take us home after."

We stepped out through the front door of Pepperidge Preparatory School for Girls, into the sunshine and onto the grass. Sue took both of my hands, pulling me closer and giving me a quick little kiss on the lips.

I knew the daily after-school kiss served two purposes. It reminded everyone in this viper nest of a school who the untouchable, deadly power couple was. And Sue would take any excuse to kiss me.

I'd be lying if I said I didn't like it.

With the enjoyable formalities over, we stomped down to the curb, where a thin, stiff figure in a pinstripe suit stood next to a shiny, blue car that was probably some particularly expensive kind. Like all the other cars pulled up in front of Pep Prep.

I nodded to Sue's butler. "Good afternoon, Winifred. Thanks for pickin' us up again. Ah hope y'all're havin' a good day."

"Very good, Mistress Avery, thank you for asking," she answered with a nod that wasn't quite completely stiff and official.

"So where're we goin', anyhoo?" I asked as I slid into the backseat with Winifred holding the door.

"Don't tell her!" Sue snapped, climbing in the other side.

Which soon enough left me looking at a tall, wide, and bleakly unadorned building somewhere in Burbank, or North Hollywood, or whatever that area is past the hills. It reminded me of a parking garage. The building, that is. Big, square, and solid. Hardly any windows. The front doors looked tiny and almost hidden in that grey expanse, and no sign anywhere identified the building's nature.

To my considerable surprise, Chris, Annie, and Peggy were there already, waiting on the sidewalk.

I stepped out of the car without waiting for Winifred to do her butler thing. Chris rushed up, took both of my hands in his, and pulled me to him for a quick little kiss almost exactly like the one I'd gotten from Sue. It came with that peculiar expression I saw so often in both of them, like they couldn't believe I was real, that they got to date someone like me, and they needed to touch me to confirm it was true. I blushed, not at the public affection, but at the open adoration in Chris's dark eyes.

Again and again it floored me that anyone could think about me that way, much less two people, and those two people being Sue and Chris.

While I stood there all flustered, Chris gave me an only slightly dazed smile. "Problem. They won't let us in, and I didn't want to..." He trailed off, because people get upset when you admit in public that your super power is mind control. Even dangerously unreliable mind control that's more like being super persuasive.

I tilted my head, looking up past my looming red boyfriend at the even more looming grey wall. "Ah thought this was the place Annie found."

Chris turned to look with me, but still held onto one of my hands. "It is, but it's very exclusive, so we had to wait for Sue."

Sue hauled a big canvas bag out of the passenger seat of her parents' car, closed the door, and Winifred drove away. Both arms wrapped around the bag, she scowled and asked, "Did you have Annie flash some fire?"

Chris paused for a moment. His face the kind of blank where you're trying to hide disapproval, he said, "You mean you have to have super powers to get in?"

"Well, at least they'd let you inside. Come on." She jerked her head for us to follow as she headed for the doors.

This place did take security, or at least exclusivity, seriously. The front room did almost nothing to give away what kind of business this was, just had a sleek desk and a couple of plastic potted plants and a few businessy waiting room chairs that looked like they'd never been used. The late teen behind the desk did have wristbands and a loose blue shirt, so there was that.

I had no time to look for more distinguishing marks. Sue never slowed down as she marched to the room's side door, glowering at the desk attendant and snarling, "Susan Perrier and *friends*."

The desk clerk took it well. Hopefully a place like this paid well enough to put up with attitude. Sue's anger got a simple nod and the reply, "Of course."

We shuffled through the side door into a very large room. A very large room indeed.

My eyes were drawn immediately to the climbing rock tower. It went up and up. It spiraled, like unless someone messed with gravity you would actually be hanging from the ledges instead of climbing them along some sections. Half the building might be this one hugely tall room to accommodate it, all the way up to distant grey rafters. It wasn't the only climbing wall, either. Most of the others were straight, and it was hard to tell how tall the others were compared to the crazy thing that dominated the room. A couple of stories at least.

Annie had looked for the tallest indoor rock-climbing setup in LA, and she clearly found it. Also, maybe it was at least kind of reasonable that something that crazy was reserved for people with super powers.

Maybe.

No, it kind of bugged me.

But I was already slavering at the idea of climbing these goofy walls covered in colorful chunks of fake plastic rock. This looked like fun. I was already noticing how strange and irregular the placement of those colorful chunks was.

In the midst of my drooling, I realized something. My hands clutched in horror at my school uniform. "Ah am not climbin' anything in a skirt."

"Covered," announced Sue. She pulled a bundle of clothing with a promising amount of blue denim out of her bag, and pressed it into my hands. The main item seemed to be a short-legged version of a pair of overalls. Yes, very pleasing. Odd little shoes with pointy toes and a sharp-edged sole. Climbing shoes, presumably.

Sue turned her attention next to the devil twins, lifting more clothing out of the bag. With an accusing stare, she thrust the clothing forward. "And I knew you two wouldn't be able to resist dressing too fancy to exercise, so I took care of you, too."

Heh. Sue had scored a big, huge old hit. Chris and Annie had probably tried to dress casually for exercise. They were merely both wearing black-and-white suits that looked rather like tuxedos. Meekly, the twins accepted the bundle of actual exercise clothes. They knew they were guilty.

Sue's gaze turned to Peggy. Dressed in loose tan pants and a tan t-shirt, Pegs raised a hand and waved it dismissively, then added, "I'll take the shoes, though."

That satisfied Sue. At least, it satisfied her about Peggy. Turning her attention back to the inadequately prepared rest of us, she circled around, put a hand each on my and Chris's backs, and pushed us towards the clearly marked locker rooms.

Soon enough I emerged from those locker rooms, much more comfortable and relaxed. My gigantic hair had been tied back into something more like a red puffball than a ponytail to keep it out of my eyes.

Sue had managed to change and be already back waiting for me. She was wearing... exactly the same as me, the denim short overalls and shirt underneath. Sue was normally perfectly comfortable in skirts, and in this ultra-tomboy outfit she looked awkward in a wonderfully adorable way.

Chris and Annie emerged at the same time, as if they'd coordinated, and dressed exactly the same. Sue had gotten them both snug, shiny black exercise shorts and shirts, and what worked as a sports bra for her merely decorated him, baring their scarlet midriffs and making it almost possible to confuse the two. Without Annie's usual heels, they were exactly the same height, and walked at the same pace, lifted up on the balls of their bare feet like prowling cats. They held the climbing shoes in their hands.

Sue sighed in not entirely believable exasperation. "I gave them exercise clothes off a rack and they look like runway models wearing it."

A woman skipped up to us. She had an odd gait, her feet barely lifting from the floor, sliding forward at a speed that didn't match the strides. She looked completely in-place for a gym, with loose, wrinkly blue shorts and a loose white shirt over a dark sports bra, sweatbands on her wrists, those special climbing shoes, and a massive canvas belt with hooks and pouches that was clearly climbing gear itself. Her brown hair wasn't long enough to make a good ponytail, but she had it pulled back anyway. I couldn't see any other customers in this giant room, but we obviously weren't the only people she'd worked with today because her face had that subtly puffy look like someone who'd sweated a lot, and smudges of chalk stained her forehead.

She had to have worked hard to get that sweat, because now that I was wearing less I could feel the faint, pleasantly cool draft that filtered through the giant room.

An employee ID tag on her shirt identified her as "Levi." Clasping her hands together, she asked like a friendly school teacher, "First time, kids? Is everybody ready?"

"Born ready," I answered, and took off, letting the thrill of eagerness replace impatience. I didn't go for the twisty tower. I had no clue how to climb on a face that leaned back, much less one that actually went upside down. But one of the regular straight up and down walls looked like just the thing.

Reaching one, I wedged my feet onto the first, well, wedges in the surface. With the irregular placement of the plastic "rocks," I had to do a bit of a jump and pull to get to the next solid spot with my feet in place and my hands holding tight grips, but I managed it. After that, things looked steady, if wandering.

The projections varied wildly in size and shape. Some were itty bitty, and I wasn't sure how to get a grip on those, so I treated them with care. Big metal clasps hung regularly from the wall all over, but those were clearly for cheaters and I ignored them.

To my delight, faint thumps, creaks, and grunts turned out to be Chris, climbing the wall a few feet to my right. He gave me a huge grin as he nearly caught up.

Levi floated up next to me on the opposite side, hovering in the air as casually as if she were standing on the floor. She held up a knotted blue rope, raised her eyebrows, and asked, "Safety training?"

"Oops," I said out loud.

Chris jumped right off the wall, from above head height, landing in a smooth crouch and standing back up. I'd have broken my ankles if I tried that. That apparently wasn't enough, because he followed up by holding his arms out in a silent invitation for me to jump into them.

Horrified, I squeaked, "Ah'll crush you!" He was five inches taller than me, and I outweighed him! Probably. I thought. I avoided scales.

The look Chris gave me was somewhere between affectionate

and scathing. Definitely a smirk. His arms still extended, he retorted, "No you won't."

I had to trust him. I jumped.

He caught me! A heavy catch, crouching nearly to the floor when I landed in his arms, but then he straightened back up smoothly and carried me over to our waiting friends as if I were only a little heavy.

Finally, he set me down, and gave me a grin.

I blushed. I blushed furiously. I felt so flattered it burned up my spine to my cheeks and paralyzed me with awkwardness, and I wasn't sure why.

The soft, cool breeze of the building's air conditioning slowly eased that down as the brown-haired woman skipped up to us. Having seen her floating in the air, the reason for her odd walk was obvious. She wasn't walking, she was keeping tenuous contact with the floor as she flew.

She introduced herself to us with a cheerful smile that looked both tired and genuine, holding up her ID tag. "Hi, I'm Levi. I'll be your coach and your safety attendant. You've already noticed my special qualifications. Most of our customers have super powers, we keep a lot of equipment designed to superhuman specifications, and you're old enough to have noticed that super powers lead to super mistakes. We'll be doing top-roping for safety on your first lesson, and if the ropes don't catch you, I will. Why don't we start with introductions, starting with the girl who loves climbing maybe a little too much?"

After whatever Chris made me feel, the embarrassment of being singled out like that was hardly anything. Besides, Levi did seem, yep, super friendly, and the drafty air—

"Yoah a magic usah! Ah "spec that's a flight spell yoah usin'?" I should have spotted it sooner! No one's clothes fluttered an inch in the breeze only I felt.

Levi hesitated only the briefest second as she got her first good earful of my sludge-thick accent. The Carolina version could be pretty, but it was still ridiculous. If she felt anything other than surprise, she hid it perfectly as she slid the fingers of one hand in the air and cocked the other on her hip. Actually, she looked a touch embarrassed herself, while grateful to talk about it. Boy, did I understand that. She started with a quick puff of a chuckle. "That's the only thing I can do with my magic. Even my light spell flickers. If you can tell..." She trailed off, giving me a long, not quite focused look, mumbling something so low I couldn't make it out. Then her eyes jerked wide. "You're that necromancer!"

Now I really winced, and groaned through gritted teeth. "Y'all've seen that awful reality show."

Being kidnapped by a deranged evil producer for her reality show about supervillain children was a terrible introduction to LA—which introduced me to the best friends a girl could have.

Everything else about that show was awful, though. I couldn't see Chris behind me, but Annie flinched, Sue facepalmed, and Peggy looked off to the side with a frown.

Levi frowned too, but only in confusion. "The what? No, but us magic folks, you know, we kind of keep track of each other. Shared hobby and all." Her frown turned defensive, and some of her hair tumbled free of the ponytail as she rubbed her hand across her forehead. "It's not like I fight crime or do villainy or anything. I don't think I've even met a hero or villain, and they wouldn't tell me if they were. But we gossip, trade spells and stuff. It's so hard to find a spellbook and they take forever to learn!"

I stared at her passionate, aggrieved scowl and her groan of frustration. I didn't know what to say. That wasn't my experience with magic at all. The hard-to-find-spellbooks part, sure, but I got lucky and a librarian handed me mine.

Back to defensive, she held up her hand, palm out, and hurriedly returned to topic. "Anyway, when the first necromancer since Alicia Blackheart herself shows up in LA, word gets around. We keep tabs on each other, especially black magic users. Not that I believe in black magic." The last sentence came out even more hurried.

I sure did. I probably wouldn't be able to cast Levi's levitation spells, or her light spell. Levi didn't look like she had cravings, either, and her power felt gentle. My powers were really good at two things: Killing people and making them get up and walk again after.

"Probably" wasn't "certainly," however. It might be worth asking for a copy of those spells.

Sue cleared her throat loudly.

Levi jerked upright, back to professional adulthood. "Right, right! Training."

Chapter Sixteen

Several minutes of lectures I probably should have paid better attention to later, I was back at the same wall, but this time with a special belt, and a blue rope tied to it. The rope was looped around something at the top of the climbing wall, and tied again to the belt of Annie, who would stop me from falling if necessary.

I was determined that wouldn't be necessary. Looking up at the three-story wall in front of me, I cracked my knuckles. That felt weird and scratchy because my hands were now covered in chalk dust from a pouch on the funny climbing belt.

Levi suggested helpfully, "You should start over here on one of the more beginner—"

I wedged my pointy shoe into one of the lower projections, grabbed one further up, and got through the awkward starting pull to my first really stable position.

After that it got easier. Sort of. It wasn't like tree climbing, where all the good support spots are next to the trunk. Rock climbing involved twisting and wandering. Both involved relying on my legs to push as much as possible. My arms tired out fast enough just helping with support.

The funky climbing shoes helped a lot. The lines of those

funny soles wedged nicely into cracks against the wall.

I loved it. I started to sweat and my muscles burned just enough to be pleasant a story up, and this giant room conveyed the wonderful sensation of being up high. It lacked the world of branches you got lost in with trees, replacing that with being surrounded by empty space in a way that standing on a floor couldn't deliver.

I was maybe two thirds of the way and definitely sweating when I heard Sue below me bark, "Move it, Prince Charming."

Making sure I had a solid grip first, I looked down to see Chris, who was roped to Levi on the floor, and Sue, who was roped to Peggy. Sue was underneath Chris at an angle, maybe because of the weird way the plastic "rock" wandered rather than going straight up and down.

Chris stuck his tongue out at Sue. Sue stuck her tongue out back at him. I giggled, then turned my focus back to climbing. I was not going to slip because I took this for granted, especially with the way I had to watch how my body leaned as the path moved me from side to side.

...and then I got a grip on the upper edge of the wall and pulled myself up with sore arms to lie on the flat top by the support poles. Whew. My muscles hurt a lot more than I'd expected from that short distance, and I was breathing hard.

But I reached the top on my first try, with no falls! I swung my legs over the edge, out of the way of Chris and Sue, and flexed my biceps. "Woo! Who's the queen of climbing?"

Farther down, Chris had moved into my space, but was also hanging from his rope trying to get a good grip back.

"The best! The best! The best!" I chanted down at my boyfriend and girlfriend, pumping my fists.

My gleeful display of bad sportswomanship ended as soon as they reached the top together. With my body braced around a support pole, I took a chalky grip on each of them and helped pull them up for that final, relieved collapse.

After that we all three sat on the edge, Chris on my right, Sue on my left, and waved down at Peggy and Annie and Levi. Chris's scarlet toes wiggled in the open air. He and Annie had never put on their shoes.

Chris waved a no longer shaky finger. "Problem. We have to climb down so Peggy and Annie can try."

Sue leaned forward enough to stick her tongue out at him. He stuck his tongue out back. I stuck my own tongue out, and twisted my head rapidly from side to side to show it to both of them. Down below, Annie stuck her tongue out, and pulled her eyelid down with the tip of her tail.

Peggy, waiting patiently with her hands in her pockets, stuck her tongue and spat, "Pbbbbbt."

We all laughed so hard I almost collapsed again.

As I straightened back up, I saw something.

Two blue-outlined figures stepped out of the locker rooms, through the wall. "Tumbled" might have been a better word, diving and rolling, not quite in control. Leaping to their feet, they kept moving around, coming together and breaking apart. I was pretty far away, and they weren't much more than outlines, but I got the vague impression one was feminine shaped and the other masculine.

If it was a fight, it was taking forever and they kept wrestling then pushing apart more than I'd ever imagined. If it was a date, it was more athletic than anything I'd ever imagined. If it was an exercise routine, that was one serious and mobile workout.

"What in the Sam Hill???" I asked, squinting harder at the ghosts.

Sue and Chris looked at me. I saw that out of the corner of my eye as I watched one of the ghosts thrown through Annie on the floor below us, and the other jump over her to intercept its fallen... opponent?

Cupping my hands to my mouth, I called down to Levi, "Hey, ma'am! Anybody die here in this ol' gym?"

Levi's open-mouthed, taken-aback expression was quite clear even from this distance, as was her high, confused tone. "I mean... not that I know about?" She knew not to argue with the necromancer.

"You'd know. You'd know right certain. I'll come down an'—"

Sue grabbed my elbow, holding it still. She looked across

me at Chris with a pleading expression. That shocked me into immobility more than her touch.

Chris put his arm tenderly around my shoulder, gave me a sweet, apologetic smile, and murmured, "This is where you practice letting go."

I pouted. "Aw, come on, this is harmless." I was getting good with ghosts. Even if I somehow messed up and gave them more power than they needed just to explain themselves, I could control them.

He tilted his face an inch down, so his dark eyes looked up knowingly into mine. "But there's always something, isn't there? Your parents were right about that. And besides... this is our time with you. Call me selfish, but I don't want to share it with ghosts."

I opened my mouth.

I closed my mouth.

I grinned hugely, then hid my face in my hands. "You guys..."

Taking a couple of deep breaths to make sure my voice didn't squeak, I called down, "Never mind, ma'am. Can y'all help us dayawn so Peggy an' Annie don't gotta wait?"

Levi floated Sue down first, then Chris. Each time, I saw her lips moving with an incantation. That reminded me that if my parents hadn't intervened, I'd be in Schleimy's pitch-black basement home pouring ice water on myself right now. It felt strange not to be doing that. Not bad, but lost.

Laughing, I shook my head and told myself, "Ah really did need that intervention, huh?"

One of the ghosts succeeded in pinning the other to the floor. I couldn't tell which. Then they disappeared, and reappeared elsewhere. Was the story starting over? No, now they were struggling over by the front wall. So, the scene being remembered in front of me was muddled as well as passionate. Maybe it wasn't even true, and I'd have to restore the ghosts to lucidity to get the real memory.

I was absolutely burning up with curiosity, an itchy sensation going right up my spine into my throat. Why were these ghosts so visible? To look like this, they should have died recently and in an obvious, public way. Did they die fighting each other? Was magic involved? Maybe these weren't ghosts, and some magic left these events printed on this spot while the original actors didn't die. Or the ghosts had been moved from their place of death. I might be the only necromancer, but I'd seen that other mages could fiddle around the edges. Or...

This was exactly what Chris had been talking about, wasn't it? I had to let go.

Swinging around, making sure my rope was still tied to me and to Annie, I started climbing down. It was a whole different kettle of anxiously mysterious fish than climbing up, thanks to these irregular rocks.

I got quite a way before Levi floated up with folded arms and an amused smile. "This is your first time. Let me. A lot of our clients are natural climbers—"

"I'm not," called out Peggy.

Levi floated me down, a sensation rather like being carried, even if I couldn't quite pin down where the arms holding me up would be. When I got to the ground, I wrapped my arms around Peggy and gave her a hug so big that I lifted her up off her feet. Tilting my head so I could look her in the face from so close up, I asked, "Y'all sure you wanna try this? We ain't no super team. We don't care none iff'n you kin lift a car or run a marathon, just that you're you."

When I put her down and she could breathe again, Peggy answered simply, "It looks like fun."

The farther to the right of the wall we were climbing, the more beginner the rock placement. The absolute farthest right was pretty much just a ladder of little ledges sticking out of the wall. Peggy considered it seriously and silently for several seconds, while Levi made absolutely sure Peggy's anchor rope was secure around my waist.

Peggy took the next slot up from the ladder, where there were lots of big rocks but they weren't actually lined up like rungs. She started her way up.

Annie, tied to Chris, took the spot Chris had, the next row easier than the one I'd gone up. Annie went up like a squirrel, her bare toes finding toeholds like a goat. She got about halfway up before she lost her grip and slumped hanging in the air from her rope. It might have been the same spot Chris fell.

Annie pointed at Peggy, a third of the way up and pausing to breathe hard. I clapped. "Go, Peggy! Slow 'n' steady wins the race!"

I meant it honestly, but Peggy looked back at me and stuck her tongue out. Suddenly everyone was sticking their tongue out at each other, and laughing so hard that Peggy fell off the wall. I had to set my weight to hold her up.

Dangling, arms and legs hanging, Peggy confessed, "I think I'm done. I'm going to be sore tomorrow."

I flexed an arm, feeling the stiff burn. "Me too."

Peggy, Chris, and Annie declared together, "No, you're not." Annie clasped her hands over her mouth after doing it, but the straight line of her black eyebrows showed amusement, not guilt.

Scales brushed against the back of my neck, and I jumped nearly a foot in the air, especially as the scales kept going down the rest of me.

No one else noticed anything, not even my bounce. Chris was standing in front of Sue, telling her, "You look really good in that." Behind him, Annie nodded. Sue did look good in those overalls, as much as you'd never expect to see her in them.

Sue edged closer to me, scowled, and looked away and down at the mat-covered floor.

The scaly sensation rolled over me again. Brr!

Someone was doing magic. Big magic, nearby, and...

...it was none of my business.

Boy howdy, was that a weird thought to get used to. I had the option of just ignoring it, like I could ignore the ghosts now locked in hand-to-hand struggle halfway through the climbing wall. The world was full of this stuff. I didn't have to do get involved.

I slipped my arm around Sue's waist, and grinned, dismissing magic for the fun topic of overalls. "I'm glad, 'cause I reckon we'll be wearin' this all the rest'a the day. I ain't goin' back to skirts just 'cause the exercise is done."

Sue twisted, got both her hands on my back, and shoved me forward, so I staggered into Chris's embracing arms. Stiffly upright, like a lecturing school teacher, Sue said, "Okay, but Wednesday I've got Marcia's permission for us to use her swimming pool, so everyone have a swimsuit ready."

"Uh..." I said, trying to catch up to the change in tone and topic.

Sue talked over me, brisk and officious, which wasn't difficult since I hadn't anything to say and she had plenty. "Right now, I'm going to call Winifred. I was thinking, Chris is big on plants, and Annie likes peace, and you like anything that's not Kentucky—" I coughed guiltily, but Sue kept going. "—so I looked up arboretums, and I don't know if there's actually a Japanese garden nearby, or just a shop with the name, but we're going to go check."

She stalked off towards the front office as if she were going to beat up her phone rather than talk to it.

Barely above a whisper, Chris said, "I'm not sure if she's angry that she's been hogging your time, or..."

When he trailed off, I whispered back. "She thinks this trip out is important an' wants it to go right. She's trying to organize it all, and she cain't be nice ta herself 'til she sees it's a success, poor darlin'."

Chris's smile strengthened, and he said just a little louder, "I'm glad we have someone who can organize on this team."

I nodded frankly. Annie nodded furiously. Peggy nodded visibly, but just barely.

Sue came back with her arms around the canvas clothing bag. "Chris and Annie, I have your clothes—"

Chris interrupted her. "We'll stay like this. We might as well all be informal together."

I giggled. "Chris, you'n Annie could make burlap sacks look lahk fashion."

The twins' expressions immediately turned distant, thoughtful.

Sue scowled furiously. I grinned so wide my face hurt like my arms, and whispered to her, "They're serious." That was how much they loved fashion.

Sue snapped her fingers, breaking the spell. "Car is waiting. Move it, fancy twins."

Since Sue was pushing us together today, Chris snagged my arm, wrapping it up in his as we walked side by side towards the door. Okay, he'd have done it even without Sue, and it was nice to be held onto. He told me and through me the group, "If this doesn't work out, there's one almost straight south of us in Hollywood. If you need excuses to do nonmagical things, we could make trips to all the different arboretums around LA."

I giggled at the lust to look at green things poorly hidden in Chris's eyes and voice.

Annie tapped my shoulder and pointed back at Peggy.

Peggy shuffled along behind us, mouth tight, looking uncharacteristically awkward and embarrassed.

My brain managed to catch this one. "Oh, right. Theyah's a lot of bugs in gahdens." Slipping free of Chris, I grabbed hold of Peggy and lifted her up for another hug. When I put her down, I said, "We'll manage, Pegs. We've got fiyah, death, and openin' holes in the wall you can make the bugs stand behind. It won't be that bad. You've hahdly summoned anything in heah."

Peggy shrugged an inch, looking more relaxed. "A few spiders. This building hardly has any bugs in it."

We'd already made it to the front room. Sue pushed open the darkened glass front doors of the building.

A dark stream of ants writhed in front of it, going around the building but until now unable to get through the door seal. People were walking on the other side of the sidewalk, keeping well clear.

I couldn't help it. I laughed. "Well, so much fer thayat. Make 'em scoot aside so we kin get to the car, wouldja, Peggy?"

The scaly feeling hit me again. A broomstick flew down out of the sky, and the tiniest heroine I'd ever seen hopped off. The top of her pink-haired head didn't reach my shoulder, although her pointy hat went up past Annie's horns—and Annie had her shoes back on.

Little Witch. I had seen her once, very briefly, coming out of the shower while I, uh… robbed her apartment. Now in full Halloween witch costume, including pink-and-purple striped stockings, she jumped off her broom and made horrified noises as she danced away from the pooling, rippling ants. Once out of danger she dismissed the insect problem and pulled two things from her big belt of pockets and pouches—a belt colored black to blend perfectly with her dress. I couldn't see what she held in her left fist, but in her right hand she held a gold loop. She lifted it in the air, and I felt the pulse of scaly magic again.

In a hard and serious voice that belied her cute appearance, Little Witch yelled, "I know you're here, robot! I don't know why, but if you surrender peacefully for exorcism, it... I guess it won't matter... *listen!*"

Reshuffling her equipment, she pulled out a silver bell bigger than both my fists together, and a little copper striking hammer. Little Witch shouted, "The ringing of the bell commands you!" and struck the bell. It went *bong*, a pretty but normal bell sound, accompanied by a very much abnormal burst of cold necromantic power.

Glass crashed across the street. A shiny white, long-haired figure that could easily be the robot from the haunted house broke the third-floor window of a building.

"The ringing of the bell commands you!" shouted Little Witch, striking the bell again and releasing another pulse of necromancy.

The robot jumped, cracking pavement when it landed on the sidewalk.

"The ringing of the bell commands you!" repeated Little Witch, hitting the bell a third time.

The robot took a step, then a second step, then a third, each faster than the last... but not towards Little Witch.

Towards me.

"Got you!" shouted the pink-haired heroine. She shoved the bell back in its pocket, and pulled a wand with a cog on the end out of another.

The robot took that time to swivel completely around and run into an alley.

Little Witch snarled, "Oh, you ffffffffiddlesticks!" She hopped on her floating broom again and soared off after her undead mechanical prey.

I stood there, cold with horror, not magic. My friends didn't know that was the same robot. There were probably dozens of crazy robots in LA. But that was the robot I'd freed, here, stalking me.

And like I'd been told, the adult superheroes were handling it.

I took a deep, slow, shuddering breath, and stepped over the trickle of ants that Peggy hadn't entire shooed out of the way. "Well, that was sure a thing that happened raht theyah. Hey, Winifred! Who all gets shotgun?"

Chapter Seventeen

That lasted all the way to Thursday.

As ever, Sue and I sat on the little fieldstone wall that separated one level of school courtyard from another, enjoying our lunch, or rather Sue enjoyed her lunch while I showered her with indignance. "Ah am nevah going swimming with any of y'all again. Ah would have thought Peggy at least would be above such pranks."

My doting girlfriend laughed, and laughed, and laughed some more, high and sharp with evil glee. Wrapping both arms around one of mine, she snuggled up closer to me.

My phone rang in my backpack.

Which was weird, because it was turned off.

I dug the phone out, both relieved that I'd avoided telling Sue that her love of teasing sometimes goes too far, and as baffled as a girl can get that I was getting a phone call at all. At least I recognized the phone number this time.

Pressing the answer button, I said, "Tonika? Yoah lucky you got through. Ah sweah ah turn this thing off for school." Every day, because those were the rules.

Her faintly nervous but otherwise neutral voice answered,

"You do, but it leaves a minimal monitoring function running. Mech has programs to reactivate someone's phone. He's almost as good at programming overrides as he is at building power armor frameworks."

I processed that for a second, then gave up and focused on the important part. "Okay, well, that's mighty peculiar, but you waited fer lunch time, so I reckon it ain't rude. What's so desperate ya gotta turn on my phone for it?"

Tonika's answer came out cold and flat like an omen of doom. "Gumshoe Ghost Girl has found someone who knew me, and knows where I lived."

Me, I lit up with a smile she couldn't see, unless Mech had really tinkered hard with that phone. "Wow, that's good news, ain't it?"

"He was my boyfriend," Tonika said, her voice still empty.

"...okay, that there's quite a shoe to drop, but it's a good one, ain't it?" I asked.

Tonika's calm split. "I'm scared," she admitted, her voice shaky. Through the phone connection I could hear her breathing hard now.

"Yeah, reckon anyone would be," I said, all quiet and gentle.

Her voice picked back up a little life. "Not you."

"Hey, I—" I started to argue. Then I remembered the moment my relationship with Chris and Sue became official. I'd been confused. I'd been shocked. I'd been overloaded. I'd been delighted that my romantic life had handed me everything on a silver platter. I'd been embarrassed. Seriously, and hoo boy, I'd been overloaded. That had been crazy.

But fear hadn't been any of the feelings in that mix. "—okay, reckon ya got me."

"I want you there. Please," Tonika whispered.

I pulled my head back and blinked at the phone. "Me? Ah ain't refusin', but why me?"

I remembered to put the phone back to my ear just in time to hear, "You make me feel safe. You make everyone feel safe."

That again. It hadn't gotten any less strange to hear. "Ah make folks feel safe?"

"Yes," Sue declared instantly. I'd almost forgotten she was

sitting next to me.

"Yes," Tonika answered, much more meek and subdued.

I furrowed my brow and squinted at the phone. "But it ain't like y'all're in danger. Mech'd be there to protect you anyhow, right?"

"I'm not scared he'll hurt me physically." There was that quiver in Tonika's voice again.

Still bewildered, I said, "Ah make you feel safe 'bout emotional stuff?"

"Yes," Tonika repeated.

Sue looked me straight in the eyes, and said emphatically, "You make your friends feel safe from everything." Then a big smirk broke that serious expression, and she added with malicious delight, "And your enemies feel like they'll never be safe again."

"When did I become a human security blanket?" I asked the world.

Whatever the world was going to say, Sue got a big, big smile on her face, and to prevent the teasing I knew was on the way I told Tonika quickly, "Ah'll do it! Ah'll do it! Ah get this is scary. Iff'n ah kin help, ah will."

Sounding relieved, or at least no longer timid, Tonika said, "Mech will talk to your parents and pick you up after school."

I wasn't sure that would go over well with my parents. The ringing of the end of lunch bell interrupted that thought, so I told Tonika hastily, "Oops, gotta shake mah tail, see y'all then."

As Sue stood up and opened the shadow door back into the cafeteria, I made certain to turn my phone off again.

Two hours later, Sue and I stepped out into the mild January afternoon LA sunshine. Clouds in the sky threatened to obscure that sun. It might even drizzle tonight.

Mech's superficially normal-looking car sat right up front on the curb, prompt and responsible. We headed down to it.

As we walked, I gave Sue a fond smile. She didn't return it. She looked... I couldn't say what that expression was. Her never-chapped lips pressed together, but if it was a frown, it was a vague, inward one. Maybe she'd been expecting to spend the afternoon with me?

"Sorry, Sue—" I started to say.

She grabbed me by the lapels poking out of the neckline of my sweater vest, yanked me close, and kissed me fiercely on the mouth. After a mere few seconds of that, she pushed me away sharply, and ordered, "Go save the day just by being you."

Red-cheeked and embarrassed for the hundredth time by Sue's need to prove our relationship to everyone we met, I climbed into the back seat of the car and strapped in.

The rear-view mirror told me Mech hadn't batted an eye. He just had on his charming, noble, clean-cut smile and was looking at the road as he pulled out into traffic, not me. Tonika's face I couldn't see. Too make sure of that, I looked out the window at cars with really great paint jobs languishing under a layer of dust. A boxy red car that looked like it belonged in a silent movie passed us, the kind that looked like it didn't have a roof so much as a flat awning over the top. The guy driving wore a huge, fur-lined purple coat and leather-and-brass pilot goggles and had a hugely long mustache which stuck out the sides off his face, then curled up at the tips. Supervillain? Or just the kind of person you met in this city? The bumper sticker "My Other Ride Is A Dog On A Motorcycle" didn't clear things up.

Tonika decided I had stewed enough, and asked, "I did hear something about you saving the world?"

I sat up sharply and shook my head. "That could not be a wildah exaggeration."

The car turned left in an intersection at a safe, responsible speed, as Mech said, "I know I should have asked you in detail long ago, but I thought you might feel too pressured. How did you stop those skeleton attacks?"

I struggled for a way to describe this that didn't sound bigger than it had been. It had been big for fifteen-year-old necromancer me, but that wasn't a high heroism bar. Flopping one hand weakly, I tried, "Ah sorta woke up an undead necromansuh. He was a weenie, but he knew wheah this super-necromancy-enhancin' doodad was, and a real hahdcoah necromancer monstah woke up in the process." I shuddered. The memory of that skeletal cat pulling my own power out of my hands like plucking a pacifier from a baby's mouth still chilled me. "But ah broke the doodad and shut them both back in the traps ah found them in. Don't get me wrong, sugah, ah'm proud of mahself, but it's hardly world-shaking."

Mech's image in the rear-view mirror raised its eyebrows. "A master necromancer with a major power enhancer and a place to hide where regular heroes can't get to him sounds like a serious problem. I'm glad we never had to face it, thanks to you. Do your parents know? It might settle their minds."

I snorted, propped my elbow on the edge of the window next to me, and stared out that window at boxy, dust-covered passing shops. "Last thing ah want them hearin' 'bout raight now is that ah'm even more a hero'n they know."

Mech kept on with his adult wisdom and kindness thing. "I think you should tell them, or at least let me tell them, but I won't force the issue. There are good reasons why we don't let what people do in costume follow them back into their day-to-day lives. Remember that, if you decide to go the 'Deathette' route. No one in our world will reveal anything that might get back to Avery Special's world."

Audibly haunted, Tonika said, "Right now, I need Avery Special's help."

Mech's smile and tone turned even warmer than usual. "I'm sure this will go well, Tonika. You'll spend tonight in your own bed, with a family that loves you. I'll miss having the help of someone who handles mission information so well, but you'll be much happier. Anyway, we're almost there."

Yes, a change of topic! I leaped on top of that. "Wheah ah we goin', anyway?"

Mech explained, "We're meeting the Bubblegumshoe Detective Agency and the person they found at Upper High. It's not far from Pepperidge Preparatory. I've considered seeing if we can get you transferred there, but that's its own complicated topic."

I cocked a bushy eyebrow. "Why there?"

"I used to go to school there," Tonika said.

Now I cocked both bushy eyebrows, and blinked besides. "Huh! Figgered you fer middle school."

With just a touch of wry self-scolding, Mech said, "So did I, which is why I checked Northeast West Hollywood Middle across the street, and I felt like a fool when Tonika's private detective checked Upper High as well."

"It turns out, I'm fourteen," Tonika said.

"Looks like a nice enough place," I commented, as we pulled up.

It did. High school and middle school stood opposite each other across a little bitty side street all to themselves. The high school was a big H-shaped, red brick building on a slightly higher hill than the J-shaped, multicolored middle school. I got a peek at a big asphalt recess ground on the other side of the middle school, with kids running around in it. Neither school had the expensive, immaculately cared for trees and bushes around it that Pep Prep boasted, and as we walked into Upper High, I encountered slightly more worn hallway tiles and more leftover holiday signs than at the expensive prison for girls I attended.

Seriously, Pepperidge Prep was a rough place.

There was something subtly, naggingly odd about Upper High. It wasn't the kid with the huge claws. Super powers were a thing. They weren't limited to heroes and villains. There were other girls at Pep Prep with super powers. I saw people on the street with obvious powers.

Maybe it was the way a couple of the teens looked surprised when they saw Mech, then looked away so deliberately that they had to know who he was. One of those teens, a heart-thumpingly pretty platinum blonde, followed up her glance at Mech by giving me and Tonika long, assessing stares.

I squirmed, my shoulders twitching. I couldn't help it. I didn't like being seen in this dumb school uniform, with the blouse and blue sweater vest and pleated, knee-length skirt.

I made sure to keep my mouth shut so that my accent didn't embarrass me even more.

On the plus side, nobody who didn't recognize Mech thought me or Tonika in her purple wig were worth a second glance.

We arrived at the school office, or rather set of offices. A larger room with a counter dividing the clerical desks from the waiting room chairs spawned side doors off either side, most of them open to provide glimpses of actual offices and more waiting rooms with their own doors. There was a lot of brown in the furnishings, whether they were wood, plastic, or cloth. No two shades of brown the same, so I guess it probably wasn't deliberate.

A slim old guy in a brown suit stepped out from behind the counter, giving Tonika the kind of official smile that strains unconvincingly to be as nice as Mech's. "You won't know me, but—" He switched his attention to Mech himself, shaking the incognito hero's hand. "Thank you for finding Tonika."

Mech held up his free hand, switching to the gentle, patient smile. Like all his smiles, I was sure it was sincere. "One step at a time. First, let's make sure this is the same Tonika."

One of the side doors had a "Counselors"sign. That led into a little brown waiting room with little brown sofas and two brown wooden side doors. Gumshoe Ghost Girl stood, feet not quite touching the ground, in the center of the room. If she'd been sitting down, her brown, transparent figure would have been invisible.

As we stepped through the door, Tonika grabbed my hand with both of hers. Her expression looked merely solemn, but she held my hand by her waist like a lifeline.

Gumshoe Ghost Girl, back arched, chin lifted, beaming with pride, announced, "Sean is in the next room. I found him by—"

Mech interrupted what sounded like the beginning of a long, long story. "Tonika, do you want someone with you, or…"

Tonika interrupted him, although he'd trailed off to make that easy. "Alone."

She squeezed my hand ferociously hard, held it for a moment, and then let go to open one of the side doors, slipping into the office beyond. The door closed automatically behind her.

The counselors' offices were admirably soundproofed. I heard absolutely nothing from this side of the door.

At least, nothing going on in that room. Ghost Cat Solvin' Mysteries prowled his pudgy brown body through the wall from the direction of the main office, slunk up to Gumshoe Ghost Girl, tapped his paw repeatedly against her ankle, and said, "Meow."

That was all the communication Gumshoe Ghost Girl needed. Without another word, she and Ghost Cat Solvin' Mysteries walked out through the doorway into the main office.

I still couldn't hear anything through the door. I knew I wasn't supposed to, but...

I looked up at Mech, feeling helpless.

Mech gave me a reassuring smile, and a brief, supportive squeeze of my shoulder. "Don't worry. Heroes all over the city are keeping watch out for that robot. It seems like it's going to specific places, then doesn't know what to do when it gets there and retreats to hide. We think it's on a revenge quest, and can't grasp that the city has changed in twenty years."

Did that mean it had gotten near me randomly at the gym? I'd been deliberately not using my powers, but I'd stumbled into a lot of magic anyway. That might have drawn it.

Speaking of which, or at least thinking of which, I finally figured out what bothered me about this school. An unpleasant, oily sensation lurked in the air, giving me the impression I smelled something rancid, except when I sniffed there was no scent but the regular dusty, plasticky smell of institutional air conditioning and old sofas.

Magic. Black magic. Magic I'd felt before. This was Barbara's awesome power, her connection to alien sources of magic that made necromancy look like a flower bed. So, Barbara went to school here.

Another sensation of magic tingled past me like glitter on the breeze. Then that bubbly magic I'd felt at the testing building. That lasted several seconds. Then Barbara's unclean-feeling magic oozed back. A particularly annoying magical aura like being gently poked with a finger took over for several seconds, before Barbara's magic returned.

How many magic users could there be in one school? Certainly Barbara's sheer power tended to crowd them out.

And all this at least twenty minutes after school had left out. These were just the magical auras of students hanging out in or near the building.

The councilor's door we'd been waiting on opened, enough for me to see an office more blue than brown behind it. The boy who emerged did have brown hair, cut short. He wasn't particularly tall, but solid. Not fat or even thick, but under his button-up shirt, the shape of his shoulders and arms hinted at muscle. There was something weird about him, too.

But his wide-eyed, stricken expression of unhappiness caught most of my attention.

The boy—Sean?—stepped up to Mech and asked the hero, "You have her home address?" He sounded as subdued as Tonika usually did.

Politely matching the boy's quiet, Mech answered just above a whisper, "The private investigator gave it to me. We wanted to make sure she's the right Tonika, first."

Sean nodded. "She is." He stared past Mech at nothing, or rather at his own thoughts. He still looked as stunned and unhappy as if someone had hit him in the face with a baseball bat.

The door opened again. Tonika stepped into it. She also looked distant, but a little sad rather than Sean's bleak mask. She kept her hands clasped behind her back, lurking in the doorway rather than daring to step into the waiting room.

"Sean, I'm sorry," she murmured, big eyes shining with guilt and pity.

The boy turned to her and bowed, deep and formal and smooth. That was the odd thing about him. Sean moved with grace and balance. The bow looked both practiced and comfortable. His voice didn't sound comfortable at all, but it did sound firm and sincere. "Don't be. I have no right to push something on you that you don't want anymore. Please don't be guilty. Take care of yourself."

Already leaning slightly away, Tonika lowered her face and mumbled, "Yes."

Sean walked out past me and Mech, with a smooth, athletic gait and a clear desire to get out of this awkward and unhappy confrontation as fast as possible.

I stepped up to Tonika, trying to search her face. She grabbed my hands in hers, clenching them tight.

Mech, thoughtful and delicate, said, "I'll wait outside," and left us alone.

I put my arms around Tonika and pulled her in for a hug. I didn't know about making people feel safe, but my arms were muscular enough to give good protective hugs.

Tonika pulled her arms up and grabbed fistfuls of my sweater vest, clinging to me tightly.

I didn't say anything. I just held her and waited.

Eventually, in a raspy whisper, she said, "He's still in love. I'm not. I don't think I'm capable of it anymore."

"Ouch," was all I could think to say. I tightened my hug a little. That was the important thing. To hold her and be big and solid.

After a few more trembling seconds, Tonika whispered, "I think the electronics in my head replaced the parts of my brain that care about romance or feel physical desire. Those feelings would have interfered with my being useful to Organism One."

"You don't need it," I murmured back, all firm and sincere. "Ah feel sorry for Sean losin' his girl, but ah bet he thought he had months ago anyhow. Datin' is nice an' all, but ah don't think you're gonna miss it once the shock is over and done."

"I'll have to take your word for it. I can't even remember what being in love feels like," she whispered.

Oof.

The truth was, I didn't know either.

That might be my guiltiest secret: I wasn't in love with Sue or Chris. I liked them. Everything Chris did made me happy, whether he was giving me flowers or showing off some new outfit or just smiling while I did my thing. Sue and I were partners. Put us together, and we worked, like two cogs in a watch. The dating part of the relationship was great. Wonderful. I wouldn't give it up for the world, although it still baffled and flattered me that two good-looking people found me so attractive.

None of that was love. I knew what being in love looked like, because I saw it in the breathless awe and longing in Chris's and Sue's faces when they looked at me. I didn't feel anything close to that.

The guilt of not loving them back clawed at my heart, but I eased it with the same thought that always helped: I may not be giving them what they deserved, but they were unmistakably happy with what they were getting.

From within my embrace, Tonika mumbled into my shirt, "Thank you. I couldn't do this without you." She sounded... better, at least. Not good, but better.

"I ain't done anything," I replied, because it was true.

"You do a lot without even knowing it," Tonika answered, hardly sniffly at all, now.

"Yeah, that's my problem," I grumped.

Tonika giggled, sniffed one more time, and stepped out of my grip. Brushing down her long, plain, indigo dress, she said, "Okay, next step. Sean knew where I live. I'm an only child, and my parents are Charles and Lucretia Edison. Let's go meet them."

With Tonika holding onto my elbow but otherwise visibly normal, the two of us walked out of the school offices together. As we entered the hall, I heard Gumshoe Ghost Girl's voice behind us. "That proves it! You're an imposter!"

The principal shouted back, "And I would have gotten away with it, if it weren't for you and your meddlesome dead cat!"

"That's Ghost Cat Solvin' Mysteries to you! And I'm the Gumshoe Ghost Girl!" declared Gumshoe Ghost Girl.

Her speech went on, but we'd gone too far for me to make out any words.

Chapter Eighteen

Mech was sweet. He didn't say anything, just smiled encouragingly as Tonika clung to me on the way to the car.

Only when we were already in the car and entering traffic did he say, "It will take a while to get you re-enrolled here, Tonika. Maybe not until Fall. You'll have time to get comfortable again. If you decide you want to return faster, I'll lean on the district. They'll hurry things as a favor for the superhero Community."

Tonika, her voice low and blank, answered, "Thank you."

Always encouraging, Mech continued, "You don't live too far away. It's almost a straight shot south."

I leaned forward, pulling against my seatbelt, and extended my arm. Tonika grabbed my hand and held it for at least a dozen blocks.

I didn't know this area. It had to be somewhere near the university, right? We passed a lot of apartment buildings. It all reminded me of large portions of Lexington, except much, much flatter.

Mech found us a place to park, and we walked up to one of those apartment buildings. It was made of dark red brick.

It was five stories tall, with little windows, half of them lit and all of them with curtains or blinds closed. It was an apartment building, like apartment buildings in Kentucky, like apartment buildings everywhere, as far as I knew. Except for the bus stop right at the corner, which you'd be lucky to find in Lexington but seemed to be everywhere in LA.

Mech got out his civilian phone and told it, "We're here."

We climbed the stoop. Tonika checked the handle of the front door. Locked.

Seconds passed. Should we do something?

The door opened. The man on the other side looked completely ordinary. No, not quite. He had some of that "high forehead, big eyes" look that made Tonika look so smart. Even in a white undershirt and jeans, his dark eyes flickered over Tonika, Mech, and me with searching intelligence.

"That's not my daughter," he snapped irritably.

My mouth hung open. That was the absolutely last thing I had expected him to say.

Especially since Tonika clasped her hands together and answered in a weak, trembling voice, "Dad?"

He bent forward a few inches, peering at her suspiciously, then demanded, "What did you do to your hair?"

"It's… this is a wig…," she stammered, reaching up to the purple fiberoptic hairline, and pulling it back until a couple of popping noises revealed the little plugs in the wig and the metal-lined holes in Tonika's skull that they fit in.

The man shook his head, scowling, and let out an exasperated sigh. "Just get inside."

Tonika lowered her head and took a step up towards the door.

One was all she got. Mech put his arm out in front of her, and gave Tonika's father a bright smile that for the first time did not look at all real. His voice was also too stiffly cheerful and perky as he said, "I'm sorry, sir, you were clearly correct the first time. This is not your daughter."

Tonika's dad's scowl deepened as he looked at Mech. Then he looked at me, and it turned into a wary stare.

Anger hit me like a bucket of ice water. Cold fury filled

me, every inch, mixing with the cold of my necromancy until I could barely feel my clenched, shaking fists. My eyes hurt and my spine stiffened like a statue.

Mech looked confused and held Tonika to him protectively. Tonika's dad looked anxious, like he was staring at a rattlesnake. My powers made bystanders hallucinate unpleasant things. I'd been told that.

He was right to be afraid. Even with all the trouble I was having with my parents, that was because my parents loved me so much. I'd known there were bad parents out there, but this…

I wanted to hurt him.

I wanted to hurt him so badly that I could barely hold still.

I was also leaking power like a broken fire hydrant. So much so that without calling them, three dim blue outlines formed around me. My ancestors.

Or maybe their own rage called them up. Alicia Blackheart, one arm wrapped around her middle and the other raised almost to her chin but with a clenched fist, hissed with as much disgust and fury as I felt. "Ah *died* giving birth to mah daughtah, and ah don't regret the trade."

Horse Skull Kid stood with his hands in his pockets, his posture casual, but his normally friendly voice held an edge. "My folks were 'bout like this, so as someone who's been there, if you want ta make him pay, I'll cheer you every step."

Namluh spat on the ground, his jolliness replaced by a snarl. "I know curses, Avery. Tell me how badly to hurt him, and I'll show you the way."

I clamped my jaw tight. I didn't dare speak.

"Just say 'yes,' and we will show him suffering like only necromancy can cause," Namluh growled.

Everyone stared at me, mesmerized.

Shaking with rage, every muscle locked, I stood there fighting with myself.

Finally, I whispered, "No."

Only then could I think in words again. If necromancy gave me the power to do a lot of debatably justified things, hurting this man was not justified. He might deserve it, but that didn't make it right for me to punish him.

But he deserved it. And I wanted to.

My ancestors faded into invisibility. As the rush of power descended back to what I would usually think of as "a lot," I was able to feel something else, an unpleasant itchiness over my back.

Chaos magic? Here? Now?

"Something's going to happen. Hold tight to Tonika," I growled at Mech. I had to work to hold my anger back enough to be that polite.

Despite that unmistakable burst of chaos magic, nothing seemed to be happening. The itchiness held on long enough for me to be sure it was chaos magic, then faded.

The girl with the light powers, Angel Cruz, walked around the corner of an alley, on the far side of me from Mech and Tonika.

Seeing me, she jerked to a halt, and with a much milder accent than I'd expected shouted, "What are you doing here? Are you following me? Are you threatening these people?"

Her power flared, a hot breeze flowing off of her. I expected our skirts to rustle, but the breeze was an illusion, only felt by mages. The only visible sign of her gathering power was her half-raised hand, palm out and fingers splayed. Ready, but not yet pointed at me in threat.

Don't turn your anger on her, Avery. You would come to the exact same conclusion if you saw yourself like this. Especially since she was a hair's breadth from being right.

I tried to stop glaring, tried to push my power down as I looked over at her. "Ah ain't here about you."

That hadn't sounded real peaceful, but I was trying.

The hot breeze turned into a baking wind as Angel's magic rose higher. Her face tightened, eyes widened, mouth curled up into a sneer. I could see the anger boiling up inside her.

I forced my fists to unclench. I still wanted to hurt Tonika's father. I wanted to hurt that vile monster so badly. I wanted to hurt *someone*. My anger hadn't gone away.

Instead, I made myself say, "Now, let's both calm down a minute. Ah know what black magic is lahk. Don't let it take over."

The girl bristled, back jerking tight, shoulders bunched up, eyes bugging out. Her voice rose to a squeak. "Black magic!? How dare you!"

Plang!

A manhole cover flew up out of the middle of the street, and a shiny white robot crawled out of the hole.

Plang! Plink. Reenreenreenreenreen...

The manhole cover hit the asphalt, bounced once, and spun to a stop.

The tall, white, feminine robot from the haunted house staggered towards us. Its hair hung lank past its waist, partly covering its torso because it leaned forward with every step. Brightly glowing white eyes fixed on Angel.

Within that metal shell, visible only to me, lurched a faint blue human silhouette. The ghost wasn't truly attached to the body like a human's. It only animated and directed the robot.

A synthesized voice squealed, "I love her. She's going to help me. We're going to get married when we grow up. I can't let you hurt her."

My most important concern wiped away the others. Turning my head, I shouted at Mech, "Get Tonika to safety!"

He was unarmed, in his civilian clothing. His powers weren't inherent. Mech relied on power armor, which meant right now he was as helpless as any normal person. With his hero's heart, he could still evacuate a civilian.

Angel took that time to point her outstretched hand at the robot and release a blast of light. It poured over the robot's surface like flame, unable to damage the metal.

What the magic did do was burn away the surface of the wobbly ghost inside every time it touched the shell.

"RUN AWAY!" I shouted at the ghost.

I was so full of power, I overdid it. The robot stopped lurching, spun around and ran with terrifying speed, much faster than I'd imagined it could be. It passed the manhole, shoved a car aside, and disappeared into an alley.

Angel's light beam seared across the sidewalk, the car, and the walls of the buildings flanking the alley, leaving pale bleached stains rather than char.

Her target gone, Angel whirled back on me, finger snapping out in accusation. "You sicced that thing on me!"

"I didn't pick this fight!" I yelled back. As soon as the words were out of my mouth, I knew they would only make things worse.

Thankfully, and I was so very thankful, the dark-haired girl in the white dress had more self-control than me. The oven heat of her power died down to unpleasant warmth as she threw her hands up in the air and yelled, "I don't need this tonight! Don't follow me, or I'll—"

She cut herself off, growled, waved her hands, and finally wheeled around to stomp back down the corner she'd come out of. Heat gusted, up and down, as her control over her powers flickered.

Then it died down and down and down, because she was getting out of range.

I looked around.

The front door of the apartment building stood closed. Tonika's horrible dad was nowhere in sight. I wasn't sure if I blamed him for running away or not. I still hated him and wanted to hurt him. I still wasn't going to.

Mech and Tonika stood by the car, Mech's arms around her. They hadn't left yet. Maybe Mech had hoped to protect me, somehow.

I... had done the right thing. Hadn't I? I thought so. Right enough. Maybe not perfect, but morally, I'd made the right choices this afternoon.

Afternoon. The sun was still high. The afternoon had barely started.

I didn't know what my parents would think, but it was more important that morally, I'd been here for Tonika and saved a clearly confused ghost and didn't hurt two people even though I'd wanted to badly, even though they maybe deserved it.

Mech, arms still around Tonika, left me to take care of myself, and turned his attention down toward the purple-wigged girl hurting much worse than me. His frown emphatic and determined, he told her, "Listen. Tonika, listen. I'm not sending you back to where you're not loved."

"Ding dang straight," I snarled, then went back to struggling to ease down the cold necromancy churning inside me.

Tonika, head tilted back, stared up at Mech, who met her gaze. Kind but firm, he continued, "I'll take care of you. I'll adopt you if you want. It will be great having you help me with my hero work some more. Maybe we'll find you a better family, I don't know. But you're not going anywhere that you're not happy."

Tonika, wide-eyed, just nodded.

Mech searched her face a few more seconds, then lifted his gaze to me. "I'll take you home, Avery, and then Tonika and I will go home together."

I... wasn't sure I was safe yet. I denied, "Ah need t' walk round on mah own for a while, yet. Thuh othah direction from—" I jerked my head the way Angel had left. "Ah'll get mah folks'r Sue to take me home."

The truth was, I was going to call Alice the moment I was out of sight, and... I didn't know. Spend a few hours cooling down up on the hills, or in whatever non-place Alice went when her door was shut, or to spend time with Sue and Chris loving me, or absorbing Peggy's easygoing calm. Or just back to my own bedroom, my space, where I couldn't hurt anyone and wouldn't want to.

Tonika stepped out of Mech's grip, walked with long, resolute steps. When she reached me, she flung unafraid arms around my shoulders and hugged me tight, or at least tight for her scrawny little body. "Thank you. I made it through this because of you," she said.

Tonika's face pressed against the side of my neck, buried in my woolly red hair, and she whispered, "We both need each other's help right now. I have plans. Call me when you're ready."

Letting go slowly, reluctantly, Tonika returned to Mech with a much slower, more subdued pace.

Mech called over to me, "The other heroes and I will step things up, Avery. We'll protect you. That robot will be destroyed before it can get near you again, I promise."

He and Tonika got into his car and drove away.

Only when they were moving did I dare to move, walking

up the street after them. My body, my heart, my brain, my thoughts, all still felt cold with anger and necromancy, and I wasn't sure I could tell the difference between them.

At least mine was the only magic I felt right now.

I watched Mech's car shrink and disappear in the distance. I'd known Tonika was smart, but what could it be like to have a brain so big that after a shock this bad, you immediately knew what to do next?

I was glad Tonika had one, because I couldn't just leave my magical problems alone anymore.

Especially if Mech was right and that poor, confused ghost needed saving, too.

Chapter Nineteen

BEEP. BEEP. BEEP.

My alarm clock.

But Saturday. Today was Saturday.

BEEP. BEEP. BEEP.

But *Saturday.*

Saturday was my day to sleep in! I reached over and fumbled for my alarm clock's Off button.

No good. My clumsy banging sent the clock to the floor, where not only did it keep beeping, the bang and thump of heavy plastic on wood finished waking me up.

Opening my eyes, I pushed myself up on one elbow and peered across the dark, beige-painted room at my alarm clock. It lay on the floor. Beside my dresser. Across the room. Way, way out of reach.

I reached out my left arm and made grabby, flailing motions. The clock, at least ten feet away, scooted a few inches. I felt the pressure on my... I wasn't sure where. My hand?

The remaining fog of sleep vanished as glorious hope swelled up in my heart, lifting me into consciousness.

Okay, focus. I felt the faint thrill of chilly magic that always streamed through my body. I focused on my regular old flesh-and-blood left hand, paying close attention, I clasped it over my right hand. Then I pulled my *other* left hand up to my face.

A little blue phosphorescent speck zoomed out of the shadows to hover in front of me. Maybe twice the size of a pinhead.

Strangling my voice to a whisper, I squeaked, "Eeeeee!" My ghost hand wasn't entirely destroyed! A speck must have been following me around, and had grown into this pea-sized thing. Not quite pea-sized. Would it heal more? Would I get the full ghost hand back? This tiny blob was weak and couldn't grip, but it could press a button and definitely might be useful.

Clumsy with excitement, I tried to climb out of bed and fell out of bed instead.

Eggs. I smelled eggs. Saturday was off to a great start. I grabbed my clothes and went to see what my father was cooking.

That required a diversion through getting cleaned up and properly dressed, but eventually I sat down in front of a pile of eggs, pancakes, fake bacon (my dad always said turkey tasted better than pork), little hot pastry things covered in honey that I think he invented, and fried bread.

The difference between my loving parents and Tonika's uncaring father hit me hard enough to hurt. Urf.

Looming like a smiling mountain over the table, my father set various syrups and spreadables in front of me. He threw in an encouraging smile for free. "Stuff yourself. I know we must feel like tyrants, cutting you down to one lesson a week, but your mom and I can tyrannize you with a full belly so you're ready for a week's worth of training."

I impaled eggs, turkey bacon, and fried bread on a fork, barely fitted the mass into my mouth, and after several seconds of mastication was free to say, "It was a good idea. Don't know if othah supah powers are like this but I kin start thinkin' about zombie airplanes or somethin', and then suddenly it's bedtime and I've spent all those houahs writin' out a huge, elaborate spell what prob'ly don't even work."

Dad flipped something that smelled savory in his frying pan, because I guess he thought I could eat my own body weight in food in one sitting. He didn't even have to watch the flipping anymore, so he raised an eyebrow at me instead. "How do you make a zombie airplane?"

"Short ansuh is, lots and lotsa dead birds. Long ansuh starts with a spell to create lots and lotsa dead birds, which I reckon does work but I ain't intendin' to find out. Ew." I shuddered, feeling guilty just thinking about it. Also, for having actually figured out such a spell.

Dad shuddered, too. "That's a relief. You know, we heard about what happened when you helped your friend try to go home."

And now I was very happy I'd just shoved a huge mass of breakfast in my mouth again and couldn't talk.

Dad dropped whatever he'd just fried into a dish and sprinkled powdered sugar on it. It apparently wasn't done, because he left it there to return to the table. Pulling out a chair, he sat down, looming slightly less as his smile turned pained and sympathetic. "It's easy—okay, easier—to hold onto your temper when you're not the strongest person in the room."

He leaned towards me, crossing his arms over the table. It reminded me of just how big and muscular he was. Not just tall. Not just broad. My dad had muscles. Big, bulky muscles. He could be cast in a TV show as a blacksmith. I didn't know how he stayed that big. I'd never seen him work out, but who knew what your parents did all day while you were at school?

I chewed. He kept up the parental sympathy. "I don't have super powers, but by the time I was fourteen, I was bigger and stronger than any of my classmates, and most of the senior athletes. Stronger than my parents. And when you're a teenager, you get angry, and sometimes it comes out of nowhere."

Swallowing, I muttered, "Kinda thought that was the black magic."

Dad grinned, but still that "parent trying to be sympathetic" kind of grin. The kind with a little wry pain in it. "It's part of the whole hormones thing. It happens to adults too, but by the time we qualify as adults we've had a decade of practicing holding onto it. Most people get that decade while they're not able to win a fight with everyone around us at the same time."

The switch to "us" stood out for me. I grimaced. "It was bad 'nuff when ah couldn't control m' powers. I was scared I'd kill someone. Now I know ah kin just hurt 'em."

An image of hitting Tonika's father with Alicia's claws popped into my head. Freezing rage exploded out of my heart, and I took long, slow breaths to let it bleed away. I hated that man so much. With luck, I would never meet him again and it wouldn't matter. But still, I wanted to punish him.

Dad saw it all, and his smile shrank to just enough to make it clear he might be troubled, but wasn't at all mad at me. "This is one of the big reasons we want you staying far away from superhero stuff. You start out thinking you're stopping a shoplifter from getting away, and things start to happen, and then you're having to make decisions about how badly you have to hurt someone who is trying to make you angry because... well, it could be a misunderstanding, or they could be a jerk, or they could be a pure, evil monster. From what I can tell, even adults get it wrong a lot. You're not ready, and we're doing what we have to so that you don't make mistakes you can never take back."

I detected an edge of steel in his words. My folks were determined. Right now, I was more intimidated by myself. "Yeah, ah... see whatcha mean."

Because I was still furious. It had been so hard not to lash out at that man. Then Angel Cruz pushed me, and we only got out of that without a fight because she'd been more patient than me. Nobody got hurt or dead out of chance, not any virtue of mine.

Looking up at the ceiling, I wailed, "Ah'm not even strong! Ah'm 'bout as weak a necromancer as it gets. Ah've met mah ancestors. Every one of 'em could squash me lahk a bug." I wasn't arguing against him, just... the injustice and despair of it all.

Morning sunlight shone through Dad's slightly red-tinged blond hair as he leaned his face forward in acknowledgment. "You're weak at something that's very good at hurting people. Like fire powers."

And Annie, who had fire powers, was terrified of those powers and hardly ever used them.

My thoughts dragged me forward, because Dad was more right than he knew. My words dragged along with my train of thought. "Except people are real good at stoppin' fire. Ain't been a necromancer in near a century. Nobody 'members how ta block mah power. The don't even know what it looks lahk, can't tell ah'm usin' it unless a corpse gets up an' walks."

A memory never far from my consciousness popped up. I owed all my new control to grimoires I picked up from the LA public library. Most of all, to Pudgy Bunny Talks To A Friend, which taught me the basics of focusing. I'd learned since that it wasn't written for natural necromancers. I said, "They have spells that othah types of mages who work hard 'nuff can use to kinda-sorta-like do what I do 'fore I even start addin' spells to the hand wavin'."

Dad leaned forward and down and tapped me twice on the forehead with his index finger. With a confidential rumble, he said, "But you didn't need an explanation. You already know that when you get mad, you can act on it. You did good helping your friend Tonika, but I'm sorry to say it's going to be years before handling your anger gets easy, if it ever does. Until then, it doesn't matter if you're a hero or a villain. You have to stay out of those situations entirely."

My parents had played the "bad cop" threat version of this conversation. Now Dad had given me the "good cop" appeal to my morals. It hurt as bad as the threats, because he was right. I was an unexploded bomb that would hurt innocent people if I kept pushing, and once that started, I'd be stuck and unable to stop. Ugh, what an awful thought. I didn't dare get into more super powered chaos.

If Tonika was right, and I was starting to think Tonika was always right, I didn't have any choice.

No, I couldn't and shouldn't blame Tonika. The ghost in that robot needed me, and it needed me now. No one else could save it and save the people it might hurt without doing a terrible injustice. They also were doing a lousy job of stopping it from jumping out at me when I wasn't ready.

Dad saw my haunted expression and gave the red puffball crowning my head an affectionate pat. "Smile, honey child, and finish your pancakes. You have good friends. They'll help keep you out of trouble. I don't think I've ever seen anyone as in love as Sue's in love with you."

Sticking a stack of pancake quarters into my maw, I brooded over that little problem. I hadn't told Sue about the robot or my Angel Cruz problem. Specifically, I hadn't told her that I felt like I had to do something about them.

One pancake pile later, my troubles padded with the joy of good eating and an overfull stomach, I declared, "Speakin' of which what all, 'spec it's time for me ta go rendezvous with her and get to mah lesson."

I jumped off my chair, ran back to my room, grabbed my magic hat and staff, didn't put on my hat, and ran out with one in each hand. I tried to close the door with my ghost hand, but the little blob wasn't strong enough. I had to close the door the old fashioned, actual hand way.

Then I ran down the street like I was heading somewhere.

Actually, I was just getting far enough to spot the side door of a random neighbor's house and use that door to call Alice and duck inside.

Chapter Twenty

I stepped out of Alice, closing the door behind me. I had my composure back. I was ready for my magic lesson.

Just as soon as I found my Master. I'd exited into a street of tightly packed shops, all closed down. Some were a little bigger than others. In the distance in one direction, I saw a fence. In the other, I just saw buildings, not the end of the road.

I was looking for a mall, right? Well, one white building was bigger than the others, visible over their rooftops. The only human being I could see had just crossed the street and disappeared along a road in that direction.

Where was everyone?

I headed after the Mystery Street Crosser. It wasn't far. I hadn't understood my phone map well enough when I'd told Alice where to go, that's all. And it didn't help that I get no reception inside Alice.

My phone beeped. It had reception back, and with it, a text message. Which I checked.

Sue: When is your lesson?

I sent back: About noon, I think.

Sue: I'll be there.

I texted back a heart, but felt guilty about it. My conversation with Tonika about love was still too fresh in my memory.

The mall had to be the correct target because it wasn't abandoned. Trucks were pulled up on the street around it, with people in uniform-ish clothes moving boxes. I was stuck with "uniform-ish" because no two wore the same uniform.

Something with feathers way too big to be a chicken shouted, "B'gawk! Bok bok bok bok! B'gawk! B'gawk!" as it raced out of a truck and around the corner out of sight, chased by a man in padded leather armor carrying a hooked pole.

This was just prep work. Whatever was going on, was going on inside. I felt the faint wisps of oiliness that meant Barbara's magic. Which surprised me, because I didn't think Barbara was into villainy. She went to high school and was Mech's magic expert, for goodness' sake!

A dark-haired, hawk-faced woman with a red robotic eye bigger than Dr. Biotic's managed to pull one of the big doors of the mall open, push it until it hit the "stay open" point, and head inside, all while carrying a plastic crate in both arms. As I peeked inside, she unpacked funny mad science things that looked like guns and telescopes but with lots of crystals, laying them in neat rows on the table. Stowing the crate under the table, she headed back out again, presumably for another crate.

As she passed, I nodded my head politely and asked, "'Scuse me, ma'am. Kin y'all tell me where I kin find Schleimy?" I hoped everyone here knew who Schleimy was. They'd have to, right?

The question stopped the robot-eyed woman dead, frozen in mid-step. Not locked up, just interrupted. She turned her head and looked me up and down slowly, with a thoughtful frown that eased steadily into curiosity. Her red, artificial eye glittered with little electronic moving lights, but had no pupil and I had to assume it was looking in the same direction as her real eye. It took me in from bushy hair to rubber-soled work boots, then back up. She glanced at my magic hat, then my staff.

As if someone flipped a switch from "robot" to "woman," she relaxed, crossed her arms loosely under her chest, and relaxed into a stance that leaned her hip to one side. A small smile crept over her mouth. She was naturally on the lean side, so the addition of curves to what had been a stick-stiff figure was downright jarring.

"Mage," she told me. "Black magic," she added, her smile widening a little, and her dark eyebrows lifting up a fraction. She seemed even more interested, now.

I nodded again, politely, becoming stiff and politely at attention as she relaxed. "Yes, ma'am. Necromancy."

After the tiniest of delays, she smiled even more, and waved a finger. "Oh, that makes you... what was the latest name? Deathette?"

I sort-of-nodded, sort-of-shook my head, by tilting it to the side for a second. "Hope not, ma'am. Ah'd rather not have one'a those names at all, iff'n you get mah meanin'."

She liked that answer. Her smile widened, although with her angular—not ugly, just angular—face, she had a grin like a hawk. She looked automatically predatory. She sounded whimsical and friendly. "I'll hold off on real introductions and on making you stop calling me ma'am until you change your mind. The little laundry bundle's table isn't set up inside yet, but that's her van there."

The van she nodded at looked like any regular moving van. Not a big one, either. The little ones you load yourself. A man lounged in the driver's seat smoking a cigarette and playing with his phone. I wasn't surprised. I couldn't imagine Schleimy driving.

Cyborg-eye woman and I moved off in opposite directions without needing farewells. I approached Schleimy's van and the driver in it. He looked... very ordinary, a little scruffy, in a brown uniform like he worked for a moving company, but with a little brown peaked hat like an old-timey taxi driver.

As I reached the car, he leaned out the window, tapping ash off his cigarette onto the street, and said, "The apprentice. Right. In back. She hates me touching her stuff anyway." He sounded vaguely sarcastic, but he did toss me a key that I caught in my hat.

Everything about this place made me feel off balance. I already had the impression everyone but me was reading from a script everyone but me could see, and I'd only spoken to two people.

Oh, well, being helpful was a good thing, and I never minded moving heavy boxes. I went around to the back of the van, unlocked the door, pushed it up—it was one of those rolling doors—and unfolded the ramp.

In the very back, or rather at the end of the storage bay nearest the cab and farthest from the door, a muffled shape moved in deep shadow. In a slightly artificial woman's voice, it said, "Late."

That would be my Master herself. No surprise to find her hiding in the total darkness of a closed storage compartment rather than up front dealing with sunlight. Like anytime she had to deal with light, she was covered in layers and layers of mismatched clothing, including a robe and a cloak, both with hoods.

I grinned hugely and corrected her. "Nope. Very early. Don't mind helping you move these."

The van was nowhere near full. A regular pickup truck could have easily handled it all. I grabbed the biggest box and hefted it up in both arms. It wasn't super heavy, but sheer size made it hard to hold.

My Master picked up a much smaller bundled wrapped in paper and tied with string. She did so with obvious effort, as if it weighed more than this big box. Maybe I'd grabbed the wrong item? Naah, her arms weren't big enough for this thing.

Schleimy hobbled out of the truck and down the ramp. The clumsiness was purely all the clothing obstructing her. Underground and free of it, my Master moved with at least as much grace as a regular person. I fell in three steps behind her, letting her lead me into and through the mall's vast main corridor to a folding table on the opposite end from the robot-eye lady's stand. Robot-eye lady had several other mad scientists setting up tables around her as well. Schleimy only had one table anywhere near hers. It contained a squat guy setting out rows of pocket and wrist watches. A fuzzy sensation brushed over my skin as I passed, so some of the watches must be very magical.

"You the apprentice?" asked the guy, squinting at me suspiciously.

"Yep!" I answered, bouncing with pride.

Me and Master set down our boxes by her table, and I gave her a grin and a friendly chirp. "You sure got a lot of friends."

Schleimy shook her head curtly. "No. Well known. Not liked."

"But yer a pip!" I exclaimed.

My heavily overdressed, mostly dark grey and blue fabric pile of a teacher grumbled, "Impudent apprentice." I did not feel chastised.

We brought in more boxes. The one Schleimy carried this time turned out to some decorations, like a dark blue tablecloth, some silver cushions for her chair, and wood or silvery display boxes. I helped set out the merchandise, but switched to just unpacking when Schleimy rearranged everything I put down into a more random-looking clutter.

The merchandise was neat. The heavy package Schleimy had brought in first and personally contained books. The big box held fancy looking rods, with crystal balls on the end and so on. Only the one that looked like it was made of amber felt magical.

On my way back to the table with the final box, a feeling like scratchy sand blew across me. It reminded me of Hodir's chaos magic. Black magic, for sure.

The power flowed off of the black cat crossing my path.

He felt me, too. We stopped, staring at each other. He was tall, broad-shouldered but not enough to be bulky. A face shaped like a cat's, a cat tail, claws on furry hands, all pitch black, and slit yellow cat eyes. He wore a neatly pressed suit as black as he was, with a navy-blue waistcoat between shirt and jacket. Not as fancy as Chris and Annie, but thanks to them I noticed that he was not only deliberately dressed up, but knew what looked good on him. Silver rings gleaming on his black-furred fingers caught the eye.

"Deathette," the cat said finally, in a perfectly human man's voice.

"Not yet," I answered cheerfully.

That was all he needed to hear. The black magic cat super-villain walked away.

I resumed my own trek, and thirty seconds later set the final box next to Schleimy's table. She sat on her higher-than-normal human chair, and waved a multiply gloved and mittened hand in my direction. "Lesson in a few hours."

"Ah'll wait," I answered, sticking my hands in the pockets of my loose jeans. The best thing about switching to Saturdays was not wearing my school uniform.

After looking around at the mall, starting to fill up with little knots of mostly physically fit people in mostly ridiculous costumes, I added, "Seems as if you're either in or not in this club."

"Yes," said my hunched and miniature mentor. It really was hard to imagine the doll-like woman underneath that disguise, and that was a shame.

"Anyway, ah enjoy yer company and I wanna watcha work," I added, flashing her a big grin.

"Bah," Schleimy muttered.

Her first customer was not long in arriving. It was that guy I'd seen chasing the oversize chicken. With a closer look at his hook pole, I could see the fastener on the hook, so it could be used to catch something. Other than that, he wore a lot of padded leather that matched his weathered, leathery face and short, badly mussed black hair.

The chicken shepherd propped his free hand on the table, leaning over it and giving Schleimy a pleading expression. "Please tell me you have more of those control collars."

My mentor's hooded head shook maybe an inch to either side. "No. How intelligent?"

The shepherd's stare turned fierce, and his tone bitter. "If they weren't clever girls, I wouldn't need the collars. Hammy has hypnotic watches, but they're too slow."

Schleimy sat for a moment. Her mitten covered fingers drummed the table. Finally, her artificially feminine voice said, "Crown of Command. High end. Too expensive for purpose. Mind control, always premium."

The shepherd scowled. "Tell me about it."

Schleimy dug into a box or rings and pulled out a shield-shaped badge. Standing a few steps to the side of the table, I couldn't make out the design carved into it. She held it up for the man's inspection, and suggested, "Stun effect pendant. Hold out like stop. Give you time to use supposed training skills."

He ignored the crack. Took the pendant in his hands, gestured with it towards me, but addressed Schleimy. "Mind if I try it out."

"Won't work on mages. Push out weak spells," she replied, sounding as practical as if that hadn't been a freaky request.

The giant chicken shepherd scowled with the expression of someone about to spend a lot of money. Me, I checked my phone, surprised I hadn't heard anything from Sue yet. No, nothing, and I did have reception even in this big building. Weird.

Haggling must have been very brief. When I looked up, the shepherd guy was hurrying away, presumably much poorer. I shuffled closer, and said to Schleimy, "Got the impression you don't like that fella." It hadn't been the sarcasm. If anything, it had been how little sarcasm there'd been, how detached Schleimy had seemed.

"Sells nonhumans," she said, and even her fake voice was thick with disgust.

I didn't ask what kind of nonhumans. The question would anger her, and I was trying to learn that level of compassion anyway.

The next customer was a villainess wearing two square feet of material, total, most of it plastic. I couldn't imagine how she hid her identity, and spent the haggling session looking at the rest of the mall. There were women and men wearing costumes this skimpy, but they weren't right in front of me. A lot of the costumes were just silly, although the skimpier the sillier, mostly. More than a few villains watched me back.

The cat guy wasn't the only one with animal features, either. A brown-green lizard man in a jumpsuit caught me looking and stared back, but I couldn't read that extended, scaly face. Another, shiny grey reptile didn't wear clothing, its fidgety whiplike body didn't look male or female, but it did sport serious fangs and claws. A strong looking purple feline woman with glints of silver shining through her fur leaned in a back corner, chatting with a man in a spandex body suit who should not be that fit and muscular with so much grey in his hair.

The prize for unusual had to be the outrageously tall, powerfully muscled woman who stalked across the hall like she intended to trample anyone who didn't get out of her way. She shone emerald green, her surface gleaming like plastic, with dark purple hair in multiple thick braids that wove together down to her waist in back.

Eventually the customer traffic died down. I was pretty sure Schleimy had made more than a million dollars. I was pretty sure the supply had cost her about that. After all, she didn't gather any of it herself. What I'd noticed was the wild price differences. A seemingly equivalent item might cost two thousand dollars or a hundred thousand, depending on the customer.

And thinking of rich people, I got out my phone again and sent a text to Sue.

Me: You okay? I expected you by now.

A few seconds passed, then…

Sue: It's not noon yet?

Me: My lesson is at noon. I've been here all morning.

Sue: Don't talk to anyone, I'm on my way!

I snorted in amusement.

And then Schleimy's boyfriend arrived.

No, really. During my training I'd seen exactly one person ever visit Schleimy's home for social purposes. This guy. He had black hair and a fluffy black animal tail, both decorated in white stripes. He was… it was impossible to pin down his age. From the looks of this room, that was hardly rare. Villainy kept people fit, and either fresh, impressively scarred, or just plain not human. He was good enough looking for an adult, and tended to wear the kind of outfits you'd imagine on a romantic poet.

As for the "boyfriend" part, the first thing he did upon stepping up to the table was scoop up Schleimy's hand, lift it to his face, and kiss the back of her mitten.

"I miss your smile," he told her, with a bittersweet smile of his own.

"Not seeing it so close to daylight," she scolded him, more playfully than angrily.

Straightening up again, the stripey guy picked up a little

gold statuette, turning it over and over and studying it as he replied, "I know. There's a time and place. But I heard some news that you shouldn't miss out on."

Schleimy folded her arms across her front. Expression invisible thanks to layered ski masks and mirrored visor glasses, she asked, "Such as?"

"Artemis has been literally sleeping on the indestructible lion pelt this whole time. Some shameless rogue stole it right out from underneath her." I had to credit this guy, he did "deadpan sly" perfectly. He merely sounded amused, like it was interesting trivia.

Schleimy's head tilted an inch to the side as she asked suspiciously, "Where is it now?"

His eyes still on the statuette, stripey guy said, "It seems Blunderella got a gift of new armor from a mysterious admirer."

She paused for a moment, looking up at him, until she asked quietly, "Why?"

Stripey guy put the statuette down. Now he looked directly at Schleimy's hidden face, answering almost as softly, "So you would have a smile for me to miss."

Leaning forward, he reached out his hand and laid it over her cheek. At least five layers of thick fabric separated hand and face, but he held her cheek tenderly, and she reached up to clasp her multiply-gloved hand over his. They stared at each other in silence, him with a wistful smile. If it weren't for the masks, I was sure they would have kissed.

This way was better. It was so sweet, watching them linger like that. When he pulled away, her hand followed his, until their outstretched fingers slid apart.

Then he was gone into the growing hubbub.

Only a handful of folks would have understood what I'd just seen. Being one of them, I was grinning like a loon when the girl in the old-fashioned dress showed up.

She almost seemed to appear out of thin air, she moved so quietly, so delicately, so gracefully. She wore an ankle-length dress, plain but with slightly puffy shoulders and a narrow skirt that would be impossible to run in. Gloves, canvas shoes, and a wide brimmed hat much like mine but without the gaudy skulls meant almost every inch of her was hidden behind soft tan fabric.

But not all of her. Unlike Schleimy, this girl's face wasn't covered, merely often hidden by her hat. When she looked up at us...

Uh, wow.

This girl was made of glass. No, "glass" wasn't a good enough word. Crystal. She was shiny, transparent, gleaming, and highlighted in glittering rainbow. Her face would be breathtaking without the crystal. Slim, but not hollow. Delicate, girlish, too refined for the teenage girl her slimness suggested she was. A full mouth, curly hair that looked all one piece. Wow again. Absolute heartbreaker. And then on top of that, she was made of exquisitely elegant glass. On top of that, literally on top of that, little pointy glass cat ears stuck out of her hair, their tips peeking through holes in the hat. A glass feline tail hovered protectively close to her legs.

I couldn't say it was love at first sight, but the last time I'd felt like this meeting someone new was Chris. This girl was pretty enough to take my breath away.

But I had a boyfriend and a girlfriend, and was mighty happy with them, and this girl didn't need a random stranger drooling at her. She wasn't here to talk to me either, I was sure of that. So, as she lingered several paces away with her hands clasped in front of her shyly, I waved at the table and encouraged, "Y'all go first. 'Spec ah'll be huh last customer today, iff'n ya catch mah drift."

She paused, like so many people did, at her first exposure to my abominable accent. Or maybe she was just that shy. Her statue-like appearance only increased with the way she stood perfectly still, gracefully poised, when not doing anything specific.

The glass girl stepped up to the sales table in front of Schleimy, moving with small, silent, delicate steps. With a similarly shy and soft voice hard to hear over the mall's hubbub, she said, "I have a question."

Schleimy waved a hand at me, and assured the girl, "Avery. My apprentice. Does not care about villainy. More important, can keep secrets."

Aw. From Schleimy, that was a lot of compliments, with more implied. I managed to grin a smidge wider.

"An apprentice magic merchant?" the girl asked in surprise.

That's it. I bust out laughing, shaking my head so far my fluffy hair pummeled my face. "No, ma'am. Miss Schleimy here's teachin' me how ta use magic safely-like."

"Oh," the beautiful glass girl acknowledged, and turned her attention back to Schleimy. "I suppose I don't know what your super power is, do I? It must be something like Little Witch's."

"Something like," Schleimy muttered.

These two shy folks needed a kick. Leaning heavily on my staff, I nodded at Schleimy while looking at the glass girl. "It ain't competition. She jes' don't like how Little Witch hoards 'er toys like a dragon."

Embarrassed, Schleimy waved her hand at me to stop. I had no intention of stopping, and just grinned wider. It just might be that the stripey guy and I were the only two people in the world who really knew Schleimy, and I finally had a chance to show off why I respected and adored what everyone else thought was a little troll. Out loud, I said, "Go on. Ask 'er. She ain't shy about it nohow."

The glass kitty's hands fidgeted together where she held them clasped at hip level. She donned a hesitant smile, and said to my Master, "She has a point. If we shall be friends, I should learn more about you, shouldn't I? You have been doing this for longer than I have been alive. You must be rich by now. You don't go out for fun, do you? What do you spend it on?"

The idea of more friends for Schleimy thrilled me, so I was pleased when my overdressed teacher slumped down in defeat. Starting at a mutter, but with rising enthusiasm, she said, "Not about money. Money nice to have. About sales. One thing humans good for, make wonderful magic, permanent magic. Should not be hidden in vaults and trophy rooms and buried temples. Magic should be alive and moving. Should be used. What a waste, treasure no one sees, no one uses."

Thrilled, grinning so hard my face hurt, I asked the glass girl, "Ain't she a pip?" They might not be normal, but my Master had morals and ideals, and they were super cool.

Slumping forward more, my Master put her mittened hands over her masked face, and grumbled, "Disrespectful human apprentice."

On a crystal face it was hard to be sure, but a hint of smile had crept over the girl's mouth, and her voice held more than a hint of approval. "She is. Schleimy, I hope we do get a chance to be friends. Thank you for the friendship you've extended to me already. Now I feel guilty that I'm here for business, but I am. I need a powerful magical binding device. I don't know how I can pay, but I am confident we'll agree on something."

Schleimy turned her head to give me a direct stare, and said sharply, "Sometimes getting rid of magic part of using it. Apprentice should pay attention."

I nodded. She was right, of course. Especially for a necromancer. I straightened up and paid attention. "Yes, ma'am."

Schleimy followed up with a heavy sigh. "But do not have anything good. Not in strength you must need. Nothing." She waved her hand over a table lightly scattered with books, dice, colorful velvet bags, rings, and knives. Nothing that said to me "lock up major magic."

"And as we might'a hinted-like, she don't like none keeping stock she ain't sellin'," I filled in.

Schleimy straightened up in her seat, and even her artificial voice growled. "Apprentice get too impudent."

Sorry, but about this, I felt no guilt. Schleimy might be a strange, misanthropic little artificial being, but she was as moral as Mech and even more fascinating in her way. I was happy, I was *proud* to force her to show off how cool she was.

The glass girl curtseyed, elegant and formal and old-fashioned. The full-blown curtsey, lifting her dress up several inches and everything. She made it look pretty rather than silly. Maybe because she was such a sincere and formal person. "Thank you anyway. I'll think of another source."

"Wait," Schleimy interrupted her. For several seconds my Master sat drumming her fingers on the table, although muffled by several layers of cloth. Finally, she said, "Know who is keeping a Fenris Chain in reserve."

Glass girl's sleek, lovely, sparkling eyebrows arched a bit higher. "*Is* it Little Witch?"

I snickered.

Schleimy slapped the tabletop, making a poufy thump. "Little Witch nuisance. Biggest hoard in the world. Almost all junk. Thirty glow rings. Apprentice wands, help cast one spell or three, do nothing for non-mages. Disrespectful they sit gathering dust, but—" She shrugged. "—baubles, not treasures. No. Little Witch's big sister. Marvelous keeping chain in case she needs it."

I'd never met Marvelous. Come to think of it, I'd never met a really, truly skilled magic user that wasn't already dead. Marvelous had a reputation of having power and beauty in big buckets.

Also, in a building full of supervillains, I was not dumb enough to miss the context of the glass girl's question and Schleimy's answer. I sighed heavily. "Which ah definitely did not heah, on account ah was too busy helpin' you pack up fer the day, Schleimy. Mah date is back."

It wasn't much of a verbal cover, but it was best not to leave anyone thinking there was anything weird about Sue bursting into the mall and hurrying up to me. Sue was wearing a dull cream skirt and blouse. The bland look accentuated her "average girl" aspects rather than her flawlessness.

My explanation covered especially well the way Sue immediately wrapped both her arms around one of mine and huddled protectively close. She looked around the place like a venomous snake could jump out of every shadow and was hiding in everyone's hair. Or power armor. Or those pouches on belts that people seemed to like since so few of them had room in their costumes for pockets.

Sue completely ignored Schleimy, and gave the glass girl the least suspicious look of anyone in the room. The glass girl must be Good People.

Certainly, Sue got the glass girl's attention. With a little bow, the glass girl faced Sue and asked, "I'm sorry. Sue, can I borrow your phone?"

Sue blinked, caught completely flat-footed. "Like, excuse me?"

Torturously gentle and apologetic, the glass girl explained, "I need to call Marcia, I don't have a phone of my own, and you must have her number."

Ooh, the mysterious Marcia was involved?

Sue looked up—it would have been slightly down if she weren't huddled gripping my arm—at me for permission. No, not permission. That was the "checking to make sure Avery is okay' expression. She fiddled with her hair clip nervous, then gave the glass girl a weak smile. The glass girl really must be Good People!

"Well... okay, like, if it's Marcia," Sue agreed.

Sue had pockets in her skirts. She pulled out her phone, called up her contacts list, pressed on the "Marcia" entry to dial, and handed the phone to the glass girl as hesitantly as if it were Sue's baby.

The glass girl took a few steps away. I heard her murmur into the phone, "It's me."

Beyond that, I didn't want to spy on someone else's conversation. I turned back to Schleimy. "Figger we're done for today? With the sellin', ah mean? Want me to help pack?"

Schleimy huffed, "Apprentice wants to get her lesson over with so she can run off for romance."

Aw. I suspected that was my Master's roundabout way of giving me room to do that. I started tucking the remaining rods back in their padded plastic case, denying, "Nope. Figure I'm still a million'r so years from full control ah my powers. Bein' Queen of the Dead don't mean I'm no good at it. Any risk'a theft?"

"Only from fools," Schleimy dismissed.

"Then ah won't lock the truck," I said.

Chapter Twenty-One

With the remaining rods packed up, I carried that big plastic box out to the moving van, then came back for the next load.

By the time I got back, the glass girl was gone and Sue had presumably regained her phone. Schleimy had been packing boxes. Returning them to the van would be easier than bringing them out, because now I knew how heavy everything was, and could carry a stack. Sue was no weakling either, and carried one of the heavier boxes as we headed back outside. I might have been a bit overambitious stacking this pile, but the muscle burn was pleasant and the process wouldn't go on long enough to get dull.

As soon as we were away from Schleimy, Sue closed up almost shoulder to shoulder with me, and said, "I'm sorry I misunderstood. I would have been here earlier," as if it were some kind of actual crime.

I flashed her a reassuring and honest grin. "Weren't nothin', sweetie. I like time with the lil goblin. She's a pip, in the best way. Where anythin' but humans is concerned, she's a better person than me. Ah know that's a mahty strange qualifiah, but weah all mighty strange people."

We deposited our boxes in the trunk. I flexed and waggled my arms as we started back, getting them limber again for the next round.

Mouth pursed and sour, Sue said, "She's not the problem. I hope you didn't talk to anyone."

"Just a couple." I laughed, and the grin I gave her was affectionate this time. "Enough t' get y'all's point. Theyah sure all desperate t' have a real necromancer in the club, ain't they? They musta had a hoot when those skeleton gangs popped up last yeah. Theyah crazy anyhow. Can you imagine me in one of those costumes? Y'all might as well strap a bikini on a refrigerator."

We'd just passed a villain going the other way, and he smirked when he overheard me.

Sue stopped in her tracks, so I stopped. She swung a warning glare around at everyone remotely near us, then gave me a hard look. A really hard look. The penetrating, searching kind that doesn't like what it sees. Some accusing, some worried, she demanded, "Has your self-esteem gotten, like, worse since we met?"

From her face and tone, it was a serious question, so I scratched the back of my head as best my fleece hair allowed, and answered with complete honesty. "Darling, ah'm wedged between a glamorous debutante and Chris, who's as pretty as sin."

Sue scowled. "With any other boy I'd argue, but he totally is."

I wanted to be as nice about this as possible. Taking one of Sue's hands in both of mine, I squeezed it, gave her an eye-to-eye contact pained smile, and told the truth. "Kinda hard not to be reminded that ah'm built like a wrestler."

That got a smirk. A bitter smirk, maybe. Definitely a smirk. Her voice dripped with sarcasm. "A women's pro wrestler, maybe."

"More lahk—"

Sue put a finger to my lips, shushing me. Pulling her phone out with the other hand, she tapped at it a few times, until I heard it switched to speaker mode and I heard it ring.

The line picked up. Sue greeted, "Hey, Prince Charming."

Chris, sweet and playful, answered back, "Can I help you, Her Highness's Third Royal Consort?"

Aw. They had pet names and in-jokes they used when I wasn't around. I loved to see it. Or hear it, anyhow.

Sue, not at all playful, snapped out, "Our princess. Shape of a women's pro wrestler?"

"Yes." Chris sounded delighted. He kept sounding more delighted with every word. "Yes, that's a perfect description." Sue might have just given him a religious epiphany.

Sue answered with similar, gushing enthusiasm. "It, like, so is. Thanks, pointy tail."

And she shut off the call.

My feeble instinct to say Chris was prejudiced flickered to life, and went out again. He hadn't known I was listening, and he'd sounded so sure and emphatic. They both sounded so absolutely sure.

I didn't say anything on the last trip to the van. I couldn't. It was so strange to be reminded that what you see in the mirror isn't what other people see looking at you. My great-great-grandmother had once said something like that, hadn't she? About not trusting how a teenage girl saw herself?

"Women's pro wrestler" wasn't a shape particularly unusual in the women around us, either. Villainy clearly demanded a lot of physical effort, and more men and women had visible muscles than not. Very few were fat, although some had a padded layer over a powerful body. One woman at least half a foot taller than me had exactly the kind of big-shouldered, bulgy-muscled, brick-wall shape I had always thought was me. The guy in the costume covered in grey skull print waggling his eyebrows at her clearly did not find that unattractive. She had big hair, too.

The whole self-image thing—it wasn't just physical. Everybody looked at me and saw someone braver, more noble, or scarier, or... just different from what I thought of myself. Some of them knew me well enough I couldn't just say they were imagining things. Sue knew me top to bottom, and thought the sun rose and set with me.

Who even was I? It left me jarred, like I was physically off balance, facing that I didn't know, not for sure.

And... what did my parents see when they looked at me? That question shook me worse, all the more after my conversation with my dad this morning. I wanted it to be something good. I wanted them to be happy, not so much with what I did, but with the person they thought I was. I'd managed to put those feelings aside when I got to Chinatown, but now they came back and hovered, more important than ever before. I physically shivered from the painful rush of it.

We got back to Schleimy, standing next to her table, four and a half feet tall and totally concealed in layer after layer of fabric. Her shiny visor turned to me. What did her one eye see? I knew I saw her completely differently from everyone else. They saw the mean little pile of clothes. I saw the beautiful white fairy creature inside, with her cute button nose, angry because she was full of love for all lives that humans trample as we pass, especially the lives we pretend don't exist.

Nobody but me and the stripey guy understood that, not even when she showed them, so she rarely bothered. She did what she was doing now, act irritable by reflex. Perching her fists on her hips, she asked me a sharp, accusing question. "Well? Are you here to learn or attend the circus?"

And she was lonely, exactly because so few people saw past the layers of fabric.

Not that that changed my answer. I grabbed my staff in my left hand and my magic hat in my right, and saluted. "Here for lessons, ma'am!"

She hissed. It came out of the voice-altering device hidden in that clothing like static. Or maybe the device hadn't bothered concealing her natural, whispery non-voice. "Might have been better to give you weekend off. Need better arrangements. No resources. Interrupts business. Maybe make Eye of Heaven arrangements with Spider. Whole apprenticeship mistake."

Even at home without the voice box, comfortable and without those piles of clothes, that would have been a long speech for Schleimy. If I wasn't mistaken, my teacher just declared her willingness to spend vast, "more than my parents made in a year" amounts of money on my training.

This was sure a day for seeing the world with new eyes.

Me and Sue followed as Schleimy hobbled along to one of the dark, empty shops that lined the walls of this mall. It was a mall, after all. They had signs and posters and advertisements in Chinese, mostly brightly colored like any ad pamphlet you'd get in the mail.

She picked a store whose windows were completely papered over. When we were all inside, she snapped at Sue, "Shut the door."

Sue didn't argue. She shut the door.

It was dark in here. Seriously dark. Not dark enough for my Master to take her hood off, but dark.

Empty metal shelves lined up in rows. All the stock had disappeared for the weekend, but not the furnishings.

In the deep shadow, Schleimy's grey and blue clothing turned into an inky silhouette that I could only guess by outline was staring at me. She said flatly, blankly, "Hear you've had fights."

I grimaced. "Haven't meant to. Ah'm takin' these lessons so's I kin stop this kinda chaos, and ah swear it's getting' worse." Ouch. That sounded like criticism, didn't it? I hurried to add, "Don't think ah'm blamin' your lessons—"

My teacher waved her hand in dismissal. "Don't think that. No magic circles in fights. No purification rituals. Like here. No tools. No props. Show me control."

Okay. Well. I laid my staff and magic hat on a shelf, stepped away from them, and called up my power as fast as I could. It felt like a blizzard, a sleet storm, washing over and into me, sucked into my skin to fill me up.

Calm and focused, Avery. That's right. I tried to hold it all, a moving but controlled current, power coming in but none escaping.

"Lower it," Schleimy ordered.

Oof. That was even harder. Real calm, now. No emotions. Like relaxing my body, drain the cold away without releasing it. Except my body was churning with ice. But I kept both focused and relaxed, and drained that ice.

"Raise," Schleimy ordered.

I didn't hold back. I was here because *I* wanted to be taught, because *I* wanted control. I brought all that power back up. I sucked in more from outside. I froze myself with necromancy until it hurt, straining to keep track of it all, keep it from slipping out of my body, out of my grip.

While I struggled to do that, and to find a little more magic to pack into myself, Schleimy shuffled circles around me. The room's meager light glinted off what looked and sounded like a tinkly, sparkly wind chime mobile hanging from one of her hands.

"How'm ah doing?" I grunted, trying to keep my jaw relaxed because real control meant everything flowed rather than fought in tension.

"Do you know that answer in combat?" Schleimy asked in her true, raspy voice.

"No, Master," I answered, getting the point. I had to learn to do this blind.

Schleimy didn't say any more. I kept practice. Lowering the power. Raising it again. Lowering it again.

The process was exhausting, painful, increasingly desperate like keeping a grip on a squirming, slippery fish. Slower, too, raising and lowering each time. But I pushed.

At one of the points where my power was at its lowest, Schleimy declared, "Stop."

Breathing hard, I let the dregs slosh around in me, and didn't raise my power again.

Her voice synthesizer back on, Master asked, "You feel magic. How much contamination?"

That was like asking someone if they had cold hands. I tried to settle down, see the shadowy store again, the empty shelves, Sue leaning against a window near the door holding my hat and staff. I paid attention to the feel of the world again, the temperature of air against my skin.

"A little," I answered, as best I could. I definitely felt a chill, but we were inside on a cool day already. Maybe more important, the oiliness of Barbara's magic completely overpowered that chill, and odd little gusts of scratchiness of wriggling or other magical auras got through. No one's magic was radiating particularly strong right now, which meant mine couldn't be either, right?

Schleimy extended her black silhouette arm, pointing at Sue, then the door. "Out."

"Like, no." The hostility in Sue's voice burned.

"Please, Sue," I asked, gently, pretty sure she couldn't see my pleading smile.

She hesitated. Even without seeing her face, just knowing her, I could feel how badly Sue wanted to argue. I could see her head turn to look between me and Schleimy. Finally, Sue stomped out, slamming the door behind her.

Nothing happened for several long seconds. The faint noise of the crowd filtered in, but distant, barely audible. Nothing moved in the cool, stripped-down store. I was still keenly aware of the hints of Barbara's rancid magic brushing me, and more vague hints of the other magic users.

Schleimy shuffled halfway to the door, lifted a foot, and stomped it on the floor, hard.

Outside, Sue's muffled voice yelped in pain.

I winced. "Please don't hurt her, Master. She's jes' tryin' to protect me." Raising my voice, I said, "Sue, no shadow tricks, 'kay?"

More still seconds passed, until Schleimy shuffled back to me. Her mittened hand grabbed a fistful of my hair, pulling me down to her diminutive level. With her back to the door, Schleimy pulled her ski masks up with her other hand, revealing her pale, human-seeming face and dark, single eye. In her real voice, into my ear, she whispered, "The trouble you've been having is not random."

I sighed, disappointment adding to my weariness. "Mah control is that bad, huh?"

Without a hint of her habitual crabbiness, Schleimy whispered, "Magic is not causing your problems. Not even chaos magic."

I swallowed, and grimaced. "Heard about that too, huh?"

It wasn't really a question, and she ignored it, whispering into my ear so quietly it was soft even to me. "Someone is directing this."

I blinked, and squeaked, "Somebody's plottin' against me?"

Only belatedly did I realize I should be whispering. Master didn't scold me for it, thank goodness. She just kept on with that teacher giving a secret lesson solemnity. "Or for you. Or you're a tool against someone else. I don't know. I've seen a thousand webs of scheming woven by these people, and I know what they look like. You are caught in one."

She pulled her masks down and fumbled with the visor to completely cover her eye. Her voice artificially feminine again, Schleimy commanded, "Now go! Collect lover. Next week will figure out better. For now, proud of you."

Gosh. Thank goodness for the dark room, because I was pretty sure I was blushing.

As soon as I stepped out the door, Sue grabbed my arm, and snapped, "Lesson over? Let's get out of here. You have no idea how totally deranged these people are. They're actually worse than the heroes."

I dragged my feet as Sue tried to haul me away, through the riot of voices and colorful costumes that had been so far away in the empty store. My own feelings at least as much of a blur, I corrected Sue, "Gettin' outta here is the plan, but ah told Tonika ah'd meet her here 'bout somethin' today. Ah think she's real shook up with the bad parent—" Just the words stirred up cold anger inside me all over,. "—thing, and apparently everyone thinks ah'm a pillar of the emotional kinda strength."

Sue stopped trying to drag me. She smiled at that description, despite herself. "How bad was it?"

Me, I couldn't smile anymore. "He didn't want her back. No hugs, barely any insults. Didn't care at all."

Sue went very, very still. Her face twitched subtly. I knew her, knew those expressions, and I watched rage pass through Sue, rage so terrible she had to lock her whole body down, which she was much better at than me. Rage worse than anything I'd felt. I saw that in her tense stillness and bleak, detached, hard-eyed frown, with none of her usual sarcastic ease.

I put my arms around her. However big they actually were, they were strong, and I held her in a tight, secure hug, being her anchor as the fury stormed through her thoughts and her heart and her body. It finally ebbed, leaving Sue panting for breath and physically shaking.

Prying her arms partly free, she hugged me back, laid her head on my shoulder, and with the croak of someone trying not to cry told me, "Okay. Go help her. I'll... see if Marcia is still available. Go help Tonika."

Sue stiffened saying Tonika's name, another wave of fury hitting her, but this one drained quickly. Straightening up, pulling away, she looked me in the eyes and ordered, "And don't talk to anybody here. They're always planning something."

Schleimy's warning came back, and sent a shiver through me. "Ah'm startin' to agree."

Flinging herself on me, Sue gave me a quick, ferocious hug, for once didn't kiss me in public, and whirled around to stalk out like a vengeful murderess. Which I was pretty sure she wasn't, only wanted to be. Almost positive.

I trusted her.

Chapter Twenty-Two

Okay. Well, if I was deliberately paying no attention to the sinister carnival around me, I knew what I had to do next. Pulling out my phone, I texted Tonika.

Me: Class let out early. Do you want to see me now?

Tonika: Please.

Me: Where are you?

Tonika: Chinatown, waiting for you.

Me, while my back stiffened and my eyebrows tried to become one with my hair: Where!?

Tonika: By the exotic animal cages.

I ran down the mall's central hallway, out the doors that were now propped open, and around the corner where I'd seen the shepherd guy leading what I knew had to have been a dinosaur and not a giant chicken.

Tonika hadn't been kidding about exotic animal cages. Cat and dog carriers, plastic rodent habitats, and lots and lots of classic metal barred cages from squirrel-sized to "that hippopotamus has six eyes and bony armor plates" size, they were stacked apparently haphazardly in the open space around this corner of the mall, in what might be the only parking lot in

Chinatown. The hippo wasn't the strangest animal in the cages, either. Some were immediately identifiable, like a Labrador-sized griffon that lay in its cage giving me puppy dog eyes that made me want so badly to rescue it. Some were disturbing, like a bug-winged, antenna'd, human-looking fairy in a mayonnaise jar. Some were just plain bizarre, like the floating pink blobby thing with the dangling mouth. It had soulful eyes, too.

My inclination to free anything dropped way down when I saw the blood and bodies. It took a second to be almost sure no one was dead. Only one human lay stretched out on the asphalt, and he winced and hissed as Tonika and Barbara, on their knees, tended to his wounds. The other bodies were feathery dinosaurs that up close were obviously velociraptors, complete with bloodstained fangs and claws. Three of them lay on their backs, motionless, all four legs sticking straight up in the air. A fourth was still awake, but nuzzled the injured human affectionately instead of attacking.

Second impressions. The injured guy was the shepherd. I didn't see the badge he'd bought. I didn't see any wounds or missing parts. I did see a lot of blood leaking past fresh bandages and armor that had been ripped open and tied back on. Tonika wore that silly bodysuit, which I suppose made sense here. She was busy tying the guy's arm armor back on over a bunch more bandages. Barbara, unconcerned about the mess blood, dirt, and asphalt were making of her fancy dress, frowned in concentration as she held up an ugly burlap doll and jabbed it repeatedly with long, thin acupuncture needles.

Barbara, as always, was a sight all by herself. Full-figured to the point of exaggeration, she enhanced that further with tight corsets and ruffly, ribbony goth dresses, today in more purple than black. Her pixie cut hair was dyed black, with alternating purple and red tips today. Black lipstick accentuated a small mouth that pouted angrily as she stabbed the rag doll again and again. Each time, I felt a precise, controlled burst of that nasty, lugubrious magic she wielded.

Behind Barbara and Tonika stood Doctor Biotic, arms folded, watching passively. She'd reduced her clothing to a bikini, and not a modest bikini, either. That exposed more bare, unnaturally pink skin, and the colorful tattoos covering that skin. Since I'd seen her last, she'd turned her body into a rainbow mural of pictures of insects, the prettiest ones, dominated by spiraling flocks of butterflies. She still had the scorpion tail and extra eyes, and a wild, shaggy red wig.

The conscious velociraptor nuzzled the shepherd some more, murmuring in a birdlike squeak, "Good girl. Good girl. Why can't the others be like you?"

Barbara reached some point in her needle stabbing where she could give the injured dino shepherd a glare and lecture, "You should be in a hospital. If you lose a limb, there's no one here who can replace it."

"I'm hard to kill. Between that and your powers, I'll be fine," refused the man, who looked as tough and leathery as his armor. If only his armor hadn't been sliced open by raptors in multiple places.

Barbara raised her hands, one holding a pin and the other the multiply-impaled doll, protesting, "This is not the kind of healing I'm good at! This isn't an allergic reaction, or a prehistoric brain parasite!"

"I remember that," commented Dr. Biotic with a faint smirk.

"That was a crazy week," chuckled the shepherd, voice rough, probably because of the whole thing where he'd been clawed and bitten by velociraptors.

"Crazy summer," muttered Barbara irritably.

"Did someone call for crazy!?" sing-songed a woman's voice right behind me.

I let out a yelp, and barely restrained hitting the ambusher with necromantic claws. As the newcomer leaped past me, Doctor Biotic's tail jabbed towards her, only to be caught right behind the stinger in the newcomer's hand.

This woman was lean, fit, probably in her late twenties, a pretty normal supervillain figure. Lustrous black hair fell behind her shoulders, atop an even more lustrous black jumpsuit. The jumpsuit didn't look like fabric. It looked like a pool of black liquid clinging to her skin.

The newcomer had one of the wildest, most manic and eager smiles I'd seen so far, and after a quick look up and down cheered, "Nice ink, Biotic!"

Doctor Biotic shrugged bare shoulders decorated with iridescent scarab tattoos. "As long as it lasts. So you're back in town, Lucyfar?"

Lucyfar let go of Biotic's tail, which curled back up in readiness behind Biotic's head. The black-clad villainess waved her arms around enthusiastically, feet dramatically apart, as she declared, "Europe is great. I desecrated so many holy sites. I spray painted them in a special demonology script that's really rare, and across the continent church scholars are consulting ancient texts to find out it says, 'I bet you feel stupid now.'"

I tried to ignore the weird adults, and crouched over Barbara, who was studying her voodoo doll carefully. With both professional and personal curiosity, I asked, "Y'all found a way to use your powers for healin'?"

Barbara slid the tip of her latest acupuncture pin over the rough brown burlap to a precise spot on the doll's left side, and slid it in. I felt a faint rush of magic, precisely controlled, just the tiniest bit of spillover. Her eyes not moving from the doll, she said, "Badly. We have to find something to do with our magic that we're not ashamed of."

The dinosaur shepherd had gotten real quiet, with his eyes closed, and I suspected Barbara had just put him to sleep. It wouldn't be right to distract her from her errand of mercy, so I looked over at Tonika, jerked my heads at the loading truck zone, and asked, "Can we talk over there?"

She didn't answer, but I got up and started walking, and Tonika fell in behind me. Doctor Biotic and Lucyfar followed us.

We got to the actual corner of the building when Tonika stopped, looked behind us, and said with quiet, solemn formality, "I'm sorry, Miss Lucyfar, but I really need to have a private conversation with my friend here."

Doctor Biotic shook her head, her mouth tight on one side with mild exasperation. The relaxed gesture reminded me of Peggy. Almost as bland, she answered, "If she leaves, she'll spy on you from a distance. You might as well keep Lucyfar where you can see her."

Lucyfar swept her head to the side, flipping her hair back,

then running a hand through it. Proudly, she declared, "When a teenager takes off running, there's trouble brewing. Good or bad, I must find out what it is."

I sighed, and told Tonika, "Sue said they wuh crazy. Maybe we shouldn't've met heah."

All meek, cybernetically enhanced stillness, Tonika gave me sad, soulful eyes and said, "We had to. There were people I needed to question, and plans to make in person where there was no possibility a hero would overhear."

The black-jumpsuited Lucyfar squeed, "Oooooooooh!" and rubbed her hands in classic gleeful anticipation. The woman looked worse than crazy. She looked like she was deliberately acting crazy just for the fun of it.

And she'd attached herself to our conversation like a leech, because that was the kind of thing that you had to expect at a gathering of supervillains. This was what they were like.

Nothing to do but bull ahead as if she weren't there. I put my hand on my hip and told Tonika, "Okay, well, 'fore the sales pitch, ah spec you oughta know somethin'. Mah teacher thinks somebody's plottin' against me."

Yay for having to say that with both Doctor Biotic and this weirdo Lucyfar listening. So much for secret.

Tonika's eyes turned down, and she frowned in thought. Deep in thought. The silence stretched. I could practically see the cyborg super brain processing data. Finally, she raised her eyes to me again, and nodded. "Yes. That makes sense. Even more reason for us to do this together."

I popped the important question. "Do what now? If it involves super powahs, ah'm surprised yoah new friends can't help."

She clasped one fist over the other, holding them to her black-vinyl-covered chest pensively. Mournful, she explained, "They would love to, and they'll do what they can, but that's the problem. None of them have much control over their powers."

I nodded. "Ah get that. Mah necromancy was dang near useless, four months ago."

Tonika nodded, too, dark brown eyes turning up to me with passionate intensity. "I know. You're my inspiration here. I've been trying to figure out what would help them, and the key to everything is a divination aid for Delphine. Unfortunately, it has to be the real thing. Magical. I hope she can train to not need it…"

From personal experience, I filled in, "But y'all need the trainin' wheels to learn how to ride without the trainin' wheels."

Tonika's face fell, and then her eyes. "Yes," she admitted.

I stuck my left hand into my hair and scratched the side of my head. "Not that ah don't want ta help, but how'm I involved?"

She lifted her gaze to me again, grimly instead of sadly solemn now. "Because Mech and the other heroes think the robot that's chasing you is just a malfunctioning weapon to be destroyed."

I jerked, moral horror the next emotion to hit me like a hammer today. Raising my hands, I sputtered, "Woah, hey there, it's way more complicated than that!"

With unbending, solemn directness, Tonika told me, "Mech won't listen. None of them will listen."

I'd almost managed to shut out Lucyfar's presence, but she flapped a hand around, pointing a finger and waving and generally waggling her forearm in a series of quick, random gestures more spastic than her almost reasonable voice. "Mech's a sweetheart and a great kisser, but not at home to moral complexity. He's *too* dedicated to good."

Folding her forearms covered in swarming ant tattoos under her chest covered in butterfly tattoos, Doctor Biotic frowned with bland, sad resignation. The resignation of experience, which came out in her frank tone. "You fight a lot of rampaging robots in this job, and you fast get used to being told that this one is different. Then, if you're lucky, you're able to save the life of the person who just said that. Besides, it's already hurting people. Not badly, yet. It's unstable and violent, and my fellows want to stop it before violence becomes murder."

"But there's a ghost in it!" I yelped, scandalized.

With no sign of approval or disapproval, Doctor Biotic explained, "Someone who's dead already. Melting down the robot is a merciful exorcism."

Tonika said, "I'm not sure I disagree with him, but I know

you disagree with him. I'm confident there's an extra factor that will keep him and the other heroes from finding the robot before it finds you." She still had her eyes fixed on mine. For someone so meek and shy, the girl had the most direct and persistent stare I'd ever encountered.

I ignored that and focused on her words. With a scowl, I flapped a hand at my frustrating ignorance. "Lahk whoever's settin' all this up, for... whatevuh ding dang cockamamie reason."

Lucyfar rubbed the palms of her hands together so fast they made a hissing noise, and she started bouncing up and down with glee. "Fun. We do it for fun. So much fun! And I am the MISTRESS of fun. I'm Lucyfar. Whatever you're getting into, I'll help turn it into beautiful chaos. THE most fun you've ever had, I guarantee it."

As I recoiled from the clown car salesman routine, Doctor Biotic raised her voice in warning. "Already taken care of, Lucy."

Lucyfar slumped and pouted. "Aw, come on! You're fun when you're tripped out on cassowary DNA, Doc, but ambiguously moral good times are my specialty!"

Tonika turned her unnervingly solemn eyes apologetic, quiet formality on the manic villainess. "Thank you, but this is serious."

I sure agreed with that. What kind of person found this kind of situation fun?

Okay, it was fun, but that wasn't enough reason to do it, not when it spread collateral damage everywhere. Not nearly enough reason.

Clasping her hands under her chin, Lucyfar pleaded, "But I can juggle babies! I tell the best Talmud jokes in LA! I've been in Europe for most of a year, and do you know how stodgy they are there? It's all public service and practical uses for super powers!"

Trying very hard to ignore Lucyfar, I told Tonika, "Ah'm surprised Doc Biotic is here."

"I needed the assistance of someone who can drive, someone who can get into Chinatown, and someone who wouldn't judge me. Mech isn't allowed here, and she sees me as someone who would never want to be here in the first place." Soft, precise, and point by point. That was how Tonika answered explanations. It was like listening to a sober, tween Sherlock Holmes.

Doctor Biotic picked up where Tonika left off. "And I disapprove, but I know this seems like the whole world at your age, and you're going to go ahead with it. You might as well have someone on your side who can minimize the damage and help you learn lessons the least hard way possible."

Lucyfar whirled on the other adult. Jabbing Doctor Biotic accusingly in the chest with an index finger, the black-haired crazy woman accused, "You're part capybara. You are, aren't you? Admit it. That's the only reason you're so mellow about all this."

Unruffled and, yes, mellow, Doctor Biotic continued, "Also I'm chilled out on capybara mutagens. Lucy, I'll make you a deal. Leave these kids alone, and we'll go over there and I'll tell you about the complete disaster of a mutation you missed while you were gone."

Lucyfar's eyes sparkled. I would swear literally, with little starry specks of light to go with her huge, hopeful smile, eagerly clasped hands, and lifting right up on her toes. "Eeeee! Were there missing body parts? Can I play with your tail?"

Maybe because of the capybara mutagens, but Doctor Biotic took all of this in stride, the same way she did teenagers mixing with supervillains. "No spoilers until we're out of earshot, and sure. I'm not the one in danger of being injected with a quart of neurotoxin."

They walked off towards the other end of the building, Doctor Biotic lazily and with swaying hips and scorpion tail, and Lucyfar hopping with joy. That is, until she reached the doorway into the mall. Grabbing it as if Biotic were physically trying to drag her away, Lucyfar shouted, "Joke time! I was but a child, listening to the great Rabbis discuss Torah in the temple, when Rabbi Hillel said to Rabbi Eliezar, 'Which one are you again?'"

Silence reigned. After a long pause, a man's voice near the door burst out laughing. Lucyfar pointed and squealed. "YES! He gets it!"

The man's muffled voice explained to someone I couldn't

see, "It's because there were... so many... oy, never mind."

Lucyfar let go of the door, miming being dragged away by a Doctor Biotic who wasn't invested enough to do any dragging.

And they were gone, or at least far enough away to be no part of my conversation with Tonika.

I turned back to the little purple-wigged girl, shaking my head. "Sue was right, that these folk ain't right. Ah see now why she's so hot ta keep me from joinin' 'em. Speaking of which, it's pretty clear what y'all want is illicit. You've got an adult with experience on your side. Why me?"

Giving me that stare again, Tonika answered, "The collection needs a mage to sort through."

I shrugged. "Hodir's stronger'n me."

Honest, no self-abuse, rumors of my power level were greatly exaggerated.

"And a chaos mage. His control may be worse than anyone's. He's also not sensitive like you. I've seen you react when you pick up other magics, even minor ones. Also, I suspect there will be puzzles." Tonika was giving me the feeling again that there was no question I could ask or protest I could make that she hadn't thought of the answer to already.

So I pointed out, "Y'all're the super brain, and ah mean it when ah say that."

"I can't solve a puzzle with no clues." A chink of humanity opened up in the robotic lecture, her mouth twisting with a hint of sourness. "Besides, when I get things wrong, I get them spectacularly wrong. I think we may need to talk to the original owner."

My brain processed that, until I blinked in realization. "... oh, yeah, call up a ghost for answers. Sure, ah kin do that. It's worked before."

Tonika nodded. The calm melted, and she lifted a hand to nibble at a fingernail. Sheepish guilt flooding her voice, she said, "Now you know the reasons I need you, and the reasons I think you should do this for yourself, so... I guess it's time for the bad part."

I set my chin, metaphorically and literally. "Uh-oh. Lay it on me."

Head hunched down as if I might hit her, Tonika said, "The objects I'm looking for are in a museum."

I winced, teeth gritted. "And that's straight-up supervillainy. Exactly what ah promised mah folks ah wouldn't do. That life ain't me, Tonika. Ah gotta refuse."

Tonika lowered her unsettling eyes, suggesting softly, "Just think about it. I don't think you can refuse. You'll have to find the robot before it finds you."

I could just let it find me. It was a ghost. I might be able to take the most powerful ghost in the world. I could certainly handle this one.

If I had the chance.

If it didn't attack me from surprise, if I was able to think clearly long enough to improvise whatever it took to save it and myself.

If it didn't break into my house.

If it didn't hurt someone badly before reaching me.

I grimaced harder, my head squeezed down, jaw and forehead and heart aching. My parents were going to lose it if I robbed a museum. They'd been straining themselves to be nice all this time.

Worse than any punishment, what would they think of me?

I couldn't face that. My heart went cold thinking about it, and not in the comfortable "necromancy" way. Everyone thought I was fearless, but this terrified me.

Shaking my head, I groaned, "Ah can't. Mah parents can't find out."

Unfazed, a stick figure in shiny black rubber and gaudy purple hair, intimidatingly solemn, Tonika gave me her focused stare again and explained, "I've researched this. Museums keep the details of super powered incidents very private. The one thing you don't have to worry about is what your parents will think.

Rrg. Was that any better? Lying to my parents about something this big? I didn't want to be a supervillain, and I was getting pushed into it! By someone with a larger villainous scheme, maybe.

Another jolt of cold anxiety shot through me. What would

Sue think? She was trying so hard to keep me out of villainy. I couldn't not tell her. I had to tell all my friends, but Sue was the one who cared, a lot. Hurting her... I couldn't.

A confused robot might break into my house and kill my parents.

"Ah'll... think about it," I mumbled.

Maybe talking to Sue would make this better. Or a lot worse.

Chapter Twenty-Three

What was I going to say to Sue?

I paced back and forth across my bedroom Sunday afternoon, literally, physically pacing from one side to the other while my thoughts swirled in chaos.

It had taken about an hour for the question to go from "needing advice" to "terror of how Sue would react." Not just that Sue would disapprove of this kind of villainy, but after her freakout about the haunted house, I didn't know how Sue would react to finding out any secret I'd been keeping from her.

Rubbing my hand over the face, I stared up at the passing ceiling and muttered, "She'll insist on comin' along. She will. Ah cain't do that."

The thought of how my own parents might react made my stomach knot. Sue's parents were superheroes, I was sure of it. Sue was bending over backwards to convince her folks that shadow powers didn't mean villainy. I couldn't drag Sue into actual villainy. I wasn't sure what could be worse than sending Sue to Pep Prep, but her parents would think of something. They'd start with cutting her off from me.

It would break Sue. I'd be miserable, but Sue would be destroyed.

I swerved my pacing to my closed bedroom door and laid my fingers on the painted wood. Longing pulled at me. I wished so badly that I could tell my folks, but the problem would be the same as with the superheroes. It all hinged on me not wanting a ghost to be killed, or re-killed, or whatever you called that. A few questions, and my explanation would fall apart. Yes, the person was dead. No, they clearly didn't have a complete mind, and the ghost was acting exactly like a bundle of memories and emotion, which most ghosts were. It just happened to have a body, and was striving for something no one could identify, something involving me. They would tell me that the ghost wasn't a living person and didn't need saving.

My pacing brought me back to the wall against the back end of our house. I swiveled around and dropped my back against it with a thump I wouldn't dare if a room was on the other side. Squeezing my eyes shut, I groaned, "But t' me, she's a person, and a person needs savin'. Right here'n now, she ain't just a blob'a memories. She thinks. She's decidin' and actin'. Don't matter how muddled that all is. Humans is muddled all the time and it don't stop us from bein' worth saving."

"Wish ah could talk to Chris about this," I whimpered as I pushed myself back up and resumed pacing.

Chris would understand. Not my reasoning, but me. He'd understand why I had to do this. And then I'd be the person being held and comforted, which I needed badly before I stepped into this abyss. Robbing a museum was not the same as exorcising a haunted house, not by a million miles.

Except there was absolutely no way I would make Chris keep secrets from Sue. Telling Peggy or Annie would have less being held and even more secrecy complications.

I paused in front of my closet door. On the other side of that folding panel hung my magic hat. Was I desperate enough to call up my ancestors?

Their moral advice consistently involved killing someone.

I had no answers, and went back to pacing.

Chapter Twenty-Four

Monday, somehow, was worse. I sat down next to Sue in class, trying to think of what to say. How to even start the conversation. How do you gently lead into "I'm going to commit supervillainy" or "I've been hiding that a haunted robot is stalking me"? "Sue, I have to talk to you" doesn't do it. That would just put the problem off one sentence.

A shadow, a regular, non-super powered shadow crossed over me. I looked up to our teacher standing over me, thin and severe in a charcoal suit and her hair in a bun. She held a ruler in one hand like a scepter, and laid the tip of it on the desk top as her cold eyes stared doom down at me.

"Miss Special, what is the volume of a cone?" she asked, with the sharp tone of accusation that I hadn't been paying attention, which I hadn't.

So no one was more shocked than me that I knew the answer to that one. Blinking up at her in awe, I half recited, half figured out, "One third'a the volume of if it was a cylinder, so I reckon that's pi times the diameter of the base, times the height, and all that divided by three."

Those blade-sharp eyes held no forgiveness, no admission

of mistake, but also no grudge. I had answered the question correctly, and my teacher walked away, back behind her desk to continue teaching.

I had escaped doom, half because I really did spend a lot of time on studying and homework, often with Sue and Chris helping. But the other half was luck. I had never found out what happens if you upset a teacher at Pepperidge Preparatory School for Girls, and I didn't want to find out. Necromancy wouldn't save me.

Forcing my fears aside, I focused on schoolwork for the rest of the day.

Of course, I couldn't focus on schoolwork at lunch, so I sat down on the stony wall in the quiet, green courtyard next to Sue and tried to think of what to say again.

"Sue…" I fumbled.

She lurched to the side. Her left arm darted around my shoulders behind me, squeezing me in a tight hug. Her head tucked down onto my shoulder, filling my view with pretty brown hair as I tried to look down and see her expression. Setting her fancy wooden food box aside, she wrapped her right arm around me too, clinging.

The breathy weakness in her voice came out of nowhere. She whispered like she was about to cry, "I love you so much. It was so good of you to help Tonika deal with her parents. She must be torn apart."

I wasn't sure what Tonika was, in many senses. Either she'd been prepared for her father to be awful, which I figured was true, or she was superhumanly good at hiding her pain, which I knew for a fact was true. Just because she looked like she'd move on didn't mean her heart wasn't bleeding shreds where no one could see.

Sue nuzzled her face deeper into my neck. She sounded so… in awe of me. "Tonika needs to know someone isn't totally abandoning her. I'm so proud of you."

Now I actually felt even more confused and conflicted. Honestly, I said, "Thanks. Ah'm trying. It ain't easy."

Sue clung to me, squeezing me… not desperately. She wasn't trembling or anything. Just tight. From "about to cry," her tone switched to "cold and hard." "I'm glad it was you. I'd have killed him for abandoning his daughter. I'd have fed my shadow into his mouth and squeezed shut his windpipe and watched him choke and die for what he did."

Well, that left me cold. I wasn't sure whether Sue was kidding or not. I didn't think her power could do that, but I didn't know. She didn't sound angry, she sounded bleak.

Not that I didn't understand her feelings. I understood them all too well. Standing in front of that man who responded to the return of his months-missing daughter with mild annoyance... magic and anger swirled up in me just at the memory.

Sue added softly, "I don't know how you kept your temper."

"It was hard." It was hard right now. But this was also my chance. I could tell Sue the story in more detail, which would include the robot attack, and would lead into everything else.

But those thoughts had delayed me, and Sue murmured with a sigh and increasing cheer. "You're so much better a person than me. And you'd better be feeling better about your looks after that talk on Saturday." Lifting her face from my shoulder, Sue gave me her evil, teasing smirk. "Or I'll have to tell you every little detail about what I like about your looks. Maybe I'll do that anyway."

Heat roared across my cheeks in a furious blush, and I squeaked, "We both have ta eat iff'n I'm going to keep looking like this."

Sue smirked, relishing her victory.

I dug into my box of Thai noodles, knowing my best opportunity to tell her was gone.

Afternoon classes came and went, with me trying to focus on them and not on my problems, which meant I was unprepared all over again when the bell rang. Sue and I picked up our backpacks and wandered out in no hurry. She slipped her hand into mine while we were still in the hall. It always felt small and warm and delicate, despite there being not much difference in size and Sue being athletic herself.

It was hard to think while holding Sue's hand, and I badly wanted not to think right now.

As we passed out the front doors, I asked her, "Do you think she gave us so much homewuhk because ah was distracted today?"

Sue shook her head sharply. "Not me, and if anyone else thinks so and says anything, they'll totally suffer for it."

A question hit me, because my thoughts really had been elsewhere all day. "Ah you taking me home today? Ah haven't been keeping track."

Maybe the sheer awkwardness of that extra time together would force me to confess?

Sue stopped, biting her lip nervously, which was not an expression I saw from her often. Awkward, drawing out her words, she answered, "I was going to, but, like, I hope you don't mind, because I had an idea. I couldn't get together with Marcia Saturday, and I don't want to hear anything about it being your fault, so stop looking guilty. Instead, I told my parents I'm going out on a date with you this afternoon, and I'm getting together with Marcia after her club. Before then, I want to do a little shopping."

That smirk crept back over Sue's face, which meant I didn't want to know about the shopping and would probably find out later in some embarrassing way. Maybe I'd be lucky and it would just be a ten-thousand-dollar sequined evening gown that Sue and Chris would swear I looked elegant in.

They might convince me I—

Sue straightened up and pointed with the hand not clasped in mine. "There's Winifred!" She turned her face to me, and her hazel eyes filled with that awed, longing, lost expression she reserved only for me. Darting her face in to give me a quick kiss, she followed it by squeezing my hand and whispering breathlessly, "I love you so much."

Then she pulled free and ran off to meet her parents' car and her butler driving it, leaving me flustered and confused and guilty.

My dad was pulling onto the street in our car anyway.

The car ride home proceeded in pensive silence. When we got home, as soon as I stepped inside I told my dad, "Ah got a lot of homework to do."

I was sure I sounded convincingly exasperated, especially

since I did have a lot of homework to do, and that wasn't rare. I had no idea how Sue did the same homework so fast.

He headed straight towards the kitchen, with a big smile on his face, calling out, "I'll make cupcakes for energy later!"

I left him behind, walked down the hall, into my bedroom, dropped my backpack on my bed, yanked open my closet, grabbed my magic hat, and slapped it onto my bushy-haired head.

"Exorcise it," declared the Horse Skull Kid's voice before I could even say anything.

My great-great-grandmother's voice slithered in a sweet attempt to be comforting. "You stress yoahself fah too much about these things, but yes, if you want to end the ghost's suffering, end its suffering."

Numlah growled eagerly, "There is nothing so much fun as ripping a spirit from its place in this world and sending it to the tedious dark of BWA HA HA HA!" His voice switched to the kind of amusement where I imagined him brushing a tear from his eye. "No, no, you think of us as much too evil, girl. Spells to make the crossing peaceful for those who died in pain and anger were my specialty. People will pay you to do that, Avery. With no competition, you'll be rich."

These were better answers than I'd expected, but not by enough. I hadn't given them voices for moral support. I snapped, "Look, I'll figure out what to do once I talk to the ghost. How do I get to it before it gets to me?"

Amused and exasperated, Alicia Blackheart said, "Summon it, honey child."

Like I hadn't thought of that? "This city is huge! I'm not strong enough."

A couple of seconds of silence followed. I couldn't see my ancestors without donating power I didn't want to give them carelessly. So I was a bit surprised when Alicia asked quietly, "Am ah that hard on her, Kid?"

"A lil, Alicia. Sorry," he answered, also quiet and abashed.

Alicia picked up a little more energy, but sad and... grandmotherly, now. "Yoah just so *adrift*, Avery. You can do so much, and the only teaching yoah getting is how to hold yourself back.

Yes, of course you can do it, honey child. It will take a lot of powuh, but that's what yoah staff is for."

"And if the ghost doesn't bite the hook, we'll help," growled Namluh in his merely sane and reasonable Southern accent. Or was that an actual Sumerian accent?

Cheerful and casual, the Horse Skull Kid speculated, "Might take us a few days to teach you how ta make a better beacon, but you kin do it."

A creepy realization struck me. "Wait. Beacon. This isn't just a big spell that uses a lot of power. It's going to get the attention of everyone and everything magical in LA, won't it?"

"Of course," answered Alicia.

"No thanks," I declared, whipping the hat off my head.

Sighing, I trudged over to my bed, and unzipped my backpack. I didn't even want to think about what a disaster lighting up a magical beacon would be, so I put the matter off another day and did my homework instead.

The cupcakes were delicious, at least. Cream cheese frosting is to die for.

Chapter Twenty-Five

Tuesday morning.

Talk to Sue, take two.

Today's strategy: Try to make a commitment before we even entered school. Even if the conversation was a disaster, even if I started it in the worst way possible, I had to at least have the conversation. I usually met Sue on the lawn in front of the door, so I would blurt out something, anything, that made her force me to tell her everything later.

I stepped out of my dad's car at the curb and marched towards the awaiting Sue.

When something more important threw my plans aside.

Sue was covered in bruises. Every inch of her face was blue or purple or green. Her hands were bruised. I rushed over to her, grabbed her sleeve, and pulled it up a few inches to confirm the ugly colors ran up her arm. I crouched and pulled her skirt up far enough to confirm bruises above her socks. Grabbing her sweater and blouse, I pulled that out of her skirt so I could get a peek at her stomach.

More bruises, everywhere. Hideous ones.

Anger stormed like a blizzard outside a window, terrible

but at a distance. What mattered was the question I asked with frigid calm. "Who did this? I'll make them pay."

Now my hands clenched into fists, and the fury, mixed with icy magic, began leaking past my defenses.

Sue threw herself onto me, face in my neck, arms squeezing me ferociously. "It's not like that," she tried to assure me.

My own arms raised, then stopped, frozen. I wanted to hug her back. I couldn't. I couldn't put pressure on those bruises. The question I should have asked first squeaked out. "Should you even be out of bed?"

Sue unwound from the hug, grabbing my hand instead and pulling me towards the door. With a calmness and a smile that made absolutely no sense, she answered, "The real damage is healed. I'll explain at lunch. You don't have to protect me."

Maybe, or maybe not. We got to the classroom last, right before the bell. Everyone looked stony-faced, pretending they didn't see Sue's glaring, colorful injuries. No one dared to make a joke about it.

But three people giggled, just loud enough for me to know who it was.

Which was the point, of course.

That had to be nipped in the bud, if Sue and I weren't going to have a whole round of trouble from people testing just how much harassment they could get away with. Besides, no one got to laugh at my Sue.

No one.

But we couldn't linger at the door when lunch rang, or those girls would just hide in the classroom. That would interfere with school, and get the teacher involved. So as kids rushed out into the hall, towards the cafeteria, I walked just a little way and stopped.

My power was already drawn up. I'd been filled with cold magic, ready to unleash it for hours. It had been an effort to pay attention to geometry.

Spending a little of that power, I whispered, "Spirits of my ancestors, attend the Queen of the Dead."

"How can we help, honey child?" came Alicia's immediate response.

"I don't know how to hurt someone at a distance. Not kill, just hurt," I whispered. Two of my targets left the classroom at the same time, and separated. One was already past me. Teenage girls in blue school uniforms milled around, carefully paying no attention to me standing there whispering to myself.

Numlah barked a jolly laugh. "Ha! I know just the spell. Oh, yes. No harm, but they learn to respect the masters of death."

I didn't care about the details. "Teach me. Fast."

I poured power icy power into the voice, and the bald, pot-bellied outline of the ancient necromancer solidified in the air, visible only to those with ghost sight—a group in this world consisting only of me.

Namluh didn't waste time. He said, "Repeat after me," and began.

There was a gesture. There were words of gibberish, probably Sumerian. All small and quiet, not attention grabbing. Cold necromancy danced in a pattern as I drew it, rippled through my musical words.

They formed something. Something invisible, but the last word felt like when you close a box and the lock clicks.

"Now, just pick your targets," instructed Namluh, his hands on his belly, his voice thick with relish.

The crowd had started to clear, with most of the students having reached the cafeteria. Not my targets. The first was one of the bleach blondes. It seemed like Pep Prep was filled with identical debutantes stamped out of a mold, with the only difference being whether they bleached their hair. I'd learned to spot the differences. This one had just rearranged her makeup, and was tucking the case back into her backpack.

I drew a little x over her with my finger. Magic rushed out of me like a cannonball.

The girl wailed, dropping her backpack, which spilled books and stationery and her tablet and makeup on the tile floor. She staggered two steps, clawed at a potted plant with both hands, holding onto it as she slid to the floor. Her hands fell free, and she lay there, maybe passed out.

I drew an x over the second girl, a brunette who could have been a less polished version of Sue, without the ability to love and the driving need to be a better person.

The brunette didn't shriek. She doubled forward, grabbing her shoulders. Even halfway down the hall, I could see her shaking. She dropped slowly to her knees, bent forward farther, but didn't quite collapse. She just held herself and whimpered.

Except that whimpering, the hallway had gone completely silent. No one dared move.

I turned. The third girl, another bleached blonde, stared at me with wide eyes. She knew what she'd done, oh yes.

I drew an x over her. More icy power dashed invisibly out of me.

She let out a squeak, breathless rather than loud. Her face a mask of horror, she fell against the brightly painted wall next to her, hands gripping her chest in the center. She slid down to a sitting position, then took a sudden, deep breath and whimpered, "My heart. It stopped. I felt it stop."

Tears were already rolling down her cheeks.

I let the spell go, sucking the power that formed the weapon back into myself as best I could. Taking tight hold of Sue's hand, I walked towards the cafeteria, the two of us surrounded by still figures.

At least, for a few seconds. The crowds began to move again. Quieter than before, but going about their business.

No one moved to help the three girls. Not even a teacher. I did hear a few snickers.

This place was a snake pit, and I would make sure those snakes knew who they didn't dare bite.

The cafeteria was also silent and subdued as Sue and I got our meals and paraded down the center to the back wall, which Sue opened with her shadow, letting us out into the garden.

The shadow hole closed behind us, and Sue swiveled, grabbed me, yanked me close, and kissed me hard.

It went on, with my hands trapped between us holding a cardboard box of food, Sue's closed eyes filling my vision, so purple they were almost black, and her mouth tightly pressed to mine.

I started to relax into that pleasant closeness. Sue's eyes fluttered back open, and she pulled away slowly, her smile sad and awed and delighted all at the same time.

She started to say something, but I cut her off to ask the question again. "Who did this?"

As if everything was fine and normal now, Sue grabbed my bicep and tugged me down to sit next to her on the edge of the wall. She waved a pair of disposable chopsticks. "Like, I did it to myself."

I stared at the hand holding those chopsticks, at its nightmarish coverage of bruises. "I don't believe that."

With both hands on her food now, she bumped my shoulder with hers, and shook her head. A bit more sheepishly, she corrected, "No, I mean… this isn't your problem."

I gaped at her. "Someone beat you like a pinata. How are you not in the hospital?"

Tears formed at the edges of Sue's black-ringed eyes, but they were tears of joy, matched with a wide smile. She stared at me blissfully, but sounded only a little breathy as she answered, "I told you, I got help. All the important damage was totally fixed. She just couldn't fix the bruises."

My horror barely dimmed, I said, "That must have been agonizing."

Sue paused. She didn't want to lie to me, so tucked her head down a bit, and admitted sheepishly, "Yes." When my face hardened , she immediately reared back up, giving me a stern look. "No! Don't you dare. Listen, Avery. I love you so much for wanting to defend me like this, but I deliberately took a risk. Marcia and I did something heroic to impress my parents, and it went badly."

And that shut me up, because I was not going to tell Sue to stop seeing her best friend, who Sue had said many times was dangerous.

Sue told me and my helpless, open-mouthed stare, "And it *doesn't involve you*. I made my choice and I accepted the consequences. I know you would have been there for me if you knew, but…" She paused, her frown turning pained, head twitching, struggling with the thought forming as she said it. "…there are risks I have to take without you, Avery."

I set my untouched food aside, grabbed Sue, and hugged

her close. Close, but gently, because those bruises had to be sore. With no one watching, I could tell she moved gingerly. Glum at the bitter truth, I said, "Ah know. Ah guess we're not supposed t' share everything."

Sue's arms came up, clutching at my shoulders from behind. Her voice by my ear took on a touch of roughness. "I want to share everything in our lives, but I… it doesn't work like that. I want it to, but it doesn't. This was one of those things that you can't be a part of."

We let each other go, and I looked her straight in those beautiful hazel eyes, promising, "But iff'n you do want mah help, ah'll be there for you always. *Always*. You understand that? Ah will drop everything to protect you. To be theyah for you."

She set her own food in her lap, clasped both of my hands in hers, and leaned forward again, laying her face against my neck. Still a touch hoarse, she whispered, "I know. Thank you so much. Thank you for understanding."

"Ah do." I did. I understood a lot now. "And ah know that if ah'm the one takin' a risk without you, you'll come running just as fast if ah get in over mah head."

She would. I knew it absolutely. I couldn't, wouldn't drag Sue and my friends into this mess with Tonika and my stalker, but that didn't change that Sue and I would drop everything when the other called.

"Always. Always always," Sue whispered. Sniffling, she rose back up, taking hold of her lunch again, but still smiled at me with shining eyes.

"Did it at least help with yoah parents?" I asked, forcing myself to accept that I shouldn't dwell on Sue's injuries or freak out any more.

She rolled her eyes, and her head, and let out an exasperated groan. "I don't know. When I reported how it went to them, they were all totally weird. I'm sure they think I was brave and acted like a hero, at least."

I started to open my own box of food, the normal thing to do at a time like this, but couldn't tear my eyes from Sue's bruised face. "Well, y'all said ya don't want me involved, but if ya do decide to tell me the whole-all story, I'll for sure want to hear.

'Spec what's important is that y'all're okay."

Downright prim and amused now, Sue looked herself over, and even smirked. "Well, I look like a monster, but nothing is seriously damaged. I was worried about how this would shake out at school, but someone wonderful stepped in and totally protected me."

I sat there for a second, processing all this, while the leafy green trees rustled above us, and an ant crawled off the stone wall over my skirt. Quietly, I asked, "Can ah ask you this? Are y'all sure you did the right thing?"

Sue gave me an equally silent, thoughtful stare, until she finally nodded. "You know... like, I am. I really am. It turned out crazy, but still, I'm proud of myself."

I smiled. After all that seriousness, it made my face ache. "Then ah'm proud'a you."

Sue took advantage of my open mouth to flick a shrimp tempura out of her box and feed it to me.

Which shut me up, and answered all the remaining questions whirling around in my head.

Although I did intend to tell Sue everything afterwards. I swear I did.

Chapter Twenty-Six

"Y'all can't possibly intend ta do villainy at five o'clock durin' rush hour on a Wednesday afternoon in downtown LA," I said, because it was five o'clock during rush hour on a Wednesday afternoon as we pulled into a parking lot in downtown LA.

Doctor Biotic, in the driver's seat next to me and focused on parallel parking, corrected, "This is Culver City."

Behind me, in the back seat, Tonika's earnest voice explained, "I promise, it will work. Between regular people with super powers, the low level of destruction associated with most supervillain crimes, and the common practice of filming on LA's streets, we will attract minimal attention. I learned it from Mech."

Tonika was back there by the door, squeezed in like a slice of cheese next to Olga, who was squeezed in next to Delphine, who was squeezed in next to Hodir, who had the door behind Doctor Biotic. I got the front passenger seat alone, for the simple reason that I was as wide as any two of them. That wasn't a judgment on my looks. I'm a big girl and they were tiny. Delphine was the only one of them who even approached adult size.

They had come down with a plague of big, lumpy grey sweatshirts that turned their torsos into a blending mass. It made me feel a little lonely for my friends, my teammates when things got tough. We wouldn't have fit, though. Even Peggy dwarfed Tonika, Olga, and Hodir.

The parallel parking ended, wedging us between two much fancier looking cars, which weren't even all that fancy. Biotic's car, as clean as she kept it, had a subtle lumpiness and color mismatch between parts that announced it had survived fire, perdition, and tornadoes filled with sharks.

I got out onto the not particularly wide sidewalk, and looked up and down a gruelingly unremarkable street of stores that had been converted from houses that had been crushed as tightly together as Tonika's friends in the backseat. I saw absolutely no sign of a museum anywhere.

The back seat's door came open, and Tonika stumbled out, practically shoved out by the pressure. As she got her balance, I asked, "Y'all swear this here'll work?"

"I've studied the situation heavily, and this time we're bringing backup sufficient to take care of surprises, including an experienced adult super combatant."

I still would be a lot more reassured if this were my friends and not Tonika's, and if Doctor Biotic weren't feeding coins into a parking meter with a blasé and barely involved air. But... "Well, alrighty. One second, then."

It had been absurdly easy to arrange this. I told my folks that I was going out with Tonika after I got my homework done, and a superhero would be picking me up and driving. It was all true, and my father had even gotten to see Tonika and Doctor Biotic wave from the car.

That did mean I hadn't brought my equipment, and I was going to need it. Trying not to think about the witnesses behind me, I knocked softly on the grey door of the skinny building in front of me with one knuckle, whispered "Alice," and ducked in.

With the door closed but still present behind me, I crossed Alice's always pleasantly cool crypt to pick up my magic hat lying atop the sarcophagus in the center, and my magic staff lying against it. I even put the hat on, tucking my hair in to hold it firm. Odds were good I would need my ancestors' advice.

Advice they didn't wait to provide. Alicia Blackheart's sweet, affectionate voice murmured. "A second of yoah time, honeysuckle. Ah have been preparing a present for you, and ah do believe you need it now."

My great-great-grandmother's sweetness always sounded predatory, and even more sinister given the timing. I replied cautiously, "What?"

Alicia's blue outline materialized, which she should not have been able to do without me. The ghost drifted across the room to the wall niche in which Revivienne lay. Patting Revivienne's hands, Alicia said, "Heah. It's a present from both of us."

I followed her. Despite my suspicion, Revivienne lay as peacefully as ever, hands crossed over a rib cage layered in purple silk ruffles, and with a purple hat much like mine but more elaborate covering the skeleton's face. I could, just barely if I focused and searched, see the blue tracery around Revivienne's fingers of masterpiece-quality necromancy that hadn't completely faded in the hundred years since this skeleton was raised from the dead. Only mostly faded.

From under those hands, I pulled out a silver chain necklace with a shiny pendant of a flower with four white petals.

"Dogwood," Alicia identified. "Ah do wish yoah parents would take you back to where ah was born sometime. It was beautiful country for a necromancer to grow up in. Try it on."

The necklace part was tight enough I had to squeeze and wriggle it down over my head, and of course I'd finally managed to get it settled around my neck before I felt the clasp I was meant to use to take it on and off. Even in this cold room, I felt magic in the pendant, a chill in those ceramic petals and a sticky sensation as it tugged at my magic when my fingers touched the surface.

Warm and approving, a silhouetted hand touching her chin, Alicia said, "It looks lovely on you. Ah wish you were mah own daughtah, and—" She sighed. "—but the dead have many regrets. Give it some powah."

Uh huh. Give it power. Alicia had taken over my body once,

so first I filled myself with cold necromancy, a barrier to keep out invasion, before touching the flower with my fingertips and feeding some of that cold into it.

Instead of invading, it yanked out a bigger drink of necromancy than I'd expected. A breeze started around me, swirling, tickling my skin as my shirt and overalls dissolved into a colorful spiraling cloud. At the same time, a cloud of black dust poured out of the necklace, joining the spiral around me.

The black sank in, until I felt fabric, not wind. My magical staff got a lot heavier. The dust of my original clothing flowed into the necklace and disappeared.

Although it wasn't really a necklace anymore. It had transformed into a loose, comfortably soft choker. I now wore a knee length dress with an uneven hem around my knees, fringed in long, ragged strips that fluttered but didn't get in the way of movement. Black stockings underneath covered all conceivably visible skin down to solid black boots. A foot-wide black belt circled most of my waist. High black lapels merged into black ruffled shoulders, whose sleeves slimmed to meet black, nearly elbow-length gloves with pointy fingertips. My magic hat had reshaped into a hood that tucked into the lapels like part of the costume. Questing fingers found a pointy tip on the back of the hood. The glove fabric was much thinner than it looked, and a single step confirmed it was easy to move in.

Thin black blades with a raven-head theme clustered around the top of my staff, turning it into a scythe.

I shook my head. "Nope. No scythe. It's dumb, it's not me, and as the only necromancer alive, I might as well be wearing an 'I'm Avery Special' sign."

With my power raised, my accent was gone again, which was always a relief to hear.

Alicia's ghost waved a silhouette hand. "Ah told Revivienne you would feel that way, and ah nevah liked them mahself, but the deah thing insisted on trying. Turn the pendant to the left."

I reached up and felt the collar around my neck. Yes, the dogwood flower was still there at the front. I twisted it. The pendant resisted slightly, turned suddenly, and clicked into a new position. The scythe blades dissolved into ash, sucked into the pendant, and the ash that flowed out coalesced replaced the blades with a big, angular crystal, probably just dark quartz, held to the tip of my staff with thorny claws.

I could handle that, but "How...?"

Amused, Alicia answered, "Honey child, if ah knew how sophisticated clothing magic worked, ah would nevah have need Revivienne. Well, except foah the company. Revivienne provides the spells, and ah provide the magic."

Irritation overrode my astonishment, and I snapped, "I meant how did you get the magic, and you know it."

Alicia Blackheart went still. After a second of that she sighed, and waved the hand poised next to her chin. "Ah would rathah keep this mysterious, but ah can see you'll get all bent out of shape about it. Sweetheart, you've been doing all this practicing, trying to use yoah magic efficiently. Ah have been... let's say, sweeping up the crumbs. Those magic circles yoah teacher is so fond of have been wondahfully convenient."

"I can barely wake Revivienne up!" I argued back.

Sympathetic and great-great-grandmotherly, Alicia said, "Yoah a beginnah, honey child. Ah've had rathah moah practice at getting the most from mah magic, and you have been doing rathah a lot of training. It's doing you a world of good."

"Where have you been storing this much magic?" I demanded next. Even for Alicia, this could not have been trivial.

The ghost turned amused. "A lady does need some secrets. Someday, darling, ah'll teach you everything ah know, if you let me. One step at a time. Raht now, you needed a disguise."

Because that was inarguably true, I reached up and touched my bare face. "Without a mask, it won't help much."

Even more delight honeyed Alicia's spectral voice. "Oh, but that's the cleverest part. Revivienne always keeps a mirrah on hand."

I knew where it was. As elegant as Revivienne's gown looked, it was covered in pockets containing sewing equipment, all hidden by ruffles and ribbons and fabric flowers. From one of them, I pulled out a small hand mirror and took a look at myself.

My face was invisible. Inky, contourless black hid it,

stretching from one side of the hood to the other, except for angular white eyes that might or might not actually be glowing. The hood already covered my distinctive hair.

I held the mirror out at arm's length. I looked like any magic-themed supervillainess. One of the more modest ones. I was already adult height, and with my face covered, in this getup, you couldn't tell I was only fifteen.

I didn't want to thank the ghost who'd been sneaking around stealing magic, and searched for something else to say. "Not sure about the heels." The boots weren't completely flat, and didn't look as practical as they felt.

"Revivienne wanted them much highah, but ah said this was foah you, not for me," Alicia said.

Silence descended.

The outline of my great-great-grandmother drifted closer, until touches of blue formed inside the silhouette, and I glimpsed a gentle smile as she said, "Ah quite undahstand, but ah want you to undahstand, honey child, that whatevah you think of us, your family is always looking out for you. Now, yoah peers ah waiting."

The invisible Numlah snorted in distain. "More like sheep she's been tasked to shepherd."

Opening the door as little as possible to slip through, I left Alice's crypt and emerged on the Los Angeles (Culver City?) sidewalk again.

Chapter Twenty-Seven

Delphine, Olga, and Hodir boggled. They were in bad costumes and cheap Halloween masks, although Hodir had managed to strap an impressive array of odd death-metal-themed accessories like shoulder pads over his pajamas, and Delphine's leotard was unquestionably sleek. A bad costume, but not bad-looking. So, this was why they'd been wearing the weird, loose hoodies.

Tonika didn't react to my new look and was in her black leather bodysuit, but with a shiny purple helmet now.

Delphine and Hodir were holding hands. It's hard not to notice something like that, even if they showed no sign of noticing themselves.

Doctor Biotic gave me a nod. I couldn't tell where her pitch-black eyes were looking. "Well done." All she had on were knee-high boots with flaps, and that bikini from Chinatown. Or maybe an even smaller one. Her strategy clearly was to draw all attention to her tattoos, and it worked for me. They were more a costume than any amount of fabric.

I told the professional superheroine, "I still feel like it's spitting in the wind. The moment I raise the dead, everyone will know who I am."

Still no accent, or only a tiny one, anyway. That always made me feel a bit more confident. I needed it. The ghost robot... I had to do this. I had to. But my parents had cracked down once, and if they found out I'd committed a supervillain robbery in costume, my life would come crashing down.

And still I had to do this.

Tonika certainly sounded confident. Well, she sounded firm. Unless she went robotically flat, the best her high, nervous voice could manage was "trying hard." "No, I thought about that. Museums have a careful relationship with heroes and villains. If we don't destroy anything, just take what we want and go, they won't even share the security footage with superheroes."

Doctor Biotic's mouth quirked up slightly on one side. "Assuming this museum has security cameras at all."

"Right. So where is this mystery museum that closes before rush hour?" I asked, looking up and down this extremely not fancy or remarkable street. I mean, I could see some restaurants, so it wasn't awful, either.

Doctor Biotic's jaded smirk pulled up a fraction more. "You just stepped out of it, and it's not your usual museum."

There was nothing to do but turn around and peer at the door, with its itty-bitty plaque that read *Museum of Jurassic Technology. Open Thursday—Sunday.*

"Museum of what now?" I asked, boggled.

Tonika stepped up, literally and conversationally. "The story goes that a wealthy creationist left a fund in his will to create a museum to house all the evidence that humans and dinosaurs lived side by side. Once the scientists who ran the museum did that, they looked around and decided they needed to put something in all the empty rooms."

Doctor Biotic affirmed, "I've been here before. It's cute."

Tonika, her taking-charge tone edged by natural shyness, declared, "At the moment, we're interested in an exhibit of unsolved magical puzzles."

"Well, my door won't get us in," I warned them, not wanting to explain Alice more than I had to.

Hodir shook a gleefully excited fist. The left one, the one not holding Delphine's hand. "Extradimensional closet! NICE. I can do those, but half the time when I open the hole again, the thing I pull out wasn't the thing I stored. One time I—" He stopped, and I just barely spotted the quiver as Delphine squeezed his hand hard.

"We'll melt the door lock with warp lightning," Tonika the Practical said.

I scowled, not comfortable with all this bad guy stuff to begin with.

My expression might be invisible, but Doctor Biotic saw something in my body language. She patted me on the shoulder. "The museum's supervillain insurance will pay for it. Just don't damage anything else."

Hodir suddenly twitched, and he started to stammer. "I, uh, I'm not good at—"

Delphine squeezed his hand again, longer and accompanied by an intense and reassuring smile. Quietly, she told the blond boy, "We can do this."

"You would know," he mumbled awkward. Then, abruptly, Hodir jerked up straight, a beaming grin on his face. "Oh, yeah, you would know! Awe—" He stopped, interrupted by another hand squeeze, and fumbled, "Right, right."

Hodir and Delphine stepped up to the door together. Hodir extended his fingertip, touching the keyhole of the old-fashioned twisty latch door lock. He looked up at Delphine with wide, cautious, questioning eyes, and got a nod back.

They both stared hard at the lock as green sparks like arcing electricity but, well, green, crawled over the metal. An itchy breeze blew past me.

The lock didn't so much melt as sag into slime. Delphine turned the handle, but the door pushed open even before she finished.

We stepped inside. The "museum" looked like a small, converted house on the inside, just like it had on the outside. Wooden walls, a reception desk, and magazine and book racks decorated the front room.

In the intrusively quiet room, Tonika murmured, "Spread

out. The collection will be labeled. Don't touch anything."

She and her friends spread out between different doors and halls. Delphine and Hodir went together, still holding hands. Holding hands tight, like they were afraid to be separated for a second. They'd known each other, what, a week? Two? They'd sure fallen for each other fast.

Then again, Sue and Chris knew they wanted me about fifteen minutes after we met. All I'd known at the time was that Chris was gorgeous and charming, and Sue and I could work with and count on each other in a pinch. Which was pretty much what I knew now, just add a lot of making out.

Thinking of Chris, it was a good thing my friends weren't here after all. Delphine and Hodir did not need Hodir's crush on my super-handsome boyfriend causing jealousy issues.

I looked up at Doctor Biotic, surprised to realize I was only looking slightly up. This costume really drove home that I was about as tall as I would ever get already. "Are you going to get in trouble for this?"

She didn't even bother to shrug, just answered blandly, "Some. That's part of why I'm here. I'll take the heat, make the excuses, and no one will ask who the kids I took on one of my crazy binges were. Not that this one is crazy. I'm expecting it to be as dull as dishwater."

I nodded, and turned my attention to business. No more worrying about my secret identity. Thanks to Alicia and Tonika and Dr. Biotic, I could put that aside and focus on the job.

I felt a faint tickle of magic. I followed it down the hall, past the little display case with a picture of Noah's ark, looped around a room whose walls were covered in pages with writing on them, and headed to the back of the building.

In back, by narrow stairs leading up, I found a room with two rows of little tables. Under plastic boxes lay a bunch of objects teasing me with different magical sensations. The walls were painted black—no, dark blue, and the lights kept dim, which seemed to be a theme for most of this museum.

Olga, her light web strung between her fingers, stepped in from the door by the stairs. She started to call out, "I found—oh."

Olga looked past me. Tonika stepped past me, heading

towards Olga as I leisurely began to circle and inspect the exhibits. Carved bones, a normal-looking jigsaw puzzle, some metal rings, several boxes, stuff like that, most of them magic. Wasn't sure about the bones. The jigsaw puzzle was super magic, for all it looked like a regular children's toy that should take half an hour to assemble.

In this quiet building, I could easily hear Olga mumbling to Tonika, "I don't know why I'm even here. I can't contribute anything."

Tonika squeezed both of Olga's shoulders, then hugged her, murmuring back, "This is step one to help you control your own powers. Until then, you're here because you're part of the team, and you're part of the team because we're friends. We would miss you if you weren't here."

Aw. Good job, Tonika.

Louder, I asked, "So what are we looking for, exactly? It's all magic. Most of it, anyway."

Currently, I'd stopped in front of a table with a little metal puzzle box. Every exhibit had a transparent plastic box over it, but the covers weren't fastened down and I lifted this one and put it aside. A little sign in front of the puzzle box read:

Discovered last year in Los Angeles, this box of uncertain age and origin is not hard to open. The mystery is what is inside. Several magicians have provided different answers to what the little black speck the box contains is, but they all agree that it's horrible. Our curator has seen it himself, and agrees.

Lying next to the box was a photo of the box with its various sliding bits pulled out, enlarging it and exposing the core. Sure enough, inside floated a little black dot. It didn't look scary.

I touched a fingertip to the metal surface and felt something awful, like the magic inside was clawing at the surface, trying to get into my finger but unable to escape the box. Whispers teased my ears, not quite understandable.

I jerked my hand back, and the sensations stopped. Yep, that was horrible. Was that what witnessing my powers was like? It would definitely explain why people freak out.

As an afterthought, I put the cover back on as well.

That had taken hardly any time, and I was startled when Tonika answered my question. "The enchanted treasure chest of Extravago the Extravagant."

And I was startled again as Alicia Blackheart yowled, "The what of who!? That's nonsense! Extravago was a fraud. A bunko artist. A literal snake oil salesman. He could be chahming when he wanted to be—" And for a moment her tone turned wistfully fond, only to harden into denial again. "—but he didn't have a speck of magic in his body."

Again, there were several big boxes with locks or apparently sealed lids, most decorated with symbols. I resumed circling, checking the plaques.

And was stopped again by another oddity. "Well, I'll be. Isn't this cuneiform?"

I couldn't read cuneiform, but the mashed together pointy arrows sure looked like it, especially imbedded in the surface of a thick tablet of dry clay, encased in a larger rectangle of perfectly see-through ice. No, crystal. It didn't give off cold. It certainly gave off magic, like the touch of old, dry paper.

Hodir stuck his head in the doorway, squeaking, "Cuneiform? Awesome! The first chaos mages were cultists in Akkadia! That's like if the city of Ur had a baby. What's it say?"

Despite being on the other side of the room, Tonika answered for me. "No one knows. It's most likely a forgery. The symbols are cuneiform, but mostly gibberish. The few readable parts describe a monster who takes over people's souls. The tablet isn't what makes it interesting. It's protected by a spell that is ancient even if its contents aren't as old as Sumeria. Any magical spell lasting more than three hundred years is impressive. Someone went to a lot of trouble to preserve a clay tablet with a fake inscription.

That was all pretty much what the sign in front of me said.

I looked back over my shoulder, even though my ancestors weren't physically there, asking, "Sumerian, huh? Can you—I'll take that as a yes."

Because Namluh had burst out laughing with uproarious glee.

The now properly invisible Alicia Blackheart, mildly amused, said, "I take it it's real."

His voice growly with feral delight, Namluh chortled, "Oh, it is, it is. It's about me!"

I raised an eyebrow no one could see. "You're saying this ancient relic is a real Sumerian story about you."

Namluh cackled, "BA HA HA HA HA HA. Did you think I was just some random priest? Namluh was a big name in my day!"

Fair enough. Any ancestor powerful enough to haunt me was big league. "So what's the story say? Condensed version."

"It's better than a story. It's a wanted poster," Namluh growled.

Horse Skull Kid started laughing now.

Oh, I could hear Namluh's smirk in the way he drawled over his words. "Old bush-beard always did hold a grudge. Let's say I stopped by the temple regularly to make sure his wife was protected from evil spirits."

Alicia joined Horse Skull Kid in hysterical laughter.

"Why can only you read it?" I demanded, still skeptical.

"Because he insisted on writing it himself, with lots of pretentious legal terms, and his spelling was terrible," Namluh explained, still wickedly gleeful, and even more so as his voice rose in sudden inspiration. "I'm sure we could use this to call him up if we worked together."

Folding my arms, which crossed my magic staff over my body, I reminded my ghosts, "I need the power for something a little more important than six-thousand-year-old gloating."

Namluh declared emphatically, "There is nothing more important than six-thousand-year-old gloating—except helping my descendants."

I paused for a second, and asked more solemnly, "Is all that really true?"

Namluh gasped. "Avery! My own blood! Would I lie?"

He got me. I snorted a laugh of my own.

Then I realized the other kids were all staring at me.

I summarized as fast and dismissively and with as much dignity as possible. "The tablet is real, it's not important, I'll tell you later. You asked for a necromancer. This is what you get."

The other kids weren't all standing together as they stared at me, though. Tonika lifted the case off of the display in front of her, and said, "This is the box."

I wandered around to take a look at it. Pretty big. Twice as long and wide as a shoe box, maybe three shoe boxes high if you included the lid. It was made of wood, painted blue, with golden but probably not gold metal edging and a series of Zodiac-shaped buttons on the lid, each in a different color. One button was missing, leaving a hole.

"Well, it's sure magic," I reported immediately. I didn't have to touch it to feel a gentle aura like writhing cotton. If you could be tickled by clouds, it would feel like this.

Tonika the researcher reported, "The Virgo symbol was believed to be a key, but it has been destroyed. The spell is too complicated to unravel. It's not empty, but no one can be sure what's inside without opening it. Breaking the box to open it would be a tragedy. I have... theories. I think the box isn't as unopenable as it looks, that the missing key is a red herring. The arguments I read about that online were convincing, but the only person who would know the truth is—"

I finished for her. "Extravago the Extravagant."

Tonika nodded, the dim lighting sending a gleam flickering over her purple helmet. How could she see in that thing? It must be like wearing sunglasses at night.

Returning to my actual problem, I asked, "How long has he been dead? Never mind, says here on the sign. About sixty years. I expect that's doable."

Alicia spoke up. "Ah hardly think you'll need us, but weah here if you do."

And hey, I didn't need seances to do this anymore. They'd been clumsy and dumb, even if they worked. Now I, the no longer completely novice necromancer, put my hand on the box lid.

Delphine pulled Hodir back to the room's doorway, which I admit was a little concerning.

Filling my voice with magic, I declared, "Extravago the

Extravagant! I avert the gaze of the seven eyes from you. I stand aside the guardians of the underworld. I open the gates and set you free. I am the Queen of the Dead, and I call you to answer me. Don't you want to tell us about this puzzle of yours?"

I was trying to not be too rough with ghosts these days, and I figured a con man would respond to a call like that.

He did. The power I'd been releasing was sucked away, a lot of it, enough to form the transparent but completely visible blue ghost of a man in a suit and cape and top hat. Visible not just to me, but to Tonika and her friends, whose heads all turned to look at him.

Flourishing his top hat, the ghost announced like a circus ringmaster, "Does someone wish to explore the mysteries known only to Extravago the GREAT JUMPING JEHOSEPHAT!"

Extravago jumped a couple inches higher in the air, cringing with his arms protectively in front of himself, and hung there.

Alicia Blackheart greeted with sly, predatory cheer, "Wah, hello theyah, Xavier." She pronounced it "eks-zayvee-er." "Fancy meetin' you heah."

Only straightening up a little, his hands fidgeting back and forth and waving his top hat, Extravago stammered, "Please don't hurt me. Look, it was all a big misunderstanding, and neither of us needs the money anymore, and Susie is gone, so there's nothing to stop us from starting over. You know I always loved you the most, but I had heroes threatening to melt my brain if I didn't give you up, and I knew you would rather I run away than be killed by anyone else. I was protecting you!"

The other kids were only looking at Extravago, so they must not have been able to hear Alicia. I was kind of captivated by the sheer chutzpah of the man myself.

"What's in the box, Xavier?" Alicia asked. Her voice sounded like candy-coated knives.

"The relics I mastered that gave me the power to pierce the veil of past and future!" Extravago answered, straightening up further, head lifted, as showmanship battled with desperation.

Delphine and Hodir grinned. Tonika held out her arm, and Hodir slipped her a low five.

Taking the conversation back, I asked the ghost, "How do I open the box?"

Some of Extravago's renewed confidence deflated. He flinched, addressing me but shooting the occasional glance at Alicia. "Oh. Well. You can't. Not without the key and the enchanted telephone receiver."

"Ahem," said Alicia, her silhouette's arms folded under her chest. Her friendly politeness oozed even more menace than anger would.

The Ghost of Extravago—he seemed like the kind of guy who would have a "the Ghost of"—waved his hat in his hand desperately, like he was warding off mosquitoes. "No, it's true! Honest! The woman who gave it to me said that the receiver forms a magical current between Libra and Sagittarius, and the key turning the lock has to be magical, too!"

I pursed my lips, thinking about that. "Since I have actual magical powers, I expect I can handle the first part. The key might be a problem. Although come to think of it, those old-fashioned keys were mighty simple, weren't they?"

Tonika, straight as a stick and looking particularly robotic in her "researcher' mode, reported, "People have tried picking the lock. It wasn't hard, but the spell still wouldn't let go."

Scratching my head with one of the thorns on my staff—and through the hood and my hair underneath I barely felt it—I decided, "I think... well, let me try this. It's not a hard puzzle, just until now nobody had the clues."

Which was exactly what Tonika predicted, right?

I stretched my right pinky and thumb between the woman holding scales button and the centaur button. I didn't have to press them. I gave them a trickle of magic instead, and felt a cold current start swimming in a circuit through my hand.

As for the key part... I held up my left hand, palm up. I focused on locking my muscles, holding it still while flailing around with the other, magical left hand. Awkward a start as that might be, I spotted the little blue blob that was left of that spectral hand bouncing around. With rapidly improving control, I slid the blob into the lock and fiddled around. The blob was pure magic, after all. It just had to fit inside and push the little lever thing that makes a lock work.

The lock clicked. The magical flow through my right hand stopped.

Everyone held their breath as I cautiously, delicately, afraid-to-damage-anythingly, raised the lid with both of my flesh and blood hands. The lid swung back easily.

The inside of the box was lined in purple velvet, and contained a ragged notebook, a little leather bag, a Ouija board, a crystal ball, and a compass. They were all magical, even the book. It was a nice magic. Smooth, gentle, a touch like soft plastic on my wrists, which were the closest part of me to the relics.

Tonika identified them in her blank cyborg voice. "The focusing tools of the Swamp Seer, Sophia Hutchins."

Alicia Blackheart gasped, and pulled back an inch. "Goodness gracious. Xavier, where did a—you stole them. You stole the relics of the Swamp Seer!" She sounded a little offended and a lot surprised.

Extravago still had that monumental chutzpah. He hardly shrank back at all anymore, and sounded more like he was making a noble declaration than begging for his afterlife. "She didn't need them anymore! Her great-great-granddaughter could barely use them."

Alicia's "surprised and a little offended" became "shocked and a little angry," which wasn't a big difference, but added a little squeaky roughness and volume to her exclamation. "You stole them from her family and heir!?"

I gave the ghost a huge grin, and suggested, "I expect you'd love to get out of here right about now."

The Ghost of Extravago gave me a very fast, very brief bow, and babbled, "Yes, great idea, thank you for summoning me!"

And with that, he took off towards the front door.

We all watched him go, everyone but Doctor Biotic looking as surprised as me. She was leaning against the wall of the hall, rubbing her knee and ignoring Extravago as he ran past her.

"I meant to send him to his rest," I told the quiet room.

Well, he couldn't do much harm before the power I'd used to summon him ran out anyway. He didn't have my relatives' ability to leech off me.

No longer stiff, official, and emotionless, Tonika patted Delphine in the back, urging her towards the box. Her visor hid her smile, but not the warmth in her tone. "All yours. See if you get a reaction from any of them."

That all wasn't my problem anymore. I gave my great-great-grandmother a puzzled look instead. "Am I missing something?"

Unusually enthused, her very transparent ghost clapped her hands together. "Darling, Sophia Hutchins was Carolina history. A legend. She used huh remarkable divination and claiyahvoyance powahs to help the Underground Railroad avoid the slave catchahs. She always said she was too cowardly to do the missions huhself, but if she slipped up once she'd have been executed. An astonishing woman."

Horse Skull Kid was barely visible, but his hands were on his hips and he sure sounded impressed. "Well, hogtie me to a mound'a black footed ferrets. Reckon we could call her up? I never got ta meet her, but I was a powerful admirer."

"Maybe if Delphine needs help with the talismans," I half-offered.

Delphine did not need help with the talismans. At that moment, Delphine lifted the crystal ball out of the chest with her right hand. Her left still held hands with Hodir. The ball glittered and began to glow. So did Delphine's eyes, in tiny, rainbow sparkles.

She blinked, and all the lights went out. In a horrified hiss, she whispered, "Someone is upstairs listening to us!"

Chapter Twenty-Eight

That someone squeaked. A woman who matched that high-pitched sound crept down the stairs, bent forward and clinging to the banister to look as harmless as possible, which she was naturally good at. Dull brown hair hung in two long, braided pigtails down her back. Her circle-framed glasses were absolutely enormous, and her white button blouse and charcoal-grey skirt hung around a stick-thin body. Rolled down white socks called attention to perfectly ordinary blue-and-white striped sneakers that somehow looked huge on her.

Magnified eyes wide with terror, she stammered, "Sorry! Sorry! Look, I won't tell anybody. I mean, I don't want to tell Steven that I left the Laika exhibit cleaning until Wednesday night because I wanted to sneak in and study—uh, anyway, hi, my name is Nicole." She finished with a forced, crooked smile.

"No, it's not," Delphine corrected her, still peering into the crystal ball.

Not-Nicole paused, her face twitching, until she stammered more defeatedly, "Okay, my name is Nicotine Fastidious, but it's easier to tell people it's Nicole."

"Personally, I think Nicotine's a great name," I said. I mean, mine was Avery Special.

Her mousy face lit up in excitement, and she rose a few inches higher in her crouch. "Yes! Names. You're, uh…"

Hoo boy. Here goes. I hadn't wanted to say this, but now that I had to, I tried to sound solemn and professional. "Deathette. With any luck this is the only time you'll ever hear of me."

I'd gotten sucked into the job itself, the joy of using my powers. It had actually taken a minute to realize that I'd just been caught doing the one thing that made it absolutely plain who I was.

Nicotine descended the stairs step by slow step, pulling at the banister as if her hands were dragging her down against her will. Her face remained lit with nervous, ecstatic hope. "You can call up ghosts! Long dead ghosts! Like from the early twentieth century?"

"A fact I'd rather not get around, if you understand me," I said, which, um, I hadn't meant to sound like a threat, but definitely did.

Although if that worked… ugh. Whatever happened, I would rather face my parents than actually hurt someone just to keep them silent. Letting her think I might was… debatably justified.

Reaching the foot of the stairs freed Nicotine (or should I call her Nicole?)'s hands to wave furiously with her shaking head and flying braids. "No no! Just… I mean… I'm doing research… would you please, please, *please* call up a ghost for me?"

"That sounds like a good way to buy her silence," Tonika said, giving me a good way to seem professional but not a bloodthirsty jerk. I appreciated the save. Boy, howdy, did I.

Doctor Biotic shrugged. She still wasn't watching, just tugging at the collar of her boot.

Feeling boxed in but not wanting to buy a pig in a poke, I hemmed and hawed. "Well… I'll consider it."

Nicole (she would probably prefer that?) pumped her fist in victory. "Yes! This way! You'll understand when I show you this." Mercy, the relief and excitement on this girl's face. Woman's face. She had to be at least five years older than me, or even twice that. But fear and desperate hope transformed her into a child.

I followed the scuttling museum worker around to the room with the paper-lined walls. They were letters. Some handwritten, mostly typed, just lots and lots of text pinned to the wall behind plastic sheets. White paper on a white wall. At first glance, the room was as exciting as a furniture construction manual, only with fewer pictures.

Nicole rattled out an explanation in the face of my lack of being impressed. Or maybe in the face of my lack of face and how that made me look like I might rip her ghost from her body at any moment. Either way, lots of babble. "We're featuring a collection of the collected letters of famous mages who lived in LA in the twentieth century. Some of them were only here for a year or two, but still. There's one... well, there's so many legends about her, it's impossible to know what's true, and until now no one has been able to ask her personally, but you could call her up, right? You're a necromancer too. You have to have heard of her. Her name is—"

Glad she couldn't see my gawking expression, I cut over her. "—Alicia Blackheart."

Behind me, Alicia Blackheart gasped. "Oh, land sakes, these are mah lettahs, aren't they? Please tell me they only put up the tasteful ones."

Horse Skull Kid's outline walked past me to peer at the far wall's letters. "This Charlie fella seems mighty happy to have met you, but he ain't goin' into specifics. Shoot, look at all these. Ah reckon ah'm jealous."

Namluh added his two shekels. "BA HA HA HA HA HA."

Ignoring the frivolity, I gave Alicia a questioning look.

She stood there for a second, stiff instead of her usual languid, then answered, "Well... alright. But ah'm only answering dignified questions."

Reaching out my left arm, I touched two fingertips to the page Horse Skull Kid was reading, and called out, "Alicia Blackheart! I feel your presence in this room. What you cared about is close."

"Yes. You," Alicia said.

I continued the fake, or at least really super easy, incantation. "Awaken from your rest, please. It has been nearly a century, but one of your fans would love to meet you."

Letting go of the paper, I held my hand out to Alicia. She laid her cold, spectral hand on mine, and I fed even colder power into her, hoping I wouldn't regret that later. The old ghost was so sneaky.

Color filling in to a merely translucent blue woman in a slinky gown, Alicia declared coquettishly, "Well, ah do always have a moment foah mah fans."

Nicole's eyes bugged out. She clasped both fists to her chin and bit her fingernails. She reached new and breathy levels of charming, geeky awe. "Oh my goodness oh my goodness oh my goodness. Ah. Ee. Uh." Straightening up and brushing down her skirt, she made a bad attempt to compose herself into seriousness, like an objective interviewer. "Miss Blackheart. I'm not just a fan. I'm writing a paper on you. There are so many unanswered questions. I... I... I'm so sorry. First, I have to be responsible and prove it's you to my colleagues. What's at the center of the Appalachian Horror Orchard?"

Alicia crossed an arm under her chest, tilted her hips to one side, and fluttered a hand around airily. "A swing set, assuming the Orchahd is still theyah. Surely it's been burned down by now."

Nicole's head vibrated in a rapid head shake that only went an inch in either direction. "No, no. It's on the historic register and it's a federal supernature preserve. Nobody's allowed in after the preacher died in 1928 and the superhero—"

Alicia cut her off with an unusually sharp and shocked declaration. "1928? Before ah died? Why did ah nevah hear about this!? Gracious, ah hope the Orchahd didn't learn to feed on blood. It wasn't supposed to be dangerous, it was just a little girl playing with dolls."

Nicole whipped out her cellphone, typing furiously. Taking notes, maybe. Squinting at the screen and typing didn't interrupt her excited flow of conversation. "So that's why there are no letters about the incident. You didn't know!"

I started to relax again. This was working. Nicole was so

energized, so enraptured by meeting her idol. This had to be the right thing to do morally, and someone this happy with how I'd helped her could be convinced to keep it a secret.

Alicia told her. Reminded her? "Ah was a bit busy at the time. Ah wasn't even in North Carolina."

Still typing, Nicole nodded. "Yes. This was a year before you got pregnant. I hope—I mean, I hope your death isn't a difficult topic—" She looked up from the screen with wide, concerned, compassionate eyes.

Alicia shrugged, languid as usual. "Ah can't say it's a pleasant memory, but ah'm not upset."

Nicole stammered, "Just… so many people tried to kill you, but then you died in childbirth."

Alicia gave her a sad smile. Maybe an honest, sad smile. "Ah was weak, honey child. Ah had to stifle mah powahs for nine months. Necromancy does not react well with… well, expecting. The magic only sees an invasion to put down, and sweetie, when you're ready to have yoah own, remember that it's not an easy or safe process unduh the best of circumstances. Ah had hoped that ah could start using mah powahs to protect us both when we reached the stage that I was carrying an actual baby, and her own necromancy developed. Unfortunately, dear Samantha didn't inherit the gift. Ah regret nothing, by the way. Nothing." She swept a hand sharply horizontal to emphasize that point.

Nicole typed away, eyes flicking back and forth between ghost and phone. "So who was the father? There are so many debates. Buster Keaton—"

Alicia broke her off with a barking, "Absolutely not. Ah hadn't seen him in yeahs, and ah won't heah a word said to ruin his reputation. He had enough of that from—well, it's unladylike to speak ill of a man's wife, but it's no wondah he went looking for othah women. Ah wish… well, you must know how difficult ah could be with men mahself."

Finally calm and adult, Nicole told the ghost, "He eventually found a woman who was good to him for the rest of his life."

Alicia let out a long sigh, shoulders sagging in visible and audible relief. "Thank you. It's nice to heah that."

Nicole adjusted her glasses, back to typing, but not back to hyperactive freakout. Like a serious interviewer, she said, "I'd like to ask you about Revivienne. No one knows where you found them. Was Revivienne someone you knew when you were alive? Or a superhero?"

The femme fatale ghost donned a coy smirk. "Honey child, ah learned early nevah to reanimate anyone yoah close to. Ah—"

Nicole chimed in, and the two chorused together, "—have always relied on the corpses of stranguhs."

With a flutter of laughter in her voice, Alicia cheerfully began the storytelling. "Revivienne was one of those once-in-a-lifetime lucky events. Ah was getting fitted by a dressmakah and just realizing ah'd found an undiscovah'd fashion genius when the poor thing had a heart attack right in front of me."

From the back of the museum, Tonika called out nervously, "Avery? I think we need you."

I stepped out of the room promptly, but trying not to hurry in a way that might scare Nicole.

Doctor Biotic was leaning against the door frame of the magic puzzles room, and was an inch of sag from "slumped" against the frame. She held a metal and plastic cartridge against her neck—no, a big, fat, fancy syringe. Breathing hard, featureless black eyes wide, she whispered, "Sorry. Sorry. Being a capybara is just so boring."

Where had she even kept that mutagen cartridge? Her bikini had been designed to show off tattoos, and wasn't big enough for a pocket. Her boots. It must have been in a boot.

The tattoos moved. Her skin rippled, wrinkled, turned orange and spotty. The tattoos disappeared like they were being sucked under the surface of bumpy orange goo instead of skin. Blue circles bubbled up to replace them.

The heroine jerked. Her collapsing body went stiff instead, back arched. She made an "mmf" noise, and squeezed her eyes shut, even the ones on the side of her head. They reopened golden, speckly, and the pupils squeezed into horizontal bars before relaxing again.

In her most emotionless and technical voice, Tonika said,

"Doctor, you're probably feeling a little disoriented right now—"

Doctor Biotic lurched up to her feet, but her shoulders leaned forward and her arms dangled like a film zombie. Her voice was plenty sharp and animated, maybe too emphatic as she interrupted Tonika. "No, not disoriented. Hungry."

The superheroine's lips pulled back from her open mouth, revealing teeth that had gone weirdly saw-edged, and dripped purple liquid. Venom?

The doctor's scorpion tail, unaltered, jerked straight up with only the stinger bent alertly forward. Tonika and I stood at equal distances from her, me in the hall and Tonika in the room, both of us out of arm's reach but too close for comfort. The doctor chose Tonika to turn towards, her arms pulled back as she crouched in a theatrical and overdone but bizarrely fluid ready-to-pounce position.

I hit her with my claws. The spell could reach that far—out of stinger's reach—and still do damage. Invisible, inaudible, it also hit with no warning, so Biotic made no attempt to dodge.

Only I saw the three magic crescents slice through her. Everyone saw her drop to her knees, tail sagging to her shoulders, and groan. Even at this distance, that was less hurt than anyone else I'd hit with necromancy.

Voice still completely calm, Tonika asked, "Wouldn't you rather have shrimp than steak?"

Doctor Biotic groaned again. Her orange-and-gold skin stopped rippling. The blue rings stopped swimming around on it, and disappeared, replaced by butterflies. This time, the butterflies moved, flying across her skin on flapping wings. The skin itself shimmered sometimes.

"That did it," she confirmed between deep breaths. Pushing herself up, looking around with six opalescent but alert eyes, she continued with merely tired good cheer, "I would kill for some teriyaki shrimp right now, but I'm almost positive that's a metaphor. And barbecue crab. Have you ever dipped crab in barbecue sauce? It's so good."

"Any other disasters to avert?" I asked anyone and everyone, holding my staff ready at my side and drawing more power out of it to replace the quite a bit I'd spent on this adventure already.

At the far end of the puzzle room stood Delphine, still hand-in-hand with Hodir, peering into the sparkling crystal ball. She answered cautiously, "No. I... I'm almost sure."

Doctor Biotic took a few more deep breaths, and gave her head a shake to clear it. "Sorry. I'm sorry. I told you, Tonika. This is who I am. I can't stop. I don't want to stop. It's the only thing that never changes."

Finally straightening up fully, Biotic ran her hand through her fake, bubblegum-pink hair, which matched the bikini and hadn't seemed strange next to all the tattoos. Bubbles rushed up her legs and over her body, some over, some behind the butterflies. Another step more alert, Biotic continued, "In all seriousness, kids, I'm impressed with how smoothly this went, and you handled the little hiccups perfectly. As an apology and congratulations, let me take you all to a seafood restaurant. And get us out of here while the robbery is still a success."

I was not thrilled to have been part of a robbery, successful or not. On the other hand, the box was open, its treasures free, and Delphine was only taking the crystal ball. Plus, the researcher woman was getting information available nowhere else. Was it exactly theft when you leave the victim with more than they had when you started?

I returned to the letters room, knocked on the door frame with my staff, and said, "Miss Nicotine? I have to go, and the spell goes with me."

She and Alicia's ghost had been huddled together close, chattering and typing. Now the museum keeper jerked her head up nervously, and stammered, "Oh, no. It's okay. Thank you. Thank you so much. Thank you both. Getting to actually talk to Alicia Blackheart is a history breakthrough."

Trying for firm but not too threatening, I reminded her, "I'd strongly rather nobody know about what happened tonight, Miss Nicotine."

Only a little nervous in the face of the faceless, black-clad supervillainess Queen of the Dead, Nicole nodded a mere half a dozen times and not even in any hurry. "That will be fine! It won't be a problem. It'll be at least a year before I publish. Maybe two. I won't say where I spoke to Alicia, or who made it possible."

I thought about it. Even if it was tracked back to me, it wouldn't be tracked back to me being supervillainous. "...yeah, that will work. Let's get going, Miss Blackheart."

Alicia drifted over to me, still smiling back at Nicole. "It was a pleasure. You're a charming young lady, Miss Nicotine, but you really should get out and have moah fun."

"I think for her this is fun," said Doctor Biotic beside me.

Alicia and I touched hands. I drew my power out of her ghost, making her fade away until even I could barely see her.

Leaning over, the now graphically animated Doctor Biotic murmured into my ear, "So you know what to expect: LA's supervillains are the world gossip champions. I don't know how, but they will know that Deathette walked tonight. What they won't do is tell the superheroes. Mech in particular won't know."

The freshly mutated heroine left me to corral super powered kids like sheep, herding them to the front door with considerably more enthusiasm than the bored heroine with the old, tedious mutations had herded us into this museum.

Tonika and I didn't need much herding, which let Tonika hang back long enough to nudge me with her shoulder and say, "I haven't forgotten about you. With Delphine's power working, I can find the time and place you need to be to deal with the robot on your terms. Give me a couple of days to work it out. I can do this."

I had to admit, this had gone well. Very well. Even if I didn't want it to have happened at all, Tonika had researched and planned everything as smooth as butter.

Nudging her shoulder back, I said with extreme sincerity, "I trust you, Tonika. But hurry, okay?"

Chapter Twenty-Nine

Just a couple more days. I just had to get through a couple more days.

That thought was bouncing around in my head as I sat down for breakfast on Thursday, and my dad said, "Where'd you get the pretty necklace?"

Chris gave it to me.

Sue gave it to me. She had money and liked giving me gifts.

Debating the exact lie to tell took enough time for guilt to hit. I didn't want to be this teenager. I was keeping enough secrets from my parents. Too many. Sure, almost all of them were debatably justified.

I would get through this crisis and figure out how and what to tell people after. Right now, I wanted to lie as little as possible.

"It's mah great-great-gramama's. She likes ta lead me to stuff she left behind in LA," I answered, poking at my grits. My mother loved grits, so grits got made.

I'd made the wrong decision. My father tensed up, and when a man that big tightened his shoulders, you could see it.

No. I'd made the right decision, just a right decision that might have ugly consequences.

"Can I hold it?" he asked, his expression noncommittal and his voice scrubbed of anything but mild curiosity.

I unhooked the chain, pulled the necklace off, and set it in his outstretched hand. I knew I might not get it back. I wouldn't mind so much, except for what that would say about how my parents didn't trust me. But it wasn't my choice, even if I was choosing for it to not be my choice. And I was pretty sure no one else in the world could activate it, or at least only I could activate it easily.

Dad fingered the short, delicate chain, turned the dogwood pendant over to look at its shiny silver back, then over again to admire its delicately curved front. It was pretty, fancy in subtle ways, like the slight curve on the petals. They weren't just flat cut-outs.

He was still working really hard to have his expression and voice neutral as he asked, "What does it do?"

Great. Another of those moral choices getting flung at me rapid-fire lately. I'd lied about too much lately. I wasn't going to fall into the trap of doing it casually. Alrighty. My policy from now on would be to tell as much of the truth as I possibly could without endangering someone else.

Unfortunately, if I didn't get to resolve the ghost robot situation myself, yes, people were in danger.

So I shrugged, and told a lot of the truth. "Somethin' to do with clothing. Alicia was simply mad about fashion. Ah can't say ah share huh tastes, but the necklace is lovely."

His eyes still on the pendant, Dad asked, "Do you talk to Alicia often?"

I winced, probably visibly. I'd known that question was inevitable.

And like a snake out of a hole, the answer burst out of me, pained and angry. "Ah don't live in the same world as regular folk, Dad. Yeah, ah talk to her way more'n ah lahk. Ah'm surrounded by stuff that normal people don't nohow have t' decide what to do 'bout, on account they don't never know it's there. Like..."

I closed my eyes, focused on my sense of touch. Because I'd been telling the truth, that didn't take more than a second.

Lifting one arm, I waved my hand towards the back of the house. "...there's somethin' magic goin' on in that there direction."

Dad's clumsy attempt to look mysterious vanished. He stood up straight and swiveled around to look at the back wall of the kitchen. His big, big fists clenched, and one of his beefy arms extended in front of me across the table, as if he could shield me with it. "What is it?"

The answer only made me more frustrated. "Ah don't know! It ain't near. Ah spec it's fah away, but terribly strong. Whether or no, ah guarantee ah'll pass something magic in the street today. Ah sit in mah bedroom and know something is happening neahby. Ah see ghosts when ah go on dates! And that there's just the big stuff. I'm doin' the best I can, but bein' a necromancer dumps a mighty amount on your head. One'a those things is my great-great-grandmama showin' up sometimes when I don't even call her, wantin' to give me advice, or treasures she left in LA, or what all, because she may not have a drop of mercy in her, but she loves huh family deahly. It's easy to not make bad decisions when you don't have to make decisions at all. The necklace is pretty and it ain't dangerous. It's some kinda clothing magic."

I stopped, panting for breath. That had all come out wild, then circled around by itself to where it began. It left my heart aching, and I wasn't sure if I felt guilty or not.

Dad slowly relaxed, at least in terms of guarding me from whatever was still going on behind the house. It was a peculiar sensation, like a bug walking over my skin, faint and occasional. It also wasn't important.

Turning back to me, his face turned back to badly masked, but the fake calm was laid over a worried frown rather than a suspicious one. He was even worse at keeping it out of his voice. "Maybe we shouldn't have brought you to LA, for your sake."

I shook my head, woolly hair flapping. "I'd still have mah powahs, ah just wouldn't know how to control theyem. Ah would'a found all the magic lurkin' in Lexington, or I spec more likely it would'a found me. This way, least ah'm kinda sorta prepared for what life and undeath throws at me."

Dad leaned over the table. His big hands, with their scratchy callouses and the flannel of his sleeve cuff, fastened the neck-lace back around my neck. Leaning further, he kissed the top of my head.

At least a little relief wrangled with the other confused emotions twisting in my heart. Disaster had been averted for a little longer, but my parents were suspicious—and with very good reason.

I tucked the pendant of the necklace under my shirt on the way out to the car, and spent the trip to school in silence, resting up from the weight of that conversation.

Sue waited for me, and as I left Dad's car behind and trudged up the grass towards her... horror replaced my grumpiness. The purple bruises all over her body had turned a hideous green. I'd expected, somewhere deep down, that having super powers and superhero parents would let Sue heal her bruises quickly, just like something had fixed the broken bones that had to have come with the bruises.

Completely unbothered, Sue gave me a quick little kiss when I stepped up to meet her. I slipped a protective arm around her shoulders as we headed inside, and watched the girls around us in case anyone thought Sue's appearance meant she was vulnerable.

Sue wasn't just unbothered. With my arm around her, she strutted through the halls like she'd won a prize.

I didn't know what to talk about during lunch, so I focused on eating. Sue didn't need or want to talk. It was one of those days when she was content to lean against me and relax with a soft, weak smile.

That made me feel a little guilty. Not because of the robot thing, but because it was another reminder that Sue was madly in love with me, and I wasn't in love back.

But... it was so, so sweet to see my friend who put on an act everywhere else let down her guard and be comfortable and at peace for a few minutes.

Lunch ended, and classes were classes. There were molecules to learn about, and school didn't care if around two o'clock I felt repeated bursts of tapping on my skin, like the lightest rain. A touch, and nothing. A touch, and nothing. It got stronger for thirty seconds, and then weaker for thirty seconds, then was gone. Something magical had passed by outside. I'd been honest with my father about that. This kind of thing happened so often I only noticed this time because that conversation had me thinking about it.

Was I getting more sensitive as my control over my powers improved? No time to think about that. Molecules.

So it was only when school was over and Sue walked out the front door, leading me towards her family's waiting car, that I asked, "Am ah goin' home with y'all today? Ah ain't been keepin' track."

Holding my arm with both of hers, Sue answered brightly, "No, you're going on a date with Chris this afternoon."

I squinted. "Feel sure I'd remember scheduling that." A second later, I added, "Not that I'm complainin'."

"I scheduled it for you, because I knew you wouldn't complain," Sue told me airily.

Which was everything I'd believed about the situation, said out loud. Since Sue was right, and I even kind of liked letting her and Chris manage my time and attention this way, I didn't complain. I did feel a little weird about it happening now, with a crazy robot lurking in the shadows.

Sue and I sat in the back seat as Winifred drove us through LA's dusty-looking streets. Sue was still quiet, her eyes closed and her head leaned back against the seat, but she held my hand tight and didn't let go for the whole trip.

I squeezed back, and tried to think about the strangeness of my life right now, but my thoughts went nowhere. They didn't even circle. I just sat there pushing against a wall in my head for the whole drive.

What flash of revelation was I expecting, anyway? Hopefully, Tonika would come through before the poor ghost was killed again, or hurt someone else in its attempts to find me.

We pulled up in front of Chris and Annie's place. Their home looked nice, a three-story brick building with a vine covered brick wall fence around it, and a metal gate. It had at some point been an expensive almost-mansion. Now, I was pretty sure the floors were separated and someone different lived on each one. The front gate wasn't closed either, and what might have once been a lawn was mostly gravel.

Sue pulled me out through her door, which was weird even if it was the one facing the sidewalk. As I emerged onto the sidewalk, I smirked down at her grip on my hand. "So y'all're comin' on this date too?"

Sue didn't look at me, marching us into Chris and Annie's yard with her eyes fixed ahead, with downright super heroic focus. "I don't let go of the package until I've made the hand over."

She got me. I made a "pfft" noise of amusement, and grinned a lot as I let her pull me up the metal stairs on the side of the building that led to the door into the Domingo apartment, or condo, or whatever you called this kind of subdivided house.

With me standing on the landing of what might have been an upgraded fire escape, Sue knocked on that door. She only got to one knock. Annie yanked the door open, already looking back over her shoulder and calling out, "Chris, your girlfriends are here!"

She obviously just wanted to say it, because before she even finished shouting Chris stepped around the corner of the hall, adjusting his cufflinks. He and Annie were dressed in identical suits today, with high-waisted slacks and long tailed jackets in cream, tan buttoned shirts, and black suspenders. It might have looked a bit silly if the waistband of the pants didn't fit them exactly. As it is, they looked lithe and old-fashioned classy. In the process, they looked even more like twins than usual. The only difference in the outfits was the shape they had to fit, and Annie's shoes having heels two inches higher than Chris's. The split in the back of the jackets, of course, let their spade-tipped tails wave freely.

As always, the red-skinned, black-haired pair were effortlessly gorgeous. Just the line of Chris's chin, a little stronger than his sister's, could make me faint. Not to mention the confident smile and the glitter in his dark, dark eyes.

The smile and glitter disappeared as he got his first look at Sue, replaced by wide-eyed, open-mouthed horror. Annie was less demonstrative, but had already stopped crowing and stared at Sue's green-and-black bruised skin.

Chris's hand dove into his pocket, fumbled, and pulled out his phone. He tossed it back into his sister's hands and rushed forward to Sue. Voice shaky, he ordered, "Annie, call 911. Don't stand up, Sue. You could be doing even more damage to—"

Before Chris's arms could close around her, Sue extended her arm and placed her finger to his lips. "Like, save it," she ordered right back, and then pointed her finger at Annie. "Don't you dare."

I gave Sue, who should have been expecting this, a sharp look, and asked the rhetorical question, "First time they've seen you this week, right?"

As exasperated as if everyone was being unreasonable and she didn't look like she'd crawled out of a morgue, Sue waved her hands in front of her. "I'm totally fine. I'll tell you more later, but there's, like, no broken bones or anything, I just look hideous."

Chris's hands fell, or at least fell far enough to take hold of Sue's. That included prying one out of its grip on my hand. Holding Sue's hands to his chest, he leaned down to give her a quick kiss, and asked softly, "You're sure?"

Sue growled and pushed him away—but waited until after the kiss to do it. Scowling at the floor and fussing with her hair, she snapped, "I hate it when you put on that sweet and considerate act." She obviously did not hate it, and knew it wasn't just an act.

"If you're sure," Chris murmured. He hesitated a moment, his eyes searching Sue's mauled face, before turning his attention to me. When he did, those eyes lit up as they always did, with that little touch of excitement just from seeing me. With only the faintest lingering touch of solemnity, he said, "Then the next obvious question is, what's this new necklace?"

Sue's head jerked up, and she looked straight at my neck. "Oh, right! Like, I didn't want to ask at school."

Hoo doggies. Time to do this again, with a friendlier audience that also trusted me to share my secrets with them. Which I wasn't this time.

But I could share a lot more secrets, so I said, "Well, uh..."

and pulled the pendant out of my shirt, dangling it for inspection. "Ah got it from ma great-great-grandmama. Didn't think school'd want it to show, but it's right pretty, so ah wanted to wear it in general, like."

Also, the way things were going, I felt like having a costume handy at all times just might be a smart idea.

Sue immediately frowned. Chris looked skeptical too, tapping his perfect chin with a fingertip. He didn't hide his entirely reasonable concern as he asked, "It's Alicia's?"

I nodded awkwardly, "Yeah, but it ain't necromancy. It's, uh... well, this here's a costume spell. Like, a supervillain, necromancer costume that—" I stopped, faced with Chris's and Annie's identical stares of fascination and lips-parted anticipation. Even more awkwardly, I finished, "Y'all want me to show you, doncha?"

"Yes," said Chris and Annie, at exactly the same time and in exactly the same tone—emphatic, almost begging.

I looked around. With the fence and the way the stairway was set back between buildings, we weren't all that visible from the street, and the windows around us were dark, and someone would have to be trying really hard to see us...

I surrendered to the inevitable with a huge sigh and a flap of my arms. "Oh, alright. Ain't sure how it'll go without mah hat and staff."

The necklace was pretty, and I wanted to wear it publicly anyway. I'd only had it tucked away for school. Pulling it out, I gave it some juice. Clouds of dust, black and white and blue, swirled around me. New clothing replaced old. Even without my magic hat, the costume still had a hood. It felt a little different, but without a mirror I couldn't check how. A hood meant my face would still be shrouded in darkness, anyhow.

All the clouds of color messed with my vision, and when they settled down I found myself faced with Sue and Chris, standing side by side, holding each other's hand. They stood very straight, and very still, gawking. Just... gawking.

Barely above a whisper, eyes fixed on me, Chris asked, "We're the lucky ones, aren't we?"

Just as quiet, just as fixated, Sue answered, "We totally are."

Aaaaaand I blushed. Really, really hard, my cheeks painfully hot and tight. It took all my effort not to squirm, and thank goodness the illusion concealed my face. It was always like this, every time. I was comfortable having a boyfriend, and it hadn't taken me long to be comfortable having a girlfriend. When they both together gave me that "hungry, lost, rapturous, passionately in love" stare like they were looking at the world's greatest treasure and it was theirs... my knees threatened to buckle beneath me.

Annie was gawking too, but with a different joy. Her eyes darted over me with the love of clothing, not the person who was wearing it.

I got control of myself enough to take hold of the pendant and say with a completely steady voice, "Not wearin' this on a date, though, so I reckon you're outta luck."

A burst of power, more swirling color, and I was back in my school uniform. That broke the spell over my romantic partners as well, or at least cracked the spell enough for Sue to release Chris's hand and take a step away.

Still a little goggle-eyed, glaring resentfully at a world that made her say this rather than anyone or anything in specific, Sue growled, "I hate to cut loose, but... like... I guess it's not always me and Avery time. You two take care of her, okay?"

Annie nodded furiously. Chris tore his eyes off of me to give Sue a warm smile, answering, "Take care of yourself, please? The only reason I'm not calling an ambulance is that I trust you. You still... just take care of yourself. Heal."

Sue laughed, a joyful sound without even a hint of cruelty. Her skirts swirled as she flounced down the staircase. The swirling was another reminder that I was still wearing my ridiculous school uniform. Would I never be free of skirts?

Well, at least Chris and Sue liked the look.

Pouncing on a new thought, I raised an eyebrow at Chris. It was my turn to sound playfully skeptical. "So, 'you two?' Is Annie chaperoning?"

Chris clasped his hands together, leaning to the side in an exaggerated display of utterly fake awkwardness. "Weeeeell, as much as I love a little kissing, or a lot of kissing—" Behind him,

Annie snickered. She was so much less shy when it was just the three of us. "—this might not actually be a date. I might go so far as to say that Annie wants to spend time with you, and she'd be too nervous if I wasn't along, so the three of us are going to a movie double feature and then the library."

"Ah love this idea!" I exclaimed, shooting up straight with excitement.

Annie lunged forward, wrapping an arm around Chris and my heads, pulling us into a hug as she squeaked, "You're both so good to me!"

Chapter Thirty

I stuffed my last few french fries into my mouth, freeing my hands to help me climb out of Mrs. Domingo's car. Chris and Annie followed, the three of us crowded together on a downtown sidewalk—although downtown sidewalks were a lot less crowded than I would have expected. Buildings were packed tighter in Glendale, honestly.

Mrs. Domingo waved through an open car window. "Bye, kids! Text me when it's pickup time! Annie, make sure they—"

"MAMA," barked Chris, cutting her off.

Suddenly, I knew where Chris got his trait of being *almost* always a good boy. I also savored the rare experience of seeing Chris blush. Even if the color wasn't visible on his already-scarlet face, his tense body language screamed embarrassment. Chris and Sue didn't experience embarrassment much. They knew exactly what they wanted: Me.

Which still didn't make sense, but boy howdy was it true.

Mrs. Domingo laughed gaily, set the windows to rolling up, and drove off.

Grinning with maybe just a touch of unavoidable smirk, I said, "You know, I ain't hardly gotten to know your folks."

"Don't," Chris grumped, shoulders still pulled up awkwardly.

Annie was not interested in her mother teasing her brother. She took my wrist and pulled me towards the entrance of the LA Main Branch Public Library, a building that loomed not by being tall, but by being a long, rambling thing that rightly should be five buildings covering multiple blocks. This side of it had a solid, blocky look, all in pale beige stone, like an Egyptian tomb. It wasn't tall, it was... massive.

Chris, happy to change the subject, took hold of my other arm, escorting me towards the undeniably imposing archway hiding the actual doors. Suave and at peace again, he gave me a twinkling smile and said, "But much more importantly, what did you think of the movies?"

"They were fun! Ah'm glad we went," I said.

Annie whipped her head around and gave me a hard look, somewhere been scold and pout. Chris burst out laughing. Together they ushered me through the front doors, and through the security sensors on the other side. I wondered again, should I return those necromancy grimoires? I had probably learned everything I could from them. If I really needed black magic spells designed by people of questionable morality, I could call up a ghost. Besides, someone else might benefit from the *Pudgy Bunny* book. That was a blessing that needed passing on.

"Ahem," Chris said, pulling me back from my distracted guilt.

I blinked. "What? They were fun!" I wasn't lying. I'd had a great time!

Annie grimaced in emotional pain. Chris grinned enormously. Slowly and carefully, clearly enjoying himself, he explained, "While we're delighted that Avery Special, Annie's friend and my girlfriend, had fun, we just watched two horror movies and we'd like to hear what Avery Special the Queen of the Dead thinks about them."

If my hands weren't both taken, I'd have slapped my forehead. "Oh! Shoot, I ain't used ta bein' able to talk to anybody 'bout this here stuff."

I took a few seconds to rearrange my thoughts, but honestly, this topic came easily. "Well, first off, you gotta understand, they don't ask a necromancer afore they film these here movies. I don't reckon they ask any type'a magic person. Now, zombies and cursed dolls and what-all don't scare me none—"

Chris broke in slyly, "Nothing scares you."

With a snort, I countered, "Wish that were true."

Annie put her finger to her lips. "Shhh! Don't distract her."

Right. Back to my topic. "Now, y'all know what I think'a modern fungus-type zombies."

"I could hear it again," said Chris. Annie nodded repeatedly and enthusiastically.

Well, fine. I rolled my eyes in disgust. "It's just sloppy. Iff'n they ain't dead, just sick, how's that even a zombie? Shoot, they might as well be werewolves. I mean, I kin take or leave boys with fur, but they got fangs'n what-all for threat rather than just relyin' on grossness. And hoo boy, the downside of all zombies is that they're gross. Bein' a necromancer don't make 'em any less nasty when they're all cut up meat and the insides rot into slime—what happens real fast-like, and is grosser'n you would believe. 'Course, necromancy kills bacteria but good, and iff'n you get the body fresh a decent reanimation'll put off the gross stages near-on forever."

Pausing for a second, I added, "Ah think ah'm getting' side-tracked heah."

"Yes, but it's a cool sidetrack," Chris assured me.

"We love it," Annie echoed.

While I'd been lost in my righteous rant about the perils of zombie raising, Chris and Annie had managed to steer me all the way through the library to one of the rooms with book racks and tables looking over the pit. I noticed this because Annie pulled me into a chair at one of those tables.

Taking a deep breath to pick my rant back up at a more movie-focused spot—

—the clatter of stomping metal feet threw all those thoughts away. Through the windows occupying the whole inside wall, I saw a metal shape at ground floor level. A robot was heading for the escalators.

But not my robot. This one was steel, not white, and had a

little girl riding on its shoulder. A guy wearing a lab coat trailed behind them.

Right. Father, daughter, mad science creation. It happened. Not everything was about me.

Chris and Annie saw the robot too, maybe just following my gaze, but their faces showed no particular interest and they didn't say anything. They didn't know there was anything to be afraid of.

Which there wasn't. It was just a robot. The library was well defended. I knew that from experience. Time to turn my thoughts back to the topic, Avery.

Here goes. "Okay, so, the thing with the fungus zombies is, y'all're running a hard time limit. Y'all're pretending it ain't magic, right? So they're not being fed power from outside to keep movin'. They still gotta use muscles and such, which means they gotta eat and drink, which they ain't doing. What I'm sayin' is, how long have they got? How long has your whole plague got, iff'n you're relying on bites to spread it? Theah zombies! If they could plan and organize they wouldn't be zombies. Theyah not following search patterns or running relays to get one suhvivin' zombie to the next gas station, so he can bite someone who goes in exactly the right direction to get to the next one. They can't drive. If they could think cleahly, they wouldn't be trying to bite you. Which is why ah loved the big reveal."

In her own chair by the window, Annie leaned back, her tail hooked around a table leg to make sure she didn't fall over. Pensive, eyes unfocused on anything but her own thoughts, she said, "A disease spreading a magical curse was an unusual plot twist. Not a zombifying fungus, but a necromantic fungus. I can see why the movie gets such high reviews. I also appreciated that they didn't fall into the trope ending that implies the heroes only think the disaster is over." Mimicking a weary hero, she quoted, "It's dead. Not undead. Just dead dead."

Shaking my hands, I agreed, "Right. Once y'all break a curse like that, it don't come back. It's gotta come from somewheres, and that somewhere ain't real healthy after havin' liquid nitrogen poured on it. I figure every zombieshroom oughta be an independent curse, but it makes just as much sense for it to all be linked back to a central spell. More, maybe. Now, ah don't reckon ah buy that the guy what made it did so accidentally, but, ya know, Hollywood. They don't ask mages what all magic is like."

"And the first movie? What did you think of it?" Annie asked, voice distant, her attention on listening rather than talking.

I smirked. "You mean 'sides the acting?"

Chris collapsed face-first onto the table, laughing. He struggled to keep it quiet, since we were in a library and all. While the choking wheezes came out, he gave my hand a tight squeeze, until finally he got his breath back. "The acting was so bad. That guy might as well have just waggled his eyebrows and gone 'blaw, blaw!'"

I tittered. It had been that bad.

Annie was still leaning back, although she frowned harder now. "Which is a shame, because the writing was excellent, and I don't think most people would ever get to notice. Having the evil ghost and the demon hate each other even more than they hate humanity was a cute twist, but their evil was also very textured. They had personality."

Chris, voice steady now, lifted his face from the tabletop and declared, "But we want to hear the necromancer's opinion."

Annie's chair rocked forward, all four feet landing with a soft *whunk* on the carpet. Eyes on me again, she nodded eagerly.

I scratched the back of my neck as I thought about it. "Well… that was actual-like a lot more spot-on as you might think. I mean, I don't know nothin' 'bout demons, no sir, but the cursed doll thing, it works. You've got to understand, a lot of necromancy, and possession, and all that there stuff, works around the idea that iff'n you've got a body lying around empty-like, somethin' might move in. A bunch'a religions would hold vigils over dead folks' bodies. You don't leave those alone until they're either rotten or in the ground. Now, there's a little bit'a 'are you really for sure that they're dead?' but the main thing is, practically anything could move in and take over a body in the first day're two. They *want* to get up. Now, dolls…"

Prickles crawled up my spine, the creepy feeling of what I

was talking about having everything to do with the problems literally haunting me. "They don't have nerves of muscle just waitin' for a signal, but still, you got a human shaped shell, it moves 'bout like a human does, maybe it needs a l'il more oomph, but a ghost can move inta that, no problem. Happens all the time. Well, occasionally."

Annie had drifted back into thoughtful, but her chair only leaned back a few inches so far. She murmured, "There are historical precedents, yes, although it's always hard to tell history from legend."

I nodded. "You'd need a right-exceptional ghost, but a doll, a mannequin, a robot, anything as is human shaped and movable, that there's a tempting target. And there's a thing… look, ah ain't never met one, but ah know it can happen. Some folks is just too ding dang cussed ornery to die. Ghosts tend to be balls'a memory and emotion, right? You get somebody what dies real happy or real upset, you get a ghost even regular folk can see. Well, sometimes you get somebody as is so full'a bile and hate, their ghost is almost human. Sometimes they move back inta their own body, and y'all get some powerful vicious zombies. A guy like that there in the movie, he was 'zackly the kinda person whose ghost would take over a doll and get to killing."

Sighing heavily, I propped my chin in my hand. "Right shame. You got to be pure awful to produce a ghost like that. More likely the kind'a ghost what gets into a doll died under some really strange magical circumstances, or had a super power what pumped up their ghost, and they ain't bad folk at all. If they lash out, it's 'cause they don't know what's goin' on. They need rescuing, not destroying. I mean, it's all well and good saying they're already dead, but the whole reason as you're in this mess is because death got interrupted, right? Undead and dead ain't the same. I should know."

Chris reached across the tables, taking my free hand in his. He lifted it to his mouth and kissed my knuckles. Black eyes watched mine as he murmured, "I love what a caring person you are. The world would be a better place if other necromancers had been as compassionate as you."

I snorted. "Well, they weren't." But inside, I squirmed a little, because the compliment made me really happy.

Maybe Chris saw it, because he stared at me silently for several long, long seconds. Only then did he turn his head and ask his sister, "Okay, Annie. What's up?"

Which got me turning my head and raising my eyebrows at the devil sister. I hadn't known something was up at all.

Her comfortable openness was gone, and Annie hunched her shoulders up, twisting her hands together nervously. She did have enough confidence to squeak, "Well, it's not about the movies..."

I nodded encouragingly. "Go on, girl. This is you'n'me friends time. Chris is here just as our excuse."

Bunching her fists up under her chin, Annie leaned sharply forwards towards me and whispered, "I want to see the costume again!"

Chapter Thirty-One

Rearing back a couple of inches, I fumbled both for words and thoughts. "Well, uh… I mean, not out here, but ah 'spec we could find a restroom, or… you know, Alice'd be right easier, and ah could show you the full, complete costume."

Annie leaped out of her seat, and pulled me out of mine, whispering, "There's an employees-only door on the back wall. You stay here."

That last was to Chris, and I nearly tripped over my first step following Annie. Not bringing Chris? Annie and Chris kept so few secrets from each other they actually shared a bedroom! They were the archetype of twin bonding!

But Chris's smile didn't waver, so he clearly didn't think this was weird, and after a couple of seconds I couldn't see him past heavily loaded metal bookshelves anyway.

We reached the employee only door, a little grey thing which blended into the wall and didn't even bother with an "employees only" sign. I performed the knock-knock-whisper "Alice" routine, and Annie and I slipped in and shut the door.

Backing between stone pillars so that she could still face me as we separated, Annie clasped her hands in front of her hips, leaned forward, and squeaked, "So...?"

Amused, and slightly embarrassed, I crossed to the burial niche in the wall where I'd left my magic hat and staff. Tucking the sun hat with its ring of miniature skulls around the crown onto my head, I gave it a flick with a finger and warned my ancestors, "No ghostly heckling."

Okay. Scooping up my staff with my left hand, I gripped the pendant in my right, and gave it power. Dust of disintegrating and reintegrating clothing spiraled around me, momentarily obscuring my vision. This time I carried my staff, and I felt it get heavier at the end.

My vision cleared to reveal Annie perched with her backside against the nearest pillar, watching me with fascination rather than the adoration I'd gotten from Chris and Sue. When the transformation stopped, she stepped away from the pillar, taking my right arm delicately in her graceful scarlet hands. Annie held my arm out straight, peering closely at the sleeve, face inches from the fabric. Examining the seams, maybe? Annie and Chris had been child models. They weren't thrilled with everything else about the job, but the passion for clothing and fashion had been true, and it stuck.

Annie's deft, lightly touching fingers moved to my collar, feeling around it, giving it slight tugs. They dropped next to my belt, giving the foot-tall, shiny, maybe-but-probably-not-leather band the same treatment. After that she moved to my staff, running her fingertips over the thorn decorations on the claws holding the crystal in place. In the utter silence of the mausoleum, even her near-whisper rang like a bell. "This is a nice touch."

I grinned, which she couldn't see, but she surely could hear my satisfaction. "Isn't it? It really gives me the 'just any old mage' look."

"Or even a mad scientist hiding the nature of their powers," Annie murmured, following the line of those grasping claws to my hand gripping the staff, and the black glove over that hand.

I tilted my head an inch to the side. "Oh, now that's clever. Do they do that?"

"I don't know. Until I met you, I didn't pay any attention to heroes and villains," she murmured, distant and distracted.

Heh. No, Annie just had a Tonika-level intellect behind that fear of every human being except Chris and me.

Annie did frown a little more as she crouched far enough to give the top of my boots a tug. Probably disappointed that they weren't high heels. Her expression quickly became moot as she circled around behind me. Her hands tugged at my skirt, swishing it from side to side. She patted my hips, squeezed my waist, and patted around my shoulders. Maybe she was very politely finding out not just how tightly the dress fit, but what underclothing came with it?

Still behind me, cheerfully curious and only a little subdued, Annie asked, "How many sessions did you have to stand to have this fitted?"

"None. I didn't even know about it until old Alicia sprang it on me yesterday," I answered truthfully.

Annie's voice turned surprised. "It's not enchanted to fit you." I wasn't going to ask how she knew that. "What kind of tailoring genius could make this with only measurements?"

I jerked a thumb at Revivienne's burial niche. "That genius."

Annie's hands lifted off of me. Awkwardly, she mumbled, "Avery... could..."

Standing there like a dress maker's mannequin, my left arm slightly out from my body and my right way out holding my staff, I told her, "Worst I'll say is no, Annie."

"I'd really like to meet Revivienne," she near-whispered.

I couldn't say no to Annie. Anyway, why should I say no? Because it would take so much power I'd be defenseless. That was with my staff, which would take all night to recharge.

I would have Chris's mind-controlling super persuasiveness power and Annie's downright terrifying fire summoning to protect me.

Oh, those were all excuses. I was going to do it to make Annie happy and the rest was fiddling around the edges, and I knew it.

Stepping out of dress-dummy duty, I walked over to Revivienne's burial niche, a rectangular hole in the wall long enough and deep enough to hold a human body, which this one did. Revivienne lay lengthwise, a skeleton in an elaborate purple dress with gloved hands folded over the chest and a ribbon-bedecked purple sun hat laid discreetly over the skull.

Lifting up the hat, I traced my own gloved fingertips over the faint blue lines wrapping the skull and poured power into them. Lots and lots of power, chill that flowed up from my feet, ice that rushed down through my staff, out through my left hand and into, not the skeleton, but the barely perceptible remains of the spells woven onto that skeleton. Spells I couldn't begin to understand.

Understand, no, but I saw the few faint lines brighten into a dense, bright-blue mesh that traced out a human face, and even sweeping hair that covered one eye. Revivienne sat up, stretching its arms out as if yawning, and then leaned lazily propped up on one hand. The wall niche was just tall enough to allow it.

What did Annie see? A skeleton? A human? She didn't look horrified. I saw the blue lines. I saw a masterpiece, necromantic spellwork of exquisite beauty and skill, a complex magic that had created an undead more sophisticated than any vampire. Let historians rave about haunted mountains, dance parties of the dead, and superheroes defeated. This was the proof that my great-great-grandmother had been a genius as well as a powerhouse, and I was in awe all over again.

While I appreciated the way the blue mesh flowed, the subtle filling out of the dress that mimicked a body no longer there, the layers of emotion and intelligence animating Revivienne's expression, I also leaned heavily on my staff and panted for breath. That had taken so much power!

"You've got—a couple minutes. Best I can do," I wheezed to Annie.

Revivienne looked Annie up and down, literally glowing with delight, and batted a gloved hand playfully. Man or woman, I couldn't tell from the voice, which held a hint of reverberation. As far as I was concerned, Revivienne was an "it." As a skeleton, the question of gender had long since become moot. But skeleton, not quite human, it's voice still drawled with the love of clothing. "Aren't you divine! I've always loved the aesthetic of tall women, and men's fashion on a woman is so alluring."

I growled under my labored breaths, "But you put me in dresses."

Revivienne heard me, but the beaming smile on that illusory face didn't waver. "Of course. Look at your darling young lady friend. What's your name?"

Annie bobbed her head and her knees in a brief curtsey. "Annie Domingo."

The elaborately dressed skeleton fluttered its fingers. "Charmed. They call me Revivienne." Attention back on me, Revivienne explained, "Annie here has sleek lines, but so womanly that the straight lines of men's clothing cannot hide them. Look at how the waistline has to pinch in a way it wouldn't on a man. That contrast is so striking, so stylish. YOU—" And Revivienne touched its fingertip to my nose while I was still trying to think of a snarky complaint. "—on the other hand, have even more curves. They beg for emphasis, even exaggeration, to take the already intense and distill it into a wild vortex of femininity. It goes so well with the color black and the magical theme."

Revivienne finished off with a dramatic growl, "Darkness is a woman, and she is coming for you."

All that... words failed me. Instead, I told Annie unnecessarily, "So, uh... this is Revivienne."

"Who is not just a dressmaker, but a philosopher of clothing," Annie remarked, hands clasped but giving the skeleton an admiring rather than nervous smile.

Revivienne leaned its head to one side, regarding Annie back. "Of course. What is art, if you have nothing to say with it?"

"So you don't think clothing should reflect the personality as well as the physical context?" Annie asked, as casually as if they were discussing... well, fashion tips.

Much of the playful drawl disappeared from Revivienne's voice, replaced by more straightforward conversation... for about three seconds. "That's a factor, of course. Your soul begs not for pants or skirts, but for truly exotic outfits. Clouds and vines, snakes and spiderwebs, abstract shapes and silhouettes. Revivienne can tell. Confidentially, I can tell because of how you keep looking at my mistress's mask."

Annie giggled bashfully, but… a pleased rather than scared bashfully.

"And yet you make the ordinary extraordinary," Revivienne gushed, then waved a lazy hand at me. "My mistress, my love, my everything, needs to see who she can be, to rise above. Also, I simply adore seeing her like this."

"I do too," Annie enthused. "How did you get her measurements so perfect?"

Revivienne dipped its head forward. "I'm afraid it's time to humble brag. I wish I could give you my secret techniques, but it's just a knack. I had it when I was alive. I know, it's unfair to my hard-working peers—" The skeleton stopped, yawning enormously, and raised its hand to its mouth. "Oh, I'm so sorry, young lady. I think I'm running—"

I dove forward, an arm around Revivienne's back and the other taking its wrist. I lowered it back into its niche before the bones could fall apart, crossing its hands over its chest and laying the hat back over the skull face.

Taking one more deep breath and letting it out again, I stood up and told Annie, "Well, there you go. The twentieth century's greatest expert on clothing magic, and maybe on just regular clothing. I hope it was what you wanted."

She pounced, arms around my shoulder, almost knocking me down with the energy of her hug. Somewhere above my head, she squealed, "It was, thank you! Now let's get you back to my brother before he gets lonely, or he draws a crowd."

Which wasn't really a joke. Chris was for sure that pretty. "Wait."

I dug in my heels, stopping a couple of feet from the crypt's currently nonexistent door. "I'm not going out there like this," I warned Annie. I activated the amulet, which thankfully didn't take much power, and when it finished doing its clothing replacement special effects I laid my hat and staff in the alcove closest to the door.

Annie pouted, lower lip jutting out. Without a hint of apology, she said, "Well, I tried. You do look so good in it. Alice, would you take us back to my brother?"

I heard a click, and looked to see that the door had returned, and stood slightly open. Now Annie nibbled on her lip, nervous again with other people potentially present. Still, she giggled and gave my hand a tug.

We headed back out to see, yep, a girl talking up Chris. She leaned over the table, over him, and he talked to her with an expression of the sweetest, most apologetic friendliness, the kindest of rejections.

My friends were so wonderful, and I loved them so much. I would much rather have them on my side than Tonika's friends as I dealt with this robot problem.

Annie pulled me far enough past the shelves to see the glass door of the room's exit. Out on the stairwell stood a superhero, unmistakable in plastic-plated spandex and holding a funny gizmo with a star of antennae that rippled with rainbow lights. Oh, boy.

But... he turned and walked away, and my heart relaxed again.

Exactly because I loved my friends so much, I was not going to drag them into this.

Chapter Thirty-Two

"I really hope Tonika fixes my problem today."

Those were the words I desperately wanted to say Friday, and couldn't. Not just because if I tried, my malignant accent would find a way to stick the word "reckon" in there somewhere. I had tied myself up but good. There was no one I could say it to, or even risk hearing me say it.

But relying on Tonika's supposedly not super brains had worked eerily well so far, so I fidgeted my way through school while Sue gave me hand squeezes because I couldn't help being on edge. She let me not talk about it at lunch, which might have been the sweetest sacrifice anyone had ever made for me.

When school let out, Sue took my hand immediately in the hall, holding it tight as we walked unhurriedly towards the exit. Everyone left us alone. If they weren't terrified of us, they'd have attacked my obvious moment of vulnerability somehow, but they were terrified, and I was safe. Sue's hand in mine was an anchor, helping me calm down and realize I had a whole afternoon and evening ahead that I could spend on things other than worrying. The robot hadn't attacked me or seriously hurt anyone yet. I was just getting paranoid because this kept dragging on.

We stepped out into the wonderful afternoon sunshine—I would never get tired of how sunny it was in LA, even in winter—and from around the street corner—

Bang! Metal feet hit pavement.

Bang! Metal hit metal.

People yelled, in shock and fear.

I flooded my body with icy power. Girls squealed and darted away from me, which meant I was doing a clumsy job and subjecting them to whatever nightmares people see when necromancy touches them.

Sue hadn't let go of my hand. She gave it a little tug, and told me dryly, "I know what it's like to have to prove you're not a villain, but I am totally not letting you run off after any random car wreck."

Oops. "Car wreck. Right." I stood still, listening hard while trying to ease down my magic and not let it spill everywhere.

Sue's hand slipped from mine, slowly and cautiously. She stepped around behind me with the same gentle movements, placed her hands on my shoulders, and with no gentleness at all began to knead. She rolled the big muscles by my neck with hands much stronger than you would think looking at her. I couldn't completely relax, and the grip hurt, but in a pleasant way.

From somewhere behind my gigantic hair, Sue murmured, "You desperately need to relax, so I contacted your parents, and you're coming home with me today. We are getting professional massages, then a spa treatment because I know you've never tried one. I am going to devote my entire evening to making *you* feel relaxed and comfortable again, and I'll deliver you to your freaky little magic mentor tomorrow morning."

My eyes stung as tears welled up in them. That all sounded so, so nice. My voice squeaked a bit as I said, "Thanks. Ah been jumpin' at shadows. No offense—"

Bang! Another metal on pavement sound rang out, followed by another, quieter but still audible even from the next street over. And another, and another. Metal footsteps running.

A shiny white robot with long white hair trailing after her leaped over a car on the road, hitting the asphalt with another audible *bang*, and raced towards me in long, loud strides.

There was still a parked car on the road between the robot and me. Inside, kids and parents struggled with their seatbelts and doors, trying to get out before the robot reached them. They didn't. The robot's arms stretched out to grab the car as she got close. Fingers closed on metal.

"Stop!" I yelled, forcing the power I still had called up into the word.

The robot's grip let go, and she tumbled over the hood in an uncontrolled somersault instead of whatever violence she had planned.

She landed shakily on her feet, standing rather than running. Lifting her arm to point at me, she declared, "I knew it! I knew it was you. I can feel you everywhere!" Well, mostly pointing at me. The arm weaved a lot, but I was at the center.

Then she lurched forward again, sprinting three steps up the hill, only to trip and fall hard on her face into the grass.

Sue, stepping up beside me, snapped her fingers in malicious contempt. "Totally not letting you touch my bae." Turning to look at me, she added, "You're up. Put it down."

Yes. I had a second to focus. I filled myself with cold again, my breath feeling like frost as it rushed through my mouth and I shouted, "Calm down!"

The robot had been climbing back to her feet. Now she collapsed, only to push back up more slowly on shaky arms. She was resistant, but not immune.

I yelled again, "Just calm down!" and switched to a loud, commanding, but also sympathetic tone. "Let's talk about this. Ah'm keen to help you."

She finished staggering back to her feet, weaving from side to side as if she were drunk. She sounded drunk, confused, and rambling. "Help me? You killed me! I wanted to be beautiful, but what you did to me—" Her upper body jerked forward, hunched over as she grabbed her head in both hands. "—and the whole time, I pleaded for you to save me from him, and then I died happy that you didn't come, because he would have killed you too. Then you freed me. You freed me, and I'm perfect. Look at me. I'm everything we wished I was. You can feel about me now the way I feel about you."

...

For a second I stood there, stunned by this barely coherent rant. The ghost thought I was at least three different people. She needed to be woken up. She was too close to living to rest, but not close enough to think clearly or understand what was going on around her.

Chilly necromancy flowed through me smoothly now, layering every word as I told the ghost, "Y'all're sure pretty, alright. All that awful stuff is over. You're safe now. Now it's time ta talk, time ta heal."

I walked down to her. Even steps, Avery. Unthreatening. Kind. I raised my arms, palms out, reaching for the robot's head so I could feed her power and stabilize the ghost inside.

My fingers touched cold metal, or maybe ceramic. Up close, the white plates didn't look like metal, but they were hard and rigid, cold even in the sunny afternoon. I cupped her cheeks.

Her arms lashed out, grabbed me by the waist, and yanked me up against her for a hug. Ow. A ribs-creaking tight hug. Ow ow ow. In a breathy whimper, she said, "I missed you. I'm glad you escaped." Then the hug relaxed a little, and the robot's head jerked up, regarding me with blank, impassive eyes as she barked, "But killing me and stuffing me into a robot once wasn't enough, was it? You're going to stuff me into that one next?"

Above me, Mech's voice said, "Stay calm, Avery. Lean your head out of the way. I've done this before. You won't be in any danger."

This was exactly the reason I hadn't wanted to randomly wait for the robot to find me. I had no control over the situation, and one little surprise sent her into an angry panic. She squeezed me tighter, forcing the breath out of me as I grimaced, and she yelled up at Mech, "You can't have her! She's the only thing you didn't take from me!"

Tilting me horizontal, she turned and ran, still gripping me in her arms.

I bounced. I hung sideways in a tight, mechanically powerful grip. It hurt. Out of reflex, I yelled, "Put me down!"

Power I'd intended to use to heal the ghost burst out in those words instead. The robot dropped me, and my shoulder and hip hit asphalt. Lying on the road, I got to watch up-close as the robot sidestepped a twinkly beam that melted, a line of pavement. Ripping a manhole cover up out of the ground, she flung it up into the sky at Mech, backflipped and dove straight down into the hole.

I rolled over onto my back, now treated to the sight of Mech in his brightly polished red armor hovering in midair using no obvious jets or other flying devices. With the sincerity of a deeply caring, unbendingly nice guy, he sighed. "Talk about the nick of time. Don't worry, Avery. I've got its scent now. This will be over by morning. Sue, take care of her. Keep her safe and help take this robot mess off her mind."

"Already planning on it," Sue answered. Her seriousness slipped into a sly, lurid grin, and she added, "By the time I'm done with her, she, like, won't even remember what robots are."

Mech laughed. "Young love. It's so pure." He barely sounded sarcastic at all. I got the impression he recognized that Sue's salacious tone was a joke.

Legs extended and arms straight by his sides, Mech zoomed off over the rooftops.

Sue ran over to me. I climbed upright, dusting asphalt dust off my school uniform as Sue circled me twice, checking me for damage. That was sweet, but ridiculous. I was at worst slightly bruised. Sue was still purple and green, and had to be in more discomfort constantly than the whole encounter had put me through. As she inspected, Sue asked in a rush, "Are you okay? That was the robot from the haunted house, right? I didn't know it was still after you!"

"Yep. That's what ah been nervous about," I muttered guiltily, staring down at my white, uniform-prescribed socks.

My vision filled with Sue's blue sweater vest instead as she threw her arms around me for a fierce hug. I hugged her back more gently, because she did still look like she'd been run over by a herd of horses.

Resting my chin on Sue's shoulder, I sighed. "Ain't no way my folks don't hear 'bout this. Ah jes' hope what they take way's zat all ah did was try'n deescalate."

My phone beeped in my backpack. I hadn't turned it back on yet, which could only mean—

Pulling out of the hug, I dug my phone out and checked. Yes, a message from Tonika.

Tonika: That was close. I've sent him in the wrong direction. We'll be done before he finds out.

Me: Now? Please mean now.

Tonika: Now. Come pick me up with your teleport chamber. Mech's place.

I stuffed the phone back. Sick guilt trickled down my throat as I grimaced at my girlfriend. "Sue... ah'm so sorry. Please, it's so unfair t' ask, but can y'all cover for me?"

Sue grabbed me for another hug, pressing her cheek to mine. With calm, serious, absolute determination, she said, "Whatever you need me to do, whether it's stand aside or take a bullet for you, I will totally do. Right now, that's cover for you, so, like, I'll cover for you. Go fix this."

Taking her cheek in one hand, I gave Sue a simple but ferocious kiss, pouring all my desperation and gratitude and love for her into the touch, even if it wasn't the same love as the passion she felt for me.

Then I broke free, ran to the nearest car, shouted, "Alice!", yanked open the car door, and ducked inside.

Chapter Thirty-Three

"Please tell me this will be quick and simple," I begged, thumping Mech's carpet with the heel of my staff. The extra heavy heel of my staff. I was in full costume now, including crystal-topped staff and my inherited magic hat transformed into a hood.

Tonika, in her bodysuit but wigless and helmetless, answered solemnly, "It will be quick. I don't know what anyone else considers simple. We're only going to one place. Is the ghost robot still on its way, Apollonia?"

After a second's pause, Delphine jerked up an inch in recognition. "Oh! Right. Not used to this costume thing." She had found a much better costume, a white robe slit up the sides, fastened by a golden belt and with lots of gold embroidery around the edges. It looked very Ancient Greek. Add to that a green, glittery masquerade snake mask, and the crystal ball held in her right hand.

Her left, of course, still held Hodir's. Those two had it bad, which had to be the nicest thing to come out of this mess.

Brisk, emotionless, businesslike, but not at all harsh, Tonika explained, "There are things we can get away with as a supervillain team that we can't as teenagers."

"My parents will think it's super cool!" squeaked Hodir. He and Olga had also gotten costume upgrades. In his case, black leather that looked armor-ish, but with a ridiculous amount of extra spikes and zigzags. His face had been painted in black-and-white lightning designs.

"I predict that," declared Delphine, tone airy and chin held high. She dissolved almost immediately into a giggle, pressing her shoulder to Hodir's. "But, um. Ghost robot."

Holding up the crystal ball, Delphine stared into its depths. The clear glass lit up with a soft white glow. Voice subtly echoey, Delphine said, "Yes. She's heading this way."

"That is the best power," Hodir told her with a huge grin.

Delphine blushed. It wasn't visible, but her head tilted an inch, her shoulders bunched up, one of her feet tucked up onto her toes—the embarrassment was obvious. As was her smile. "I'm not the one who can melt things and summon monsters and teleport."

Ignoring the litany of two teens with a massive crush on each other, Tonika addressed me instead, now with a guilty frown. "I'm sorry about—" and she jerked her head towards the bathroom door in Mech's underground base that I'd used Alice to ferry her teammates through.

I did not like having to reveal Alice's existence to her friends. At all. An apology helped a lot.

Tonika continued, "But you see now why timing was crucial. Helping Delphine with her powers let me know when and where I could get you and the robot together without interference or innocents in danger. We have to be in the right place at the right time, and both are near. We should get going now."

Surrendering to necessity, I trudged back towards the bathroom door to call Alice. "Where to?"

Tonika shook her head. "No. We don't need to go anywhere except downstairs."

I looked around the comfortable little round living room, with its silent robots and plush furniture. "It's in Mech's base? How is a ghost in a robot shell going to wander in here?" As I said it, I savored again that being in full costume and powered up for action turned off my accent. Being a supervillainess would almost be worth it for that.

"It will be easier to show you. Follow me," Tonika answered, too blandly matter-of-fact to sound mysterious.

So we followed her, down a nice, carpeted, curving staircase all in the same variations on cream and light brown as the rooms above. This place felt like a penthouse apartment or one of those fancy homes on the hills more than a superhero base—although being secret and underground would make the land cost zero, which had to make a difference. We emerged into a circular hallway in the same theme, but the doors around the outer side looked into rooms either fancier or a lot more practical. The white-walled room with all the pedestals holding trophies for sure caught my interest. Maybe I could find a discreet way to ask Mech for a tour.

Tonika ignored all of them, leading us to another stairway going down, leading to another hallway the same as the one above. This seemed to be the bottom floor, though. No further stairways. At least, not until Tonika ushered her me and her friends into a small room jammed with the kinds of sensor equipment I saw when those scientists were studying our powers. Most of the equipment was in use, humming faintly or emitting colorful arcs of energy at items like a hammer and a head-sized pink crystal globe.

The opposite wall slid open. I could barely call it a secret door, it had been so seamlessly perfect until it opened. There hadn't been any sign of what Tonika did to open it, either. I guess a big-league mad scientist like Mech could secret it up way better than regular people.

We had left the base. I was sure of that, because the decorating scheme changed wildly. Beyond the door lay a rough shaft cut through rock, with metal bars driven into the wall to make a stairway spiraling down the sides and a big enough hole in the center for someone to fall or fly down. Me, I stuck close to the wall in this wildly unsafe descent, and Delphine held Hodir close to the wall with a grip on his bicep. His eyes shone with eagerness to look down the center pit, but he let her keep him safe.

We went down a few floors, until this shaft cut into a much

more official looking tunnel, like a two-lane underground street, arched over smooth pavement. Our section was maybe the size of a bus, with big, solid, buttressed doors at either end that looked like they would shrug off tank shells. It was all grey, grey stone ceiling, lighter grey pavement floor, grey metal doors, except for some big red symbols painted on the doors that made no sense to me.

The tunnel sloped, and Tonika faced the down direction, held up what looked like an electronic car key, and pushed its button. The massive door lifted up into the ceiling.

Okay, the tunnel looked like a road because it was a road. Inside was a parking garage, one lane with parking spots on either side. Scorch marks and gouges marked the walls and floor. Most of the parking spots lay empty, but black wreckage lurked in a few, and farther back, a few blackened, blocky, hulking humanoid robots. Maybe vehicles. They were big enough. The whole thing curved like a donut, but I couldn't be sure if it made a complete circle.

Hodir went, "Ooooooh." I kept the cold necromancy in my hand mingled with the reservoir in my staff, ready for a fight. This place could not possibly be safe.

Tonika clicked another button. It opened a slightly undersized hatch door on the inner wall. One by one, we stepped through into a room that would be pretty big if it weren't crowded with slabs, rails, and the kind of mechanical arms you saw in car factories. The upper half of a charcoal dark robot like a mannequin lay on one of the slabs, its assembly interrupted.

A side door from that room led into a surgery. A fancy surgery, lots of mad-sciency arms hovering around the surgical table like spider legs. Some of the arms were slender and delicate, especially the ones clustered around the head end of the bed. On the walls hung or sat stacked on shelves high-tech parts with a very cyborgy replacement body part look.

One final door led into a round room at the center of the complex. What looked like computers lined the domed walls, ringed with pipes, some filled with water, others opaque. Wires ran from every machine down to a waist-high metal cube with an open top.

We'd reached the end of the road, and it was time for me to ask the question. "What *is* this place?"

Tonika climbed over the rim of the cube and stood in its center. Some of the wires ran through the box rather than hooking into it, and she lifted up cords, sorting through them and picking the occasional plug to fasten into the jacks in her head. As she did, she explained, "This is where Organism One launched its first attempt to destroy humanity, by exploiting the time change when computers worldwide switched to the year two thousand and attempting to take control of all of them, everywhere. That was before Mech became a superhero. He built his base over this spot after later incidents, because someone had to protect it and he had the knowhow. He's actually much better at computer overrides than building power armor."

I blinked. "Organism One? Like…"

"The supervillain who replaced part of my brain with a computer, erased most of my memories, and derailed my life completely, yes," said Tonika, voice blank as she twisted another plug into place with an audible click.

I winced, and lowered my voice in sympathy. "Being here must be mighty uncomfortable."

Still detached in tone, Tonika answered, "I have people to help. People I care about."

Looking around again, I said, "I can't help but notice it's… mighty snug in here. I'd have expected a bigger base." Seriously. If more than Tonika and I tried to crowd into this middle room, we'd all be tangled up in wires and each other.

Tonika finally smiled, impishness returning to her face and voice. "Organism One didn't get out much. We'd better get started."

I held up a finger. "One more question first?"

"For you? Of course."

I waved my arm around the room. "What's with all the weird red symbols?"

Because that was the major decorating theme of the whole base. Weird red symbols painted onto machines. Weird red symbols on bands around the base of wires. Weird red symbols on plaques on the walls. The construction room had plain white walls, the cyborg surgery pale blue, and the control room a dark, oppressive, shadow-filled grey, but red symbols turned all of them into a crazy fresco. The symbols sat in little clumps, like abstract pictograms. Circles, straight lines, triangles. Rounded brackets contained little markings like a pair of upwards-pointing arrows, like an Egyptian cartouche. Stuff like that.

Also, the fact that I knew the word cartouche meant my fancy prep school education was working.

Tonika's smile became a grin. Next to me, just inside the cyber-surgery, Hodir grinned, too. He chirped eagerly, "It's Ancient Catlantian!"

"A conlang, of course," Tonika added. "Invented by a woman named Blavatsky. Catlantis never existed. No one knows why Organism One likes this fake language so much. My personal theory is that Organism One started out as an artificially super-evolved cat."

I looked around some more, taking in the threatening mad-scienceness of it all. "I like cats as much as the next sorceress, but it would sure explain the megalomania and sociopathy."

What I didn't want to say was that I'd seen symbols an awful lot like this in a buried, magically sealed city hundreds of years older than Los Angeles.

Tonika looked past me at her friends. "Cat's Cradle, you know what to do?"

In response to her code name, Olga hunched forward, hands clasped together with the rainbow wires of her one creation twisted around her fingers. "I'm scared," she mumbled.

Delphine slipped her hand into that grip, pulling the right hand and the tangled web away, holding that hand and turning a reassuring smile down at the little mad scientist. Hodir took her other hand, clasping it in both of his. Delphine murmured warmly, "We're with you."

With Hodir still holding her left hand, and Delphine her right, Olga climbed up onto the surgical bed and lay down with her head nestled in a little raised clamp. She squeezed her eyes tight, and squeezed the hands she held tighter, but otherwise lay still.

My eyes widened as my whole body tensed up, and I

protested, "Woah, you're not going to—"

Tonika interrupted me, soft and confident. "Of course not. Organism One found ways to stimulate super powers, that's all. I'm helping all my friends, all at once."

She closed her own eyes. Little LEDs lit up on the computers lining the walls. Mostly the red symbols lit up, but lights also streaked rhythmically down the wires connected to Tonika's skull. Water gurgled through pipes, and with a soft hum, the air conditioning in the walls turned on.

I looked at the computers. I looked at the wires. I looked at Tonika connected to that. I said, "Okay, I was wrong. New question. Is that safe?"

"Almost no one has the equipment or knowledge to use these systems. Mech is one. Thanks to my implants, I'm another," she answered quietly, eyes still closed.

I nodded impatiently. "I figured that. I mean, isn't that begging to be taken over?"

The tiny, bald girl in the shiny black bodysuit and the wires plugged into her head shook that head just slightly, setting the wires to swaying. "No. The interface where Organism One would control me is dead, on the organic side where nothing he can do here would fix it."

Gritting my teeth, I grumbled, "I hope you're right," because this worried me. A lot.

Her voice still quiet, distracted, and completely calm, Tonika said, "Mech checked repeatedly, and Delphine is sure Organism One taking control of me today isn't a possibility. Are you ready, Cat—" She interrupted herself, and finished in a more gentle, affectionate tone, "Olga?"

"As I can be," the equally tiny middle school kid on the table answered.

Tonika stood absolutely still, not even breathing that I could tell. The computers around the walls began to whir. A light from the surgery ceiling drifted up and down Olga and the bed she lay on. Another pair of padded robotic arms clasped her temples, holding her head still.

I could just barely see something move under Olga's neck.

She jerked upright into a sitting position, so fast she ripped free of the clasps that hadn't let go of her head. Loudly, face tight and eyes saucer-wide in awe, she declared, "Everything is connected!"

Olga relaxed, panting for breath, head bent forward so she could feel the back of her neck with a hand she withdrew from Hodir's grip. My angle wasn't great, but I got a glimpse of what sure looked like a computer chip stuck there.

Still breathing hard, with mingled regret and wonder, she said, "It's fading, but… it's still there, in the background. I'm not making anything right now, but I will. It worked" Head jerking up again, she squealed in delight, "I'm a mad scientist!"

Tears ran down her Olga's cheeks. Hodir and Delphine swooped in, hugging the little brunette from both sides. In the cube, Tonika opened her eyes and smiled with the kind of relief so intense it looks pained. She told her friends, "Save a hug for me. I have to help Deathette now, and then everyone's problems will be solved."

Me, I had to hold my hands still and not scratch the back of my neck. Not scratch everything. I itched. No surprise that Hodir would be leaking power at an emotional moment like this. That little kid had crazy amounts of power. I was a mite jealous.

Computers whirred some more. Doors thumped open out of sight. Distracted and eyes closed again, Tonika stood in the center of her electronic web and said, "With this equipment, I can locate and try to take control of any robot in the city. I can't completely control the one that's stalking you, but I can lure it down the access tunnels Organism One used for its own robot agents."

Action time. My staff was full. Cold magic flowed in slow, perfectly controlled currents through my body. I was focused and only a little nervous. "What does that mean for me?"

Face slightly pinched with effort, Tonika said, "Go out in the tunnel, and wait. I know this has to be all you, but we'll be behind you wishing you good luck."

Gratitude wriggled through the magical chill as I made my way back out of the base. This was exactly the scenario I'd been hoping for, handed to me on a silver platter. I did still feel extremely uncomfortable returning to the stark, rock-walled exit tunnel. The outer hatch had peeled back, revealing that the tunnel extended on into darkness.

I tapped my hood with the end of my staff and told my ancestors, "Be ready, but no telling me to just kill her."

Namluh growled hungrily, "But when you need to drive her into—BA HA HA, yes, yes, we all support you, greatest of granddaughters."

Horse Skull Kid chipped in enthusiastically, "And me, I think y'all're might noble. Just 'cause I wouldn't do it myself don't mean I don't admire it."

Great-great-grandmother Alicia said, "Honey child, even if you yoahself off a cliff, ah will try to teach you to fly on the way down. But at least have some descendants fuhst, so you can haunt them."

Chapter Thirty-Four

I stood alone in the middle of a big, empty tunnel, with Tonika and her friends way behind me in the garage, and only one direction the robot could approach from. This was perfect. Just me and the robot, and she couldn't come at me by surprise. A nice, open area to talk her down, and use my power on it gently.

"Almost perfect. Wish I knew her name," I said aloud.

"Would that help?" Tonika asked behind me.

I blinked in surprise and looked back around at her. "You know it?"

"No, but I know who knows it," she answered. Pulling her phone out of a pocket tucked protectively inside the neckline of her bodysuit, she dialed and tossed the phone to me. I caught it one-handed. Awkwardly, but I caught it.

It was already set to speaker phone. Someone picked up, a woman's voice I didn't know. "Bubblegumshoe Detective Agency. Two hundred years of mysteries solved by an annoying dead girl and her even more annoying dead—I'M ON THE PHONE, GRAMMA!"

Faint, in the phone's background, Gumshoe Ghost Girl announced, "A clue! Good work, Ghost Cat Solvin' Mysteries!"

I might be taken aback, but I didn't have time to indulge confusion, and bulled ahead. "I need to speak to the Gumshoe Ghost Girl quickly. She has information from an already solved case I need right now."

Did that sound rude? I hoped not. The ghost robot could get here any second and I had to make this quick.

Faint movement noises echoed through the speaker. Gumshoe Ghost Girl said, "Hi, I'm Gumshoe Ghost Girl, and this—"

"Meow."

"—is—"

I didn't let them finish. "I'm so sorry, but I think I hear her footsteps. What's the name of the girl who got turned into a robot at the haunted house?"

Joyous with pride, Gumshoe answered, "Sam Washington! I deduced—"

"So, so sorry," I told her, and hung up, tossed the phone back to Tonika, and turned to face the corridor where I had been hearing the clip clop of footsteps. Louder, pushing plenty of power into my voice, I commanded, "Step into the light!"

The approaching figure lit up, a beacon of white light in the darkness. It might be sheathed in white and have long hair, but it wasn't the robot. It was Angel Cruz. She said something in Spanish, and I didn't need to see her scowl. It *sounded* menacing.

Hoo boy. I had a translator ghost. Should I get it out? No, with the kind of translator I had, things would just get more confused.

So I shook my head and tried really hard to sound calm and friendly. "I don't speak Spanish, sorry."

Now annoyed as well as angry, she declared, "I said I bring my own light, supervillains!"

I gawked at her. "Supervillains? Us?"

She lashed out an arm, pointing an accusing finger at me. "Don't you dare try to gaslight me! You know I'm the good guy here!"

Oops. Um. I was wearing a pitch-black dress with a black-magical face mask, wasn't I? And Tonika and her friends were all in costumes. We were, technically, supervillains right now, and definitely looked the part.

Clank clank clank clank. That was running metal feet echoing down the hallway. Tonika yelled, "You don't have time. Fix the ghost. We'll deal with her, and all your problems will be solved!"

Deal with Angel? How? With Hodir's lightning, directed by Delphine's prognostications, and backed up by whatever Olga now knew her web could do?

"No! That's exactly what I don't want!" I shouted.

I wanted my friends here, so bad. Chris's mind control would be a great way to defuse this situation. Peggy's bugs would make anyone pause long enough to act nonviolently. Sue—

I winced. Right. What Sue would do. The robot was on her way, but Angel was here now. I waved my hands out to the side, and called out, "I'm sorry! When someone attacks me, Sue hits first and asks questions later. I'm grateful for the loyalty, but I'd rather work things out peacefully. Just let me rescue this poor ghost and we'll talk."

Angel stared at me like I was crazy, but importantly, she didn't actually do anything.

I could see the sleek white robot approaching now. I pulled power from my staff and shouted to it, "Sam! Sam Washington! Listen to me! I am the Queen of the Dead, and I am here to help you. You've been sick and hurting for a long time, but if you are calm, if you let me, I will take away the pain and you will finally wake up."

Doing it this way felt weird, uncomfortable, groping for a new style of magic. Dominating the ghost would have been easier, but that wasn't how I wanted this to go. Plus, Angel needed to see what kind of necromancer I was.

The name worked. At the sound of her name, the robot stumbled to a halt, and stood there listening to the rest of my crude, improvised spell.

Holding my right arm out, hand extended and tilted at an angle, I approached the wobbly robot. I kept talking, kept feeding my words power so they would touch the ghost in a way mere sound couldn't. "Shhhh. It's okay. Rest."

I reached the white, segmented, mannequin-liked robot. Clasping my hand to its cheek, I trickled just a little necromancy through the shell into the faint blue silhouette of the ghost inside. It dropped abruptly to its knees, like someone so relieved that their knees gave out underneath them.

Angel got her voice back. The dark girl in the pure white dress demanded, "Why did you call me here? Why do you keep calling me?"

I kept stroking the robot's head, kept feeding it soothing power, keeping myself cold and calm and focused as I replied, "I've never called you that I know about, but strong magic calls to other strong magic."

Necromancy was not penetrating the robot shell easily. This was a strange ghost. I needed it calm, and stroked its hair, trying to feed it just enough to slowly solidify it. If I powered it up enough without it panicking, it should become fully conscious. Then we could talk.

Glaring again, angrier by the second, Angel made a fist and accused, "You called my powers black magic!"

I nodded, just an inch, and slowly, respectfully. "Sorry. I know black magic sounds bad. Your powers are some kind of magic."

The anger disappeared from Angel's face, the nearly violent tension from her posture. She lowered her fist, grumbling and sulking, "Don't be sorry. It's better than the alternative."

Understanding dawned. Oh, yes, I knew where she was coming from. "Oof. Everyone thinks the white light makes you good?"

Her pout just got deeper, more sour and haunted. I winced, not that she could see it. "More than that, an angel?"

She flashed her teeth, looking away for a second, with a grimace not meant for me or anyone present. "Mostly just... destined to be a hero. I'm from a little town in the middle of nowhere. One reason my parents immigrated was to get me away from that, but our neighbors, my aunts and grandparents..."

She trailed off, so I picked up. "Been there, done that." From the opposite end. "But it's worse than expectations, because your powers don't feel angelic. They're angry and exciting, and you get drunk on them, but mostly you just can't use them as much as you want because they don't really do much except destroy. All that's even beside the point, because they make life weird and you can get carried away with them, but they're not *you*. They don't define who you are and what you want."

The voice of Alicia Blackheart that only I could hear murmured, "Quite true. Ah wanted fun, not an empiah of death."

I barely registered her, because Angel reared back and yelled, "I don't want to be a hero!"

The robot, Sam Washington, jerked under my hand. I bent over her, whispering, "Shhhh. Shhhh. It's okay," and she settled down again.

This was working. Tonika had been right. If I played this gently, I could fix my problems and go back to trying to live a life where my powers were only a part of it.

Heat blasted off of Angel. Not real heat, the feel of her magic rising, pouring out of her without control. She glowed as her fists balled up again, and she complained, "But if it's not you, why does a voice keep calling me? Why does it pull me to you?"

Her power had a real problem with making her angry, and it had sprung back up again. She had all my sympathy for that. At least necromancy was cold and focusing. Too focusing, sometimes, but that was better than these flashes of hot rage.

I only had an eyeblink to be sympathetic. Maybe it was the heat, or the sudden outburst, or bad timing. Sam leaped to her metal feet, yelling, "You won't hurt me again!"

She'd jumped out of my grip, but I pressed my palm to her cold, segmented chest plates, and slid up to her shoulder, whispering to this scared, half-aware, traumatized victim I wanted to save, "Shhhh, it's okay. Sam. Sam, it's okay. Listen to me, Sam. You're safe."

Blue light shone down the tunnel. The light belonged to Mech's armor, zipping into view and landing a few yards from me, boots crunching solidly on the paved floor. Loudly, but with earnest reassurance, he told us all, "I'm here. Everyone will be safe."

No one was reassured. Everyone panicked, instead. An already edgy, angry Angel opened her palms and called up two of those floating glowing orbs. Tonika's friends squeaked and milled around. That included Hodir stepping in front of Delphine, and while he didn't do anything visible, I felt the itchy rush as he called up his own magic.

And with all that going on, Sam freaked out. She went from standing in front of me, twitching and wobbling, to lashing out one arm with snake-bite speed, grabbing me by the neck. Still, balanced, upright, and ready to fight again she ranted, "You tricked me again! I won't let you hurt her. It's not worth this to be a beautiful girl!"

My blood didn't run cold because it already was, with my power, but this was bad. Rigid mechanical fingers held me by the throat, and I already knew those fingers were superhumanly strong. If Sam squeezed, she would crush my spine. It would take her a second, tops, to kill me.

But she hadn't squeezed yet, and I had a weapon that moved faster, that she couldn't see coming. The claw spell I'd inherited from Alicia. If I focused it rather than lashing out, I could cut the ghost's arm off like I'd severed my own to make a poltergeist. She would be unable to squeeze. This close, I could cut her head off before she knew it was happening, dissipate the ghost and end this confrontation and most of my problems.

No one would debate whether that killing was justified, and almost no one would see it as a killing.

But I would, and I didn't want to be that person, even if I was an inch from being murdered myself.

I didn't strike.

Others weren't that restrained. Angel acted first, flinging those two balls of light at Sam's head. She wasn't far away, but the globes moved like thrown baseballs, not bullets. Sam threw herself to the side, dropping me as she did. The robot and I hit the floor and rolled in opposite directions.

As the room whirled, it occurred to me that making the robot dodge might have been the point.

Sam and I both stopped rolling. The ghost-possessed robot sat up and lunged for me, only to have to roll away again as a sparkling beam shot from Mech's gauntlet, leaving a melted smear on the floor when it hit. Sam dodged, and kept dodging, eluding destruction as Mech made sure the beam always stayed between her and me rather than focusing first on chasing her down.

For the first time, I heard Tonika shout in panic. "You weren't supposed to be here! This wasn't the plan!"

Delphine hunched up, hands raised protectively as if Tonika would hit her, and squealed with desperate guilt, "I'm sorry! It's not what I saw!"

Sam's head snapped from watching me as she dodged to watching Tonika. She snarled, "You did this! You and your IQ and your obsession with death!"

She leaped to her feet in a run towards Tonika, inhumanly fast again, but she'd lost too much time ranting. Mech's weapon intercepted her hips. The metal flashed hot and melted, accompanied by another flash as one of Angel's light balls knocked the robot's top half away from the bottom.

It didn't stop Sam, not completely. She wheezed, "I'd rather die than be killed again."

Something started whirring inside her.

It didn't have time. Unable to dodge, the robot melted into slag as Mech played his beam over it, its final gambit unfinished.

The glow from the melting metal was painfully bright, and I raised a hand, blocking it out. Heaviness settled on my heart as I recognized what had just happened.

Mech switched to melting down the robot's legs, his sympathy audibly sincere as he said, "I'm sorry, Avery. You're a good person and you wanted to end this peacefully, but I can't let it kill people." He turned his attention to Angel, and told her, "Good job, Miss. Nice reflexes." Then to Tonika, and he raised his voice because she was farther away. "I'm proud of you for supporting Avery like this, Tonika. You have a good heart."

Anger sparked and then died in my heart. I couldn't hate Mech. He was so obviously a hero, in action and in his heart, doing his best to save a bunch of kids from real danger.

Alicia Blackheart's phantom voice gasped. "Honey child, look!"

The Horse Skull Kid added, "Trouble, Avery!"

The pile of slag was too bright to look at, but I peeked around my hand as far as I could.

Sam's robot body might be melted, but her ghost was up and moving. She was murkier in shape than most ghosts, in general shape thin and with long hair like the robot, but blobby and featureless despite being clearly visible. To me, anyway.

Nobody else could see her lurching down towards the base entrance, where Delphine, Olga, and Hodir stood clustered anxiously together. Olga and Hodir had their arms wrapped around Delphine, who watched the scene fish-eyed with guilt.

Tonika had to look guilty alone.

"Sam Washington!" I shouted. I was too surprised to put much power into my voice, and that ghost was so naturally resistant. She didn't waver at all. She finished her staggering run and dived into Tonika.

It was a weird motion. The ghost head hit the physical head first, and stuck, while the rest of Sam got sucked into Tonika like someone smoothing out bubbles in cellophane with their hand. Now Tonika looked like she had in the hospital bed when I first saw her, with a blue ghost overlaid on her body, inside her, wearing the body but not part of it.

I'd had a second to gather my power again, and I put that power into my voice this time. A lot of power. "Sam Washington!"

Tonika jerked, back arched, like a marionette whose string had been yanked. She recovered with a stagger, but a clear voice. "I hear you. I'm awake. I'm finally awake. Was I a beautiful robot, or was that part of the dream?"

It might be Tonika's voice, but it was obviously Sam talking, and I felt... relieved. She might be catching up on events, but she sounded coherent. You could work things out with someone who was lucid.

So much relief. Body-aching relief. This wasn't over.

While I put some lucidity back together myself, Sam raised Tonika's hands, and looked herself over. With rising cheer, she said, "I wanted to be the robot, but I like this."

Nope. Not letting that thought take hold. I held up a hand. "This body's not yours, Sam, but we'll talk about it. I'm positive we can find you a body you're happy with, especially if you liked being a robot."

"A beautiful robot," Sam insisted.

Okay, well, to each their own. This mess might not be resolved, but it was getting easier to clean up. Mech's relentless, rigid nice-guyness would want to help a ghost that's friendly and no threat to anybody, even if he didn't believe it was really alive.

And with Sam sane again, I could safely tell her, "Hang tight. Let me talk to my friend here."

Everybody had been reduced to staring, working out for themselves what was going on. When I looked up at Angel, her blank expression turned to an irritable pout, and she folded her arms under her chest. "'Friend' is pushing it, but I'm willing to talk."

That was all I needed to hear. I told her cheerfully and frankly, "I don't know why you're being called. Magic calls magic, but it's nothing like you're describing for me, and I wasn't using enough magic to bother with until you arrived."

The anger in Angel's face faded slowly into curiosity. She unlocked her arms, summoned another of those white balls, and tossed it between her hands like a toy. "You really think my power is black magic?"

I shrugged. "Seems like it to me. It's for dead sure magic."

"Woo, black magic kids club!" shouted Hodir at the end of the tunnel.

Lashing a finger out in his direction, I scolded, "Not the time, Hodir!"

The little blond tween went back to hugging his gradually less-traumatized-looking girlfriend. Sam-in-Tonika watched them, me, all of us with fascination.

Angel pursed her lips again, suspicion warring with temptation. I could hear the burning, badly suppressed hope when she asked, "As in, I could cast spells magic?"

I nodded. I didn't need to be encouraging, just tell her the truth. "That kind. Black magic doesn't like to bend to other magics much, but it does bend. Listen, I barely understand necromancy. If you want to contact a real expert, I can... what's your phone number?

Angel pulled her phone out of a little pouch on her belt. There wasn't really any space for pockets on her dull white dress. I got to my feet and hunted around my costume until I found where the magic-clothes-changing pendant had hidden my phone. I turned it on, and held it up next to Angel's. Hers was primitive, not a smartphone. It wasn't my place to pry about that. Right now we were peacemaking.

Her phone number was on her screen, so I dialed it into my message app, and a second later, sent a group text to Angel and Barbara.

Me: Barbara, meet a new magic user our age. Black magic, I think. She needs advice. This is so she can contact you when she's ready.

Would Barbara see this quickly? Apparently so, because before Angel or I got tired of waiting, we got a reply.

Barbara: I will be happy to. Take your time, new mage. There is always a rocky period with our powers, and two things I can promise are that I won't judge your powers, and I won't judge you.

Out loud, I said, "She means it. She's friends with the best and the worst."

"Personally, I think you have the makings of a true hero," declared Mech, completely failing to read the room.

Angel looked disgusted at his praise, but put it aside to raise a still-suspicious eyebrow at me. "Are you going to stop calling me? Summoning me? Whatever?"

I spread my hands. "Can't. I don't think it's me doing it. Barbara will help you find out what's going on, and until then, I'm happy if you ignore those calls and keep going around your own business."

She stared at her phone for a second, then up at me with a sour frown. "Good. If I never see you again it will be too soon, and I mean that in the best way possible."

Whirling around, long hair billowing like a cape, Angel Cruz stalked back up the tunnel out of sight.

I sighed heavily, letting out all the tension I'd been carrying from that problem. It might have paled next to the crazy robot danger, but Angel's animosity and her popping up whenever things were already difficult had been weighing on me.

Straightening up, I reached into my hood to brush down my massive hair a little. Not that I could, but for the millionth time I tried and failed. Now I could give Sam my full attention, and called over to her, "Alright, Sam. Glad you're finally with us to be helped. How'd you even take over Tonika, anyway? Why her?"

Sam-in-Tonika didn't look at me. She stared off to the side at one of the pieces of wreckage in the garage, and answered distractedly, "The computer in her head."

Oof. I snapped my fingers, warning, "I think you're losing yourself again, Sam. Don't worry. I'll help."

She shook her head, but gingerly, like she had a headache. "No, it's… there's something else in here, and it's biting me."

What? That didn't… *sound* like Tonika fighting for her body?

I was already approaching her. I squinted, studying hard the blue shape inside Tonika's body.

A second ghostly outline twitched inside Tonika's head. Something spidery.

"What is that?" I asked out loud.

Alicia answered, "You have me confounded. Ah have nevah seen the like."

Numlah rumbled, "Reminds me of a magic leech."

Horse Skull Kid spit on the ground. Or at least, it sounded like he did. "Had those in the Colorado River. Nasty varmints. Weren't quite like this."

"Didn't you have to take somethin' out of the child's head to wake huh up foah the first time?" Alicia reminded me.

I gritted my teeth. That was exactly what this thing looked like, and it couldn't be good. Raising my voice, I said, "Sam, step out and inhabit something else."

Tonika's body turned away and walked into the garage, instead.

My heart knotted. This had gone bad. I couldn't knock the parasite out of her from this distance.

I could cast Namluh's spell?

No! I now knew two combat spells, and that was two too many.

Brisk and businesslike, Tonika said, "Registering Organism—"

"Stop her!" shouted Mech.

"—Two as new administrator," Tonika finished.

The garage door slammed shut behind her.

Chapter Thirty-Five

Like the top superhero he was, Mech held up a gauntleted hand, palm out. "Stay calm, kids. I've dealt with this problem before. Avery, what happened?"

There wasn't a hint of ego in his voice, either. Just sober, professional confidence.

"Deathette," said Olga, from the huddled mass of Tonika's friends.

I'd have been happier if that name disappeared down a memory hole, but she must have had a point because Mech sounded ever so slightly guilty as he nodded. "Of course."

Me, I sounded sheepish and awkward enough to cut through my panic over the situation. I confessed to the famous hero who'd been helping me for months, "Sometimes a teenager or a hero can't help people, but a villain can."

"Then let's work together to save Tonika, Deathette," Mech replied, because he was just that nice a guy.

Also he had asked me a question way more important than my guilt, so I jumped back to it. "Right. Getting hit by necromancy killed the thing Organism One left in her head. Looks like getting hit by necromancy again reanimated it. Just plain bad luck. I imagine we'd better hurry, because it's going to try to destroy humanity, right?"

His visored face on his helmeted head on his armored body turned to look at the massive door into the bunker. "It will, but we sabotaged this place pretty heavily, and it's going to take time she doesn't have to find out how, and more to fix it. Then she has to restore contact to Organism One to do any major damage, which also takes time. Meanwhile, I know things about this installation I never recorded anywhere."

With no further prompting, the garage door slid up into the ceiling. Everything inside looked the way we left it, except the hatch door into the base itself was closed.

Mech looked at Olga, Delphine, and Hodir next. With sincere empathy, he said, "Kids, I know you want to help your friend, but now's not the time. Stay out here. Deathette—"

"You need my powers. I'm with you," I answered before he asked the question.

Warm and approving and condescending only in the way adults always are to teenagers, Mech said, "A villain with a hero's heart. I have a bad loadout for catching non-powered children. I have tranquilizers, but a dose that might knock out a supervillain will kill her several times over."

While I could go after the ghost directly. I nodded. "Got it. You can handle the physical stuff."

"We understand each other. Let's move."

Hodir squeaked suddenly and angrily, "We want to help!"

"Tonika is our friend!" exclaimed Delphine, shoulder to shoulder with the blonde boy.

Mech waved his hand in emphatic denial and repeated. "You kids are in way over your head already. I need Deathette's powers."

The unspoken truth hung in the air. If Mech could do this without me, there was no way he would take a fifteen-year-old child into this fight.

This time the message stuck. Hodir, Delphine, and Olga didn't argue any more, they just watched us with varying expressions of pain, anxiety, and regret.

More than once Chris, Annie, and Peggy had said that some

people lead, and some people can't. Sue and I could lead, and miraculously, lead in the same direction.

I could also follow if that was what circumstances called for. I watched Mech, who ignored the upset teenagers and focused his attention on the hatch on the other side of the garage. It swung open.

But the huge garage door in front of us slammed shut.

Mech didn't do anything visible, but the garage door slid open once more.

And slammed shut again, with a thump and a gust of wind that echoed up the passage. The metal door was at least six inches thick. It was *massive*.

Open.

Shut, with another boom.

Brisk and only slightly amused, slightly frustrated, Mech said, "Cute. Organism Two's strategy is going to be delay, Deathette. Until it reestablishes contact with Organism One, it will be unable to do much damage, and won't have the resources or power to take on my suit. It can see and hear us, by the way, but I don't mind admitting I'm not fond of it having access to—"

The door slid open. The door slammed partly shut, but this time Mech stepped forward, lifting one arm and grabbing the garage door on its way down. Metal clanged and squeaked, but he held it as he finished, "—Tonika's brain."

The door pulled back up into the ceiling, dragging Mech with it, until his fingers scraped off the lower edge. As Mech fell down to the floor, the tremendously heavy garage door slammed down on top of him.

Uselessly. Mech caught it with his hand again on the way down, and while it drove him against the floor with an ear-splitting crack, the force barely bent Mech's knees. The next time it tried to pull him up, Mech let go, and caught the door again when it tried to crush him.

Trusting that Mech had this, I bent low and scooted past him into the murky garage.

Mech waved his free hand. An almost invisible force, just hints of sparkly aquamarine blue, gently pushed Tonika's friends away from the door and into the alcove with the spiraling stairs.

Bystanders safely out of the way, he stepped into the garage himself. The door stopped banging and remained open.

Instead, metal squealed on metal, an engine chugged, and one of the piles of wreckage zoomed out of the darkness towards us. Whatever the vehicle had been, now it was a charred, shattered frame that clung to the ground, spraying sparks, screeching and weaving. But it moved, and moved fast.

Except not quite towards us. Mech held out his hand and those blue sparkles hovered in the air in front of me, but he didn't need to. Instead, the mass of already burned metal plowed into the hatch that had been our next goal, blocking the base entrance with a twisted lump of steel.

Staring at the new obstacle, Mech explained, "That is how Tonika thinks. The door bought her a few seconds to get one of the remaining drones active. It blocking the door is giving her time to activate her next stage of defense. We need to free her, and not just for her own sake. This city doesn't need a second Spider."

Whatever that meant, Mech sounded decidedly grim about it.

Grabbing the destroyed vehicle with both hands, Mech yanked it out from in front of the door. Amazingly, the wreck still wasn't finished, and its wheels spun and whirred and squealed where they touched the pavement, trying to spin around again.

The inner hatch popped open, no doubt in response to a remote signal from Mech. Like the garage door, it immediately set to swinging open and then shut, over and over.

In the darkness down the curving garage, a larger, humanoid shadow moved. One of the robots trudged out of its parking place. All I could see was a silhouette, which looked nearly as battered as the vehicle Mech as fighting.

But it moved.

Mech spun in place, flinging the not-broken-enough vehicle into the air, sending it sailing towards the approaching robot. When the hatch did its next swing open, he grabbed it in one hand, and me in the other.

A blocky metal forearm lifted me off the floor and squeezed

me uncomfortably against a blocky, metal chestplate as Mech hunched forward and darted through the doorway, weaving through the cluttered workshop and surgery. I could hardly see anything except the floor and blue twinkles. Above me, a couple of thumps might have been Mech breaking interior doors off their hinges as Mech stampeded through them, but I couldn't be sure. Buzzing and sparking and scraping noises filtered through from the other side of Mech's power armor as things attacked him.

They didn't drown out Mech telling me, "And every second we let her delay us, we fall further behind."

Mech wasn't letting Tonika delay us anymore. By the time he finished saying that, he was straightening up and setting me back onto the floor of the control room at the center of the tiny base.

It hadn't changed much. Wires, big and small, still ran from computer-y boxes that lined the dome to the cube in the middle. It was still badly lit. Like last time, Tonika stood in the open-topped cube, fixing plugs into the sockets on her head with a faint frown of concentration. She didn't look like she was hurrying, or paying us any attention.

Mech placed his nearly indestructible back against the door. Deep in the grey shadows on the grey walls, another grey door lurked on the opposite side of this one, but it didn't seem to be in a hurry to open up and let in mechanical monsters. Anything trying to fight in here would have to rip through dozens of wires to do it.

Mech folded his arms, solid as a wall between me and danger, and said, "Your turn. I'm helpless against evil ghosts. You have an advantage." Raising his voice, he called out, "I know you're in there, Tonika, and I know you're fighting, because I know you could have tried to kill Deathette and you didn't."

...What now? What was this about killing me?

I pushed that useless thought aside, and suggested the easy, obvious solution. "You could cut all those wires, there."

Now Tonika noticed us. She didn't look at us, but she smirked and sounded both evil and smug. "He doesn't dare, and he knows why."

Me, I didn't care why. I didn't have time to care. The easy solution wouldn't work, so I'd move on to the next, trying the thing that had worked last time. I lashed out with my ghost hand to grab the parasite and rip it free from both Tonika and Sam's ghost. I could see the blue, fuzzy outline of Sam nestled just inside Tonika's skin, and the multi-legged monstrosity twitching in her head.

The problem was, I didn't have a ghost hand this time. I had a ghost blob, which darted forward and poked the parasite fiercely and persistently, trying to force it out of Tonika's head. Even with just a little pea-sized blob, the effort wasn't completely ineffective. I pushed the parasite a few inches out, but it clung like a stubborn octopus to Sam's ghost.

Irritated now, Tonika warned, "Tell her to quit it, Mech, or I'll discharge the chemicals. I will *make* my host kill her."

That was confirmation that Tonika was fighting. If the parasite was having trouble overriding just Tonika, maybe what we needed was to make it fight both the people it has possessed.

So I swirled cold necromancy through my body and out through my words, shouting, "Sam Washington! The Queen of the Dead calls you, Sam! Is this body a robot? Is this what you wanted, Sam? Is this what you died for? Now another killer wants to use you?"

Tonika's head jerked. Her eyes widened. "What?" she asked, unfocused and confused. Raising her hands, she stared at them and whispered, "That's right, I'm—"

Another sudden change. Tonika bent forward now, grabbing her own head, fumbling with the wires. Her voice whimpering with effort, she begged, "Mech, unhook me while you can!"

I hurried to the edge of the cube, which didn't take much hurrying because it was only a few feet away. The whole control room was about the size of my bedroom back home, and much more tightly packed.

Tonika stopped my reaching hands by holding out her own. She wheezed, "Guard Deathette. Please."

"Done wrong, this could cause permanent brain damage, or even kill her," Mech explained. He had already abandoned his post at the door, and despite the metal gauntlets his hands moved nimbly as they popped free plug after plug, disconnecting Tonika from the facility. Tonika removed a few herself, but her shaking hands couldn't keep up with his.

The last cable clicked free. Tonika hunched farther forward, shuddering. Arms crossed and gripping each other, she whispered, "Capture field. Get me past the bunker's cage before it repairs my antenna."

Tonika knew Mech's armor and what it could do. As she requested, he laid his hand on her head, and a bubble popped into just barely visible being around Tonika, all baby blue and twinkly like his force fields. We didn't waste time. He guided the bubble as we rushed back out through the silent surgery and robot repair room, both of which now featured several of their robotic arms snapped off and scattered around. Mech had to kick open the door into the garage, pushing the hatch past the wreckage of both drone car and big clunky robot.

The robot wasn't completely shut down. It turned, raising a fist clumsily.

Mech raised his own hand and blasted his sparkle beam through its head. I circled well around the hot, glowing remains.

And then we were out into the tunnel. With nothing trying to stop us, navigating the tiny base had taken thirty seconds, tops. Most of that was crossing the parking garage.

"Tonika!" cheered Hodir, Olga, and Delphine simultaneously. Her friends rushed out of the stairway, gathering around the bubble. Inside, Tonika's mouth moved, but no sound got through the barrier.

Mech lifted his hand. The bubble popped. Tonika dropped half an inch to land steady on her feet on the floor. Steady, but still hunched forward, with one hand clutching her face and the other outstretched to ward off her friends.

"Not yet! I love you all, but not yet!" she whimpered, hoarse and desperate.

Mech sounded much more calm, and stood at ease as he said, "Even if it reactivates your connection, it can't reach the base or the city from here. Deathette, destroy the thing in her head."

Tonika spasmed, her head jerking away from me, and she pleaded, "Pull it out of me first. Get it out. Get it out! I don't want to lose me again!" Her whole body shook as she fought for control.

I knew what to do now. I shoved my little pea-sized poltergeist into Tonika's head, through Sam's ghost, and pushed as hard as I could at the spidery artificial ghost tormenting them. I couldn't dislodge it, but I pushed some of it out past the surface of Tonika's skin. Just a couple of inches.

A couple of inches was plenty. Switching my staff to my right hand, I filled my left with necromancy and grabbed the protruding edge of the bug-thing. It clung to its victims, fighting me, but I dragged it out inch by inch.

For extra measure, I yelled, "Out, Sam Washington! Out! This is not the beautiful robot you were promised!"

Sam came flying out of Tonika, tossed to the floor like a living person, with the parasite still attached to her head. I positioned myself between them and Tonika to stop them from possessing her again, and raised my left hand, focusing on a very sharp claw like the one I'd used in the ghost hand ceremony. I spent another breath of power to order, "Now, hold still, Sam."

She didn't. She leaped up like a spring and dove into Mech instead. I saw her outline expand, filling and shaping herself to his armor like she had to Tonika.

My eyes bulged. I fought the urge to freeze in panic, and shouted instead, "Hodir, Olga, help!"

Delphine grabbed me and Tonika, dragging us to the floor, and I let her. Hodir and Olga dove on top of us. Olga threw out her web, which stuck in the air, the web containing the kaleidoscope of raw chaos magic Hodir blasted into it. The itchy back blast made me twist around uncontrollably in discomfort, but not enough that I didn't see the sparkles going past the rim of that shield, bouncing off it to melt chunks of the tunnel's surface and floor. No holding back this time. The parasite was trying to kill us.

But not for long. A couple of seconds later it flew past the web into the garage, and the heavy garage door slammed shut. So did the door to the outer tunnel. We'd have been trapped if not for the staircase up to Mech's base.

Not that being trapped was the problem.

Hodir's colorful mess dissolved. Olga yanked on a string of her web, and it collapsed, flying back into her hand. I stood up and looked at the garage door, which locked us out and locked Mech, possessed by a ghost possessed by a servant of Organism One, in.

Chapter Thirty-Six

Mouth dry and a little croaky, I asked out loud, "Is that as bad as I think it is?"

"*Yes*," exclaimed Tonika, emphatically. She sat on the floor, face screwed up in misery, tears running from the corners of her eyes. Her voice turned into a sobbing croak. "And it's my fault!"

Back on his feet, Hodir grabbed one of her shoulders in both hands and insisted, "It wasn't you!"

Gritting her teeth, Delphine clutched her crystal ball in both hands, head bent over it as she whimpered, "It was my fault. I should have seen Mech showing up!"

Angry, fists on her hips, little Olga corrected all three of them. "It's Organism One's fault for putting that thing in your head."

Tonika sniffled, rubbing at her red-veined eyes. "No, it's my fault! You don't understand. The parasite forced me to think for it. This was my plan! It and I didn't have the knowledge together to fix the connections and contact Organism One, so we put together a fake resistance plan to keep you and Mech too focused to realize that it could use the ghost who possessed me to possess Mech!"

Staff holding hand hanging at my side, my left fist propped on my hip, I admitted, "Well, that's freaky smart."

Tonika threw her hands up, protesting, "It's not! I just ask questions like what if I can't win, can I win by losing? I'm not smart. I'm—"

Sobbing replaced words. Tonika staggered to her feet, twisting away when her friends tried to hug her. She staggered into the stair-lined open shaft leading up to Mech's base, and in the center of that hole pulled her phone out and held it in a shaky hand.

Peering at the screen, she croaked, "One bar. It's enough," and started dialing.

Still trying to catch up mentally and emotionally, I asked, "What are you doing?"

Hunched over the phone, Tonika whimpered, "I'm lost. I've destroyed the world. I can't do this anymore. I need an adult, and… and there's only one I know to call."

She must have set the phone to speaker, because I heard the click as someone picked up, and Doctor Biotic asked, "Mech?" After the briefest of pauses, her cheerful tone disappeared, turned flat and serious. "Not Mech. Tonika?"

Stuttering with sobs, Tonika whispered into the phone, "It's bad, Doctor Biotic. It's really bad. I've ruined everything. So many people—"

Doctor Biotic interrupted her with a soft, soothing, but insistent tone. "Shhhh. I know you can control yourself. Report, like you would for Mech. Where are you, and what happened?"

It helped. Tonika's eyes were still red, and her cheeks shone with tears, but her miserable voice stabilized. "I'm in the access shaft from Mech's base to Organism One's bunker. Deathette, Olga, Hodir, and Delphine are with me. The doors are sealed. Mech is inside. A ghost fused with a parasite Organism One put in my brain have taken control of Mech."

A hideous noise came out of the phone, like nothing I'd ever heard before. Not animal or mechanical. Unearthly. A grinding but vocal noise.

Because it was important, I corrected, "Control of his armor. I don't think they can control Mech, unless his armor can."

Her voice getting more and more shrill and panicky, Tonika said, "It will have put him in Impact Mode to keep him from interfering. Doctor Biotic, it's going to—"

"I know what it's going to try to do," she said quietly.

Tonika started sobbing again, bent over the phone, tears dripping onto the screen. "I'm so sorry. I was so stupid. So selfish."

More firm, more businesslike, more... like Mech, Doctor Biotic asked, "Mech is alive, correct?"

Tonika sniffed a couple of times before she could answer. "It won't want to kill him. That would shut down his armor."

Patient and even, Doctor Biotic said, "Then right now, Tonika, you've had a painful learning experience. If Mech dies, and only if Mech dies, you'll have made a mistake you can never take back. Start planning a way to prevent that. I'll be in touch again as fast as I can. Okay?"

Voice hollow, but tears stopped, Tonika whispered back, "Okay."

The line cut out with a click.

Silence reigned for a few seconds. Hodir, Delphine, and Olga stood in the tunnel, watching Tonika with eyes full of worry. I did the same, but from the bottom step of the stairs. Tonika remained bent over the phone.

She took a deep breath and whispered. "I can do this." Straightening up, suddenly completely calm despite tear-tracked cheeks, she said, "I have turned off my emotions. If I don't give in, we can do this. First, Delphine, listen to me. It's not your fault. Super powers fail. Everyone's powers go wrong. Ask Hodir."

Putting his fists on his hips, chin lifted, Hodir declared proudly, "That's all my powers ever do!"

But, despite his bravado, his right hand left his hip and slipped into Delphine's, holding it tight.

Tonika continued, not quite robotically flat in expression and voice, "I chose to ignore that, and used you to justify my ego, thinking I had planned out everything."

"Uh... excuse me?" I asked, half-raising a hand.

"Yes?" Tonika asked, her head tilting in curiosity, which her cyborg implant must not turn off.

"So that means you expected Angel to be here?" Because that was sure what it sounded like when only Mech surprised Tonika and Delphine.

Tonika waved a hand in her friends' direction. "I called her. Or rather, I made Hodir call her, but I don't think he knew what he was doing."

A memory struck me. That unexplained burst of itchy chaos magic just before Angel showed up at Tonika's father's home. I put another two together with two and two.

I did not like the result I got. Frowning, anger snaking up like frost through my body, I thought out loud. "You've called her before. And Sam. That's it. *You're* the person who's been plotting against me this whole time, aren't you?"

"For you," Tonika corrected dispassionately. "I didn't try to make Angel hate you, or know Sam would happen, but once they did, I needed you on edge so that you would let me fix your problems and I could fix everyone else's problems in the process."

I glared. Ice spiked through my heart. "By manipulating me!? Tonika, this is… this is borderline evil stuff. You know that? Where did you learn this? From that thing in your head?"

"From you," she answered.

The ice tower of my rage collapsed. "Say what now?"

From the tunnel, Hodir squeaked, "It's true! You got your tools that let you master your powers by stealing them. You did villainy stuff for a good cause, and it worked."

Olga, suddenly puffed up and stubborn in defense of her friend, declared, "I've known other people who did the same."

Tonika looked me in the eyes, and explained, "My memories of a normal life are gone. I was working off of the examples I had. When I turn my emotions back on, Avery, I'll be so sorry I won't be able to function. I told you once that when I'm stupid, I'm stupider than any regular person can be. I didn't just mean saying socially awkward things."

I paused, although not to think. To feel, maybe. My emotions writhed around, until they reached a point I could say, "I'm not in a position to judge, and we need to act now while this is still just a dumb choice."

"It's going to be difficult. Hodir, try to destroy the door," Tonika ordered, waving a black-vinyl-sheathed arm at it.

Olga darted out of the way behind Hodir. Way out of the way. Delphine took a step back, but just one step back, still holding Hodir's right hand in her left.

Hodir extended his left hand, and out of his hand flared green, twisting lighting, bathing the tunnel in freakish highlights and shadows, and bathing me in itchiness so bad I had to fight to keep my fists clenched and still.

The raw power of that little boy was... it awed me. With lightning blasting out like that, on and on, his face paint and spiky, black-leather armor no longer looked ridiculous.

Eventually, the lightning stopped. Hodir wasn't even breathing hard.

But he hadn't destroyed the door. Who knew what it was made of, but that monolithic barrier had been built to take abuse. Its previously ridged surface now warped and rippled. The red Catlantian symbols were now a network of interlocking lines and circles, but squiggly rather than geometric. Green crystals that gave off an itchy aura grew out of the surface in three places.

That was all surface damage. It still looked impregnable.

Undaunted, never daunted, Hodir declared, "I might be able to make a gate through it to the other side, with Delphine's help."

The goofy little blond boy smiled up at the brown-haired, cookie-cutter-pretty rich girl. She smiled back, her remaining guilt and fear melting into gratitude.

The remaining icy anger in my heart melted, too. Those two were just so *cute*.

Tonika shook her head an inch either way. "We have a better teleport option."

Skittering and clinking sounded in the shaft above me and Tonika. I edged out into the open center and looked up.

Doctor Biotic was approaching us fast. On all fours, she leaped between levels of stairs twice, landing perched with all four feet together. The last few yards she crawled down the rock wall, arms and legs outstretched, claws on hands and feet digging into the stone.

When she reached head height, she jumped off the wall and landed with a perfectly human uprightness next to me and Tonika.

Curiosity flickered in Tonika's expression again, raising the ridges where other people had eyebrows. Organism One really, really must not like hair. "How did you get here so fast?"

Doctor Biotic had mutated again. What drew my eye first was that the metal plate and red robotic eye in her face were gone, replaced with an eye that while it had a huge, dark iris and pupil ringed by only tiny hints of white, was normally flesh and blood. That was only the first change. There were the big, hooked claws on fingers and toes, which made her wear sandals that her toes and their claws stuck over the edge of. Her other main eye was still a pool of green and brown with a black bar through the middle, but the smaller eyes on the side of her head all looked different. On this side, I saw a purple slit-pupiled eye and an eye dominated by a wide, white horizontal band and a rainbow band at the center of that.

Her face had changed. The whole shape of her head had changed, but subtly. It sloped forward, farther than a human face, but not as far as an animal's muzzle. The effect was elfin—odd, but not ugly. She had what was probably real hair now, short and dark grey around her ears, with a streak of white inside that, brown inside that, and black at the middle, all running back from a point between her eyes to her neck. Fluffy fur in the same pattern grew out of the segments of her scorpion tail now, which did not make it look less dangerous.

Her skin was still golden orange, but a lot less of it showed. This mutation was far more modest, wearing a basic exercise outfit of snug Velcro from wrists to stomach and from hips to knees. A butterfly design still occasionally flapped across her midriff from one item of clothing to the other.

She wore a pouch on a belt around her waist. Clothing like that didn't have pockets.

Still pointy fangs flashed between her lips as she gave a crisp answer. "I made a deal with someone to do something I'd rather not do, but which won't make me feel guilty. I don't think any other help will get here in time. You're already making plans?"

Tonika nodded. "Yes. If Deathette agrees, and she will, we can get in."

I didn't have much choice about it. We'd wasted too much time already.

Looking down at Tonika with a frown and a serious expression clear even on that distended, six-eyed face, Doctor Biotic told her, "Alright. There's one thing you need to do first to prepare."

Curious again, Tonika tilted her head. "What?"

Six eyes bored into Tonika's two. "Turn your feelings back on."

Tonika tilted her eyebrows in confusion. "That's—"

The robot turned off. The little girl's face twisted up in misery, tears welling up in the corners of her eyes again. Her mouth remained open, but no words came out.

Doctor Biotic took the single step forward to close the gap between them, put her arms around Tonika, and held the little girl in a gentle hug. Tonika hugged back, clinging to the species-spliced doctor with ferociously gripped fistfuls of Doctor Biotic's elastic top. Sniffles and sobs came out of where Tonika's face pressed to Biotic's neck.

"I'm sorry. I'm so sorry, everyone," Tonika whispered.

Cheek laid on top of Tonika's bald head, Doctor Biotic murmured, "Then you need to fix it, and take it from me, pure logic is just another altered frame of mind, not a better one."

Tonika's sobs and sniffles slowed down, replaced by heavy breathing.

Me, I asked, "While we're blaming everybody, why didn't you folks just destroy this bunker the first time?"

Her face still lying atop Tonika, Doctor Biotic turned her eyes up to me and answered quietly, "Mad scientists can't bring themselves to destroy a machine capable of contacting every computer on Earth simultaneously, especially since not even Organism One can build another. This facility has been used for more good than evil. Mech used it to help stop an alien invasion. But at times like this, your way sounds better to me." Lifting her head, she looked down at Tonika and asked, "Okay. You got control of yourself?"

Tonika gave one more sniff, wiping her nose in a vinyl sleeve and making it slightly more shiny. She nodded. Her voice now just a bit hoarse, she said, "Mech will have access to many more defenses than I did. We need to skip as many of them as possible."

Which was what I expected to hear. "Got it. Up the stairs, folks. As fast as you can."

Making the point, I took off, leaping up the stairs two at a time, racing towards the top. Speed was important, and I loved the burn of climbing stairs like this at a run. Doctor Biotic picked Tonika up like a sack of flour with one arm, and ran up the stairs three legged, skipping whole sections by jumping across now and then. That looked suicidally dangerous, but her clawed feet and hand grabbed the rung on the other side every time.

Olga grabbed the side of her head, face pinched up, and giggled. Whatever was going on, she seemed happy, so I didn't slow down. I was up a couple of spirals when strings of colored light shot up the center of the shaft. Below me, a giddy Olga shouted, "Come on!" and a second later Olga, Delphine, and Hodir went shooting up the center like they were being bounced on a rubber band, all wrapped together by the web. A few seconds after that, squeals and yelps sounded above me, followed by a lot of laughter.

Olga's voice echoed down. "Well, that was almost a good idea."

So did Hodir's. "We made it, didn't we?"

Hodir's head peered over the edge of the top of the stairs, then was yanked back.

I, the most physically fit person here who didn't get that way from super mutagens, was the last person to the top. That did not seem fair.

A moment of flippancy helped push back the looming terror. I was going to confront Mech, who had force fields, heat rays, knockout drug weapons, and stuff I couldn't imagine, and this Mech didn't have any moral restraints about using them. I was walking into a death trap, because I didn't have any choice. I was the only person who could do it.

As I climbed the last few steps, maybe slightly winded and feeling some stiffness in my laterals, I shouted, "Alice!"

I only got a glimpse of the secret door from this side. In Mech's base, it had been invisible. Here it stood out like a sore thumb, a slab of metal with an embedded handle in a crude rectangular hole cut into the already crude vertical stone tunnel. That was my glimpse, before the door slid open to reveal the wonderfully cool crypt of Alice. It was actually pretty stuffy in that underground base.

Everyone piled in, me last, and Alice slid the door shut behind me. I got the feeling she didn't like exotic doors that weren't rectangles swinging in or out.

I stopped a few steps in, taking a deep breath, letting the ache disappear from my lungs and legs, soothed by the subtle flow of necromancy inside a ghost room. My composure back, I swept the heavy, crystal-laden head of my staff around the room, pointing at everyone in turn. "Nobody tells anybody about Alice. Especially Mech. I'm not real thrilled with how many folks know already."

Doctor Biotic, who probably didn't have to look around with those eyes on the side of her head, nodded amicably. "I would want this kept secret if I owned it."

Tonika, only traces of hoarseness left in her voice, fluttered a hand at her friends lined up next to her. "I will make sure they understand."

"I'll make sure Hodir understands," Delphine declared.

"I don't understand," said Hodir.

Everyone giggled, even if Tonika sounded strained. Doctor Biotic didn't actually giggle. She made a weird hissing noise that sounded less animal and more like air escaping from a tire.

I flexed my gloved left hand, and clenched and relaxed my right hand around my staff. I pulled a little power in from it, partly to refill me, mostly to create that connection where magic flowed in and out from it as easily as if the staff were part of my body. "Alrighty. There's a closed door on the other side of the control room. No way the ghost parasite thingy will expect us. Alice? Hook us up, but don't open yet."

I turned to look at the door. Yes, it was now a bolted ship hatch type door.

I took a deep breath. Time for the climactic battle.

Chapter Thirty-Seven

Out loud, I said, "If there's a climactic battle, we are going to get creamed."

Tonika, her frown calm but very, very serious, said, "Correct. We have to do this fast. Given more than a few seconds, Mech's armor can kill us all. Hodir, wreck the room. If we fail, Organism One cannot be allowed to take control of this facility."

Doctor Biotic extended a freakishly long tongue, slid it around her bulging face to smooth down the furry stripe down between her eyes, and followed up with, "I can distract Mech for a few seconds and live. Deathette, can you hit the target through me?"

I thought about that, and whether my ghost sight would show me the parasite through Doctor Biotic's body. Both seemed likely, but I warned, "Not without hurting you."

"If it hurts but doesn't kill me, do it. The same with Mech," she said, prying open the Velcro of her belt patch and pulling out a pair of gloves with metal claw covers that she slipped onto her hands. Not just covers like blades. Covers with circuitry-looking tiny lights threaded over them.

She was right. Making Mech feel awful with necromancy

but doing no permanent damage was a clear moral choice here. But... "Doesn't he have a force field?"

Tonika had thought of that already, and answered, "It didn't stop a ghost. He can't detect a pure necromancy attack, much less counter it. Delphine, will this plan work?"

Delphine paused in pulling Hodir away from the sarcophagus in the center of the room. Lifting her crystal ball, she stared into it. Even Hodir calmed down as the seconds passed. Delphine started to shake, but the ball remained dull and unlit. She stammered, "I—I can't—it's not working."

Tonika grimaced, touched with a sad, sympathetic smile. She grabbed the taller girl and gave her a tight hug, telling Delphine, "Then it isn't. Nobody is all powerful. You'll always be one of us. Olga, if Doctor Biotic and Deathette fail, set your web to do whatever it can to shield us or slow down Mech, and everyone runs back in here. Hodir destroying the room will foil Organism One, and we'll have to hope someone else can save Mech."

And Sam. Poor Sam, who never deserved any of this, starting twenty years ago when she was scooped up by a killer psycho. Except that nobody but me would even try to save Sam.

Hold on, Sam. I was on your side. You deserved to be saved.

Which meant I had to stop ignoring my own options just because I was squeamish about villainy. I thumped my hood with a finger. "Namluh. Help me with that spell again."

I figured I remembered it. The more complicated a spell, the easier it was to remember, somehow. I still couldn't afford to get this wrong.

"I'm proud of you, girl," said Namluh's jolly voice.

"Me, too," echoed Horse Skull Kid.

"And me," grunted a voice I recognized as the Creepy Old Mountain Man, who I hadn't even known was awake and haunting me.

Alicia Blackheart followed up. "Moah than I can say. Now hurry."

Namluh rattled off the spell. I recited it with him, drawing the symbol that came with it in the air. The spell clicked into place. I felt the weapon it created floating in front of me, like you feel anything too near your skin, and like the feeling that something in your body is held tense.

"It's taken us too long already. Everyone ready?" I asked the room.

Everyone nodded, although Olga looked wide eyed and petrified, and Delphine was still sniffly and depressed.

I waved at the door. Alice swung it open.

Doctor Biotic moved like lightning. I barely got a chance to see Mech standing in the cube, with two of the boxy computers above him open and his hands plunged into them. Doctor Biotic leaped on top of him, with the claws of both hands and feet. His subtle blue haze of shield flashed brightly and went out. Doctor Biotic opened her jaws freakishly wide, biting down over his face plate. She hooked her claws into the seams in his armor, a foot into his waist and another in his left wrist, fingers in his right shoulder and elbow, her body twisted and writhing chaotically as she clung to him. More threatening than her claws or fangs, the point of her stinger jammed itself into the joint of his left shoulder, wriggling its way in steadily deeper.

Hodir yelled gibberish in a scratchy voice. Gibberish that just might be death metal lyrics in some Scandinavian language? As with all the best spells, the magic was in the music. Good spell or bad, kaleidoscope jagged lines splintered around the ceiling of the room, writing around and leaving boxes twisted and wires made of random materials. Those would not be interfacing with anything.

Forget all that, Avery. You have your own part to play.

"His right arm!" I shouted, because I could see the parasite. It wasn't in Sam's head, it was in her hand in Mech's glove, reaching its legs into the ceiling. It was making contact with its creator.

Doctor Biotic moved as fast as before, planting a foot over Mech's visor in place of her mouth, hooking the claws of one hand into his elbow, the other into his shoulder, and slamming her stinger home into his wrist. As strong as Mech's armor was, she only had to hold him for a moment.

I didn't need to aim. The spell did that for me. I just drew an x with my finger over the parasite ghost.

The spell caught. I felt the necromantic bullet yanked out of me, and while I couldn't see it hit, I heard the screech from Mech's armor, and saw it buck and wobble.

Hating to do this, I drew another x around where Mech's shoulder must be, through Doctor Biotic. As the invisible projectile launched, I ran to the cube in the center of the room, jumped up onto it, jumped onto Doctor Biotic's back as she and Mech keeled over, and I grabbed the transparent blue parasite with my left hand where it flopped out of the gauntlet. Sam was too stunned by my spell to maintain a good hold on Mech's suit.

I hauled the ghost half out of Mech's armor, whispered, "Sorry, Sam," and hit her hand and the attached parasite with Alicia's claws. Not sharp this time, not refined, or strong, like I'd used on my own hand. A weak, blunt mess. I still heard Sam's ghostly shriek, and the parasite's screech. Sticklike spectral legs flailed as the parasite came loose from Sam, and I shoved the ghostly little monster into one of the skulls of my magic hat. In hat form they'd decorated the brim. Now they lurked around the base of the hood.

Either way, the skull did what it was designed to do—it sucked the ghost in and held it there.

Sam, a flopping shape no longer human, wriggled like a transparent blue eel up into the ceiling and disappeared.

"Mech!" wailed Tonika, recognizing that I'd succeeded. She ran into the room, up to the cube that Mech now flopped over instead of standing inside. Climbing past both me and Doctor Biotic, her hands took hold of Mech's helmet, fingers fiddling with things I couldn't see.

The helmet hissed and came loose. Tonika pulled it loose and cupped a hand under the back of Mech's head supportively.

Dazed, his copper skin gleaming and his short hair matted with perspiration, Mech gave her a tired grin that was still absurdly noble and handsome. "You did it," he whispered.

Doctor Biotic pushed herself up off of Mech, making that hideous grinding sound I'd heard her make over the phone. "Congratulations, Deathette. That felt awful." She staggered a couple of steps with one hand clasped to her head before stabilizing.

Me, I was astonished that she was already upright.

Mech sure wasn't, but he grinned even wider as he looked around. His voice was pretty shaky as he confirmed, "It did. Congratulations to all of you. You did the right thing. Forget your doubts and guilt. Today, you saved the world."

Tonika giggled awkwardly and pointed at me. "Again."

I held up my hands, one arm crossed over the other that held the staff. "I barely, maybe, saved LA the first time."

Mech didn't pick up the argument. Like the serious hero he was, he asked me, "The program in Tonika's head. Can it come back?"

I pursed my lips, watching the little lights from the tiny glowing crystals Hodir's power had left decorating the ceiling reflect off Mech's armor. Doctor Biotic helped him carefully to his feet while Tonika at least tried to contribute from the other side.

I gave my judgment. "I can't be totally sure, but I'm pretty sure it's gone forever." You couldn't revive something that was just imprisoned, not dead, after all. "Not a lot of sources of Necromancy to test the idea, anyway. I'm sure not going to."

Mech took a deep breath, standing on his own feet now, although Doctor Biotic still stayed close and Tonika was reluctant to let go. He flashed a new grin. "Perfect. There's nothing left any of you have to worry about. Let's get out of here."

The door held ajar by Alice shut, then sprung open again, but with a room full of technology on the other side. The door into the nursery also swung open, and I heard more doors thump open all around the bunker.

We shuffled out, silently. Doctor Biotic stretched upwards, making her spine look too long, too fluidly bendy, and she ran her clawed hands through her hair a few times. Mech blinked when he entered the brightly lit surgery room and gave his head a vigorous shake. Delphine and Hodir had their arms around each other. Tonika finally let go of Mech and looped her arm around Olga's shoulders. Olga had gone back to playing cat's cradle with her light web.

As we squeezed into the robot assembly room, I heard clinking and clanking. A young woman laughed in maniacal glee, adding a couple of words that sounded suspiciously like Spanish profanity. When I reached the garage door, I saw the damaged robot vehicle from earlier running up the tunnel towards the outside world.

Everyone stopped in their tracks, but the robot was heading away, not towards us, and was already out of sight.

"What was that?" asked Mech.

I managed a tired smirk. "Just a guess, but I'd say someone is trying out villainy to spite her neighbors." I'd never heard Angel Cruz laugh, but the voice had sounded right.

That got another grin from Mech, and hissy chuckles from Doctor Biotic.

The garage lay in darkness and silence as we trudged through it. Everything but us was still, pacified, the threat defeated.

When we emerged into the brightly lit tunnel, Doctor Biotic stopped, and gave Mech a hard look. Probably a hard look. Her new face wasn't easy to read. She certainly sounded serious as she said, "Mech, you're going to offer to feed all these kids, take them home, and tell their parents how heroic they are, but only if they ask you to, right?"

Mech, with a hardened athlete's recovery time, was back to walking easily. His smile beamed with pride as he looked us over and said, "I think they all deserve for me to brag about them, but it's their choice."

Me, I deactivated my pendant with relish, swirling clouds of fabric putting away my supervillain look and returning me to a school uniform that right now felt downright welcome. Pulling off my magic hat, I let it and my staff hang at my sides and said, "I ain't askin' for none of it. Ah will call Sue, and let huh take care of me."

Mech watched my transformation sequence. His eyebrows went up, and his grin got as sardonic as it was capable of—not much. He radiated too much sincere admiration. "I'm impressed. If I ever see Deathette again, I'll treat her like any adult villainess who spends all her time teaming up with heroes instead of doing evil."

Doctor Biotic grinned now, with a row of scary sharp white

teeth, today more dagger-shaped than triangular. "Those are remarkably common. I think it's the stylish black costume."

I tilted my head forward graciously. "Deathette does have a great costume, don't she? It's a shame, but ah 'spec nobody'll be seeing it much. Ah'm sure Deathette also forgives anybody what got her into all this."

Did I sound sincere? I did. I knew I did, because Tonika grabbed the shoulders of my blouse and sweater vest, pulled herself close and tight to me, burying her face in my shoulder and trembling in relief and gratitude for several seconds before letting go.

As she stepped back, Mech—still smiling, of course—leaned over to look down at the little bald cyborg genius, to make it clear who was the adult and who was the tiny barely-teen. "As for you, young lady, you saved me and the day, and had the brains, the bravery, and the moral fortitude to fix your mistakes. I'm proud to have you as my ward, and I hope you'll keep being my assistant."

Tonika froze. Instead of smiling back, her jaw clenched. She trembled, although maybe only Mech and I were close enough to see it. Her face went blank, and she tried to blank her voice, but she hadn't shut off her emotions because her voice shivered too much with nervousness. "Actually, no." She took a deep breath, stretching things out another second before confessing, "I'd rather Doctor Biotic adopt me."

Doctor Biotic recoiled, dropping to all fours, back raised and arched, fuzzy scorpion tail raised with stinger threateningly forward. Her mouth dropped open, and she let out that awful, grating, alien noise again, louder than ever before. All six eyes went wide, staring at Tonika.

The crabby noise trailed off. Doctor Biotic's stance relaxed, slightly. Staring up at Tonika, Doctor Biotic asked in confusion verging on horror, "Me? I... you don't want me. I'd be a terrible parent. I'm dangerous. I'm a mutagen junkie, Tonika. I won't be the same person tomorrow, or that person next week. I can afford to raise you, but Mech is rich, and he's a better person, and he can take care of you in ways a teenager needs."

Now absolutely calm, in a tunnel where no one else made

a sound, Tonika answered, "I don't need to be taken care of the way other teenagers need. I need someone who understands what it's like to be flawed."

Slowly, gracefully, her elongated face still a mask of shock, Doctor Biotic unfolded, rising cautiously and fluidly upright. Her voice dropped to match Tonika's quiet. "Are you sure?"

Tonika clasped her hands in front of her, face tilted down, but her two dark eyes tilted up to meet Doctor Biotic's mismatched six. "Yes, I'm sure. I'm sorry, Mech, but... I need imperfect, and Doctor Biotic has always been imperfect for me."

Mech gave her the smile of a super nice guy who did not understand what was going on at all, and told her with radiating sincerity, "I want you to do what's best for you."

Composed again, even formal, Doctor Biotic pointed at the pavement in front of her and told Tonika, "If you're sure, come here."

Tonika shuffled over and stood meek and still as Doctor Biotic glowered down at her, with the seriousness of any angry parent. In that stiff tone, she told the little girl in front of her, "Mech and I both told you not to do this. I told you from the beginning, and every step along the way."

Her face a mask of guilt, helpless in front of the mother she'd chosen, Tonika nodded.

Doctor Biotic leaned forward, wrapped her arms around Tonika's torso, and hauled her tiny new daughter up into the air, hugging her tight. Quietly, more explanation than scold or sympathy, the doctor said, "You messed up. You messed up bad, but you got through it. You'll mess up again, and we'll get through it next time, too. Over time you'll mess up less, and hopefully never this bad again. Okay?"

"Okay," Tonika whimpered. Her eyes squeezed shut, and she hugged Doctor Biotic back so hard her arms shook, her face squeezed into Biotic's neck. Muffled sobs snuck out of their embrace.

Doctor Biotic held her silently for a few more seconds, before looking over at the rest of us. "Mech?"

"Yes, Doctor?" Mech acknowledged, watching Tonika with kindly concern.

"If Tonika is my responsibility now, I'm going to take her home, and we're going to order pizza and watch bad movies. Terrible, awful, cheesy movies. The worst I can find. Make sure those other kids know they're all heroes, and I'm sure they'll see Tonika tomorrow," Doctor Biotic said solemnly.

That was my cue to wave my hand. "Ah'm getting' outta here, too. You got good friends, Tonika. I'll see you too, but not tomorrow."

With that I turned, and walked up the tunnel. I heard the occasional click of claws behind me, but by the time I saw the exit clearly ahead, Doctor Biotic and Tonika hadn't caught up.

I pulled my phone out of my backpack and dialed Sue. My job wasn't done. Sam wasn't dead. The ghost who could possess robots found out she could travel through the internet. I would save Sam, but I was going to do it the way I should have from the start—with my own friends as backup, and I was going to tell my parents.

Chapter Thirty-Eight

My finger was hovering over the call button when I changed my mind. I would call my friends last. First, I had to do the right thing.

I dialed up my father, instead.

He picked up immediately and asked with a joviality that hit me like a shock after the seriousness of the afternoon, "Hey, Avery. How's the pool party? I thought you were done with those after the last one, but I know how convincing girlfriends can be."

"Is Mom home?" I asked first.

Dad's tone instantly turned concerned. "You sound upset."

I nodded, even if he couldn't see it. "Ah know. One thing at a time. Is Mom home?"

Half-amused, half-concerned, he answered, "She said it will be at least a half hour. Traffic is especially bad downtown. She said she's thinking about using surface streets rather than freeways from now on."

"Then you'll just have to tell her for me." I took a deep breath. Here goes. "Y'all're gonna be mad. Y'all're gonna be furious. Punish me however. Ah don't care anymore, nohow. This has to be done, and ah'm gonna do it. A ghost of a kid what got murdered really rough has been stalking me, and ah ain't sneakin' around about it no more. Nobody else wants to help her. They just want to get ridda her. Ah don't care if you and Mom think a ghost is already dead, ah think this is right and ah'm gonna do it. Ah'm gonna do it now, and not lie about it no more, or care whether this is villain stuff or hero stuff or what all. It's prob'ly gonna cause trouble, too, but ah'll face it 'cause ain't nobody else will do this, maybe nobody else can, and I can't—ah *won't* let her suffer."

Silence.

Not a long silence. Patient, maybe a bit stern, Dad said quietly, "I'm upset, but not as upset as I'm sure you expected. I know that I can't understand half of what you're going through. I have one question that you need to answer, for me and for yourself. Are you sure you're doing the right thing?"

Was I?

Was I sure I was doing the right thing?

I'd purged a haunted house, releasing a murdered child from one torment into another. I'd stolen from a museum, but had given them new treasures in the process. I'd established a supervillain identity I didn't want but had made official anyway. I'd lied a lot. Like, a lot, a lot, mostly by keeping secrets from my parents and my friends, even Sue who trusted me more completely than it was safe for any person to trust another. I still wasn't going to tell my parents about Alice, maybe ever, and I was going to hide the supervillain identity also, whether or not I successfully buried it.

I said, "No, but ah'm sure ah'm doin' the best I can. Ah'm dead sure that doing nothin' is the wrong thing."

Dad absorbed that, then said, "Then what you need is advice, not rules or punishment, and I don't have advice to give. Have you talked to your magic teacher?"

"I'mma call her next." That had been the plan.

"We got you a magic teacher for a reason. If she thinks you're doing the right thing, your mom and I will too," Dad said, voice soft, concerned again, with no trace of scolding.

I sniffled. It hurt, having such good parents that I wasn't at all sure I deserved. "Thanks, Dad. Ah'll see ya soon. The dangerous parts for me are over, ah spec, but not the dangerous parts for other folks. That matters. It matters to me."

"I love you," Dad said.

I hung up before I started bawling and babbling.

Okay. Calm. Control. Absorb the sunlight. Absorb the cars going past on a street maybe a dozen yards away, completely unaware of how close they were to an underground doomsday weapon.

My strength back, I dialed Schleimy next. I wasn't sure she would have her phone handy, or answer if she did. She wasn't exactly socially connected. But I was going to try.

One ring. Two rings. Three rings. I was willing to wait.

On the fourth ring, Schleimy picked up. She was breathing hard, like she'd had to run to get to the phone, and I knew she was in private because she whispered, "Apprentice. What is wrong?"

I didn't have to cry with Master, didn't hesitate to tell it to her straight, but what I had to stay still stung. "Ah been lettin' other folk try to fix the ghost problem for me, and that's gone so blasted wrong that I had ta hurt Sam to pull some kinda techno-ghost parasite thingy offa her. Ah'm going ta summon her, and bring her back to lucidity, and let her decide what all she wants. I got the techno-ghost bottled, and ah'd 'preciate yoah help deciding what to do about it, but that's all later-like. Right now, ah got a question. Is theyah some way ah can get mah hands on a mindless robot, fast? Best if it looks lahk a pretty girl, and also real roboty, but raht now ah ain't picky. Sam has a powah ah have nevuh seen in a ghost. Ah think perhaps it's a super power that crossed ovuh. She can possess computers."

Again I waited while an adult who I desperately wanted to approve of me thought about what I said. Finally, Schleimy whispered, "Thank you for reminding me that humans can learn to be better."

My knees wobbled, and I had to focus to keep from falling to my knees. My eyes stung painfully as tears tried to well up in them again, and I successfully fought down the urge to cry. I knew Master would approve, but that wasn't the same as hearing it.

Maybe the faint sounds I made told Master I wasn't ready to talk yet. She went on. "I have ideas. If I can't get an empty vessel to you in time, store Sam in your hat. We will save her together."

My voice a little croaky, I said, "If I have to. Putting this off and lettin' other folk fix it has been a right bad idea so far. Iff'n I can, I'll fix it now."

It was hard to read emotion in Master's whispery non-voice, but she answered, "You are responsible as well as caring. You know that any spell big enough to pull in a specific ghost from long distance will pull in other things? Are you ready?"

I sniffed once, just to clear my nose. "Ain't nobody can be, but this time I'll have friends ah trust to help me, rather'n me helping someone I just like."

"Then I will hurry and try to find you a robot," Schleimy whispered, and hung up.

Okay. One more. More hopeful than Schleimy, more scary than my parents.

I dialed Sue.

On the third ring, Sue picked up. Sort of. I heard banging and thumping like she dropped the phone. When she got it again, she was breathing as hard as Schleimy had been. It was an odd little flattering fact in the midst of all this chaos that I was important enough to people that they rush to the phone.

In the background, someone giggled.

"Avery? Are you okay?" asked Sue, the panting giving her voice an edge of desperate worry.

"More or less," I reassured her. "I've been lettin' other folk lead me around, and that don't work for me."

I found out Sue had me on speaker phone, because in the background Chris laughed and said, "I could have told you that. One thing I love about you is that you're a leader, not a follower."

Except where romance was concerned, anyway, but I had more serious things on my mind and couldn't indulge in the sweet sound of Chris's laughter.

Also, I was more than a little surprised. "Chris is there?"

Now that she knew I was alright, Sue was back to her usual purring, sly amusement. "And Annie, too. Like, what better way to make a cover story?"

I nodded. "That works. Listen, ah'm gonna cast a spell and save a suffering ghost. Ah need a ride, because ah'm not sneakin' around to do this. And ah need mah friends with me, to look out for me whatever happens. That was mah dumbest mistake, not goin' to you all first."

"We... I... I accept that we have stuff to do alone, but...," Sue stammered.

I picked up for her, warmth rushing into my heart and voice. "Yeah. That oughta be the exception, not the rule. Ah like bein' your partner, Sue, in everthin'."

Sue groaned, loud and long. "Being in love is so totally complicated!" Her voice rasped with that special, wounded frustration of someone finding out everyone who'd kept telling her that had been right. A slap sounded, and a touch muffled, I heard her shout, "Move your pointy-tailed butt, Red! We are going out to protect our princess!"

Chapter Thirty-Nine

Winifred pulled up to the curb. Annie, Sue, and I opened our respective car doors. Winifred turned around in the driver's seat to ask formally, "Did you wish me to stay?"

I inclined my head gratefully. "No, ma'am. This is me and mah friends."

"I quite understand, Mistress Avery." For the first time, Winifred's butler-y reserve cracked, enough for the faintest of wry smiles. "I have been there."

Me, Annie, Chris, and Sue, all of us piled out of the car and onto the sidewalk in front of my home. It stood bright in the late afternoon sunshine, because even in January the sun went down ridiculously late in L.A. The little, straight house looked like it had been sand blasted, and so did the brief lawn, because everything in this city looked like that, even during the wet season.

To anyone from Kentucky, calling a Los Angeles winter "wet' was hilarious. Every once in a while it did actually rain, not just drizzle.

My sweet moment turned bittersweet. My father was surely inside that house, and maybe my mom. Should I...? No. I'd already told them what I was doing, and if I started talking to them now, I wasn't sure I could stop.

I flicked my head at my girlfriend. "Sue. Y'all're good at explainin'. Go get Peggy. If she ain't at her house she'll be at the Stubbs's down the street. Chris and Annie, stand guard, but ah don't reckon anythin'll happen before they get back. Ah gotta prepare."

I turned my eyes down to my hat, which held the best and worst advisers possible. Putting it on, I invoked, "Ah need help. Can ah do this?"

Horse Skull Kid remarked cheerfully, "Shouldn't be complicated. Y'all know the ghost's name, and she wants to find you. Connection is already there."

I waved my hands, one of which held my staff now lighter and gloriously free of a big, completely honking useless crystal. "I don't know if she's… zipping around all the world's computers on the internet, or just took a wire up to the surface and possessed a car, or what all."

My imagination supplied Alicia Blackheart, hips tilted to one side, one hand cupping the elbow of her other arm that fluttered a fan coyly. "Well, we can certainly come up with a summoning ritual that will bring huh from anyweyah, but it would take preparation. Yoah in an understandable hurry, so try the simple way first."

"Just focus, put out the call, and keep callin' 'til she responds," advised Horse Skull Kid.

"And take off your shoes," gruffed Namluh.

After the briefest delay, Alicia asked archly, "Ah beg yoah pardon?"

The shameless Namluh acknowledged no reproof, and explained jovially, "Contact with the Earth. Standing in running water would be better."

I snorted. "Not a lot of that in LA." But I did crouch down and unlace my shoes, then peel off my ridiculous school-mandated knee socks. I'd never believed those silly schoolgirl costumes were real until I'd been forced to wear one. No time to go grab decently comfortable and practical overalls now.

My toes digging into the dry dirt between my lawn's sparse

grass, I listened to Horse Skull Kid say, "He's right, though. Not sure what it is, but I always did have more control when ah I barefoot."

Namluh declared, "It clears the sacred path from Enki through Enlil to you. BA HA HA HA HA."

From the silence, nobody got the joke. I sure didn't.

But when I stood up, I did see Sue and Peggy on the way.

Which left no honest reason to procrastinate further. Step one. Focus my power.

Setting the butt of my staff against the dirt as well, I chanted, "O Pluto, quamvis per vallem mortis ambulo, nihil mali timebo, quia canis in valle sum vilissimus."

Cold swirled up my body from my legs, in from my arms, exploding from my heart. I didn't let it whirl about chaotically, but set it to flowing in steady, constant streams around and around.

I sang again, "O Pluto, quamvis per vallem mortis ambulo, nihil mali timebo, quia canis in valle sum vilissimus."

My staff was a part of me, a seamless part of the flow of magic, a deep well for it to fill, flow out of, and refill.

I had no magic circle, but I didn't need it. All my emotions had been let go, rather than pushed aside. Icy magic filled me, and I controlled it perfectly. I was ice. I was necromancy.

Inevitably, the first trouble arrived. But that was going to be my challenge, to hold on to this control with no props, while the world flung its chaos at me.

The chaos began with a dark-blue sedan, perfectly ordinary except for the big yellow arrows that pointed to each other and curved around the surface in a pattern that covered the whole car. It pulled up right in front of my house where Winifred had been parked.

Manipulator got out, in big mad-science goggles, a waist-length deep purple cape, dark-blue leather pants and jacket with long, pointy, almost military shoulders, and yellow boots and gloves. He swaggered with exaggerated villain to the back of the car and opened up the trunk.

Out of the trunk he pulled a doll. For a doll, it was huge. It nearly came up to my shoulders. From the effort he displayed lifting and carrying it out to set in front of me, it couldn't be hollow. It was certainly pretty, in an elaborate green dress with white ruffles, and a bonnet over lustrous brown hair tied in two huge braids that fell almost to the ground. I got a glimpse of white stockings and shiny black shoes before he set it down again. It stood up without help, arms folded over its stomach, eyes closed and pouting lazily.

Manipulator looked me up and down, smirking, and drawled, "I was hoping to deliver this to Deathette." He had either grown or glued on a convincing long, thin mustache, and twisted the end with his fingers for that extra note of sinister theater.

I didn't laugh. I was cold inside. But I did smile. Cold did not mean angry, or unhappy. "I'm afraid she's left me to receive it. What did Schleimy negotiate?"

He shrugged, head twisting to the side, lips pursed, his diffidence as exaggerated as everything else. "Nothing much. This is a spare, from a haunted doll themed game I wanted to play but didn't get the chance. Deathette can just owe me a favor."

So, his game was pretending to be silly and harmless. I warned, "Not if it's open ended and she might regret it."

He laughed, bright and delighted, and behind the goggles his eyes flashed with predatory glee. He was clearly enjoying the game, whether he won or lost. The next shrug was much more human and normal. "Fine, fine. Just tell Deathette to show up in costume the next time she visits Chinatown. Rumor has it she's the height of style, and everyone wants to see."

I was impressed by just how badly these other villains wanted a necromancer supervillain. Manipulator had surely found a way to benefit himself with this promise, but the promise itself was harmless. Mostly. Harmless enough. It's a trade I would make for Sam with no regrets. I smirked a touch more, and it's easy sound sarcastic when you're made of ice and magic. "Deal. Did I mention how super creepy you are?"

Manipulator laid a hand to his stomach and bent forward in a stiff bow. "Thank you. I put a lot of effort into it."

That was enough. He left the doll standing silent and mindless in front of me, got back into his arrow-covered car, and drove off.

And I still held my power in complete control This was perfect. Time to begin.

"Sam Washington! You wanted to be a beautiful robot girl. I have her ready for you to be!" I shouted, with so much ice in my words that I expected to see fog and frost when I breathed.

Nothing happened, but I hadn't expected it to.

As much as I preferred to do it Schleimy's way, this was not a time for asking. I shouted again. "Sam Washington! By Enlil the Earth, by Enki under the Earth, by the authority they have granted me to be Queen of the Dead, I command your presence! By the wish you have made, I summon you to me."

I thumped the heel of my staff against the ground. Namluh had been right. I felt the cold magic rippling through the ground with the soles of my feet.

My spell was definitely reaching out, because a wasp the size of a bear came buzzing up the street. The huge, hard-shelled, yellow-and-black thing hovered not quite a man's height off the ground, its wings buzzing too fast to see, body hanging vertically, and I knew the front legs that ended in big spiky claws were not wasp standard.

It stopped, huge-eyed bug head turning to stare at me, feelers waving erratically.

Peggy cleared her throat. The wasp turned to look at her instead. She pulled a hand out of her corduroy jeans pocket and pointed down the street the way Manipulator had gone. It flew off that way.

Chris folded his arms, grinning down at the relentlessly casual Peggy. "Okay, but you got the easy one."

Everyone, even Peggy, giggled. Everyone but me. I did smile.

I smacked the ground with my staff again. "You hear me, Sam Washington! I know your name, and I know you. You have spoken your love of me. The connection is made between us, and I pull you to me by that cord."

I'd been calling using the format of seances and spells I'd read in old books, but to my surprise, this time it came literally true. Something brushed against me, a flickering, invisible presence like a wet, cold wire. I could see it or feel it like an object, but I felt the cold of its magic, and grabbed it in my free hand. Feeling that wriggling cold in my grip I pulled, and pulled again. Necromancy rushed over me, from the outside rather than within, and faded.

Sirens wailed down the street, getting rapidly louder. A police car drove up, and pulled to a sharp, screeching stop in front of my house. The window rolled down, and the driver leaned out and demanded, "What's going on here?"

Chris stepped up, horned and tailed and red-skinned, in a fantastic suit of white blouse and pants that looked fashionably mussed, like he'd just hopped out of bed. He was the least-inno-cent-looking person in the world, but he had a smile as charm-ing as Mech's and harmlessly spread hands. "You were chasing the giant bee that's chasing the supervillain, right?" he asked instead of answered.

This cop was tough, resistant to mind control—but not immune. He asked again, much less confident, "Yes, but what's going on here?"

Chris shrugged. His tailtip twitched rhythmically behind him. "Just a bunch of kids who can tell you which way they went. They fled that way, and they're getting farther away by the second. You'd better hurry!"

Another policeman, in the passenger's seat, grumbled, "Forget it, Jake. It's Glendale."

"Now hit the gas!" Chris barked suddenly.

"Now hit the gas!" echoed the policeman in the passenger's seat.

The driver did, sending the police car screeching away in as sudden a hurry as it arrived.

Chris walked back to my friends, one hand extended, and Sue slapped palms with him in congratulations.

I continued my summoning. "The Queen of the Dead calls, Sam Washington, and you cannot resist. You are hurting. You are scared. I am your ruler, but also your refuge. The cure for your pain is here. I have brought a home for you, where you will be safe. Hurry, Sam Washington. Your queen is waiting to save you."

I swore I could feel the spell hanging over me like a cloud, now.

In my backpack, my phone beeped a text. I had a moment. Digging my phone out, I checked the message.

Angel Cruz: Is that you?

I typed back.

Me: It's me. Ignore me.

Angel Cruz: Happily.

A few seconds later, just as I was about to put it back, my phone beeped again. I checked and saw:

Barbara: I feel it too. I don't know who Sam Washington is, but good luck.

I tucked my phone back into the easiest to reach pocket and prepared for another round of summoning.

Instead, a witch floated down out of the sky, sitting side-saddle on a flying broomstick. Not just a witch, the superheroine called Little Witch, and for a second I almost lost my grip on my magic and the spell. It's not just that I once broke into her base. I might have kind of broken into this particular heroine's base twice, robbed her, and destroyed her apartment last semester. Also, I couldn't help but notice how much alike her heroine and my villain costume were. Dress with spiky hem, boots, stockings, fluffy sleeves. She wore a pointy witch hat instead of a hood and held a wand instead of a staff, but the style was similar.

I was struck again by what a tiny, adorably round-cheeked woman she was, fully adult but shorter than Tonika and Olga, with long, pink hair that curled up at the tips. In her witch costume, she looked like a cute and harmless holiday decoration. Her scowl couldn't threaten a puppy.

Her voice, on the other hand, snarled with queenly impatience. "Do you know what you're doing?"

My power still flowed evenly within me. I was still cold. I was still in control. I felt the spell hovering around me. I said, "I'm sending out a signal to a lost soul, and if everyone can hear it, then it's working."

Clinging to her broom with both hands, the heroine leaned forward and scolded me furiously, "This is not a good week for random magic. There is a dragon awake and listening to you right now, and I don't know what he's thinking."

Calm, unintimidated, I answered, "He's thinking I'm one high note in the magical chorus this city drowns in." The spell needed another jolt, so I gave it one. "Sam Washington! You have the trail, Sam Washington! Follow it!"

Little Witch leveled her wand at me, waved it towards my friends, then turned it back to me. She sounded tired, exasperated, and completely, unstoppably determined. "Look, I hate to beat up kids, but you're causing chaos, and unless you have a very good reason, I have to shut you down."

"Someone is hurting, and I'm going to save her," I answered.

She was truly a heroine, angry or not. That explanation stopped her, and with visible effort, she shoved aside her feelings and merely complained, "...okay, but when you see me covered in claw and sucker marks because I had to calm down those magically sensitive cats AND the octopus nymph in the aquarium, realize it's your fault and there's a reason I don't like you."

Her desire to talk to me completely expended, Little Witch and her broomstick flew up into the sky and away towards Downtown, or maybe Hollywood.

During the pause, as I prepared for my next cast, I looked over at my friends. Sue had strolled right up to the sidewalk, arms folded, looking up and down the street with a face as stern and implacable as Little Witch. She met my gaze, and told me, "I am ready for my turn. I will protect you."

"I don't think anyone else gets a turn. I hope. I feel something," I told her in return.

I did. A gust of chilly power that wasn't my own, behind me.

My phone beeped, screeched electronically, and a ghost popped out. I grabbed the phone, then threw it onto the dirt as it spit sparks and caught fire. Before I could stomp on it, Sue's shadow slithered over and yanked the phone away, smothering the flames.

I turned my attention to the ghost, an eel-like, stretched out blue blob. I reached for it, and it slithered away in panic.

"Sam Washington!" I shouted, halting in its tracks on the sidewalk.

I tapped the doll with my staff. "Your body awaits, Sam. Claim it."

The ghost, Sam, scurried around in anxious loops instead, unable to flee, too scared to come closer. I felt... bad. My heart ached. I'd hurt Sam badly to save Mech and the world and Sam herself, bludgeoning her with magic to detach the parasite. She wasn't even slightly coherent now. If I let her go now, she would fade into nothing before morning, like the dead naturally do.

But if she was that weak, it was my fault, not a reason to abandon her. I felt that slithering again, the cord I'd pulled on earlier. I grabbed it, pulling slowly, reeling Sam in like a fish as she leaped and writhed and flailed from side to side.

When her writhing body touched the doll, it sucked her inside, snapping her into its shape like a lock closing.

I pulled the remaining power left from my staff and dropped the stick to the ground. Placing my hands on Sam's cold, plastic-textured cheeks, I fed magic into her, not too fast for her to absorb without harm, not slow enough for her to lose focus and pull away. I was shocked by how little magic I had left. What had felt like a few simple recitations like made up any séance had used up vast amounts of power, far more than I'd spent saving Tonika and Mech.

But I had enough to restore the ghost in this mechanical shell.

The doll twitched, but otherwise lay still and allowed me to feed it.

Finally, when I was almost out of power and starting to feel the fatigue that had hidden behind the cold, the doll opened mismatched eyes, one blue and one green.

Panting a little, I asked, "Are you in there, Sam? Do you understand me? Do you know who I am?"

The doll girl's head tilted up, and I heard the faint whir of robotic muscles behind that action. She frowned. Her stiff-feeling face was remarkably expressive. Surprised, she answered, "No. You're not her. You're not him. Who *are* you?"

I sighed in deep relief, took off my hat, and wiped my forehead with my sleeve. Giving the blue, beautiful, empty California sky a quick look of gratitude, I turned my attention back down to the doll and told her, "Ah'm Avery Special. Ah'm just the necromancer what wanted ta help a lost ghost, that's all."

"You got me this body?" she asked, raising her hands. She looked at them, moving each joint of segmented fingers in turn. Then she pulled down one sleeve to look at the complicated seams of her wrist and elbow joints.

"And you kin keep it," I promised.

Sam straightened out her sleeve carefully, reached around back, and pulled forward one of her arm-thick braids. As she held it out in front of her to study, she said softly, her voice higher in this body than the original, "It's not what I imagined, but... I like it. I'm pretty."

"Y'all are that," I acknowledged, completely honest. I hadn't thought the original was all that pretty, but this little doll was a work of art.

The doll's faint, growing smile snapped suddenly into a scowl. Black-handled knives appeared in her hands, gripped with deadly ferocity as she snarled, "Where is he? I'll find him. I'll kill him for what he did!"

I winced, forcing myself to not squeeze my eyes shut in the process. Of course, any robot body a supervillain gave me had weapons. Sam was sounding unhinged again, and I wasn't sure I could touch her safely or had enough power to control her again if I did.

Reason. I would have to try reason and hope I'd restored her right the first time.

"Someone did that for you already, twenty-odd years ago," I told her, as simply as I could.

Sam's anger froze, replaced by wide-eyed shock. "Twenty years!?"

Now I did flinch. Sam was coherent, but... I was completely unqualified for this. I could bring a ghost fully to life. What to do with that life after was beyond me.

But... but I was the only option Sam had.

As I struggled for direction, she lowered her knives, and her voice turned thoughtful. "That's right. I went looking for my family, and they weren't there."

I fumbled ahead, lost but trying. "Look, ah'm... ah mean, mah part'a things is to get you here, but ah ain't gonna just abandon you. There are folks what can help you with the next step. Mah Master'll care, and have ideas."

My friends had all been watching this, and now Sue took a step forward, waving a hand horizontally from side to side with helpful disgust. "There's this crazy old couple who are totally obsessed with helping robots find new lives. I can get their number."

Annie whipped out her phone and started tapping words into the web browser. Chris crowded over to look over Annie's shoulder.

Beside them, Peggy shrugged, but she did watch Sam with soft, sympathetic eyes.

"Meow!" declared a cat loudly from the street.

"I knew you could do it, Ghost Cat Solvin' Mysteries! The trail went cold, but no trail is too cold for the Bubblegumshoe Detective Agency!" called out Gumshoe Ghost Girl.

The sepia-toned, nineteenth-century ghost child zoomed up the street on transparent ghostly roller skates strapped to her crude shoes. Ghost Cat Solvin' Mysteries jumped from car to car in front of her, leaping off the last one to come strutting up into my front yard.

My jaw fell open.

How?

Why???

And then I realized what a doofus I was. This was the first thing I should have expected. I sent out a ghost summoning, and ghosts answered. Ghosts connected to Sam, and connected to me. This wasn't luck, it was what I'd asked for. Loudly. Repeatedly. Shouted to an entire city, while its magical inhabitants yelled at me to keep the noise down.

Spinning to a graceful halt in front of us, Gumshoe Ghost Girl addressed the doll grandly, "And you are Sam Washington, whose dream was to be a beautiful robot girl, which I deduce was accomplished with the help of necromancer Avery Special and her contacts in the supervillain community! From the look of the robot, I deduce—"

Sam stumbled a couple of steps on her short new legs, and grabbed Gumshoe Ghost Girl's hands in her own, holding them up and together underneath Sam's wide-eyed, pleading face. I made a note that being operated by a ghost let Sam's robot body touch other ghosts.

"Are my parents looking for me?" asked Sam, squeaky with anxiety and hope.

Gumshoe Ghost Girl, queen of gentle tact and empathy that she was, announced, "Your parents passed on seven years ago, but you were close to your older brother, and he remembers you so well that he recently hired an expert in ghost mysteries to find out what happened to you! That expert was the Gumshoe Ghost Girl, and fortunately for you, when he hired me he also hired Ghost Cat Solvin' Mysteries!"

"Meow!" contributed Ghost Cat Solvin' Mysteries, pushing its head up against Sam's leg in the universal kitty language of demanding to be petted.

I sighed in relief. Deep, utter, bone-weary relief, the relief of the last important problem letting go. Sam Washington would be fine. I had saved her, and other people could and would take it from here.

Chris saw that sigh, and took it as a signal to rush over and wrap me up in a hug. "You did it!" he cheered. Seconds later Sue, Annie, and Peggy plowed into us, adding to the embrace.

Until a black shape fell from the sky, hitting the pavement with a deafening CRACK! that demanded everyone's attention.

An old man wrapped in black rags stood in the middle of a shattered square of cement, leaning on a cane. They weren't bandages, but irregularly sized strips of black cloth wrapped and tied awkwardly over a faded black suit, tying it tight to an emaciated figure. A repeatedly and clumsily patched black top hat perched on a head completely concealed by wrapped-up cloth, although a tiny slit between layers hinted at eyes. The edges of gloves peeked around the wrists of his wrapped-up hands, and shabby wingtip shoes sported rags tied over them like spats. He leaned on an ebony cane whose brass compass handle was the only thing that didn't match the theme.

The nearly stick figure moved like an old man, stiffly,

awkwardly, cane wobbling to the point of uselessness as he stepped off the broken sidewalk and into my yard. His feet sank at least an inch deep into the hard-packed dirt when he put his weight on one.

Sue wriggled free of the group hug and placed herself in front of me, arms out to either side. Chris, Annie, and Peggy tensed up to fight.

I extended an arm ahead and pushed all of them, even Sue, gently back out of the way, letting the mysterious figure approach me.

In a perfectly normal, scratchy old-man voice, the towering, not quite bone-thin figure said, "It seems I missed the excitement. Unfortunate. There is a ghost I have wanted to talk to for a long time, and I heard that Deathette could help me."

Tired as I was, I give him my biggest, goofiest grin. "Well, ah don't know 'bout this here Deathette person. Sounds like you need to talk to Avery Special, the Queen of the Dead!"

About the Author

Richard Roberts is drawn to dark, strange fairy tales, which of course is why he got famous for his perky middle school supervillain stories instead.

That presents the two halves of his work, the fun and crazy, and the dark and weird. In both cases, he does his best to entertain, to look at old ideas to see how strange they are if you think them through, and to make a story where his characters earn their happy endings.

Bibliography

Please Don't Tell My Parents Series

Book 1: *Please Don't Tell My Parents I'm a Supervillain*
Book 2: *Please Don't Tell My Parents I Blew Up the Moon*
Book 3: *Please Don't Tell My Parents I've Got Henchmen*
Book 4: *Please Don't Tell My Parents I Have a Nemesis*
Book 5: *Please Don't Tell My Parents You Believe Her*
Book 6: *Please Don't Tell My Parents I Work for a Supervillain*
Book 7: *Please Don't Tell My Parents I'm a Giant Monster*

Stand Alone Novels

You Can be a Cyborg When You Grow Up
Quite Contrary
Sweet Dreams are Made of Teeth
Wild Children
A Spaceship Repair Girl Supposedly Named Rachel

Curious about other Crossroad Press books?
Stop by our site:
http://store.crossroadpress.com
We offer quality writing
in digital, audio, and print formats.